KU-167-038

CRIME
for Christmas

CRIME
for Christmas

Foreword by Peter Cushing OBE

Edited by Richard Dalby

MICHAEL O'MARA BOOKS LIMITED

First published in 1991 by
Michael O'Mara Books Limited,
9 Lion Yard, Tremadoc Road, London SW4 7NQ

Crime for Christmas copyright © 1991 by
Michael O'Mara Books Limited

All rights reserved. No part of this publication may be
reproduced, stored in a retrieval system, or transmitted, in
any form or by any means, without the prior permission in
writing of the publisher, nor be otherwise circulated in any
form of binding or cover other than that in which it is published
and without a similar condition including this condition being
imposed on the subsequent purchaser.

A CIP catalogue record for this book is available from
the British Library

ISBN 1-85479-034-X

Typeset by DP Photosetting, Aylesbury, Bucks
Printed and bound in Great Britain by
Richard Clay Limited, Bungay, Suffolk

CONTENTS

FOREWORD

But there are moments which he calls his own.
Then, never less alone than when alone,
Those that he loved so long and sees no more,
Loved and still loves—not dead—but gone before,
He gathers round him;

The sentiment expressed in that lovely passage from Samuel Rogers's 'Human Life' could also be applied to much-loved books, and rather belies the somewhat cynical remark which is attributed to him: 'When a new book is published, read an old one.'

Richard Dalby supplies us with a rich harvest of both new and old Christmas crime stories in this anthology. Among his chosen authors are Agatha Christie, who delighted her readers—and incidentally, grateful actors!—with such characters as the gentle Miss Marple and the flamboyant Belgian sleuth, Hercule Poirot; Edgar Wallace, a master of the so-called 'thriller'; Thomas Hardy, a great writer of epic-drama; Wilkie Collins, here represented by a rare short novel with an intriguing theatrical background; and Arthur Conan Doyle, the man of medicine, who created that most celebrated of fictional detectives—the one and only Mr Sherlock Holmes.

'You takes yer pick', but I have a feeling that there will be few readers who will not enjoy each and every one of this excellent and seasonable selection, and—like Oliver Twist—they'll ask for more.

Peter Cushing OBE
Whitstable, Kent

THE TRINITY CAT

Ellis Peters

Ellis Peters (pseudonym of Edith Pargeter b. 1913) is one of the most popular crime novelists working today. Her series of books starring the 12th century monk detective Brother Cadfael have achieved 'cult' status. 'The Trinity Cat' first appeared in *Winter's Crimes 8* (1976).

H e was sitting on top of one of the rear gate-posts of the churchyard when I walked through on Christmas Eve, grooming in his lordly style, with one back leg wrapped round his neck, and his bitten ear at an angle of forty-five degrees, as usual. I reckon one of the toms he'd tangled with in his nomad days had ripped the starched bit out of that one, the other stood up sharply enough. There was snow on the ground, a thin veiling, just beginning to crackle in promise of frost before evening, but he had at least three warm refuges around the place whenever he felt like holing up, besides his two houses, which he used only for visiting and cadging. He'd been a known character around our village for three years then, ever since he walked in from nowhere and made himself agreeable to the vicar and the verger, and finding the billet comfortable and the pickings good, constituted himself resident cat to Holy Trinity church, and took over all the jobs around the place that humans were too slow to tackle, like rat-catching, and chasing off invading dogs.

Nobody knows how old he is, but I think he could only have been

[1]

about two when he settled here, a scrawny, chewed-up black bandit as lean as wire. After three years of being fed by Joel Woodward at Trinity Cottage, which was the verger's house by tradition, and flanked the lych-gate on one side, and pampered and petted by Miss Patience Thomson at Church Cottage on the other side, he was double his old size, and sleek as velvet, but still had one lop ear and a kink two inches from the end of his tail. He still looked like a brigand, but a highly prosperous brigand. Nobody ever gave him a name, he wasn't the sort to get called anything fluffy or familiar. Only Miss Patience ever dared coo at him, and he was very gracious about that, she being elderly and innocent and very free with little perks like raw liver, on which he doted. One way and another, he had it made. He lived mostly outdoors, never staying in either house overnight. In winter he had his own little ground-level hatch into the furnace-room of the church, sharing his lodgings matily with a hedgehog that had qualified as assistant vermin-destructor around the churchyard, and preferred sitting out the winter among the coke to hibernating like common hedgehogs. These individualists keep turning up in our valley, for some reason.

All I'd gone to the church for that afternoon was to fix up with the vicar about the Christmas peal, having been roped into the bell-ringing team. Resident police in remote areas like ours get dragged into all sorts of activities, and when the area's changing, and new problems cropping up, if they have any sense they don't need too much dragging, but go willingly. I've put my finger on many an astonished yobbo who thought he'd got clean away with his little breaking-and-entering, just by keeping my ears open during a darts match, or choir practice.

When I came back through the churchyard, around half-past two, Miss Patience was just coming out of her gate, with a shopping bag on her wrist, and heading towards the street, and we walked along together a bit of the way. She was getting on for seventy, and hardly bigger than a bird, but very independent. Never having married or left the valley, and having looked after a mother who lived to be nearly ninety, she'd never had time to catch up with new ideas in the style of dress suitable for elderly ladies. Everything had always been done mother's way, and fashion, music and morals had stuck at the period when mother was a carefully-brought-up girl learning domestic skills, and preparing for a chaste marriage. There's a lot to be said for it! But it had turned Miss Patience into a frail little lady in long-skirted black or grey or navy blue, who still felt undressed without hat and gloves, at an age when Mrs Newcombe, for instance, up at the pub, favoured shocking pink trouser suits and red-gold hairpieces. A pretty little old lady Miss Patience was, though, very straight and neat. It was a pleasure to watch her walk. Which is more than I could say for Mrs Newcombe in her trouser suit, especially from the back!

'A happy Christmas, Sergeant Moon!' she chirped at me on sight. And I wished her the same, and slowed up to her pace.

'It's going to be slippery by twilight,' I said. 'You be careful how you go.'

'Oh, I'm only going to be an hour or so,' she said serenely. 'I shall be home long before the frost sets in. I'm only doing the last bit of Christmas shopping. There's a cardigan I have to collect for Mrs Downs.' That was her cleaning-lady, who went in three mornings a week. 'I ordered it long ago, but deliveries are so slow nowadays. They've promised it for today. And a gramophone record for my little errand-boy.' Tommy Fowler that was, one of the church trebles, as pink and wholesome looking as they usually contrive to be, and just as artful. 'And one mustn't forget our dumb friends, either, must one?' said Miss Patience cheerfully. 'They're all important, too.'

I took this to mean a couple of packets of some new product to lure wild birds to her garden. The Church Cottage thrushes were so fat they could hardly fly, and when it was frosty she put out fresh water three and four times a day.

We came to our brief street of shops, and off she went, with her big jet-and-gold brooch gleaming in her scarf. She had quite a few pieces of Victorian and Edwardian jewellery her mother'd left behind, and almost always wore one piece, being used to the belief that a lady dresses meticulously every day, not just on Sundays. And I went for a brisk walk round to see what was going on, and then went home to Molly and high tea, and took my boots off thankfully.

That was Christmas Eve. Christmas Day little Miss Thomson didn't turn up for eight o'clock Communion, which was unheard-of. The vicar said he'd call in after matins and see that she was all right, and hadn't taken cold trotting about in the snow. But somebody else beat us both to it. Tommy Fowler! He was anxious about that pop record of his. But even he had no chance until after service, for in our village it's the custom for the choir to go and sing the vicar an aubade in the shape of 'Christians, Awake!' before the main service, ignoring the fact that he's then been up four hours, and conducted two Communions. And Tommy Fowler had a solo in the anthem, too. It was a quarter-past twelve when he got away, and shot up the garden path to the door cf Church Cottage.

[3]

He shot back even faster a minute later. I was heading for home when he came rocketing out of the gate and ran slam into me, with his eyes sticking out on stalks and his mouth wide open, making a sort of muted keening sound with shock. He clutched hold of me and pointed back towards Miss Thomson's front door, left half-open when he fled, and tried three times before he could croak out:

'Miss Patience . . . She's there on the floor—she's bad!'

I went in on the run, thinking she'd had a heart attack all alone there, and was lying helpless. The front door led through a diminutive hall, and through another glazed door into the living-room, and that door was open, too, and there was Miss Patience face-down on the carpet, still in her coat and gloves, and with her shopping-bag lying beside her. An occasional table had been knocked over in her fall, spilling a vase and a book. Her hat was askew over one ear, and caved in like a trodden mushroom, and her neat grey bun of hair had come undone and trailed on her shoulder, and it was no longer grey but soiled, brownish black. She was dead and stiff. The room was so cold, you could tell those doors had been ajar all night.

The kid had followed me in, hanging on to my sleeve, his teeth chattering. 'I didn't open the door—it was open! I didn't touch her, or anything. I only came to see if she was all right, and get my record.'

It was there, lying unbroken, half out of the shopping-bag by her arm. She'd meant it for him, and I told him he should have it, but not yet, because it might be evidence, and we mustn't move anything. And I got him out of there quick, and gave him to the vicar to cope with, and went back to Miss Patience as soon as I'd telephoned for the outfit. Because we had a murder on our hands.

So that was the end of one gentle, harmless old woman, one of very many these days, battered to death because she walked in on an intruder who panicked. Walked in on him, I judged, not much more than an hour after I left her in the street. Everything about her looked the same as then, the shopping-bag, the coat, the hat, the gloves. The only difference, that she was dead. No, one more thing! No handbag, unless it was under the body, and later, when we were able to move her, I wasn't surprised to see that it wasn't there. Handbags are where old ladies carry their money. The sneak-thief who panicked and lashed out at her had still had greed and presence of mind enough to grab the bag as he fled. Nobody'd have to describe that bag to me, I knew it well, soft black leather with an old-fashioned gilt clasp and a short handle, a small thing, not like the hold-alls they carry nowadays.

She was lying facing the opposite door, also open, which led to the stairs. On the writing-desk by that door stood one of a pair of heavy brass candlesticks. Its fellow was on the floor beside Miss Thomson's body, and though the bun of hair and the felt hat had prevented any great spattering of blood, there was blood enough on the square base to label the weapon. Whoever had hit her had been just sneaking down the stairs, ready to leave. She'd come home barely five minutes too soon.

Upstairs, in her bedroom, her bits of jewellery hadn't taken much finding. She'd never thought of herself as having valuables, or of other people as coveting them. Her gold and turquoise and funereal jet and true-lover's-knots in gold and opals, and mother's engagement and wedding rings, and her little Edwardian pendant watch set with seed pearls, had simply lived in the small top drawer of her dressing-table. She belonged to an honest epoch, and it was gone, and now she was gone after it. She didn't even lock her door when she went shopping. There wouldn't have been so much as the warning of a key grating in the lock, just the door opening.

Ten years ago not a soul in this valley behaved differently from Miss Patience. Nobody locked doors, sometimes not even overnight. Some of us went on a fortnight's holiday and left the doors unlocked. Now we can't even put out the milk money until the milkman knocks at the door in person. If this generation likes to pride itself on its progress, let it! As for me, I thought suddenly that maybe the innocent was well out of it.

We did the usual things, photographed the body and the scene of the crime, the doctor examined her and authorised her removal, and confirmed what I'd supposed about the approximate time of her death. And the forensic boys lifted a lot of smudgy latents that weren't going to be of any use to anybody, because they weren't going to be on record, barring a million to one chance. The whole thing stank of the amateur. There wouldn't be any easy matching up of prints, even if they got beauties. One more thing we did for Miss Patience. We tolled the dead-bell for her on Christmas night, six heavy, muffled strokes. She was a virgin. Nobody had to vouch for it, we all knew. And let me point out, it is a title of honour, to be respected accordingly.

We'd hardly got the poor soul out of the house when the Trinity cat strolled in, taking advantage of the minute or two while the door was open. He got as far as the place on the carpet where she'd lain, and his fur and whiskers stood on end, and even his lop ear jerked up straight. He put his nose down to the pile of the Wilton, about where her shopping bag and handbag must have lain, and started going round in interested circles, snuffing the floor and making little throaty noises that might have been distress, but sounded like pleasure. Excitement, anyhow. The chaps from the C.I.D. were still busy, and didn't want him under their feet, so I picked him up and took him with me when I went across to Trinity Cottage to talk to the verger. The cat never liked being picked up, after a minute he started clawing and cursing, and I put him down. He stalked away again at once, past the corner where people shot their dead flowers, out at the lych-gate, and straight back to sit on Miss Thomson's doorstep. Well, after all, he used to get fed there, he might well be uneasy at all these queer comings and goings. And they don't say 'as curious as a cat' for nothing, either.

I didn't need telling that Joel Woodward had had no hand in what had happened, he'd been nearest neighbour and good friend to Miss Patience for years, but he might have seen or heard something out of the ordinary. He was a little, wiry fellow, gnarled like a tree-root, the kind that goes on spry and active into his nineties, and then decides that's enough, and leaves overnight. His wife was dead long ago, and his daughter had come back to keep house for him after her husband deserted her, until she died, too, in a bus accident. There was just old Joel now, and the grandson she'd left with him, young Joel Barnett, nineteen, and a bit of a tearaway by his grandad's standards, but so far pretty innocuous by mine. He was a sulky, graceless sort, but he did work, and he stuck with the old man when many another would have lit out elsewhere.

'A bad business,' said old Joel, shaking his head. 'I only wish I could help you lay hands on whoever did it. But I only saw her yesterday morning about ten, when she took in the milk. I was round at the church hall all afternoon, getting things ready for the youth social they had last night, it was dark before I got back. I never saw or heard anything out of place. You can't see her living-room light from here, so there was no call to wonder. But the lad was here all afternoon. They only work till one, Christmas Eve. Then they all went boozing together for an hour or so, I expect, so I don't know exactly what time he got in, but he was here and had the tea on when I came home. Drop round in an hour or so and he should be here, he's gone round to collect this girl he's mashing. There's a party somewhere tonight.'

I dropped round accordingly, and young Joel was there, sure enough, shoulder-length hair, frilled shirt, outsize lapels and all, got up to kill, all for the benefit of the girl his grandad had mentioned. And it turned out to be Connie Dymond, from the comparatively respectable branch of the family, along the canal-side. There were three sets of Dymond cousins, boys, no great harm in 'em but worth watching, but only this one girl in Connie's family. A good-looker, or at least most of the lads seemed to think so, she had a dozen or so on her string before she took up with young Joel. Big girl, too, with a lot of mauve eye-shadow and a mother-of-pearl mouth, in huge platform shoes and the fashionable drab granny-coat. But she was acting very prim and proper with old Joel around.

'Half-past two when I got home,' said young Joel. 'Grandad was round at the hall, and I'd have gone round to help him, only I'd had a pint or two, and after I'd had me dinner I went to sleep, so it wasn't worth it by the time I woke up. Around four, that'd be. From then on I was here watching the telly, and I never saw nor heard a thing. But there was nobody else here, so I could be spinning you the yarn, if you want to look at it that way.'

He had a way of going looking for trouble before anybody else suggested it, there was nothing new about that. Still, there it was. One young fellow on the spot, and minus any alibi. There'd be plenty of others in the same case.

In the evening he'd been at the church social. Miss Patience wouldn't be expected there, it was mainly for the young, and anyhow, she very seldom went out in the evenings.

'I was there with Joel,' said Connie Dymond. 'He called for me at seven, I was with him all the evening. We went home to our place after the social finished, and he didn't leave till nearly midnight.'

Very firm about it she was, doing her best for him. She could hardly know that his movements in the evening didn't interest us, since Miss Patience had then been dead for some hours.

When I opened the door to leave the Trinity cat walked in, stalking past me with a purposeful stride. He had a look round us all, and then made for the girl, reached up his front paws to her knees, and was on her lap before she could fend him off, though she didn't look as if she welcomed his attentions. Very civil he was, purring and rubbing himself against her coat sleeve, and poking his whiskery face into hers. Unusual for him to be effusive, but when he did decide on it, it was always with someone who couldn't stand cats. You'll have noticed it's a way they have.

'Shove him off,' said young Joel, seeing she didn't at all care for being singled out. 'He only does it to annoy people.'

And she did, but he only jumped on again, I noticed as I closed the door on them and left. It was a Dymond party they were going to, the senior lot, up at the filling station. Not much point in trying to check up on all her cousins and swains when they were gathered for a booze-up. Coming out of a hangover, tomorrow, they might be easy meat. Not that I had any special reason to look their way, they were an extrovert lot, more given to grievous bodily harm in street punch-ups than anything secretive. But it was wide open.

Well, we summed up. None of the lifted prints was on record, all we could do in that line was exclude all those that were Miss Thomson's. This kind of sordid little opportunist break-in had come into local experience only fairly recently, and though it was no novelty now, it had never before led to a death. No motive but the impulse of greed, so no traces leading up to the act, and none leading away. Everyone connected with the church, and most of the village besides, knew about the bits of jewellery she had, but never before had anyone considered them as desirable loot. Victoriana now carry inflated values, and are in demand, but this still didn't look calculated, just wanton. A kid's crime, a teen-ager's crime. Or the crime of a permanent teenager. They start at twelve years old now, but there are also the shiftless louts who never get beyond twelve years old, even in their forties.

We checked all the obvious people, her part-time gardener—but he was demonstrably elsewhere at the time—and his drifter of a son, whose alibi was non-existent but voluble, the window-cleaner, a sidelong soul who played up his ailments and did rather well out of her, all the delivery men. Several there who were clear, one or two who could have been around, but had no particular reason to be. Then we went after all the youngsters who, on their records, were possibles. There were three with breaking-and-entering convictions, but if they'd been there they'd been gloved. Several others with petty theft against them were also without alibis. By the end of a pretty exhaustive survey the field was wide, and none of the runners seemed to be ahead of the rest, and we were still looking. None of the stolen property had so far showed up.

Not, that is, until the Saturday. I was coming from Church Cottage through the graveyard again, and as I came near the corner where the dead flowers were shot, I noticed a glaring black patch making an irregular hole in the veil of frozen snow that still covered the ground. You couldn't miss it, it showed up like a black eye. And part of it was the soil and rotting leaves showing through, and part, the blackest part, was the Trinity cat, head down and back arched, digging industriously like a terrier after a rat. The bent end of his tail lashed steadily, while the remaining eight inches stood erect. If he knew I was standing watching him, he didn't care. Nothing was going to deflect him from what he was doing. And in a minute or two he heaved his prize clear, and clawed out to the light a little black leather handbag with a gilt clasp. No mistaking it, all stuck over as it was with dirt and rotting leaves. And he loved it, he was patting it and playing with it and rubbing his head against it, and purring like a steam-engine. He cursed, though, when I took it off him, and walked round and round me, pawing and swearing, telling me and the world he'd found it, and it was his.

It hadn't been there long. I'd been along that path often enough to know that the snow hadn't been disturbed the day before. Also, the mess of humus fell off it pretty quick and clean, and left it hardly stained at all. I held it in my handkerchief and snapped the catch, and the inside was clean and empty, the lining slightly frayed from long use. The Trinity cat stood upright on his hind legs and protested loudly, and he had a voice that could outshout a Siamese.

Somebody behind me said curiously: 'Whatever've you got there?' And there was young Joel standing open-mouthed, staring, with Connie Dymond hanging on to his arm and gaping at the cat's find in horrified recognition.

'Oh, no! My gawd, that's Miss Thomson's bag, isn't it? I've seen her carrying it hundreds of times.'

'Did *he* dig it up?' said Joel, incredulous. 'You reckon the chap who— you know, *him!*—he buried it there? It could be anybody, everybody uses this way through.'

'My gawd!' said Connie, shrinking in fascinated horror against his side. 'Look at that cat! You'd think he *knows* . . . He gives me the shivers! What's got into him?'

What, indeed? After I'd got rid of them and taken the bag away with me I was still wondering. I walked away with his prize and he followed me as far as the road, howling and swearing, and once I put the bag down, open, to see what he'd do, and he pounced on it and started his fun and games again until I took it from him. For the life of me I couldn't see what there was about it to delight him, but he was in no doubt. I was beginning to feel right superstitious about this avenging detective cat, and to wonder what he was going to unearth next.

I know I ought to have delivered the bag to the forensic lab., but somehow I hung on to it overnight. There was something fermenting at the back of my mind that I couldn't yet grasp.

Next morning we had two more at morning service besides the regulars. Young Joel hardly ever went to church, and I doubt if anybody'd ever seen Connie Dymond there before, but there they both were, large as life and solemn as death, in a middle pew, the boy sulky and scowling as if he'd been press-ganged into it, as he certainly had, Connie very subdued and big-eyed, with almost no make-up and an unusually grave and thoughtful face. Sudden death brings people up against daunting possibilities, and creates penitents. Young Joel felt silly there, but he was daft about her, plainly enough, she could get him to do what she wanted, and she'd wanted to make this gesture. She went through all the movements of devotion, he just sat, stood and kneeled awkwardly as required, and went on scowling.

There was a bitter east wind when we came out. On the steps of the porch everybody dug out gloves and turned up collars against it, and so did young Joel, and as he hauled his gloves out of his coat pocket, out with them came a little bright thing that rolled down the steps in front of us all and came to rest in a crack between the flagstones of the path. A gleam of pale blue and gold. A dozen people must have recognised it. Mrs Downs gave tongue in a shriek that informed even those who hadn't.

'That's Miss Thomson's! It's one of her turquoise ear-rings! *How did you get hold of that, Joel Barnett?*'

How, indeed? Everybody stood staring at the tiny thing, and then at young Joel, and he was gazing at the flagstones, struck white and dumb. And all in a moment Connie Dymond had pulled her arm free of his and recoiled from him until her back was against the wall, and was edging away from him like somebody trying to get out of range of flood or fire, and her face a sight to be seen, blind and stiff with horror.

'You!' she said in a whisper. 'It was you! Oh, my God, *you* did it—*you* killed her! And me keeping company—how could I? How could *you!*'

She let out a screech and burst into sobs, and before anybody could stop her she turned and took to her heels, running for home like a mad thing.

I let her go. She'd keep. And I got young Joel and that single ear-ring away from the Sunday congregation and into Trinity Cottage before half the people there knew what was happening, and shut the world out, all but old Joel who came panting and shaking after us a few minutes later.

The boy was a long time getting his voice back, and when he did he had nothing to say but, hopelessly, over and over: 'I didn't! I never touched her, I wouldn't. I don't know how that thing got into my pocket. I didn't do it. I never . . .'

Human beings are not all that inventive. Given a similar set of circumstances they tend to come out with the same formula. And in any case, 'deny everything and say nothing else' is a very good rule when cornered.

They thought I'd gone round the bend when I said: 'Where's the cat? See if you can get him in.'

Old Joel was past wondering. He went out and rattled a saucer on the steps, and pretty soon the Trinity cat strolled in. Not at all excited, not wanting anything, fed and lazy, just curious enough to come and see why he was wanted. I turned him loose on young Joel's overcoat, and he couldn't have cared less. The pocket that had held the ear-ring held very little interest for him. He didn't care about any of the clothes in the wardrobe, or on the pegs in the little hall. As far as he was concerned, this new find was a non-event.

I sent for a constable and a car, and took young Joel in with me to the station, and all the village, you may be sure, either saw us pass or heard about it very shortly after. But I didn't stop to take any statement from him, just left him there, and took the car up to Mary Melton's place, where she breeds Siamese, and borrowed a cat-basket from her, the sort she uses to carry her queens to the vet. She asked what on earth I wanted it for, and I said to take the Trinity cat for a ride. She laughed her head off.

'Well, _he's_ no queen,' she said, 'and no king, either. Not even a jack! And you'll never get that wild thing into a basket.'

'Oh, yes, I will,' I said. 'And if he isn't any of the other picture cards, he's probably going to turn out to be the joker.'

A very neat basket it was, not too obviously meant for a cat. And it was no trick getting the Trinity cat into it, all I did was drop in Miss Thomson's handbag, and he was in after it in a moment. He growled when he found himself shut in, but it was too late to complain then.

At the house by the canal Connie Dymond's mother let me in, but was none too happy about letting me see Connie, until I explained that I needed a statement from her before I could fit together young Joel's movements all through those Christmas days. Naturally I understood that the girl was terribly upset, but she'd had a lucky escape, and the sooner everything was cleared up, the better for her. And it wouldn't take long.

It didn't take long. Connie came down the stairs readily enough when her mother called her. She was all stained and pale and tearful, but had perked up somewhat with a sort of shivering pride in her own prominence. I've seen them like that before, getting the juice out of being the centre of attention even while they wish they were elsewhere. You could even say she hurried down, and she left the door of her bedroom open behind her, by the light coming through at the head of the stairs.

'Oh, Sergeant Moon!' she quavered at me from three steps up. 'Isn't it *awful*? I still can't believe it! *Can* there be some mistake? Is there any chance it *wasn't* . . . ?'

I said soothingly, yes, there was always a chance. And I slipped the latch of the cat-basket with one hand, so that the flap fell open, and the Trinity cat was out of there and up those stairs like a black flash, startling her so much she nearly fell down the last step, and steadied herself against the wall with a small shriek. And I blurted apologies for accidentally loosing him, and went up the stairs three at a time ahead of her, before she could recover her balance.

He was up on his hind legs in her dolly little room, full of pop posters and frills and garish colours, pawing at the second drawer of her dressing-table, and singing a loud, joyous, impatient song. When I came plunging in, he even looked over his shoulder at me and stood down, as though he knew I'd open the drawer for him. And I did, and he was up among her fancy undies like a shot, and digging with his front paws.

He found what he wanted just as she came in at the door. He yanked it out from among her bras and slips, and tossed it into the air, and in seconds he was on the floor with it, rolling and wrestling it, juggling it on his four paws like a circus turn, and purring fit to kill, a cat in ecstasy. A comic little thing it was, a muslin mouse with a plaited green nylon string for a tail, yellow beads for eyes, and nylon threads for whiskers, that rustled and sent out wafts of strong scent as he batted it around and sang to it. A catmint mouse, old Miss Thomson's last-minute purchase from the pet shop for her dumb friend. If you could ever call the Trinity cat dumb! The only thing she bought that day small enough to be slipped into her handbag instead of the shopping bag.

Connie let out a screech, and was across that room so fast I only just beat her to the open drawer. They were all there, the little pendant watch, the locket, the brooches, the true-lover's-knot, the purse, even the other ear-ring. A mistake, she should have ditched both while she was about it, but she was too greedy. They were for pierced ears, anyhow, no good to Connie.

I held them out in the palm of my hand—such a large haul they made—and let her see what she'd robbed and killed for.

If she'd kept her head she might have made a fight of it even then, claimed he'd made her hide them for him, and she'd been afraid to tell on him directly, and could only think of staging that public act at church, to get him safely in custody before she came clean. But she went wild. She did the one deadly thing, turned and kicked out in a screaming fury at the Trinity cat. He was spinning like a humming-top, and all she touched was the kink in his tail. He whipped round and clawed a red streak down her leg through the nylon. And then she screamed again, and began to babble through hysterical sobs that she never meant to hurt the poor old sod, that it wasn't her fault! Ever since she'd been going with young Joel she'd been seeing that little old bag going in and out, draped with her bits of gold. What in hell did an old witch like her want with jewellery? She had no *right*! At her age!

'But I never meant to hurt her! She came in too soon,' lamented Connie, still and for ever the aggrieved. 'What was I supposed to do? I had to get away, didn't I? *She was between me and the door!*'

She was half her size, too, and nearly four times her age! Ah well! What the courts would do with Connie, thank God, was none of my business. I just took her in and charged her, and got her statement. Once we had her dabs it was all over, because she'd left a bunch of them sweaty and clear on that brass candlestick. But if it hadn't been for the Trinity cat and his single-minded pursuit, scaring her into that ill-judged attempt to hand us young Joel as a scapegoat, she might, she just might, have got clean away with it. At least the boy could go home now, and count his blessings.

Not that she was very bright, of course. Who but a stupid harpy, soaked in cheap perfume and gimcrack dreams, would have hung on even to the catmint mouse, mistaking it for a herbal sachet to put among her smalls?

I saw the Trinity cat only this morning, sitting grooming in the church porch. He's getting very self-important, as if he knows he's a celebrity, though throughout he was only looking after the interests of Number One, like all cats. He's lost interest in his mouse already, now most of the scent's gone.

A HAPPY
SOLUTION

Raymund Allen

Raymund Allen contributed many intriguing
short mystery stories to the *Strand* magazine
which published a great range of crime and
detective stories by the best writers in the genre.
Allen's stories included 'One Black Knight'
(1892), 'The Winning Move' (1913), 'Allah
Knows Best' (1914), and 'The King's Enemies'
(1916). 'A Happy Solution' first appeared in the
Christmas Number of the *Strand*, December
1916.

The portmanteau, which to Kenneth Dale's strong arm had been little more than a featherweight on leaving the station, seemed to have grown heavier by magic in the course of the half-mile that brought him to Lord Churt's country house. He put the portmanteau down in the porch with a sense of relief to his cramped arm, and rang the bell.

He had to wait for a few minutes, and then Lord Churt opened the door in person. His round, rubicund face, that would hardly have required any make-up to present an excellent 'Mr Pickwick', beamed a welcome. 'Come in, my dear boy, come in. I'm delighted to see you. I wish you a merry Christmas.'

It was Christmas Eve, and his manner was bubbling over with the kindliness appropriate to the season. He seized the portmanteau and carried it into the hall.

'I am my own footman and parlour-maid and everything else for the moment. Packed all the servants off to a Christmas entertainment at the village school and locked the doors after 'em. My wife's gone, too, and Aunt Blaxter.'

'And Norah?' Kenneth inquired.

'Ah! Norah!' Churt answered, with a friendly clap on Kenneth's shoulder. 'Norah's the only person that really matters, of course she is, and quite right too. Norah stayed in to send off a lot of Christmas cards, and I fancy she is still in her room, but she must have disposed of the cards, because they are in the letter-bag. She would have been on the look-out for you, no doubt, but your letter said you were not coming.'

'Yes, I know. I thought I couldn't get away, but today my chief's heart was softened, and he said he would manage to do without me till the day after tomorrow. So I made a rush for the two-fifteen, and just caught it.'

'And here you are as a happy surprise for your poor, disappointed Norah—and for us all,' he added, genially.

'I hope you approve of my fiancée,' Kenneth remarked, with a smile that expressed confidence as to the answer.

'My dear Kenneth,' Churt replied, 'I can say with sincerity that I think her both beautiful and charming. We were very glad to ask her here, and her singing is a great pleasure to us.' He hesitated for a moment before continuing. 'You must forgive us cautious old people if we think the engagement just a little bit precipitate. As Aunt Blaxter was saying today, you can't really know her very well on such a short acquaintance, and you know nothing at all of her people.'

Kenneth mentally cursed Aunt Blaxter for a vinegar-blooded old killjoy, but did not express any part of the sentiment aloud.

'We must have another talk about your great affair later,' Churt went on. 'Now come along to the library. I am just finishing a game of chess with Sir James Winslade, and then we'll go and find where Miss Norah is hiding.'

He stopped at a table in the passage that led from the hall to the library, and took a bunch of keys out of his pocket. 'She was sending you a letter, so there can be no harm in our rescuing it out of the bag.' He unlocked the private letter-bag and turned out a pile of letters on to the table, muttering an occasional comment as he put them back, one by one, in the bag, in his search for the letter he was looking for. 'Aunt Emma—ah, I ought to have written to her too; must write for her birthday instead. Mrs Dunn—same thing there, I'm afraid. Red Cross—hope that won't get lost; grand work, the Red Cross. Ah, here we are: "Kenneth Dale, Esq.,

[15]

31, Valpy Street, London, S.W."' He tumbled the rest of the letters back into the bag and relocked it. 'Put it in your pocket and come along, or Winslade will think I am never coming back.'

He was delayed a few moments longer, however, to admit the servants on their return from the village, and he handed the bag to one of them to be taken to the post office.

In the library Sir James Winslade was seated at the chessboard, and Churt's private secretary, Gornay, a tall, slender figure, with a pale complexion and dark, clever eyes, was watching the game.

The secretary greeted Kenneth rather frigidly, and turned to Churt. 'Have the letters gone to post yet?'

'Yes; did you want to send any?'

'Only a card that I might have written,' Gornay answered, 'but it isn't of any consequence'; and he sat down again beside the chess players.

Churt had the black pieces, black nominally only, for actually they were the little red pieces of a travelling board. He appeared to have got into difficulties, and, greatly to the satisfaction of Kenneth, who was impatient to go in quest of Norah, the game came to an end after a few more moves.

'I don't see any way out of this,' Churt remarked, after a final, perplexed survey of the position. 'You come at me, next move, with queen or knight, and, either way, I am done for. It is your game. I resign.'

'A lucky win for you, Sir James,' Gornay observed.

'Why lucky?' Winslade asked. 'You told us we had both violated every sound principle of development in the opening but could Black have done any better for the last few moves?'

'He can win the game as the pieces now stand,' Gornay answered.

He proved the statement by making a few moves on the board, and then replaced the pieces as they had been left.

'Well, it's your game fair and square, all the same,' Churt remarked good-humouredly. 'I should never have found the right reply for myself.'

Gornay continued to study the board with attention, and his face assumed an expression of keenness, as though he had discovered some fresh point to interest him in the position. At the moment Kenneth merely chafed at the delay. It was an hour or so later only that the secretary's comments on the game assumed for him a vital importance that made him recall them with particularity.

'If the play was rather eccentric sometimes, I must say it was bold and dashing enough on both sides,' Gornay commented. 'For instance, when Lord Churt gave up his knight for nothing, and when you gave him the

WHITE.

BLACK.

Black to play and win.

choice of taking your queen with either of two pawns at your queen's knight's sixth.' He turned to Churt. 'Possibly you might have done better to take the queen with the bishop's pawn instead of with the rook's.'

'I daresay, I daresay,' Churt replied. 'I should have probably got into a mess, whatever I played. But come along, now, all of you, and see if we can find some tea.'

Kenneth contrived, before entering the drawing-room, to intercept Norah for an exchange of greetings in private, and her face was still radiant with the delight of the unexpected meeting as they entered the room.

After tea Sir James carried off the secretary to keep him company in the smoking-room, and Churt turned to Norah. 'You must sing one of the Christmas carols you promised us, and then you young folk may go off to the library to talk over your own private affairs. I know you must both be longing to get away from us old fogies.'

'Thank you, Lord Churt, for "old fogies", on behalf of your wife and myself,' Aunt Blaxter commented, with a mild sarcasm that somehow failed of its intended playful effect. But Norah had sat down at once to the piano, and her voice rang out in a joyous carol before he could frame a suitable reply.

A second carol was asked for, that the others might join in, and in the course of it Kenneth's hand came upon the letter in his pocket. He was opening the envelope as Norah rose from the piano. Her eye caught her own handwriting and she blushed very red. 'Be careful, Ken. Don't let anything fall out!' she cried in alarm.

Thus warned, he drew the letter out delicately, being careful to leave in the envelope a little curl of brown hair, a lover's token that she would have been shy to see exposed to the eyes of the others. But, in his care for this, a thin bit of paper fluttered from the fold of the letter to the carpet, and all eyes instinctively followed it. It was a Bank of England note for a thousand pounds.

Kenneth looked at Norah in wonder, but got no enlightenment. Then at Lord Churt, as the bare possibility occurred to his mind that, in a Christmas freak of characteristic generosity, he might have somehow contrived to get it enclosed with her letter. But Churt's dumbfounded expression was not the acting of any genial comedy. His hands trembled as he put on his glasses to compare an entry in his pocket-book with the number on the note. He was the first to break the amazed silence. 'This is a most extraordinary thing. This is the identical banknote that I put into the Red Cross envelope this afternoon as my Christmas gift, the very same that I got for the purpose of sending anonymously, and that you ladies were interested to inspect at breakfast time.'

Each looked at the others for an explanation, till all eyes settled on Norah, as the person who might be expected to give one.

Churt looked vexed and troubled, Aunt Blaxter severely suspicious, as she saw that the girl remained silent, with a face that was losing its colour. 'As the note was found in a letter sent by Norah, she would be the natural person to explain how it got there,' she remarked.

'I haven't the remotest notion how it got there,' Norah replied. 'I can only say that I did not put it there, and that I never saw it again since breakfast time, until it dropped out of my letter a few moments ago.'

'Very strange,' Aunt Blaxter remarked, drily. Kenneth turned upon her hotly. 'You don't suggest that Norah stole the note, I imagine!'

'My dear people,' Churt intervened, soothingly, 'do let us keep our heads cool, and not have any unpleasant scene.'

Kenneth still glared. 'If Norah had put the note into this envelope, she would have referred to it in her letter. I suppose you will accept my word that she doesn't.'

'Read out the postscript, Ken,' Norah requested. 'Miss Blaxter may like to suggest that it refers to the note.' The girl looked at her with a face that was now blazing with anger, and Kenneth read out: 'P.S. Don't let anybody see what I am sending you!' It had not occurred to him that it could be

[18]

taken as anything but a jesting reference to the lock of hair, the note of exclamation at the end giving the effect of 'As though I should ever dream you would', or some equivalent. The matter was growing too serious for any shamefacedness, and he produced the lock of hair in explanation. It was cruel luck, he reflected, that the unfortunate postscript should be capable of misconstruction. He had counted on Norah's making a triumphant conquest of the Churt household, and it was exceedingly galling to find her, instead, exposed to an odious suspicion. Aunt Blaxter's demeanour was all the more maddening that he could think of no means to prove its unreasonableness. He looked gratefully at Lady Churt, as her gentle voice gave the discussion a fresh turn. 'How long has Mr Gornay been with us?' she asked her husband.

Churt looked shocked. 'My dear, we mustn't make any rash insinuations in a matter of this kind. What possible motive could Gornay have for putting the note into Norah's letter, if he meant to steal it? Besides, my evidence clears him.'

'Would you mind telling us what you did with the note after you showed it at the breakfast table this morning?' Kenneth asked.

'I'll tell you exactly,' Churt answered. 'When it had made the round of the breakfast table, I put it back in my pocket-book and kept it in my pocket till this afternoon. It was while we were playing chess that I remembered that the bag would be going to post earlier than usual, and I put the note in the Red Cross envelope with the printed address and stuck it down and put it into the bag. I came straight back to the library, and I remember being surprised at the move I found Winslade had played, because he was offering me his queen for nothing. Just at that moment it occurred to my mind that Norah had probably already put her letters into the bag, and that, if so, I might as well lock it at once, for fear of forgetting to do so later. I looked at the chessboard for a few minutes, standing up, and then went and found that Norah's letters were in the bag, and I locked it, and came back and took Winslade's queen.'

'But I don't quite see what all that has to do with Mr Gornay, or how it clears him,' Lady Churt remarked.

'Why, my dear, whoever took the note out of one envelope, and put it into the other must have done so in the few minutes between my two visits to the bag. It was the only time that the letter was in the bag without its being locked. And during that time Gornay was watching the chess, so it can't have been him.'

'Was he in the library all the time you were playing?' Kenneth asked.

'I can't say that,' Churt replied. 'I don't think he was. I didn't notice

[19]

particularly. But I am positive that he did not enter or leave the room while I was standing looking at Winslade's move, and he must have been there when Winslade offered his queen and when I took it, because he was commenting on those very moves after the game was finished, and suggesting that I might have done better to take with the other pawn. You heard him yourself.'

'Yes,' Kenneth answered. 'I follow that. But there is such a thing as picking a lock, you know.'

'The makers guarantee that it can't be done to this one,' Churt answered, 'and the key has always been in my possession, so he couldn't have had a duplicate made, even if there had been any time.'

Norah interposed in a voice that trembled with indignation. 'In short, Lord Churt, you think the evidence conclusive against the only other person, except Sir James Winslade, who was in the house. I have only my word to give against it.'

'It is worth all the evidence in the world,' Kenneth cried, and she thanked her champion with a bright glance.

'Lady Churt is quite right,' Kenneth went on. 'I'd stake my life it was that sneaking Gornay. Have him in here now, and see if his face doesn't show his guilt when I call him a thief.'

'Not for the world!' Churt exclaimed, aghast. 'We should have a most painful scene. This is no case for rash precipitancy.' He assumed the air of judicial solemnity with which, from the local bench, he would fine a rascal five shillings who ought to have gone down for six months. 'I entirely refuse to entertain any suspicion of anybody under this roof, guests, servants, or anyone else. It will probably turn out that some odd little accident has occurred, that will seem simple enough when it is explained. On the other hand, it is just conceivable that some evil-disposed person from outside should have got into the house, though I confess I can't understand the motive of their action if they did. In any case, I feel it my duty, for the credit of my household, to have the matter cleared up by the proper authority.'

'What do you mean by the proper authority?' Lady Churt asked. 'I didn't think the local police were very clever that time when poor Kelpie got stolen.'

The Aberdeen terrier at her feet looked up at the sound of his name, and Churt continued: 'I shall telephone to Scotland Yard. If Shapland is there, I am sure he would come down at once in his car. He could be here in less than two hours. Until he, or somebody else, arrives I beg that none of you say a word about this affair to anyone who is not now present in this room.'

'Quite the most proper course,' Aunt Blaxter observed. 'It is only right that guilt should be brought home to the proper person, *whoever* that person may be.'

With a tact of which Kenneth had hardly thought him capable, Churt turned to Norah. 'I have no doubt Shapland will clear up the mystery for us satisfactorily. Meantime, my dear girl, you and I find ourselves in the same boat, for there is only my word for it that I ever put the note into the Red Cross envelope at all.'

The kindness of his manner brought the tears to her eyes, and Kenneth took her away to the library.

'Fancy their thinking I was a thief—a thief, Ken—a common mean *thief!*'

'Nonsense, my darling girl,' he said. 'Nobody could believe any such rubbish.'

'That odious Aunt Blaxter does, at any rate. She as good as said so.' She sat down in a chair, and began to grow calmer, while he paced about the room, angry but thoughtful.

'I was glad I had you to stick up for me, Ken, and Lord Churt is an old dear.'

'He's a silly old dear, all the same,' he answered. 'He has more money than he knows what to do with, but fancy fluttering a thousand-pound note through the Christmas post, to get lost among all the robins and good wishes!'

They were interrupted at this point by the entry of Gornay.

'I am not going to stay,' he said, in answer to their not very welcoming expressions. 'I have only come to ask a quite small favour. I am having a great argument with Sir James about character-reading from handwriting, and I want specimens from people we both know. Any little scrap will do.'

Kenneth took up a sheet of notepaper from a writing table and wrote, 'All is not gold that glitters', and Norah added below, 'Birds of a feather flock together.' It seemed the quickest way to get rid of him.

Gornay looked at the sheet with a not quite satisfied air. 'I would *rather* have had something not written specially. Nobody ever writes quite naturally when they know that it is for this sort of purpose. You haven't got an old envelope, or something like that?'

Neither could supply what he wanted, and he went off, looking a little disappointed.

'I wonder whether that was really what he wanted the writing for,' Kenneth remarked, suspiciously. 'He's a quick-witted knave. Look how sharp he was to see the right move in that game of chess. It wasn't very obvious.'

The chessboard was lying open on the table, where Churt had left it before tea. He glanced at it, casually at first, and then with growing interest. He took up one of the pieces to examine it, then replaced it, to do the same with others, his manner showing all the time an increasing excitement.

'What is it, Ken?' Norah asked.

'Just a glimmer of something.' He dropped into a chair. 'I want to think—to think harder than ever in my life.'

He leant forward, with his head resting on his hands, and she waited in silence till, after some minutes, he looked up.

'Yes, I begin to see light—more than a glimmer. He's a subtle customer, is Mr Gornay, oh, very subtle!' He smiled, partly with the pleasure of finding one thread of a tangled web, partly with admiration for the cleverness that had woven it. 'Would you like to know what he was really after when he came in here just now?'

'Very much,' she answered. 'But do you mean that he never had any argument with Sir James?'

'Oh, I daresay he had the argument all right—got it up for the occasion; but what he really wanted was this.' He took out of his pocket the envelope in which the banknote had been discovered. 'The character-reading rot was not a bad shot at getting hold of it, and probably his only chance. But no, friend Gornay, you are not going to have that envelope—not for the thousand pounds you placed in it!'

'Do explain, Ken,' Norah begged.

'I will presently,' he answered, 'but I want to piece the whole jigsaw together. There is still the other difficulty.'

He dropped his eyes to the hearthrug again, and began to do his thinking aloud for her benefit. 'Churt's reasoning is that Gornay must have been in here, watching the game, at the only time when the letters could have been tampered with, because he knew afterwards the move that was played just at the beginning of that time, and the move that was played just at the end. But why might not Winslade have told him about those two moves while Churt was letting me in at the front door? That would solve the riddle. I should have thought Winslade would have been too punctilious to talk about the game while his opponent was out of the room, but I'll go and ask him. I needn't tell him the reason why I want to know.'

He came back almost immediately. 'No, there was no conversation about the game while Churt was out of the room. Very well. Try the thing the other way round. Assume—as I think I can prove—that Gornay *did* tamper with the letters, the question is how could he tell that those two moves had been played?'

He took up the chessboard again and looked at it so intently and so long that, at last, Norah grew impatient.

'My dear boy, what *can* you be doing, poring all this time over the chess?'

'I have a curious sort of chess problem to solve before the Sherlock Holmes man turns up from Scotland Yard. Follow this a moment. If there was any way by which Gornay could find out that the two important moves had been played, without being present at the time and without being told, then Churt's argument goes for nothing, doesn't it?'

'Clearly; but what other way was there? Did he look in through the window?'

'I think we shall find it was something much cleverer than that. I think I shall be able to show that he could infer that those two moves had been played, without any other help, from the position of the pieces as they stood at the end of the game; as they stand on the board now.' He again bent down over the board. 'White plays queen to queen's knight's sixth, not taking anything, and Black takes the queen with the rook's pawn; those are the two moves.'

For nearly another half-hour Norah waited in loyal silence, watching the alternations of his face as it brightened with the light of comprehension and clouded again with fresh perplexity.

At last he shut up the board and put it down, looking profoundly puzzled.

'Can it not be proved that the queen must have been taken at that particular square?' Norah inquired.

'No,' he answered. 'It might equally have been a rook. I can't make the matter out. So many of the jigsaw bits fit in that I know I must be right, and yet there is just one little bit that I can't find. By Jove!' he added, suddenly starting up, 'I wonder if Churt could supply it?'

He was just going off to find out when a servant entered the room with a message that Lord Churt requested their presence in his study.

The conclave assembled in the study consisted of the same persons who, in the drawing-room, had witnessed the discovery of the banknote, with the addition of Shapland, the detective from Scotland Yard. Lord Churt presided, sitting at the table, and Shapland sat by his side, with a face that might have seemed almost unintelligent in its lack of expression but for the roving eyes, that scrutinized in turn the other faces present.

Norah and Kenneth took the two chairs that were left vacant, and, as soon as the door was shut, Kenneth asked Churt a question.

'When you played your game of chess with Sir James Winslade this afternoon, did he give you the odds of the queen's rook?'

Everyone, except Norah and the sphinx-like detective, whose face gave no clue to his thoughts, looked surprised at the triviality of the question.

'I should hardly have thought this was a fitting occasion to discuss such a frivolous matter as a game of chess,' Aunt Blaxter remarked sourly.

'I confess I don't understand the relevance of your question,' Churt answered. 'As a matter of fact, he did give me those odds.'

'Thank God!' Kenneth exclaimed, with an earnestness that provoked a momentary sign of interest from Shapland.

'I should like to hear what Mr Dale has to say about this matter,' he remarked. 'Lord Churt has put me in possession of the circumstances.'

'I have an accusation to make against Lord Churt's private secretary, Mr Gornay. Perhaps he had better be present to hear it.'

'Quite unnecessary, quite unnecessary,' Churt interposed. 'We will not have any unpleasant scenes if we can help it.'

'Very well,' Kenneth continued. 'I only thought it might be fairer. I accuse Gornay of stealing the thousand-pound banknote out of the envelope addressed to the Red Cross and putting it into a letter addressed to me. *I accuse him of using colourless ink, of a kind that would become visible after a few hours, to cross out my address and substitute another*, the address of a confederate, no doubt.'

'You must be aware, Mr Dale,' Shapland observed, 'that you are making a very serious allegation in the presence of witnesses. I presume you have some evidence to support it?'

Kenneth opened the chessboard. 'Look at the stains on those chess pieces. They were not there when the game was finished. They were there, not so distinctly as now, about an hour ago. Precisely those pieces, and only those, are stained that Gornay touched in showing that Lord Churt might have won the game. If they are not stains of invisible ink, why should they grow more distinct? If they are invisible ink, how did it get there, unless from Gornay's guilty fingers?'

He took out of his pocket the envelope of Norah's letter, and a glance at it brought a look of triumph to his face. He handed it to Shapland. 'The ink is beginning to show there, too. It seems to act more slowly on the paper than on the polish of the chessmen.'

'It is a difference of exposure to the air.' Shapland corrected. 'The envelope has been in your pocket. If we leave it there on the table, we shall see presently whether your deduction is sound. Meanwhile, if Mr Gornay was the guilty person, how can you account for his presence in the library at the only time when a crime could have been committed?'

'By denying it,' Kenneth answered. 'What proof have we that he was there at that particular time?'

'How else could he know the moves that were played at that time?' Shapland asked.

Kenneth pointed again to the chessboard. 'From the position of the pieces at the end of the game. Here it is. I can prove, from the position of those pieces alone, *provided the game was played at the odds of queen's rook*, that White must, in the course of the game, have played his queen to queen's knight's sixth, not making a capture, and that Black must have taken it with the rook's pawn. If I can draw those inferences from the position, so could Gornay. We know how quickly he can think out a combination from the way in which he showed that Lord Churt could have won the game, when it looked so hopeless that he resigned.'

The detective, fortunately, had an elementary knowledge of chess sufficient to enable him to follow Kenneth's demonstration.

'I don't suggest,' Kenneth added, when the accuracy of the demonstration was admitted, 'that he planned this *alibi* beforehand. It was a happy afterthought, that occurred to his quick mind when he saw that the position at the end of the game made it possible. What he relied on was the invisible ink trick, and that would have succeeded by itself, if I hadn't happened to turn up unexpectedly in time to intercept my letter from Norah.'

While Kenneth was giving this last bit of explanation, Shapland had taken up the envelope again. As he had foretold, exposure to the air had brought out the invisible writing so that, although still faint, it was already legible. Only the middle line of the address, the number and name of the street, had been struck out with a single stroke, and another number and name substituted. The detective handed it to Churt. 'Do you recognize the second handwriting, my lord?'

Churt put on his glasses and examined it. 'I can't say that I do,' he answered, 'but it is not that of Mr Gornay.' He took another envelope out of his pocket-book, addressed to himself in his secretary's hand, and pointed out the dissimilarity of the two writings. Norah cast an anxious look at Kenneth, and Aunt Blaxter one of her sourest at the girl. The detective showed no surprise.

'None the less, my lord, I think it might forward our investigation if you would have Mr Gornay summoned to this room. I don't think you need be afraid that there will be any scene,' he added, and, for an instant, the faintest of smiles flitted across his lips.

Churt rang the bell and told the servant to ask his secretary to come to him.

'Mr Gornay left an hour ago, my lord. He was called away suddenly and doesn't expect to see his grandmother alive.'

'Poor old soul! On Christmas Eve, too!' Churt muttered, sympathetically, and this time Shapland allowed himself the indulgence of a rather broader smile.

'I guessed as much,' he observed, 'when I recognized the handwriting in which the envelope had been redirected, or I should have taken the precaution of going to fetch the gentleman, whom you know as Mr Gornay, myself. He is a gentleman who is known to us at the Yard by more than one name, as well as by more than one handwriting, and now that we have so fortunately discovered his present whereabouts I can promise you that he will soon be laid by the heels. Perhaps Lord Churt will be kind enough to have my car ordered and to allow me to use his telephone.'

'But you'll stay to dinner?' Churt asked. 'It will be ready in a few minutes, and we shall none of us have time to dress.'

'I am much obliged, my lord, but Mr Dale has done my work for me here in a way that any member of the Yard might be proud of, and now I must follow the tracks while they are fresh. It may not prove necessary to trouble you any further about this matter, but I think you are likely to see an important development in the great Ashfield forgery case reported in the newspapers before very long.'

'Well,' Churt observed, 'I think we may all congratulate ourselves on having got this matter cleared up without any unpleasant scenes. Now we shall be able to enjoy our Christmas. I call it a happy solution, a very happy solution.'

His face beamed with relief and good humour as he once more produced his pocket-book. 'Norah, my dear, you must accept an old man's apology for causing you a very unpleasant afternoon; and you must accept this as well. No, I shall not take a refusal, and it will be much safer to send a *cheque* to the Red Cross.'

[*The solution of the endgame given in this story, and the proof that a white queen must have been taken by the pawn at Q Kt-3, is given on page 279.*]

THE ADVENTURE OF THE BLUE CARBUNCLE

Arthur Conan Doyle

Sherlock Holmes usually took a holiday from
sleuthing over the Christmas period. The sole
exception was 'The Adventure of the Blue
Carbuncle', which first appeared in the *Strand*
magazine in January 1892.

I had called upon my friend Sherlock Holmes upon the second
morning after Christmas, with the intention of wishing him the
compliments of the season. He was lounging upon the sofa in a
purple dressing-gown, a pipe-rack within his reach upon the right, and a
pile of crumpled morning papers, evidently newly studied, near at hand.
Beside the couch was a wooden chair, and on the angle of the back hung
a very seedy and disreputable hard-felt hat, much the worse for wear, and
cracked in several places. A lens and a forceps lying upon the seat of the
chair suggested that the hat had been suspended in this manner for the
purpose of examination.

'You are engaged,' said I; 'perhaps I interrupt you.'

'Not at all. I am glad to have a friend with whom I can discuss my
results. The matter is a perfectly trivial one'—he jerked his thumb in the
direction of the old hat—'but there are points in connection with it
which are not entirely devoid of interest and even of instruction.'

I seated myself in his armchair and warmed my hands before his crackling fire, for a sharp frost had set in, and the windows were thick with the ice crystals. 'I suppose,' I remarked, 'that, homely as it looks, this thing has some deadly story linked on to it—that it is the clue which will guide you in the solution of some mystery and the punishment of some crime.'

'No, no. No crime,' said Sherlock Holmes, laughing. 'Only one of those whimsical little incidents which will happen when you have four million human beings all jostling each other within the space of a few square miles. Amid the action and reaction of so dense a swarm of humanity, every possible combination of events may be expected to take place, and many a little problem will be presented which may be striking and bizarre without being criminal. We have already had experience of such.'

'So much so,' I remarked, 'that of the last six cases which I have added to my notes, three have been entirely free of any legal crime.'

'Precisely. You allude to my attempt to recover the Irene Adler papers, to the singular case of Miss Mary Sutherland, and to the adventure of the man with the twisted lip. Well, I have no doubt that this small matter will fall into the same innocent category. You know Peterson, the commissionaire?'

'Yes.'

'It is to him that this trophy belongs.'

'It is his hat.'

'No, no; he found it. Its owner is unknown. I beg that you will look upon it not as a battered billycock but as an intellectual problem. And, first, as to how it came here. It arrived upon Christmas morning, in company with a good fat goose, which is, I have no doubt, roasting at this moment in front of Peterson's fire. The facts are these: about four o'clock on Christmas morning, Peterson, who, as you know, is a very honest fellow, was returning from some small jollification and was making his way homeward down Tottenham Court Road. In front of him he saw, in the gaslight, a tallish man, walking with a slight stagger, and carrying a white goose slung over his shoulder. As he reached the corner of Goodge Street, a row broke out between this stranger and a little knot of roughs. One of the latter knocked off the man's hat, on which he raised his stick to defend himself and, swinging it over his head, smashed the shop window behind him. Peterson had rushed forward to protect the stranger from his assailants; but the man, shocked at having broken the window, and seeing an official-looking person in uniform rushing towards him, dropped his goose, took to his heels, and vanished amid the labyrinth of small streets which lie at the back of Tottenham Court Road. The roughs had also fled at the appearance of Peterson, so that he was left in possession of the field of battle, and also of the spoils of victory in the shape of this battered hat and a most unimpeachable Christmas goose.'

'Which surely he restored to their owner?'

'My dear fellow, there lies the problem. It is true that "For Mrs Henry Baker" was printed upon a small card which was tied to the bird's left leg, and it is also true that the initials "H.B." are legible upon the lining of this hat; but as there are some thousands of Bakers, and some hundreds of Henry Bakers in this city of ours, it is not easy to restore lost property to any of them.'

'What, then, did Peterson do?'

'He brought round both hat and goose to me on Christmas morning, knowing that even the smallest problems are of interest to me. The goose we retained until this morning, when there were signs that, in spite of the slight frost, it would be well that it should be eaten without unnecessary delay. Its finder has carried it off, therefore, to fulfil the ultimate destiny of a goose, while I continue to retain the hat of the unknown gentleman who lost his Christmas dinner.'

'Did he not advertise?'

'No.'

'Then, what clue could you have as to his identity?'

'Only as much as we can deduce.'

'From his hat?'

'Precisely.'

'But you are joking. What can you gather from this old battered felt?'

'Here is my lens. You know my methods. What can you gather yourself as to the individuality of the man who has worn this article?'

I took the tattered object in my hands and turned it over rather ruefully. It was a very ordinary black hat of the usual round shape, hard and much the worse for wear. The lining had been of red silk, but was a good deal discoloured. There was no maker's name; but, as Holmes had remarked, the initials 'H.B.' were scrawled upon one side. It was pierced in the brim for a hat-securer, but the elastic was missing. For the rest, it was cracked, exceedingly dusty, and spotted in several places, although there seemed to have been some attempt to hide the discoloured patches by smearing them with ink.

'I can see nothing,' said I, handing it back to my friend.

'On the contrary, Watson, you can see everything. You fail, however, to reason from what you see. You are too timid in drawing your inferences.'

'Then, pray tell me what it is that you can infer from this hat?'

He picked it up and gazed at it in the peculiar introspective fashion which was characteristic of him. 'It is perhaps less suggestive than it might have been,' he remarked, 'and yet there are a few inferences which are very distinct, and a few others which represent at least a strong balance of probability. That the man was highly intellectual is of course obvious upon the face of it, and also that he was fairly well-to-do within the last three years, although he has now fallen upon evil days. He had foresight, but has less now than formerly, pointing to a moral retrogression, which, when taken with the decline of his fortunes, seems to indicate some evil influence, probably drink, at work upon him. This may account also for the obvious fact that his wife has ceased to love him.'

'My dear Holmes!'

'He has, however, retained some degree of self-respect,' he continued, disregarding my remonstrance. 'He is a man who leads a sedentary life, goes out little, is out of training entirely, is middle-aged, has grizzled hair which he has had cut within the last few days, and which he anoints with lime-cream. These are the more patent facts which are to be deduced from his hat. Also, by the way, that it is extremely improbable that he has gas laid on in his house.'

'You are certainly joking, Holmes.'

'Not in the least. Is it possible that even now, when I give you these results, you are unable to see how they are attained?'

'I have no doubt that I am very stupid, but I must confess that I am unable to follow you. For example, how did you deduce that this man was intellectual?'

For answer Holmes clapped the hat upon his head. It came right over the forehead and settled upon the bridge of his nose. 'It is a question of cubic capacity,' said he; 'a man with so large a brain must have something in it.'

'The decline of his fortunes, then?'

'This hat is three years old. These flat brims curled at the edge came in then. It is a hat of the very best quality. Look at the band of ribbed silk and the excellent lining. If this man could afford to buy so expensive a hat three years ago, and has had no hat since, then he has assuredly gone down in the world.'

'Well, that is clear enough, certainly. But how about the foresight and the moral retrogression?'

Sherlock Holmes laughed. 'Here is the foresight,' said he, putting his finger upon the little disc and loop of the hat-securer. 'They are never sold upon hats. If this man ordered one, it is a sign of a certain amount of foresight, since he went out of his way to take this precaution against the wind. But since we see that he has broken the elastic and has not troubled to replace it, it is obvious that he has less foresight now than formerly, which is a distinct proof of a weakening nature. On the other hand, he has endeavoured to conceal some of these stains upon the felt by daubing them with ink, which is a sign that he has not entirely lost his self-respect.'

'Your reasoning is certainly plausible.'

'The further points, that he is middle-aged, that his hair is grizzled, that it has been recently cut, and that he uses lime-cream, are all to be gathered from a close examination of the lower part of the lining. The lens discloses a large number of hair-ends, clean cut by the scissors of the barber. They all appear to be adhesive, and there is a distinct odour of lime-cream. This dust, you will observe, is not the gritty, grey dust of the street but the fluffy brown dust of the house, showing that it has been hung up indoors most of the time; while the marks of moisture upon the inside are proof positive that the wearer perspired very freely, and could therefore, hardly be in the best of training.'

'But his wife—you said that she had ceased to love him.'

'This hat has not been brushed for weeks. When I see you, my dear Watson, with a week's accumulation of dust upon your hat, and when your wife allows you to go out in such a state, I shall fear that you also have been unfortunate enough to lose your wife's affection.'

'But he might be a bachelor.'

'Nay, he was bringing home the goose as a peace-offering to his wife. Remember the card upon the bird's leg.'

'You have an answer to everything. But how on earth do you deduce that the gas is not laid on in his house?'

'One tallow stain, or even two, might come by chance; but when I see no less than five, I think that there can be little doubt that the individual must be brought into frequent contact with burning tallow—walks upstairs at night probably with his hat in one hand and a guttering candle in the other. Anyhow, he never got tallow stains from a gas-jet. Are you satisfied?'

'Well, it is very ingenious,' said I, laughing; 'but since, as you said just now, there has been no crime committed, and no harm done save the loss of a goose, all this seems to be rather a waste of energy.'

Sherlock Holmes had opened his mouth to reply, when the door flew open, and Peterson, the commissionaire, rushed into the apartment with flushed cheeks and the face of a man who is dazed with astonishment.

'The goose, Mr Holmes! The goose, sir!' he gasped.

'Eh? What of it, then? Has it returned to life and flapped off through the kitchen window?' Holmes twisted himself round upon the sofa to get a fairer view of the man's excited face.

'See here, sir! See what my wife found in its crop!' He held out his hand and displayed upon the centre of the palm a brilliantly scintillating blue stone, rather smaller than a bean in size, but of such purity and radiance that it twinkled like an electric point in the dark hollow of his hand.

Sherlock Holmes sat up with a whistle. 'By Jove, Peterson!' said he, 'this is treasure trove indeed. I suppose you know what you have got?'

'A diamond, sir? A precious stone. It cuts into glass as though it were putty.'

'It's more than a precious stone. It is *the* precious stone.'

'Not the Countess of Morcar's blue carbuncle!' I ejaculated.

'Precisely so. I ought to know its size and shape, seeing that I have read the advertisement about it in *The Times* every day lately. It is absolutely unique, and its value can only be conjectured, but the reward offered of £1,000 is certainly not within a twentieth part of the market price.'

'A thousand pounds! Great Lord of mercy!' The commissionaire plumped down into a chair and stared from one to the other of us.

'That is the reward, and I have reason to know that there are sentimental considerations in the background which would induce the Countess to part with half her fortune if she could but recover the gem.'

'It was lost, if I remember aright, at the Hotel Cosmopolitan,' I remarked.

'Precisely so, on December 22nd, just five days ago. John Horner, a plumber, was accused of having abstracted it from the lady's jewel case. The evidence against him was so strong that the case has been referred to the Assizes. I have some account of the matter here, I believe.' He rummaged amid his newspapers, glancing over the dates, until at last he smoothed one out, doubled it over, and read the following paragraph:

'Hotel Cosmopolitan Jewel Robbery. John Horner, 26, plumber, was brought up upon the charge of having upon the 22nd inst., abstracted from the jewel case of the Countess of Morcar the valuable gem known as the blue carbuncle. James

Ryder, upper-attendant at the hotel, gave his evidence to the effect that he had shown Horner up to the dressing-room of the Countess of Morcar upon the day of the robbery in order that he might solder the second bar of the grate, which was loose. He had remained with Horner some little time, but had finally been called away. On returning, he found that Horner had disappeared, that the bureau had been forced open, and that the small morocco casket in which, as it afterwards transpired, the Countess was accustomed to keep her jewel, was lying empty upon the dressing-table. Ryder instantly gave the alarm, and Horner was arrested the same evening; but the stone could not be found either upon his person or in his rooms. Catherine Cusack, maid to the Countess, deposed to having heard Ryder's cry of dismay on discovering the robbery, and to having rushed into the room, where she found matters as described by the last witness. Inspector Bradstreet, B division, gave evidence as to the arrest of Horner, who struggled frantically, and protested his innocence in the strongest terms. Evidence of a previous conviction for robbery having been given against the prisoner, the magistrate refused to deal summarily with the offence, but referred it to the Assizes. Horner, who had shown signs of intense emotion during the proceedings, fainted away at the conclusion and was carried out of court.

'Hum! So much for the police court,' said Holmes thoughtfully, tossing aside the paper. 'The question for us now to solve is the sequence of events leading from a rifled jewel case at one end to the crop of a goose in Tottenham Court Road at the other. You see, Watson, our little deductions have suddenly assumed a much more important and less innocent aspect. Here is the stone; the stone came from the goose, and the goose came from Mr Henry Baker, the gentleman with the bad hat and all the other characteristics with which I have bored you. So now we must set ourselves very seriously to finding this gentleman and ascertaining what part he has played in this little mystery. To do this, we must try the simplest means first, and these lie undoubtedly in an advertisement in all the evening papers. If this fails, I shall have recourse to other methods.'

'What will you say?'

'Give me a pencil and that slip of paper. Now, then:

'Found at the corner of Goodge Street, a goose and a black felt hat. Mr Henry Baker can have the same by applying at 6:30 this evening at 221B Baker Street.

That is clear and concise.'

'Very. But will he see it?'

'Well, he is sure to keep an eye on the papers, since, to a poor man, the loss was a heavy one. He was clearly so scared by his mischance in breaking the window and by the approach of Peterson that he thought of nothing but flight, but since then he must have bitterly regretted the impulse which caused him to drop his bird. Then, again, the introduction of his name will cause him to see it, for everyone who knows him will direct his attention to it. Here you are, Peterson, run down to the advertising agency and have this put in the evening papers.'

'In which, sir?'

'Oh, in the *Globe, Star, Pall Mall, St James's, Evening News Standard, Echo,* and any others that occur to you.'

'Very well, sir. And this stone?'

'Ah, yes, I shall keep the stone. Thank you. And, I say, Peterson, just buy a goose on your way back and leave it here with me, for we must have one to give to this gentleman in place of the one which your family is now devouring.'

When the commissionaire had gone, Holmes took up the stone and held it against the light. 'It's a bonny thing,' said he. 'Just see how it glints and sparkles. Of course it is a nucleus and focus of crime. Every good stone is. They are the devil's pet baits. In the larger and older jewels every facet may stand for a bloody deed. This stone is not yet twenty years old. It was found in the banks of the Amoy River in southern China and is remarkable in having every characteristic of the carbuncle, save that it is blue in shade instead of ruby red. In spite of its youth, it has already a sinister history. There have been two murders, a vitriol-throwing, a suicide, and several robberies brought about for the sake of this forty-grain weight of crystallized charcoal. Who would think that so pretty a toy would be a purveyor to the gallows and the prison? I'll lock it up in my strong box now and drop a line to the Countess to say that we have it.'

'Do you think that this man Horner is innocent?'

'I cannot tell.'

'Well, then, do you imagine that this other one, Henry Baker, had anything to do with the matter?'

'It is, I think, much more likely that Henry Baker is an absolutely innocent man, who had no idea that the bird which he was carrying was of considerably more value than if it were made of solid gold. That, however, I shall determine by a very simple test if we have an answer to our advertisement.'

'And you can do nothing until then?'

'Nothing.'

'In that case I shall continue my professional round. But I shall come back in the evening at the hour you have mentioned, for I should like to see the solution of so tangled a business.'

'Very glad to see you. I dine at seven. There is a woodcock, I believe. By the way, in view of recent occurrences, perhaps I ought to ask Mrs Hudson to examine its crop.'

I had been delayed at a case, and it was a little after half-past six when I found myself in Baker Street once more. As I approached the house I saw a tall man in a Scotch bonnet with a coat which was buttoned up to his chin waiting outside in the bright semicircle which was thrown from the fanlight. Just as I arrived the door was opened, and we were shown up together to Holmes's room.

'Mr Henry Baker, I believe,' said he, rising from his armchair and greeting his visitor with the easy air of geniality which he could so readily assume. 'Pray take this chair by the fire, Mr Baker. It is a cold night, and I observe that your circulation is more adapted for summer than for winter. Ah, Watson, you have just come at the right time. Is that your hat, Mr Baker?'

'Yes, sir, that is undoubtedly my hat.'

He was a large man with rounded shoulders, a massive head, and a broad, intelligent face, sloping down to a pointed beard of grizzled brown. A touch of red in nose and cheeks, with a slight tremor of his extended hand, recalled Holmes's surmise as to his habits. His rusty black frock-coat was buttoned right up in front, with the collar turned up, and his lank wrists protruded from his sleeves without a sign of cuff or shirt. He spoke in a slow staccato fashion, choosing his words with care, and gave the impression generally of a man of learning and letters who had had ill-usage at the hands of fortune.

'We have retained these things for some days,' said Holmes, 'because we expected to see an advertisement from you giving your address. I am at a loss to know now why you did not advertise.'

Our visitor gave a rather shamefaced laugh. 'Shillings have not been so plentiful with me as they once were,' he remarked. 'I had no doubt that the gang of roughs who assaulted me had carried off both my hat and the bird. I did not care to spend more money in a hopeless attempt at recovering them.'

'Very naturally. By the way, about the bird, we were compelled to eat it.'

'To eat it!' Our visitor half rose from his chair in his excitement.

'Yes, it would have been of no use to anyone had we not done so. But

I presume that this other goose upon the sideboard, which is about the same weight and perfectly fresh, will answer your purpose equally well?'

'Oh, certainly, certainly,' answered Mr Baker with a sigh of relief.

'Of course, we still have the feathers, legs, crop, and so on of your own bird, so if you wish—'

The man burst into a hearty laugh. 'They might be useful to me as relics of my adventure,' said he, 'but beyond that I can hardly see what use the *disjecta membra* of my late acquaintance are going to be to me. No, sir, I think that, with your permission, I will confine my attentions to the excellent bird which I perceive upon the sideboard.'

Sherlock Holmes glanced sharply across at me with a slight shrug of his shoulders.

'There is your hat, then, and there your bird,' said he. 'By the way would it bore you to tell me where you got the other one from? I am somewhat of a fowl fancier, and I have seldom seen a better grown goose.'

'Certainly, sir,' said Baker, who had risen and tucked his newly gained property under his arm. 'There are a few of us who frequent the Alpha Inn, near the Museum—we are to be found in the Museum itself during the day, you understand. This year our good host, Windigate by name, instituted a goose club, by which, on consideration of some few pence every week, we were each to receive a bird at Christmas. My pence were duly paid, and the rest is familiar to you. I am much indebted to you, sir, for a Scotch bonnet is fitted neither to my years nor my gravity.' With a comical pomposity of manner he bowed solemnly to both of us and strode off upon his way.

'So much for Mr Henry Baker,' said Holmes when he had closed the door behind him. 'It is quite certain that he knows nothing whatever about the matter. Are you hungry, Watson?'

'Not particularly.'

'Then I suggest that we turn our dinner into a supper and follow up this clue while it is still hot.'

'By all means.'

It was a bitter night, so we drew on our ulsters and wrapped cravats about our throats. Outside, the stars were shining coldly in a cloudless sky, and the breath of the passers-by blew out into smoke like so many pistol shots. Our footfalls rang out crisply and loudly as we swung through the doctors' quarter, Wimpole Street, Harley Street, and so through Wigmore Street into Oxford Street. In a quarter of an hour we were in Bloomsbury at the Alpha Inn, which is a small public-house at the corner of one of the streets which runs down into Holborn. Holmes pushed open the door of the private bar and ordered two glasses of beer from the ruddy-faced, white-aproned landlord.

'Your beer should be excellent if it is as good as your geese,' said he.

'My geese!' The man seemed surprised.

'Yes. I was speaking only half an hour ago to Mr Henry Baker, who was a member of your goose club.'

'Ah! yes, I see. But you see, sir, them's not *our* geese.'

'Indeed! Whose, then?'

'Well, I got the two dozen from a salesman in Covent Garden.'

'Indeed? I know some of them. Which was it?'

'Breckinridge is his name.'

'Ah! I don't know him. Well, here's your good health, landlord, and prosperity to your house. Good-night.'

'Now for Mr Breckinridge,' he continued, buttoning up his coat as we came out into the frosty air. 'Remember, Watson, that though we have so homely a thing as a goose at one end of this chain, we have at the other a man who will certainly get seven years' penal servitude unless we can establish his innocence. It is possible that our inquiry may but confirm his guilt; but, in any case, we have a line of investigation which has been missed by the police, and which a singular chance has placed in our hands. Let us follow it out to the bitter end. Faces to the south, then, and quick march!'

We passed across Holborn, down Endell Street, and so through a zigzag of slums to Covent Garden Market. One of the largest stalls bore the name of Breckinridge upon it, and the proprietor, a horsy-looking man, with a sharp face and trim side-whiskers, was helping a boy to put up the shutters.

'Good-evening. It's a cold night,' said Holmes.

The salesman nodded and shot a questioning glance at my companion.

'Sold out of geese, I see,' continued Holmes, pointing at the bare slabs of marble.

'Let you have five hundred tomorrow morning.'

'That's no good.'

'Well, there are some on the stall with the gas flare.'

'Ah, but I was recommended to you.'

'Who by?'

'The landlord of the Alpha.'

'Oh, yes; I sent him a couple of dozen.'

'Fine birds they were, too. Now where did you get them from?'

[37]

To my surprise the question provoked a burst of anger from the salesman.

'Now, then, mister,' said he, with his head cocked and his arms akimbo, 'what are you driving at? Let's have it straight, now.'

'It is straight enough. I should like to know who sold you the geese which you supplied to the Alpha.'

'Well, then, I shan't tell you. So now!'

'Oh, it is a matter of no importance; but I don't know why you should be so warm over such a trifle.'

'Warm! You'd be as warm, maybe, if you were as pestered as I am. When I pay good money for a good article there should be an end of the business; but it's "Where are the geese?" and "Who did you sell the geese to?" and "What will you take for the geese?" One would think they were the only geese in the world, to hear the fuss that is made over them.'

'Well, I have no connection with any other people who have been making inquiries,' said Holmes carelessly. 'If you won't tell us the bet is off, that is all. But I'm always ready to back my opinion on a matter of fowls, and I have a fiver on it that the bird I ate is country bred.'

'Well, then, you've lost your fiver, for it's town bred,' snapped the salesman.

'It's nothing of the kind.'

'I say it is.'

'I don't believe it.'

'D'you think you know more about fowls than I, who have handled them ever since I was a nipper? I tell you, all those birds that went to the Alpha were town bred.'

'You'll never persuade me to believe that.'

'Will you bet, then?'

'It's merely taking your money, for I know that I am right. But I'll have a sovereign on with you, just to teach you not to be obstinate.'

The salesman chuckled grimly. 'Bring me the books, Bill,' said he.

The small boy brought round a small thin volume and a great greasy-backed one, laying them out together beneath the hanging lamp.

'Now then, Mr Cocksure,' said the salesman, 'I thought that I was out of geese, but before I finish you'll find that there is still one left in my shop. You see this little book?'

'Well?'

'That's the list of the folk from whom I buy. D'you see? Well, then, here on this page are the country folk, and the numbers after their names are where their accounts are in the big ledger. Now, then! You see this other page in red ink? Well, that is a list of my town suppliers. Now, look at that third name. Just read it out to me.'

'Mrs Oakshott, 117, Brixton Road—249,' read Holmes.

'Quite so. Now turn that up in the ledger.'

Holmes turned to the page indicated. 'Here you are, "Mrs Oakshott, 117 Brixton Road, egg and poultry supplier."'

'Now, then, what's the last entry?'

'"December 22nd. Twenty-four geese at 7s 6d."'

'Quite so. There you are. And underneath?'

'"Sold to Mr Windigate of the Alpha, at 12s."'

'What have you to say now?'

Sherlock Holmes looked deeply chagrined. He drew a sovereign from his pocket and threw it down upon the slab, turning away with the air of a man whose disgust is too deep for words. A few yards off he stopped under a lamppost and laughed in the hearty, noiseless fashion which was peculiar to him.

'When you see a man with whiskers of that cut and the "Pink 'un" protruding out of his pocket, you can always draw him by a bet,' said he. 'I daresay that if I had put £100 down in front of him, that man would not have given me such complete information as was drawn from him by the idea that he was doing me on a wager. Well, Watson, we are, I fancy, nearing the end of our quest, and the only point which remains to be determined is whether we should go on to this Mrs Oakshott tonight, or whether we should reserve it for tomorrow. It is clear from what that surly fellow said that there are others besides ourselves who are anxious about the matter, and I should—'

His remarks were suddenly cut short by a loud hubbub which broke out from the stall which we had just left. Turning round we saw a little rat-faced fellow standing in the centre of the circle of yellow light which was thrown by the swinging lamp, while Breckinridge, the salesman, framed in the door of his stall, was shaking his fists fiercely at the cringing figure.

'I've had enough of you and your geese,' he shouted. 'I wish you were all at the devil together. If you come pestering me any more with your silly talk I'll set the dog at you. You bring Mrs Oakshott here and I'll answer her, but what have you to do with it? Did I buy the geese off you?'

'No; but one of them was mine all the same,' whined the little man.

'Well, then, ask Mrs Oakshott for it.'

'She told me to ask you.'

'Well, you can ask the King of Proosia, for all I care. I've had enough of it. Get out of this!' He rushed fiercely forward, and the inquirer flitted away into the darkness.

'Ha! this may save us a visit to Brixton Road,' whispered Holmes. 'Come with me, and we will see what is to be made of this fellow.' Striding through the scattered knots of people who lounged round the flaring stalls, my companion speedily overtook the little man and touched him upon the shoulder. He sprang round, and I could see in the gaslight that every vestige of colour had been driven from his face.

'Who are you, then? What do you want?' he asked in a quavering voice.

'You will excuse me,' said Holmes blandly, 'but I could not help overhearing the questions which you put to the salesman just now. I think that I could be of assistance to you.'

'You? Who are you? How could you know anything of the matter?'

'My name is Sherlock Holmes. It is my business to know what other people don't know.'

'But you can know nothing of this?'

'Excuse me, I know everything of it. You are endeavouring to trace some geese which were sold by Mrs Oakshott, of Brixton Road, to a salesman named Breckinridge, by him in turn to Mr Windigate, of the Alpha, and by him to his club, of which Mr Henry Baker is a member.'

'Oh, sir, you are the very man whom I have longed to meet,' cried the little fellow with outstretched hands and quivering fingers. 'I can hardly explain to you how interested I am in this matter.'

Sherlock Holmes hailed a four-wheeler which was passing. 'In that case we had better discuss it in a cosy room rather than in this wind-swept market-place,' said he. 'But pray tell me, before we go farther, who it is that I have the pleasure of assisting.'

The man hesitated for an instant. 'My name is John Robinson,' he answered with a sidelong glance.

'No, no; the real name,' said Holmes sweetly. 'It is always awkward doing business with an alias.'

A flush sprang to the white cheeks of the stranger. 'Well, then,' said he, 'my real name is James Ryder.'

'Precisely so. Head attendant at the Hotel Cosmopolitan. Pray step into the cab, and I shall soon be able to tell you everything which you would wish to know.'

The little man stood glancing from one to the other of us with half-frightened, half-hopeful eyes, as one who is not sure whether he is on the verge of a windfall or of a catastrophe. Then he stepped into the cab, and in half an hour we were back in the sitting-room at Baker Street. Nothing had been said during our drive, but the high, thin breathing of our new companion, and the claspings and unclaspings of his hands, spoke of the nervous tension within him.

'Here we are!' said Holmes cheerily as we filed into the room. 'The fire looks very seasonable in this weather. You look cold, Mr Ryder. Pray take the basket-chair. I will just put on my slippers before we settle this little matter of yours. Now, then! You want to know what became of those geese?'

'Yes, sir.'

'Or rather, I fancy, of that goose. It was one bird, I imagine, in which you were interested—white, with a black bar across the tail.'

Ryder quivered with emotion. 'Oh, sir,' he cried, 'can you tell me where it went to?'

'It came here.'

'Here?'

'Yes, and a most remarkable bird it proved. I don't wonder that you should take an interest in it. It laid an egg after it was dead—the bonniest, brightest little blue egg that ever was seen. I have it here in my museum.'

Our visitor staggered to his feet and clutched the mantelpiece with his right hand. Holmes unlocked his strongbox and held up the blue carbuncle, which shone out like a star, with a cold, brilliant, many-pointed radiance. Ryder stood glaring with a drawn face, uncertain whether to claim or to disown it.

'The game's up, Ryder,' said Holmes quietly. 'Hold up, man, or you'll be into the fire! Give him an arm back into his chair, Watson. He's not got blood enough to go in for felony with impunity. Give him a dash of brandy. So! Now he looks a little more human. What a shrimp it is, to be sure!'

For a moment he had staggered and nearly fallen, but the brandy brought a tinge of colour into his cheeks, and he sat staring with frightened eyes at his accuser.

'I have almost every link in my hands, and all the proofs which I could possibly need, so there is little which you need tell me. Still, that little may as well be cleared up to make the case complete. You had heard, Ryder, of this blue stone of the Countess of Morcar's?'

'It was Catherine Cusack who told me of it,' said he in a crackling voice.

'I see—her ladyship's waiting-maid. Well, the temptation of sudden wealth so easily acquired was too much for you, as it has been for better men before you; but you were not very scrupulous in the means you used. It seems to me, Ryder, that there is the making of a very pretty villain in you. You knew that this man, Horner, the plumber, had been concerned in some such matter before, and that suspicion would rest the more readily upon him. What did you do, then? You made some small job in my lady's room—you and your confederate Cusack—and you managed that he should be the man sent for. Then, when he had left, you rifled the jewel case, raised the alarm, and had this unfortunate man arrested. You then—'

Ryder threw himself down suddenly upon the rug and clutched at my companion's knees. 'For God's sake, have mercy!' he shrieked. 'Think of my father! of my mother! It would break their hearts. I never went wrong before! I never will again. I swear it. I'll swear it on a Bible. Oh, don't bring it into court! For Christ's sake, don't!'

'Get back into your chair!' said Holmes sternly. 'It is very well to cringe and crawl now, but you thought little enough of this poor Horner in the dock for a crime of which he knew nothing.'

'I will fly, Mr Holmes. I will leave the country, sir. Then the charge against him will break down.'

'Hum! We will talk about that. And now let us hear a true account of the next act. How came the stone into the goose, and how came the goose into the open market? Tell us the truth, for there lies your only hope of safety.'

Ryder passed his tongue over his parched lips. 'I will tell you it just as it happened, sir,' said he. 'When Horner had been arrested, it seemed to me that it would be best for me to get away with the stone at once, for I did not know at what moment the police might not take it into their heads to search me and my room. There was no place about the hotel where it would be safe. I went out, as if on some commission, and I made for my sister's house. She had married a man named Oakshott, and lived in Brixton Road, where she fattened fowls for the market. All the way there every man I met seemed to me to be a policeman or a detective; and, for all that it was a cold night, the sweat was pouring down my face before I came to the Brixton Road. My sister asked me what was the matter, and why I was so pale; but I told her that I had been upset by the jewel robbery at the hotel. Then I went into the back yard and smoked a pipe, and wondered what it would be best to do.

'I had a friend once called Maudsley, who went to the bad, and has just been serving his time in Pentonville. One day he had met me, and fell into talk about the ways of thieves, and how they could get rid of what they stole. I knew that he would be true to me, for I knew one or two things about him; so I made up my mind to go right on to Kilburn, where he lived, and take him into my confidence. He would show me how to turn the stone into money. But how to get to him in safety? I thought of the agonies I had gone through in coming from the hotel. I might at any moment be seized and searched, and there would be the stone in my waistcoat pocket. I was leaning against the wall at the time and looking at the geese which were waddling about round my feet, and suddenly an idea came into my head which showed me how I could beat the best detective that ever lived.

'My sister had told me some weeks before that I might have the pick of her geese for a Christmas present, and I knew that she was always as good as her word. I would take my goose now, and in it I would carry my stone to Kilburn. There was a little shed in the yard, and behind this I drove one of the birds—a fine big one, white, with a barred tail. I caught it, and, prying its bill open, I thrust the stone down its throat as far as my finger could reach. The bird gave a gulp, and I felt the stone pass along its gullet and down into its crop. But the creature flapped and struggled, and out came my sister to know what was the matter. As I turned to speak to her the brute broke loose and fluttered off among the others.

'"Whatever were you doing with that bird, Jem?" says she.

'"Well," said I, "you said you'd give me one for Christmas, and I was feeling which was the fattest."

'"Oh," says she, "we've set yours aside for you—Jem's bird, we call it. It's the big white one over yonder. There's twenty-six of them, which makes one for you, and one for us, and two dozen for the market."

'"Thank you, Maggie," says I; "but if it is all the same to you, I'd rather have that one I was handling just now."

'"The other is a good three pounds heavier," said she, "and we fattened it expressly for you."

'"Never mind. I'll have the other, and I'll take it now," said I.

'"Oh, just as you like," said she, a little huffed. "Which is it you want, then?"

'"That white one with the barred tail, right in the middle of the flock."

'"Oh, very well. Kill it and take it with you."

'Well, I did what she said, Mr Holmes, and I carried the bird all the way to Kilburn. I told my pal what I had done, for he was a man that it was easy to tell a thing like that to. He laughed until he choked, and we got a knife and opened the goose. My heart turned to water, for there was no sign of the stone, and I knew that some terrible mistake had occurred.

I left the bird, rushed back to my sister's, and hurried into the back yard. There was not a bird to be seen there.

'"Where are they all, Maggie?" I cried.

'"Gone to the dealer's, Jem."

'"Which dealer's?"

'"Breckinridge, of Covent Garden."

'"But was there another with a barred tail?" I asked, "the same as the one I chose?"

'"Yes, Jem; there were two barred-tailed ones, and I could never tell them apart."

'Well, then, of course I saw it all, and I ran off as hard as my feet would carry me to this man Breckinridge; but he had sold the lot at once, and not one word would he tell me as to where they had gone. You heard him yourselves tonight. Well, he has always answered me like that. My sister thinks that I am going mad. Sometimes I think that I am myself. And now—and now I am myself a branded thief, without ever having touched the wealth for which I sold my character. God help me! God help me!' He burst into convulsive sobbing, with his face buried in his hands.

There was a long silence, broken only by his heavy breathing, and by the measured tapping of Sherlock Holmes's fingertips upon the edge of the table. Then my friend rose and threw open the door.

'Get out!' said he.

'What, sir! Oh, Heaven bless you!'

'No more words. Get out!'

And no more words were needed. There was a rush, a clatter upon the stairs, the bang of a door, and the crisp rattle of running footfalls from the street.

'After all, Watson,' said Holmes, reaching up his hand for his clay pipe, 'I am not retained by the police to supply their deficiencies. If Horner were in danger it would be another thing; but this fellow will not appear against him, and the case must collapse. I suppose that I am commuting a felony, but it is just possible that I am saving a soul. This fellow will not go wrong again; he is too terribly frightened. Send him to jail now, and you make him a jail-bird for life. Besides, it is the season of forgiveness. Chance has put in our way a most singular and whimsical problem, and its solution is its own reward. If you will have the goodness to touch the bell, Doctor, we will begin another investigation, in which, also, a bird will be the chief feature.'

AN UPRIGHT
WOMAN

H.R.F. Keating

H.R.F. Keating (b. 1926) has written nearly
thirty highly acclaimed mystery novels since
1959, over half of them featuring Inspector
Ghote of the Bombay CID. He has also edited
the invaluable *Whodunit? A Guide to Crime,
Suspense and Spy Fiction* (1982) and *The Bedside
Companion to Crime* (1989). 'An Upright
Woman' originally appeared in
Winter's Crimes 2 (1970).

Mrs Prothero liked to keep an ordered Christmas. It meant a good deal to her that things should be done in the same way each year. So at precisely eleven o'clock in the morning on the day before Christmas Eve, a Saturday, she began putting up the simple decorations she and Mr Prothero liked. They neither of them wished for anything extravagant, but it was right that the season should be marked and so mark it they did.

She began by cutting out two silver angels to hang one on each side above the fireplace. In a few minutes Mr Prothero would come home with a small bunch of holly, just enough to put one sprig above each picture in the sitting-room.

Snip, snip went the big cutting-out scissors between Mrs Prothero's strong and somewhat work-roughened fingers. Piece by piece the unwanted edges of the sheet of tinfoil dropped to reveal the emerging figure of the angel—one figure only since both were cut at the same time

[45]

from the folded sheet, thus ensuring a proper symmetry. Mrs Prothero had been making angels for a good many Christmases now, ever since foil became readily available and an article on 'Make Your Own Clever Xmas Decorations' had caught her eye in the Church magazine. Soon the angels, long trumpets raised to their lips, angular and decisive, were released from the stiff foil.

Mrs Prothero put them on top of the bureau next to the telephone and glanced at the fob watch she had got into the habit of wearing in her nursing-sister days.

Arthur was a little late. But then with Christmas Day falling on a Monday there was bound to be an extra rush this morning. But thank goodness the bank did at least close on Saturdays leaving him free to go out into the hurly-burly of the town's shopping streets to get the last things that could not be bought earlier. It was good of him to do this each year, though no more than his duty.

However the angels had hardly begun to swing to and fro a little in the heat from the fire below when there came a scuffly sort of bump on the flat's front door and Mrs Prothero hurried out to the hallway.

She pictured Arthur standing outside, his arms—they were rather short—clutching an assortment of parcels, unable to get at the latch-key in his trouser pocket, fastened by a chain to one of his braces buttons. It happened every year.

A rare twinkle of pleasure lighting up her large grey eyes and quite transforming the helmet-severe face with its long straight nose and uncompromising lower jaw, she hastened across to the solid door and turned back the latch. And there he was, just as she had pictured.

'You poor dear,' she said. 'You must have had an awful time.'

She closed the heavy door firmly behind him.

'It was pretty rough,' her husband agreed, waddling forward and laying down the bundle of holly he had been clutching on the top of the bureau, the only clear space he could see.

Mrs Prothero quickly relieved him of the rest of his purchases and took them through into the spick-and-span kitchen she prided herself on.

'I tell you what,' she called while her husband went to hang his overcoat in the hall cupboard, 'we'll make a little change for once. Let's have our start-of-Christmas drink now, and I'll tidy these away while you put up the holly before luncheon.'

For a moment a really quite apprehensive look appeared on Mr Prothero's round, twinkling-eyed face at this departure from tradition.

But then he gave a little squaring-up shrug of his shoulders under his black bank-manager's jacket.

'Right ho,' he called. 'Let's do that, and be damned.'

He strutted boldly over to the hanging corner-cupboard where he kept his cellar and poured two glasses of ginger wine, adding a tot of whisky to his own.

He held the latter bottle up after he had finished, and assessed the quantity remaining in it.

'The senior staff certainly punished this at our little do the other day,' he said as Mrs Prothero came back in.

She looked severe.

'It was Mr Perkins,' she said. 'Considering he's your second-in-command, he ought to be more restrained.'

Mr Prothero sighed. Then he brightened up.

'But I thought the whole affair went better than in some other years,' he said.

Mrs Prothero considered.

'Yes,' she said, 'the juniors behaved well. Especially young Smith. He spoke to me quite nicely, asking about our Christmas and so forth. Really showing an interest.'

Mr Prothero puffed out his pink cheeks dubiously.

'I try to like him,' he said. 'I feel I ought to. But he will dress in that provocative manner.'

'No,' said Mrs Prothero firmly. 'I was quite impressed. I shall revise my opinion of him.'

Her husband handed her her glass.

'Shall we drink to him?' he asked, only half in joke.

'No,' said Mrs Prothero decidedly, 'we'll drink to Christmas.'

'To Christmas,' said Mr Prothero, raising his glass.

'To three whole days of perfect peace,' his wife replied.

She took a modest sip and sat herself down in her customary chair to one side of the fire, her toes just resting on the black-leaded surround.

'Well,' she said, 'I do think it was one of the wisest things we ever did, to say we'd never go away for Christmas. This little spell of quiet means more to me than any amount of junketing.'

'Perfectly so,' agreed Mr Prothero, though it was hard, for all his pink benevolence of face, to conceive of him doing much in the way of junketing.

Mrs Prothero took another sip of her wine and gave an unexpected chuckle.

[47]

'Such a funny thing yesterday afternoon,' she said. 'I quite forgot to tell you last night what with all the rush.'

'What was that?'

'A man called. You know how they do sometimes, even though our door is so tucked away inside the flats. It's being on the ground floor, I think.'

'Yes, yes. I often feel something should be done about such people. Some sort of notice. Only chaps like that are just the kind to ignore notices.'

'Yes. Well, I tried to tell him I never deal with hawkers, but he had me answering all sorts of questions before I got rid of him. And can you guess how I did that?'

Mrs Prothero wore a look of mild triumph.

'No,' said Mr Prothero. 'Did you take a broom to him?'

He chuckled.

'Oh, I would if necessary,' Mrs Prothero answered. 'But nothing like that was needed. You see, in the end I got it out of him what he was meant to be selling. Insurance. And then I told him who you were. I've never seen a face fall so quickly. "Just my luck," he said, "think I'm interesting a client and it turns out to be the wife of the bank manager."'

But Mr Prothero appeared not to appreciate the joke to the full.

'Questions,' he said. 'You say he asked questions. What sort of questions?'

'Oh, dozens. And perfectly ridiculous some of them. Like were we going out to church late on Christmas Eve.'

'I don't like the sound of this,' said Mr Prothero, a look of almost pantomime shrewdness appearing on his round face.

'Oh, he had his reasons,' his wife replied. 'It was a dangerous time to be out in the cold, he said. What if one of us slipped and broke a leg?'

'You told him we weren't going out?' Mr Prothero asked.

'Oh, yes. But whatever makes you so serious?'

Mr Prothero gave a man-of-the-world shake of his head.

'Because I very much suspect,' he said, 'that your insurance salesman was nothing but a crook. That's an old dodge for spying out the lie of the land, you know. And these fellows often go about their business over the holiday period.'

Mrs Prothero took a moment or two to digest this example of duplicity.

'Well,' she said at last, 'he certainly learnt this flat wouldn't be empty over Christmas. Quite providential really.'

She looked comfortably over at her husband.

But he was not looking at her. Instead he was sitting open-mouthed in his cosy wing-chair staring at the door behind her.

Mrs Prothero turned to see what had transfixed him.

In the half-open doorway of the room a man was standing. He was aged about thirty, dressed in a trench-coat mackintosh in spite of the sharpness of the weather, hatless, and with a thin face from which two big brown eyes looked out with an uneasy mixture of bravado and pain. At his throat was the somewhat greasy knot of a striped Club tie.

And now Mr Prothero found his tongue.

'Who the devil are you?' he demanded. 'And how did you get in here?'

But Mrs Prothero knew the man.

'Arthur,' she said, her voice suddenly hollow with unexamined fears. 'Arthur, this is the person I was telling you about.'

'That's right,' the intruder said with a jerk of brashness, 'I popped in yesterday. Mrs Prothero and I had a chat.'

'You know my name then?' Mr Prothero said, a small tremor of doubt taking away somewhat from the determination with which the question was meant to have been put.

The man smiled, almost ingratiatingly.

'We had to know all about you both,' he explained. 'Just the same as we had to pull your front-door key from your pocket last week and take an impression from it. It's all part of the job.'

The door beside him was pushed wide and a second man entered. He was older than the first, between forty-five and fifty, short, broad-shouldered and with a fat, aggressive belly pushing open his heavy overcoat.

'Keep your bloody mouth shut, Tony,' he said curtly.

'What is this?' Mr Prothero demanded again. 'Who are you?'

The self-confident newcomer ignored this pouter-pigeon question.

'Just listen to me, and do what you're told,' he said with a cheerful briskness that suited his bustling manner.

'I certainly will not. I don't even know your name.'

The small mouth in the mottled face split into a quick grin at this.

'Proper introductions, is it, mate? All right then. The name's Dawson. And I'm here to do your bank. We're going to go in underground. Tunnel beneath that alleyway to the building on the other side.'

'That won't get you anywhere,' Mr Prothero snapped back, ruffled but undaunted. 'You'll not find a penny piece that's not in the main safe, and you won't get into that in a hurry.'

[49]

Dawson grinned again, standing solidly on short legs.

'What about the deposit boxes, cock?' he said. 'You've got the key to the gate for them, ain't you?'

Mr Prothero's round pink face positively paled.

'How did you know that?' he asked petulantly.

Dawson turned and called out in a loud, larky voice.

'Here, Dennis boy, you'd better come and show your spotty face.'

A young man of nineteen or twenty entered the room a little sheepishly. Dawson was right: there was at least one blatantly inflamed pimple on his pale face, just below and to the left of the thin nose.

'Smith,' exclaimed Mr Prothero at the sight of him.

The boy gave him a belligerent look.

'Yes,' he said, 'that's how we know all about what goes on in the bank, sir.'

The last word was an open jeer.

Mr Prothero ignored it.

'You have betrayed your trust,' he said.

For all the schoolmasterishness of the remark there was a dignity to it. It was a condemnation.

For an instant Smith had nothing to answer. Then he gushed words.

'You bet I've betrayed my trust,' he said. 'What sort of trust do you think you bought for my measly so-called salary? I'm making some real money now, something to make a show with.'

It was a moment of triumph for him. A declaration of independence.

But he was not allowed to savour it. His new boss trampled on his fine thoughts just as unfeelingly as his old one had done.

'All right, lad,' he said, 'you'll get your cut.'

He turned to Mr Prothero.

'So we want your key to the safe-deposit gate, mate,' he said. 'Where do you keep it? Over here?'

He marched down on the well-polished dark-oak bureau.

Mr Prothero scuttled up behind him.

'Get out of here this instant,' he said.

Dawson turned and the two short men stood confronting one another. The indignant cock robin and the small, aggressive bird-of-prey.

'I'll give you till I count five,' Mr Prothero said. 'And then I ring for the police.'

He glared pointedly at the telephone on top of the bureau, magnificently ignoring the fact that Dawson stood, straddle-legged, between him and it with the salesman Tony and young Smith watching from in front of the cheerful little fire.

'One. Two. Three—'

'Arthur,' said Mrs Prothero, breaking in unsteadily. 'Arthur, there are three of them.'

'Leave this to me, Ellen.'

It was the Manager speaking.

'Four,' he counted. 'Five.'

He gave Dawson a push. He might as well have pushed at a solid stone statue.

'Phone's cut off anyhow,' Dawson said, 'so just let's have that key.'

His right hand dipped into the sagging pocket of his open overcoat and came out holding a strip of dulled brass.

'You know what this is?' he said. 'It's the brass knuckles.'

He slipped the vicious-looking instrument over his fingers.

'Arthur,' said Mrs Prothero urgently. 'It's no good trying to outfight a man like this.'

'Quite right, old lady,' Dawson said. 'So come on, cock.'

'No,' squawked Mr Prothero.

And he darted sideways to the end of the bureau, picked up the bunch of holly he had put there only a few minutes earlier and rammed it hard into Dawson's face.

Dawson gave a howl of agony and Mr Prothero swung sharply on his heel and headed for the open door of the room.

Only to come bang into collision with yet another intruder, a dark, curly-headed man in a white polo-necked sweater, broad as a barn-door. Mr Prothero was sent staggering backwards.

And then Dawson, his mottled face pinpointed with blood drops, caught him by the shoulder and swung him round.

The brass knuckles came up from below with terrible force.

The crack they made as they hit Mr Prothero's jaw was like a pistol-shot, clean and sharp. Mr Prothero fell as if he was a tree under the axe. The back of his head struck the black-leaded fireplace surround with a sound that was quieter than Dawson's blow but as sickening.

Almost at once Mrs Prothero was on her knees beside him.

The man at the door spoke.

'What in the name of goodness did you do that for?' he asked Dawson in a strong Welsh accent.

'You never saw what the bastard did to me,' Dawson replied sharply. 'He jabbed that holly right in my face.'

[51]

'But you shouldn't have hit him like that, man,' the newcomer said. The Welsh accent enabled him to voice a wealth of shocked dismay. But Dawson was not easily put in the wrong.

'Listen, Morgan,' he said, 'when I want advice from you I'll ask for it.'

'Yes, but—'

'Get over to that desk and look for the key to the gate.'

Morgan gave one glowering look from his sombrely handsome Welsh face and then went over to the bureau, flapping the front down with unnecessary violence and starting to rummage.

'And where's the peterman?' Dawson snapped at him.

'Making himself at home in the bedroom, if you must know,' Morgan answered.

'Yes, I must know,' Dawson replied. 'He's the bloke who's going to blow the big safe. He's important.'

Morgan's white-sweatered back eloquently expressed his feelings at the implication that he himself was not important. But he said nothing.

Down on the floor beside the fireplace Mrs Prothero had been examining her husband with quiet competence. Now she looked up.

'He's badly hurt,' she said. 'He must on no account be disturbed till the doctor's seen him.'

'No doctor,' Dawson said.

It took Mrs Prothero, down on her knees on the floor, some two or three seconds to absorb this. Then she rose in two stiff movements.

'Listen to me,' she said to Dawson, 'I was a nursing sister for years. I can recognise a serious injury when I see one. My husband must be got to hospital.'

'You'll have to nurse him here,' Dawson said brutally. 'I know your sort. I've been in hospital. And right nasty bitches you are. Well, see what good it does him.'

He glanced down at the tubby little unconscious figure on the floor.

'Here, Morgan,' he said, 'you and Tony carry him into the bathroom. That's right it hasn't got an outside window?'

He flicked a look across at the boy Smith, standing where he had been ever since the sudden explosion of violence and looking paler than before.

'I told you,' the boy said hurriedly. 'I took a good look round during the party.'

'Then get him out,' Dawson said.

White-sweatered Morgan and Club-tie Tony exchanged glances, but seemed to find nothing to say. They moved over towards Mr Prothero.

'Don't jerk him,' his wife said. 'Whatever you do don't jerk.'

The two of them knelt almost with reverence and slowly lifted Mr Prothero up. Mrs Prothero followed them out, grim-faced.

Smith scuttled into the little hall of the flat and opened the bathroom door for them.

In the sitting-room Dawson went over to the bureau and tried to open the top drawer. He had just burst it open with the coal-shovel and had started into it like a gutsy hen with a dish of scraps when Tony came back in.

'She isn't liking it,' he said.

'And you'd want her to like it, eh?' Dawson answered, paying little attention. 'You'd like everyone to be merry and bright all the way along.'

Suddenly he swung round.

'Well, they ain't always merry and bright, not unless they bloody well make sure of it for themselves.'

In his hand there dangled a ring with two keys on it.

Tony's eyes lit up.

'Is that the one?' he asked.

''Course it is. That and the front-door mortise here, by the look of it. But there's fifteen feet of solid earth between us and the bank, so get into that kitchen and get the boards up.'

At midnight the fire in the sitting-room was still burning well, something quite unprecedented. But the little fireplace was scattered with ash in a fashion which Mrs Prothero would never have tolerated. Above, the tinfoil angels swung in high perturbation.

But if the empty sitting-room was untidy, the kitchen beyond was chaos. The polished yellow-and-grey linoleum had been torn right across. Three floorboards had been removed wholesale and lay piled beside Mrs Prothero's ironing-table. The corner of the room where normally the vegetable rack plumply held potatoes, carrots and onions was heaped with chunks of clay and dirt-encrusted brick from the foundations of the flats.

On the spotlessly kept kitchen table sat Dawson, swinging stubby legs and sipping coffee which Morgan, divested long since of his white sweater, had just made, neatly ranging cups, saucers and teaspoons in a fashion that did credit to his upbringing. Tony, his face dirt-streaked and unhappy, sat exhaustedly on one of Mrs Prothero's two kitchen chairs. Young Smith, his pimple inflamed to a yet angrier red by hours of hard work, sat on the other, elbows on knees, body slumped.

'Well,' Dawson barked abruptly, 'how much did you add just now?'
Tony looked up quickly.

'At least another foot,' he said.

'Nine inches,' said Morgan.

'Nine inches?' Dawson echoed with a touch of a snarl. 'Now listen, that's too bleeding slow.'

'We've been having to do a bit of shoring-up like,' Morgan explained, sulkily.

'Shoring-up? What the hell do you think you're making? The Channel Tunnel? Get back down and dig.'

'It isn't as if we're getting all that much help, is it?' Morgan answered.

'You'd like me down there, wouldn't you?' Dawson said. 'And what'd happen when some nosy neighbour came knocking at the door? That old bitch in the bathroom would start screaming, and we'd have a police-car outside in no time.'

Morgan glared at the grey and yellow checks of Mrs Prothero's desecrated lino.

'Well, what about the peterman?' he said. 'Playing bloody Patience in that bedroom. Not even coming out for his coffee. Why can't he take a turn?'

'Not in his contract, mate,' Dawson answered, with a return of his old cheerfulness. 'He comes to blow the safe, and he doesn't—'

He broke off.

From outside in the hallway there had come a tattoo of muffled knocks.

'It's them,' young Smith whispered hoarsely. 'The police.'

'It's the old bitch,' Dawson replied. 'Go and shut her up.'

'But last time . . .'

Dawson moved one stubby fist. Young Smith positively scuttled for the door.

He was not gone long.

'She wants to talk to you,' he said, putting his head shamefacedly only just back into the room.

'Did you tell her to stop that row?' Dawson said.

The boy looked as if he would have liked to have ducked his head back and stayed out of sight till things had calmed down. But plainly he did not dare.

'I told her it was no use asking to talk to you,' he offered.

A sharp grin flicked across Dawson's mouth.

'So you come and ask?' he said.

'But she said Mr Prothero's really bad,' Smith pleaded. 'She said something about a fracture of the skull. I don't know.'

'All right, so he's got a fractured skull,' Dawson said. 'Who cares?'

From behind Smith the thumping on the locked bathroom door began again. Smith stood where he was, half in, half out.

'All right,' Dawson said at last. 'Bring her in.'

Smith disappeared quickly as a schoolboy let off a punishment. In a moment Mrs Prothero came marching into the kitchen ahead of him.

The hours locked away with her injured husband had worked on her. Her features had lost what feminine softness they had had. Her eyes were deep sunk. And they blazed.

'So,' she said, going straight up to Dawson, 'here you are quietly relaxing as you go about your money-grubbing moles' work. Well, here's a fact to slap into your dream of unending riches. Not three yards from where you sit lies a man facing his Maker. And it is at your hand he is dying.'

She got no reaction from Dawson, swinging his legs on the table. But she clearly had an effect on the others. Tony shifted on his neatly painted chair and darted a glance of entreaty at Morgan. And Morgan went stony-faced as a rock from his native mountains.

Soon enough Dawson answered her.

'Okay, but I don't believe a word of it.'

He jumped down, forcing Mrs Prothero to take half a pace back.

'Now,' he said, 'back you get inside there, and don't let's have any more trouble.'

Mrs Prothero looked at him with conviction burning on her helmet-like features.

Dawson grinned.

'You can take a coffee,' he said. 'Or two, one each.'

'Coffee,' Mrs Prothero retorted. 'You are faced with a man who will be dead before Christmas Day is gone, and you offer him coffee.'

Suddenly she swung round to the others.

'No,' she said, 'I won't allow you to let him die. Isn't there one of you with the courage to speak up?'

But Dawson was undismayed.

'All right,' he said, 'let's see if anyone's chicken.'

He looked at them one by one. Then abruptly jerked back to stare at Tony.

'Do you believe the lady?' he asked. 'Come on, don't be scared to say. Do you believe the old geezer's dying?'

Tony reddened.

'Oh, shut up, for heaven's sake,' he said. 'Of course I don't believe it. He can't be.'

Behind Dawson young Smith's face registered almost comical relief to have escaped the dilemma.

Dawson turned to Morgan.

'Well, how about you, Welshie? Do you think he's dying?'

Morgan contrived to put on a judicial look.

'I expect the good lady's a bit hysterical like,' he said.

Dawson grinned his twisty little grin.

'Yes, hysterical,' he said. 'You can ignore her then, can't you, boy? Hysterical women are something a nice young man making his way in the world, with his own Health Club and all, doesn't have to have anything to do with.'

Morgan bit his lip.

'And ain't it a pity,' Dawson went on, 'that that Health Club got so rotten into debt that nice Mr Morgan has to rob a bank?'

Morgan started out of his chair, but thought better of it.

Now Dawson turned to young Smith.

'Well, do you believe your former employer'll never get his gold watch for fifty years' devoted service?' he said.

'No, no,' Smith almost shouted. 'No, I don't believe the stinking cow.'

But he was not going to escape so lightly.

Mrs Prothero marched up till her long implacable face was within inches of his.

'No,' she said. 'You have seen my husband. You are going to tell the truth.'

'I—I didn't get more than a glimpse.'

'You took your look. I was watching. Answer me.'

Young Smith had no answer.

'Come on, laddie,' Dawson said. 'Answer up.'

The boy tautened his whole body.

'No,' he flung out. 'No. I tell you I don't believe a word she says. He's all right. Old Prothero's all right, I tell you.'

Dawson pushed his stocky frame behind him and Mrs Prothero.

'Too bad, Ma,' he said. 'It didn't come off. Now back inside.'

'I'm tired,' Morgan protested when Dawson woke the three of them next evening.

'Tired?' Dawson snapped. 'You've just had an hour's kip, haven't you?

Do you think I have? Do you think I've closed a blessed eye ever since we've been here?'

'I don't see why you couldn't have done,' Morgan answered.

'Don't you? Well, I'll tell you why not. Because if I did Smithie here'd let that bitch out before anyone knew it. Anybody can see he's fallen for that story of hers.'

'I could have kept watch on him,' Morgan said.

Dawson darted him a look.

'Do you think the boy's scared of you?' he asked. 'He knows you're a sight too worried about what the neighbours'd think to belt him one. He'd get his little dander up and tell you to go to hell. And then where'd we all be?'

He turned away and studied the clock on the mantelpiece.

'Just gone half past six,' he said. 'We'll be in there by half seven now. That gives the peterman all and more of his blessed three hours to muffle the safe and set his stuff right, and then we blow it just as the old church bells start going hammer and tongs. As planned.'

He stood there with his stumpy legs astraddle, and a gleam of something like visionary light in his eyes.

It was abruptly extinguished.

'Smithie,' he said, 'go and have a look in the bathroom.'

But young Smith jibbed.

'Me again. Why does it always have to be me?'

Dawson looked at him. Then he swiftly crossed the room to where his overcoat lay flung on a chair. He dipped his hand into a pocket and pulled out the knuckle-duster.

Young Smith needed no further hint.

But he was out of the room for only a few seconds before he came in again following Mrs Prothero.

'Christ,' said Dawson, 'you've not let her out again?'

Mrs Prothero ignored this.

'No,' she said harshly to Dawson, 'he is not dead. That's what you sent the boy to find out, isn't it?'

'If he was going to die,' Dawson replied, maintaining an appearance of calm, 'I might send to ask. But as he isn't, I don't.'

From the door Smith put in a word.

'He looks pretty rough now though.'

'Does he?' Dawson answered. 'Perhaps you're setting up as a doc, are you? Seeing you've given up a career in banking.'

'No,' said Smith, 'but he's rotten. You can see he is.'

[57]

Mrs Prothero pounced.

'Exactly,' she said. 'You can't get away from that fact, can you? So you had better persuade your friends to let me go for help.'

'Don't be blasted silly,' Smith burst out at this. 'Do you think ambulance men are going to come and fetch him and leave us getting on with what we're doing.'

'Then you'll have to stop what you're doing, won't you?' returned Mrs Prothero implacably.

'We can't stop it, we can't,' Smith shouted. 'We're in sight of it now. More money than I ever dreamt of having. And then I'll show them. Out in South America I'm going to have cars by the garageful, and suits. And the dollies'll come crawling, you'll see.'

'Money,' retorted Mrs Prothero. 'A little money, and a human life. You've got to choose.'

'No,' the boy yelled. 'I tell you he isn't that bad. All I saw was a face with a lot of bandage round it. He might be fit as a fiddle for all I know.'

'You know he is not. And I am not budging from this spot till I've made you act on that.'

But now Dawson stepped in.

'Tony,' he said curtly, 'put her back.'

'Me?' Tony exclaimed, a look of hurt outrage beaming out of his liquid brown eyes.

'Yes, you,' Dawson said. 'I'm doing the telling now, and don't you forget.'

Tony went up to Mrs Prothero.

'You'll have to go, you know,' he said.

Mrs Prothero ignored him.

Tony offered her his arm in a gesture of slick over-politeness.

'Allow me to have the pleasure?'

Again she ignored him.

'Tony,' Dawson said.

A look of childish fury darkened Tony's face and he seized Mrs Prothero by the arm and dragged her out, slamming the door violently behind him. Out in the hallway, where quantities of dirty soil from the tunnel had by now encroached, he shouted loudly.

'For God's sake, stop all this.'

Then he abruptly lowered his voice.

'And anyhow it's no damn use. You don't know Dawson. He's got young Smith so scared he wouldn't do a thing, even if he wanted to. And I don't much suppose he wants. He's a nasty-minded little tick.'

Mrs Prothero whispered too. But it was a fierce whisper.

'And you're not nasty, are you? You'd like everyone to be nice and comfortable, wouldn't you? I know, you see.'

Tony shrugged his shoulders.

'Well, there's nothing wrong in wanting to have a good time and wanting others to have a good time, too,' he answered.

'And so you persuade yourself my husband is having a good time,' Mrs Prothero whispered sharply. 'A good time as he slips nearer and nearer the grave.'

'No,' said Tony, almost speaking aloud. 'But, I mean, all that's just a trick, isn't it? It's okay for keeping Dawson in his place, and I don't blame you. But you can tell me, you know.'

'All right, I will tell you. As a secret between the two of us.'

Mrs Prothero's grey eyes looked into his.

'My husband is dying,' she said. 'Get that into your head. Just one unpleasant fact. He is dying, and you are letting him die.'

'Look,' answered Tony, casting a look desperately round. 'I'd like to help. But I can't. I'm just as much trapped as you are.'

'Pull yourself together, man,' Mrs Prothero snapped, with a glance of simple disgust. 'We're going back in there, and you are going to tell the others it's time my husband had help.'

'No,' Tony pleaded.

'Get in,' said Mrs Prothero.

She went over and jerked the sitting-room door open.

Tony went in, with Mrs Prothero close behind.

Dawson looked at him.

'I thought I told you to lock her up,' he said.

'Yes. Yes. Look, Mrs Proth—'

'Tell him,' Mrs Prothero said.

Tony turned to Dawson, almost all the way.

'For God's sake,' he suddenly burst out, 'she's right. We all know she is. The fellow's dying. We can't just let him.'

Now at last his eyes found Dawson's.

'You're going to let her go for help,' he said. 'Or I'll bloody shout out of this window.'

He swung away and began to make for the window. Dawson caught him by the elbow almost before he had moved. He spun him round and sent him smack back against the wall by the bureau. Then he stooped to the chair where he had let the knuckle-duster fall on top of his coat and picked up the little strip of heavy brass.

He stood in front of Tony and jabbed at his face until he fell to the floor.

Tony did not lie long where he had fallen. Dawson saw to that. He sent young Smith for water, splashed it over Tony, pulled him to his feet and sent him back down the tunnel, all within ten minutes.

But then something happened which had not at all entered Dawson's scheme of things. The tunnel fell in.

It fell partly on top of Smith, and Dawson himself went down and hauled the boy, who was in a dead faint, out by his wrists. Then he went down again and with the aid of one of Mrs Prothero's saucepans dug through the fall and got at Morgan.

When he eventually scrambled out Smith was still unconscious on the soil-strewn kitchen floor with Tony, his spaniel face terribly distorted with bruises and cuts, sitting looking hopelessly down at him.

Dawson sent him to fetch Mrs Prothero.

'Get a look at the lad,' he said to her when Tony brought her in. 'Find out what's the matter with him. We've had a bit of trouble.'

Without a word Mrs Prothero knelt beside Smith, as earlier she had knelt beside her husband. She went to work with cool expertness and at the end of five minutes looked up.

'It's only his foot as far as I can tell,' she said. 'But that's badly crushed. It's impossible to tell how badly. Otherwise he's fainted, but he should come out of that soon enough. Poor lad.'

'All right,' Dawson said, 'do what you have to do for him.'

'What I have to do?' retorted Mrs Prothero, still kneeling on the earth-stained linoleum. 'It's not a question of what I can do. This boy must go to hospital.'

Dawson gave her one of his savage little grins.

'Hospital nothing,' he said. 'You told me he's just hurt his foot. You can deal with that. You missed your chance though, didn't you? You ought to have added him to your list of the dead and dying.'

Mrs Prothero had been busy with her patient. Now she gave Dawson a brief glance.

'Isn't it about time you stopped this nonsense of pretending my husband isn't as bad as I've said?' she asked.

Dawson made no reply. For a little he walked about the kitchen, where he could for earth and rubble. Then he went and stood over Mrs Prothero again.

'Listen,' he said, 'you're going to get that boy patched up so we can

leave here as planned with all our nice gift-wrapped parcels full of money
as the crowds come out of the Midnight service at the church. If need be,
we'll carry the lad and pretend he's drunk. But we're going then, and
we're going with the money. Understand that.'

Mrs Prothero looked up.

'And what if I won't do as you say?'

Dawson's answer came without hesitation.

'You saw me deal with Tony here. You'll get the same. Woman or no
woman.'

Mrs Prothero looked at him quite calmly.

'Then I shall have to help you,' she said.

Dawson glanced at Smith. He was, for all his youth, a full six feet tall
and he occupied a lot of the kitchen floor.

'Here,' Dawson said, 'I'll dump him out in the hall. With the doorkey
in my pocket you'll be as safe there as anywhere, and we can get on with
the digging. There's a whole lot more earth to be shifted now. I'll have to
take a hand myself.'

He left the kitchen and Mrs Prothero heard him with a sudden switch
to considerable deference asking the man who had all the while occupied
the bedroom in solitary state whether he could as a special favour guard
the bathroom key and 'keep an eye on the old bitch'. Apparently he
agreed because Dawson came back in, unceremoniously picked up
Smith's thin body and dumped him on the hall carpet next to the earth-
pile there. When she followed she caught a glimpse of the mysterious
safe-blower. He was lying propped on one elbow on her bed, with his
shoes on. And spread out on her husband's bed were two packs of
playing-cards in an elaborate game of Patience.

Young Smith recovered consciousness soon after Dawson had gone
back to the tunnel. Mrs Prothero wiped his forehead with the dampened
tea-towel she had brought from the kitchen.

'Well,' she demanded briskly, 'and how are we feeling now?'

Smith admitted in a croaky voice to not feeling too bad. He demanded,
querulously, to know what had happened and Mrs Prothero told him,
right down to Dawson's instructions to her to get him well enough to
leave with the money some three hours hence.

'It'll get better, my foot, in the end, won't it?' Smith asked.

'Provided you get proper attention,' said Mrs Prothero dryly.

'I'll get that,' Smith assured her eagerly. 'They've got good hospitals in
South America, same as anywhere else. And I'll be able to pay. I will, too.
I want to be able to go about, hit the night-clubs, live it up.'

Mrs Prothero looked at him.

'You poor fish,' she said, very quietly and confidentially. 'They still won't care tuppence for you, the girls.'

Wide-eyed horror appeared on Smith's face. Blasphemy had been spoken.

'Look,' he whispered feverishly, 'when I've got money girls'll come running. Running.'

'To you? If you want that sort of success—and heaven knows that's pitiful enough—you've got to be the sort of person who earns some respect. And do you think that just because you've let that Dawson frighten you into committing a crime, and letting an innocent man die, you're any different?'

'I am. I am.'

'Don't be silly,' replied Mrs Prothero, as if she was in one of the children's wards. 'You're worth nothing, and you never will be.'

She looked him straight in the eyes.

'Not unless,' she added, 'when the time comes here you go the right way and go it hard.'

Smith looked away.

Mrs Prothero rose and went to the door of her bedroom. She addressed the man lying on her bed.

'I want to go and attend to my husband,' she said. 'Will you kindly unlock the bathroom door?'

The peterman gave her a stony look from little pale blue eyes. But he swung himself off the bed and did as she had asked.

In spite of the setback the tunnellers had suffered the church bells had been battering the night air with their clangour for only five minutes when Morgan unlocked the bathroom door and told Mrs Prothero the big safe was about to be blown.

'That peterman insisted on having a coffee first,' he said. 'It seems it's his right. So I brought you a couple of cups.'

Mrs Prothero looked at him.

'Do you still really believe my husband is fit enough to drink coffee?' she asked.

Morgan studied the hall carpet.

'You know, we're all very sorry that had to happen,' he said.

'Who's sorry?' Mrs Prothero countered. 'Do you think Dawson's sorry?'

Morgan bit his full lower lip.

'Well, not exactly.'

He looked up for an instant.

'In many ways,' he said, 'I wish I'd never got involved with that chap.'

'In many ways,' Mrs Prothero echoed ironically. 'But never in the way of doing anything about it. You're involved with him in what in a very few hours will be murder. The law says that you are equally guilty. And the law is right.'

Morgan looked pained.

'I wish you'd understand,' he said. 'There was a strict agreement there was to be no violence in this business. I said I wouldn't come in, unless. And he had to have me, you know, for my mining experience. Before I went in for the physical culture. It was only because that got in such a terrible jam that I had to consider this business at all.'

'And now you'll end up doing a life sentence,' Mrs Prothero capped him grimly.

But she failed to quench him.

'Oh, no,' he said. 'That's where you're wrong, see. What you haven't taken into account is how damn clever Dawson is. I've watched him, you know. And he's smart all right. He'll have us all off to South America before ever this business is known about.'

'Exactly,' said Mrs Prothero. 'Dawson is clever. Too clever for you.'

It took Morgan several seconds to absorb this. The thoughts crossing his mind could clearly be seen on his mobile Welsh face.

They had come to forming, almost aloud, the word 'Cheated' when from the tunnel in the kitchen there woofed up the sound of a single sharp boom.

'The safe,' Morgan said.

And the next moment faintly but shrilly through the tunnel there came the sound of a bell ringing and ringing.

Mrs Prothero was first to realise what must have happened.

'It looks as if your Mr Dawson is not so clever after all,' she said. 'There must have been an alarm bell he didn't neutralize.'

Morgan without a word tried to open the front door. But the mortise key was still in Dawson's pocket. He looked all round and then started off for the sitting-room and its windows. But he was not quick enough.

There was a thumping sound from the kitchen and Dawson himself came staggering out of the tunnel.

'Morgan,' he shouted. 'The bathroom key, quick. I've got to know where that bell is.'

In an instant Mrs Prothero ran across to the bathroom door and spreadeagled herself in front of it.

[63]

'You will not touch him,' she declared as Dawson came into the hall. 'Anything could be the end of him now.'

'Get out of my way.'

Dawson took a step forward, fist bunched.

And then the alarm stopped ringing.

Tony, coming in from the kitchen looking panic-stricken in every feature, stopped.

'The peterman,' he said. 'He must have found it. He was going round like a scalded rabbit when I left.'

Smith hobbled in from the kitchen, still holding an incongruously festive sheet of Christmas wrapping paper, and full of plaintive questions. Even when Dawson had tersely answered him they stood where they were, as if none of them could believe the alarm was over. And they had still scarcely shifted when the peterman came up out of the tunnel.

'Well,' he said without ceremony to Dawson, 'what you going to do?'

Dawson thought.

'Wait here,' he said eventually. 'Give it a few minutes more to see if anyone heard. It must have been some old bell. We certainly did the one that rings at the police station.'

'All right,' the peterman said.

He went over to the front door and tried it.

'You'd better unlock this, mate,' he remarked. 'If we have to go, we'll have to go quick.'

Dawson took the mortise key from his pocket and turned it in the lock. Then, with an assumption of complete calm, he strolled into the sitting-room and plumped himself down in Mrs Prothero's armchair.

The others followed him in.

'Look,' Tony said, 'shouldn't we all wait round the corner somewhere? We could come back when we were sure it was all clear.'

'And have you scuttle off out of it?' Dawson said. 'We stay here, chum.'

He looked round at the rest of them, coming to rest eventually on limping, white-faced Smith.

'Scared as hell, aren't you, lad?' he said.

'No, no, I'm not. Really, I'm not.'

It was plain that, however scared or not scared he might be of the police coming, he was frightened stiff of Dawson.

'Well,' Dawson said to him, 'you can calm down, sonny. No one's heard that bell. You can take it from me.'

From just inside the door Mrs Prothero intervened.

'It would have been better for you, far, if that bell had been heard.'

'I tell you it can't have been heard,' Dawson replied.

'And if it hasn't, and you carry out your plan and leave me here with Arthur when you go, they'll find a dead man in with me.'

Dawson's little grin returned.

'That's not going to worry me,' he said. 'I'll be far away.'

'And what then?' asked Mrs Prothero sternly.

'What then? Then I'll be up on the top side. Then it'll be my turn to rub faces in the dirt.'

He stuck out his muscled belly in defiance. But his boast had only confirmed Mrs Prothero in her diagnosis of him.

'Let me tell you something,' she said. 'Once I may not have understood a man like you. But there's some use to be made of long dark hours locked away with a dying man. I can see you now, right down to the very depths. And I'll tell you what you'll do when you get to South America and start living this life you've dreamt of so long. You'll curl up and die.'

Dawson jumped to his feet.

'You'll die,' Mrs Prothero continued unperturbed. 'You'll die because the only thing that's kept you going has been the thought of your turn to rub faces in the dirt. And when you feel you've got that, you'll be finished. I don't know what way it will take you. Gambling, I should say. You'll gamble yourself into the gutter, and then you'll creep into a hole and die.'

And it was clear then that Mrs Prothero had at last won her battle. Dawson stood without an atom of fight left in him. Above his head the trumpeting angels lazily swung.

'Well,' Mrs Prothero barked, turning to the others, 'are you going to take your chance now? Here's a decision you can make for yourself, Smith. And you, Tony, you can act in the real world, for once. And, Morgan, do you still believe this creature's so clever?'

'I'm getting out of here,' Morgan announced.

He started towards the hall.

But a voice halted him.

Small, dry-faced and insignificant, the peterman stood there and uttered one word.

'Stop.'

Morgan turned.

'You're a lot of fools,' the peterman said. 'I've blown that safe for you.

There's all the money you want just lying there. And you're running out just because of an old bitch's sharp tongue.'

'Yes,' said Morgan slowly, 'the money is there after all. It'd be stupid not to take it now.'

And Dawson was quick to scramble back into leadership.

'I should bloody well hope so,' he said. 'Not a soul's heard that bell. Inside again, quick.'

He hurried out into the earth-mounded hall, the others at his heels.

But not at his orders. Not all of them.

'No,' young Smith shouted suddenly at the back. 'I've seen you down, and I'm going.'

He was nearer the front door than any of them. He turned and got a hand to the Yale knob.

But Dawson was still formidable. He had wheeled round in an instant at Smith's hysterical shout and now he lunged.

And Smith, turning back, struck out. Blindly, but hard.

His fist connected with Dawson's face and stopped him. It stopped him just long enough for a frantic twist at the Yale knob, for the door to swing wide, for the boy to get out into the corridor.

'Help, help, police, help.'

The cries echoed loud, and the thump and thud of young Smith's lame run echoed too.

It was followed at once by a stampede of other running feet. Only the peterman stayed for a few seconds, stayed to deliver a parting valediction.

'You win, you hag,' he snarled at Mrs Prothero. 'You win, but I hope he does die. I hope he dies in agony.'

Then he too was off, at a fast, wary run.

Mrs Prothero turned to the bathroom door.

'Arthur,' she called, 'did you hear that? He hopes you'll die. You can come out now.'

A BOOK FOR CHRISTMAS

Christopher Hallam

Christopher Hallam (b. 1947) is a corporate
adviser whose short stories have been broadcast
on local radio and published in magazines. As
well as writing fiction, he also contributes
articles on legal and financial matters to business
magazines. 'A Book for Christmas' was written
especially for this anthology.

'Can I help you?' Albion Street, his fingers nimbly parcelling a
book for despatch in the evening's post, spoke to the lady who
had just entered the shop.

Mrs Evelyn Harcourt glanced uncertainly round the small premises
packed overwhelmingly with books.

Her winter coat was flecked with sleet, watery jewels evaporating in
the warmth which was provided by burbling gas heaters, their fumes
tainting the air. She hooked her umbrella on the edge of the counter and
regarded Street, a short, waistcoated man with greased black hair.

'I'm looking for a book—a Christmas present for a friend,' she replied.
Her measured, educated tones matched her elegant fortysomething poise
which, together with her quality clothes, categorized her in Street's eyes
as 'in the money'. A customer to attend to dutifully.

'Plenty to choose from here,' he said affably, knotting the parcel and
cutting the string.

As proprietor of Crowley's Books (antiquarian and collectable), he was proud of his reputation of being able to supply sought-after books, especially signed first editions.

Shelves of books climbed the walls. Library steps were available to gain access to the higher reaches. Heavily laden gondolas filled the floor space leaving only the narrowest of aisles between them. Dusty chandeliers cast a mellow glow.

'I may need some help in making my selection,' suggested Mrs Harcourt, venturing away from the counter.

The doorbell pinged, a young man entered, and began browsing.

'What sort of book, madam? Fact? Fiction?'

'Fiction.'

'They're in this section,' he said, leading her to them. Dust-free strips showed where books had recently been removed, considered, and pushed back.

'So many to choose from,' she remarked.

'Does your friend collect a particular author?'

She shook her head.

'Oh, then perhaps a particular type of fiction, say the genre of M.R. James,' encouraged Street, knowing he had a fine first edition by the famous writer. 'Ghost stories are popular at Christmas,' he added.

'Hmm, maybe. It's so difficult when one can't remember the title. My friend mentioned a book and I thought I'd be sure to remember the title.'

'Any idea of the story?'

Mrs Harcourt looked around for inspiration, watched the young man fondly handling a dusty volume an inch thick, and said: 'I rather think it was to do with swindling. You know, one person doing another out of money rightfully theirs.' Her green eyes gave Street a deep look.

'I'll take this book,' called the young man.

'With you in a moment, sir,' replied Street. Then to Mrs Harcourt: 'You try these: authors between 1950 and 1990. Must be a good yarn about swindling among those. Excuse me, please.'

'Swindling,' not a word he liked, stabbed his conscience and, while he wrapped the man's purchase and processed the cheque, Street's mind went back a few years.

Out of idle curiosity one lunchtime Street had entered the shop. The then owner, Frederick Crowley, a hunchbacked seventy-year-old wearing thick-lensed spectacles, had been earnestly flipping through a box of books. Street, who previously had not been interested in book collecting, had asked Crowley what he was searching for as he rapidly glanced at the opening pages of each book.

Crowley, oblivious to Street's impertinence, had said curtly: 'First editions. Preferably signed.' Street had learned something. 'You interested in books?' Crowley had asked. 'Collector?' Street had said he was. Anything to add some life to his boring daily routine of tick, stamp and vouch for a firm of accountants. Unqualified assistants like Street had no career prospects.

But here was a man, on his own, making a living out of dealing in old books. The prospect of being self-employed and doing the same had immediately appealed.

A plan formulated in his mind and Street became a regular visitor to Crowley's Books, buying first editions. He studied catalogues and trade journals, developing his knowledge so that he could talk authoritatively on spine-splitting, foxed pages and the many other aspects of book quality as well as becoming familiar with authors' works.

His visits became so regular and his interest so keen that he talked Crowley into letting him work in the shop on Saturdays.

Crowley's health was declining, his bones were softening and his spine remorselessly bending forward. His wife had died some years earlier and he had no family except for cousins who rarely visited him.

It was when Crowley spoke of having to sell the business because of his health that the opportunity arose for Street to buy it. Who else could Crowley entrust a life's work to but this personable young man?

A contract was drawn up by Crowley's solicitor.

'I can't pay all the money on completion,' Street had told Crowley the day before the contract was to be completed. 'I'll have to pay by instalments.'

Crowley had reluctantly agreed, overruling his solicitor's advice, such was his faith in Street.

The deposit paid on exchange of contracts was all Crowley saw until he called into the shop several days after the first instalment became due.

'Business is very poor, Fred. Interest rates are high. I'm really struggling,' Street had pleaded.

'So am I, Albion. A contract is a contract. I need the money from the sale. I've nothing else to live on. This shop was my life, my pension fund.'

The conversation was the same each time an instalment was due and each time Street would write out a cheque for a few hundred pounds. Nothing like what Crowley wanted but enough to appease him and tide him over. And there was always the promise of the arrears next time.

With Crowley's by then rapidly deteriorating health, Street knew he would not have the stamina to fight him through the courts for his money. His death would be Street's release from debt; he'd planned for that eventuality, too.

'I don't know what to choose,' announced Mrs Harcourt.

'There has to be a book for you,' assured Street, returning to her side. 'Have you considered something new, like a Jeffrey Archer?' Street peered along the shelves. 'Here's a first edition, signed, of *Kane and Abel*.'

Mrs Harcourt took the book, opened it, saw it was indeed signed and in good condition. 'Possibly,' she said, handing it back.

'What else, what else,' mused Street, tapping his lips with his forefinger.

'The other aspect of the story was forgery,' recalled Mrs Harcourt.

'Forgery,' repeated Street, reflectively.

Another customer who had been browsing was now waiting at the counter. Street excused himself and attended to the sale.

And that reference to forgery jarred, too.

When Crowley died Street ensured that he would not pay any more money for the business. He wrote out a receipt acknowledging a sum of money in full satisfaction of the balance due. He then carefully signed Crowley's wavy signature and dated it shortly before Crowley was admitted to hospital.

Copying signatures had been in Street's plan ever since he'd talked with Crowley about the difference a signature made to the price of a first edition. Consequently he had put a lot of effort into copying signatures and so revaluing the stock of books.

He bought old pens and bottles of ink from antique shops for upgrading the aged books. For the new ones he attended actual signing sessions, bought a book, and then several of the pens used by the author.

Street's enhancing of the flyleaf was so perfect that the original was indistinguishable from the copies. He saw no harm in what he was doing. Fulfilling collections' one-upmanship egos was how he saw it.

'I know, madam,' pronounced Street after bidding his latest customer hours of happy reading, 'how about *Not a Penny More, Not a Penny Less*?'

'My friend has that one.'

'Oh dear,' he said, deflated.

Then Mrs Harcourt said: 'I've decided on a traditional Christmas book. Charles Dickens.' Street smiled for he had a good selection. 'A *Christmas Carol*. And do me a favour. I've been here so long that I'm going to run short of time for my other shopping. You find the book for me—you will have it?'—Street nodded—'and I'll be back in an hour or so.' Collecting her umbrella, she crossed to the door. 'I did say, a signed first edition, didn't I?'

'Er, it'll be expensive.'

'I can afford it,' she said haughtily.

'I can't be sure about a signed one.'

'Oh, really! I've never heard of Crowley's letting a customer down, have you?'

The door closed after her and Street watched her walk away under the festive streetlights, then turned the sign on the door to 'Closed'. From the dusty shelves he took a first edition, the red leather chafed, and in the back office deftly converted it into a signed copy. Dickens's signature was always a challenge, he reflected, admiring his handiwork.

The 'Closed' sign concerned Mrs Harcourt. She pressed the bell again and, while she waited, fiddled in her bucket-style handbag. She left the top unfastened.

'Do come in,' urged Street, holding the door open. 'Successful time?' he asked, noting the large black case she carried.

'Thank you. And the book. You aren't going to disappoint me?' The green eyes weighed upon him.

'Of course not. Here you are,' he said, proudly handing the book to her. She put down her case and, holding the book in gloved hands, opened it and studied the signature and quality of the book.

'Very nice for its age. Quite scarce,' began Street, softening her up before telling her the price.

'And it is genuine?'

'Genuine!' exploded Street. 'Really! Crowley's reputation . . .'

He stopped speaking as Mrs Harcourt opened the black case and from it produced several works of Dickens and Archer, laying them open on the counter at the title page. She crossed the room, noticed a space where earlier there had been Dickens's *A Christmas Carol*, selected the two Archer books she had been shown earlier, and placed them with the others on the counter.

'Look at these signatures, Mr Street.'

He peered closely. 'Very nice, good quality books. Perfect.'

'Too perfect, Mr Street.' He waited. 'You will see, if you look carefully, that the Dickens and Archer signatures are respectively identical.'

'Certainly very similar.'

'Identical. Microscopically checked!'

'So?'

'No one ever signs exactly the same twice.'

'Really?'

'And all these came from this shop! I can produce invoices . . .'

'I don't see what you are getting at?'

'Then look at this.' She turned the pages of the Dickens books. 'If they had been signed when new, the ink would not have penetrated the paper so deeply. Old paper can't cope with fresh ink in the same way.'

Street was staring at the heavy shadow on the back of the signed pages. 'They're forgeries, Mr Street. Good attempts, though.'

'Of course they're not,' rebutted Street. 'I'll buy the books as proof they're genuine.'

She shook her head.

'I'm a handwriting expert. Assigned to the Association of Book Collectors. You've been too efficient in supplying these "masterpieces",' she said sharply.

'I'm very lucky to be able to acquire the books customers want.'

'Forge for customers the books they'd really like,' she corrected.

'No!'

'Yes! that *Christmas Carol* was unsigned on your shelf. There's a space where you took it from. I looked earlier. It is already covered with my fingerprints. That can easily be proved. Now it is signed. And I haven't fingered it. My gloves are still on!'

'Damn you,' cursed Street, lunging at her.

'Come in, NOW,' yelled Mrs Harcourt into her handbag.

As Street knocked her to the floor, a two-way radio fell from her bag. Moments later, police officers rushed into the shop.

A PAIR OF
MUDDY SHOES

Lennox Robinson

Lennox Robinson (1886–1958) was one of
Ireland's leading authors and playwrights. He
was manager of the Abbey Theatre, Dublin,
from 1910 to 1914, and from 1919 to 1923,
and director of the Abbey from 1923 to 1956.
Among his full-length plays *The Lost Leader*
(1918) and *The Whiteheaded Boy* (1920) are
outstanding. He also edited *The Golden Treasury
of Irish Verse* (1925) and *The Oxford Book of
Irish Verse* (1958). 'A Pair of Muddy Shoes' is
taken from *Eight Short Stories* (1919).

I am going to try to write it down quite simply, just as it happened. I
shall try not to exaggerate anything.

I am twenty-two years old, my parents are dead, I have no brothers
or sisters; the only near relation I have is Aunt Margaret, my father's
sister. She is unmarried and lives alone in a little house in the country in
the west of county Cork. She is kind to me and I often spend my holidays
with her, for I am poor and have few friends.

I am a school-teacher—that is to say, I teach drawing and singing. I am
a visiting teacher at two or three schools in Dublin. I make a fair income,
enough for a single woman to live comfortably on, but father left debts
behind him, and until these are paid off I have to live very simply. I
suppose I ought to eat more and eat better food. People sometimes think
I am nervous and highly strung: I look rather fragile and delicate, but

really I am not. I have slender hands, with pale, tapering fingers—the sort of hands people call 'artistic'.

I hoped very much that my aunt would invite me to spend Christmas with her. I happened to have very little money; I had paid off a big debt of poor father's, and that left me very short, and I felt rather weak and ill. I didn't quite know how I'd get through the holidays unless I went down to my aunt's. However, ten days before Christmas the invitation came. You may be sure I accepted it gratefully, and when my last school broke up on the 20th I packed my trunk, gathered up the old sentimental songs Aunt Margaret likes best, and set off for Rosspatrick.

It rains a great deal in West Cork in the winter: it was raining when Aunt Margaret met me at the station. 'It's been a terrible month, Peggy,' she said, as she turned the pony's head into the long road that runs for four muddy miles from the station to Rosspatrick. 'I think it's rained every day for the last six weeks. And the storms! We lost a chimney two days ago: it came through the roof, and let the rain into the ceiling of the spare bedroom. I've had to make you up a bed in the lumber-room till Jeremiah Driscoll can be got to mend the roof.'

I assured her that any place would do me; all I wanted was her society and a quiet time.

'I can guarantee you those,' she said. 'Indeed, you look tired out: you look as if you were just after a bad illness or just before one. That teaching is killing you.'

The lumber room was really very comfortable. It was a large room with two big windows; it was on the ground floor, and Aunt Margaret had never used it as a bedroom because people are often afraid of sleeping on the ground floor.

We stayed up very late talking over the fire. Aunt Margaret came with me to my bedroom; she stayed there for a long time, fussing about the room, hoping I'd be comfortable, pulling about the furniture, looking at the bedclothes.

At last I began to laugh at her. 'Why shouldn't I be comfortable? Think of my horrid little bedroom in Brunswick Street! What's wrong with this room?'

'Nothing—oh, nothing,' she said rather hurriedly, and kissed me and left me.

I slept very well. I never opened my eyes till the maid called me, and then after she had left me I dozed off again. I had a ridiculous dream. I dreamed I was interviewing a rich old lady: she offered me a thousand a year and comfortable rooms to live in. My only duty was to keep her clothes from moths; she had quantities of beautiful, costly clothes, and she seemed to have a terror of them being eaten by moths. I accepted her offer at once. I remember saying to her gaily, 'The work will be no trouble to me. I like killing moths.'

It was strange I should say that, because I really don't like killing moths—I hate killing anything. But my dream was easily explained, for when I woke a second later (as it seemed), I was holding a dead moth between my finger and thumb. It disgusted me just a little bit—that dead moth pressed between my fingers, but I dropped it quickly, jumped up, and dressed myself.

Aunt Margaret was in the dining-room, and full of profuse and anxious inquiries about the night I had spent. I soon relieved her anxieties, and we laughed together over my dream and the new position I was going to fill. It was very wet all day and I didn't stir out of the house. I sang a great many songs, I began a pencil-drawing of my aunt—a thing I had been meaning to make for years—but I didn't feel well, I felt headachy and nervous—just from being in the house all day, I suppose. I felt the greatest disinclination to go to bed. I felt afraid, I don't know of what.

Of course I didn't say a word of this to Aunt Margaret.

That night the moment I fell asleep I began to dream. I thought I was looking down at myself from a great height. I saw myself in my nightdress crouching in a corner of the bedroom. I remember wondering why I was crouching there, and I came nearer and looked at myself again, and then I saw that it was not myself that crouched there—it was a large white cat, it was watching a mouse-hole. I was relieved and I turned away. As I did so I heard the cat spring. I started round. It had a mouse between its paws, and it looked up at me, growling as a cat does. Its face was like a woman's face—was like my face. Probably that doesn't sound at all horrible to you, but it happens that I have a deadly fear of mice. The idea of holding one between my hands, of putting my mouth to one, of—oh, I can't bear even to write it.

I think I woke screaming. I know when I came to myself I had jumped out of bed and was standing on the floor. I lit the candle and searched the room. In one corner were some boxes and trunks; there might have been a mouse-hole behind them, but I hadn't the courage to pull them out and look. I kept my candle lighted and stayed awake all night.

The next day was fine and frosty. I went for a long walk in the morning and for another in the afternoon. When bedtime came I was very tired and sleepy. I went to sleep at once and slept dreamlessly all night.

It was the next day that I noticed my hands getting queer. 'Queer' perhaps isn't the right word, for, of course, cold does roughen and coarsen the skin, and the weather was frosty enough to account for that. But it wasn't only that the skin was rough, the whole hand looked larger, stronger, not like my own hand. How ridiculous this sounds, but the whole story is ridiculous.

I remember once, when I was a child at school, putting on another girl's boots by mistake one day. I had to go about till evening in them, and I was perfectly miserable. I could not stop myself from looking at my feet, and they seemed to me to be the feet of another person. That sickened me, I don't know why. I felt a little like that now when I looked at my hands. Aunt Margaret noticed how rough and swollen they were, and she gave me cold cream, which I rubbed on them before I went to bed.

I lay awake for a long time. I was thinking of my hands. I didn't seem to be able not to think of them. They seemed to grow bigger and bigger in the darkness; they seemed monstrous hands, the hands of some horrible ape, they seemed to fill the whole room. Of course if I had struck a match and lit the candle I'd have calmed myself in a minute, but, frankly, I hadn't the courage. When I touched one hand with the other it seemed rough and hairy, like a man's.

At last I fell asleep. I dreamed that I got out of bed and opened the window. For several minutes I stood looking out. It was bright moonlight and bitterly cold. I felt a great desire to go for a walk. I dreamed that I dressed myself quickly, put on my slippers, and stepped out of the window. The frosty grass crunched under my feet. I walked, it seemed for miles, along a road I never remember being on before. It led up-hill; I met no one as I walked.

Presently I reached the crest of the hill, and beside the road, in the middle of a bare field, stood a large house. It was a gaunt, three-storied building, there was an air of decay about it. Maybe it had once been a gentleman's place, and was now occupied by a herd. There are many places like that in Ireland. In a window of the highest story there was a light. I decided I would go to the house and ask the way home. A gate closed the grass-grown avenue from the road; it was fastened and I could not open it, so I climbed it. It was a high gate but I climbed it easily, and I remember thinking in my dream, 'If this wasn't a dream I could never climb it so easily.'

I knocked at the door, and after I had knocked again the window of the room in which the light shone was opened, and a voice said, 'Who's there? What do you want?'

It came from a middle-aged woman with a pale face and dirty strands of grey hair hanging about her shoulders.

I said, 'Come down and speak to me; I want to know the way back to Rosspatrick.'

I had to speak two or three times to her, but at last she came down and opened the door mistrustfully. She only opened it a few inches and barred my way. I asked her the road home, and she gave me directions in a nervous startled way.

Then I dreamed that I said, 'Let me in to warm myself.'

'It's late; you should be going home.'

But I laughed, and suddenly pushed at the door with my foot and slipped past her.

I remember she said, 'My God,' in a helpless, terrified way. It was strange that she should be frightened, and I, a young girl all alone in a strange house with a strange woman, miles from any one I knew, should not be frightened at all. As I sat warming myself by the fire while she boiled the kettle (for I had asked for tea), and watching her timid, terrified movements, the queerness of the position struck me, and I said, laughing, 'You seem afraid of me.'

'Not at all, miss,' she replied, in a voice which almost trembled.

'You needn't be, there's not the least occasion for it,' I said, and I laid my hand on her arm.

She looked down at it as it lay there, and said again, 'Oh, my God,' and staggered back against the range.

And so for half a minute we remained. Her eyes were fixed on my hand which lay on my lap; it seemed she could never take them off it.

'What is it?' I said.

'You've the face of a girl,' she whispered, 'and—God help me—the hands of a man.'

I looked down at my hands. They were large, strong and sinewy, covered with coarse red hairs. Strange to say they no longer disgusted me: I was proud of them—proud of their strength, the power that lay in them.

'Why should they make you afraid,' I asked. 'They are fine hands. Strong hands.'

But she only went on staring at them in a hopeless, frozen way.

'Have you ever seen such strong hands before?' I smiled at her.

'They're—they're Ned's hands,' she said at last, speaking in a whisper.

She put her own hand to her throat as if she were choking, and the fastening of her blouse gave way. It fell open. She had a long throat; it was moving as if she were finding it difficult to swallow; I wondered whether my hands would go round it.

Suddenly I knew they would, and I knew why my hands were large and sinewy, I knew why power had been given to them. I got up and caught her by the throat. She struggled so feebly; slipped down, striking her head against the range; slipped down on to the red-tiled floor and lay quite still, but her throat still moved under my hand and I never loosened my grasp.

And presently, kneeling over her, I lifted her head and bumped it gently against the flags of the floor. I did this again and again; lifting it higher, and striking it harder and harder, until it was crushed in like an egg, and she lay still. She was choked and dead.

And I left her lying there and ran from the house, and as I stepped on to the road I felt rain in my face. The thaw had come.

When I woke it was morning. Little by little my dream came back and filled me with horror. I looked at my hands. They were so tender and pale and feeble. I lifted them to my mouth and kissed them.

But when Mary called me half an hour later she broke into a long, excited story of a woman who had been murdered the night before, how the postman had found the door open and the dead body. 'And sure, miss, it was here she used to live long ago; she was near murdered once, by her husband, in this very room; he tried to choke her, she was half killed—that's why the mistress made it a lumber-room. They put him in the asylum afterwards; a month ago he died there I heard.'

My mother was Scotch, and claimed she had the gift of prevision. It was evident she had bequeathed it to me. I was enormously excited. I sat up in bed and told Mary my dream.

She was not very interested, people seldom are in other people's dreams. Besides, she wanted, I suppose, to tell her news to Aunt Margaret. She hurried away. I lay in bed and thought it all over. I almost laughed, It was so strange and fantastic.

But when I got out of bed I stumbled over something. It was a little muddy shoe. At first I hardly recognized it, then I saw it was one of a pair of evening shoes I had; the other shoe lay near it. They were a pretty little pair of dark blue satin shoes, they were a present to me from a girl I loved very much, she had given them to me only a week ago.

Last night they had been so fresh and new and smart. Now they were scratched, the satin cut, and they were covered with mud. Some one had walked miles in them.

And I remembered in my dream how I had searched for my shoes and put them on.

Sitting on the bed, feeling suddenly sick and dizzy, holding the muddy shoes in my hand, I had in a blinding instant a vision of a red-haired man who lay in this room night after night for years, hating a sleeping white-faced woman who lay beside him, longing for strength and courage to choke her. I saw him come back, years afterwards—freed by death—to this room; saw him seize on a feeble girl too weak to resist him; saw him try her, strengthen her hands, and at last—through her—accomplish his unfinished deed ... The vision passed all in a flash as it had come. I pulled myself together. 'That is nonsense, impossible,' I told myself. 'The murderer will be found before evening.'

But in my hand I still held the muddy shoes. I seem to be holding them ever since.

THE UNKNOWN MURDERER

H.C. Bailey

The fame of H.C. Bailey (1878–1961) rests on
his classic detective stories featuring the
inimitable Reggie Fortune. 'The Unknown
Murderer' is one of his very best tales, and
features all the aspects that made Fortune
celebrated in detective fiction: his intuitive 'feel'
for a crime; his medical and toxicological
knowledge; and his ruthless administration of
summary justice where he felt the law would be
inadequate. This story is taken from *Mr
Fortune's Practice* (1923).

O nce upon a time a number of men in a club discussed how Mr
Reginald Fortune came to be the expert adviser of the Home
Office upon crime. The doctors admitted that though he is a
competent surgeon, pathologist and what not, he never showed
international form. There was a Fellow of the Royal Society who urged
that Fortune knew more about natural science than most schoolboys,
politicians, and civil servants. An artist said he had been told Fortune
understood business, and his banker believed Fortune was a judge of old
furniture. But they all agreed that he is a jolly good fellow. Which means,
being interpreted, he can be all things to all men.

Mr Fortune himself is convinced that he was meant by Providence to
be a general practitioner: to attend to my lumbago and your daughter's
measles. He has been heard to complain of the chance that has made him,

knowing something of everything, nothing completely, into a specialist. His only qualification, he will tell you, is that he doesn't get muddled.

There you have it, then. He is singularly sensitive to people. 'Very odd how he knows men,' said Superintendent Bell reverently. 'As if he had an extra sense to tell him of people's souls, like smells or colours. And he has a clear head. He is never confused about what is important and what isn't, and he has never been known to hesitate in doing what is necessary.

Consider his dealing with the affair of the unknown murderer.

There was not much interesting crime that Christmas. The singular case of Sir Humphrey Bigod, who was found dead in a chalk-pit on the eve of his marriage, therefore obtained a lot of space in the papers, which kept it up, even after the coroner's jury had declared for death by misadventure, with irrelevant inventions and bloodthirsty hints of murder and tales of clues. This did not disturb the peace of the scientific adviser to the Criminal Investigation Department, who knew that the lad was killed by a fall and that there was no means of knowing any more. Mr Fortune was much occupied in being happy, for after long endeavour he had engaged Joan Amber to marry him. The lady has said the endeavour was hers, but I am not now telling that story. Just after Christmas she took him to the children's party at the Home of Help.

It is an old-fashioned orphanage, a huge barrack of a building, but homely and kind. Time out of mind people of all sorts, with old titles and new, with money and with brains, have been the friends of its children. When Miss Amber brought Reggie Fortune under the flags and the strings of paper roses into its hall, which was as noisy as the parrot house, he gasped slightly. 'Be brave, child,' she said. 'This is quiet to what it will be after tea. And cool. You will be much hotter. You don't know how hot you'll be.'

'Woman, you have deceived me,' said Mr Fortune bitterly. 'I thought philanthropists were respectable.'

'Yes, dear. Don't be frightened. You're only a philanthropist for the afternoon.'

'I ask you. Is that Crab Warnham?'

'Of course it's Captain Warnham.' Miss Amber smiled beautifully at a gaunt man with a face like an old jockey. He flushed as he leered back. 'Do you know his wife? She's rather precious.'

'Poor woman. He doesn't look comfortable here, does he? The last time I saw Crab Warnham was in a place that's several kinds of hell in Berlin. He was quite at home there.'

[81]

'Forget it,' said Miss Amber gently. 'You will when you meet his wife. And their boy's a darling.'

'His boy?' Reggie was startled.

'Oh, no. She was a widow. He worships her and the child.'

Reggie said nothing. It appeared to him that Captain Warnham, for a man who worshipped his wife, had a hungry eye on women. And the next moment Captain Warnham was called to attention. A small woman, still pretty though earnest, talked to him like a mother or a commanding officer. He was embarrassed, and when she had done with him he fled.

The small woman, who was austerely but daintily clad in black with some white at the neck, continued to flit among the company, finding every one a job of work. 'She says to one, Go, and he goeth, and to another, Come, and he cometh. And who is she, Joan?'

'Lady Chantry,' said Miss Amber. 'She's providence here, you know.'

And Lady Chantry was upon them. Reggie found himself looking down into a pair of uncommonly bright eyes and wondering what it felt like to be as strenuous as the little woman who was congratulating him on Joan, thanking him for being there and arranging his afternoon for him all in one breath. He had never heard any one talk so fast. In a condition of stupor he saw Joan reft from him to tell the story of Cinderella to magic lantern pictures in one dormitory, while he was led to another to help in a scratch concert. And as the door closed on him he heard the swift clear voice of Lady Chantry exhorting staff and visitors to play round games.

He suffered. People who had no voices sang showy songs, people who had too much voice sang ragtime to those solemn, respectful children. In pity for the children and himself he set up as a conjurer, and the dormitory was growing merry when a shriek cut into his patter. 'That's only my bones creaking,' he went on quickly, for the children were frightened; 'they always do that when I put the knife in at the ear and take it out of my hind leg. So. But it doesn't hurt. As the motor-car said when it ran over the policeman's feet. All done by kindness. Come here, Jenny Wren. You mustn't use your nose as a money-box.' A small person submitted to have pennies taken out of her face.

The door opened and a pallid nurse said faintly: 'The doctor. Are you the doctor?'

'Of course,' said Reggie. 'One moment, people. Mr Punch has fallen over the baby. It always hurts him. In the hump. Are we downhearted?

No. Pack up your troubles in the old kit bag—' He went out to a joyful roar of that lyric. 'What's the trouble?' The nurse was shaking.

'In there, Sir—she's up there.'

Reggie went up the stairs in quick time. The door of a little sitting-room stood open. Inside it people were staring at a woman who sat at her desk. Her dress was dark and wet. Her head lolled forward. A deep gash ran across her throat.

'Yes. There's too many of us here,' he said, and waved the spectators away. One lingered, an old woman, large and imposing, and announced that she was the matron. Reggie shut the door and came back to the body in the chair. He held the limp hands a moment, he lifted the head and looked close into the flaccid face. 'When was she found? When I heard that scream? Yes.' He examined the floor. 'Quite so.' He turned to the matron. 'Well, well. Who is she?'

'It's our resident medical officer, Dr Emily Hall. But Dr Fortune, can't you do anything?'

'She's gone,' said Reggie.

'But this is terrible, doctor. What does it mean?'

'Well, I don't know what it means. Her throat was cut by a highly efficient knife, probably from behind. She lingered a little while quite helpless, and died. Not so very long ago. Who screamed?'

'The nurse who found her. One of our own girls, Dr Fortune, Edith Baker. She was always a favourite of poor Dr Hall's. She has been kept on here at Dr Hall's wish to train as a nurse. She was devoted to Dr Hall. One of these girlish passions.'

'And she came into the room and found—this—and screamed?'

'So she tells me,' said the matron.

'Well, well,' Reggie sighed. 'Poor kiddies! And now you must send for the police.'

'I have given instructions, Dr Fortune,' said the matron with dignity.

'And I think you ought to keep Edith Baker from talking about it.' Reggie opened the door.

'Edith will not talk,' said the matron coldly. 'She is a very reserved creature.'

'Poor thing. But I'm afraid some of our visitors will. And they had better not, you know.' At last he got rid of the lady and turned the key in the lock and stood looking at it. 'Yes, quite natural, but very convenient,' said he, and turned away from it and contemplated a big easy chair. The loose cushion on the seat showed that somebody had been sitting in it, a fact not in itself remarkable. But there was a tiny smear of blood on the arm still wet. He picked up the cushion. On the under side was a larger smear of blood. Mr Fortune's brow contracted. The unknown murderer cuts her throat—comes over here—makes a mess on the chair—turns the cushion over—and sits down—to watch the woman die. This is rather diabolical.' He began to wander round the room. It offered him no other signs but some drops of blood on the hearthrug and the hearth. He knelt down and peered into the fire, and with the tongs drew from it a thin piece of metal. It was a surgical knife. He looked at the dead woman. 'From your hospital equipment, Dr Hall. And Edith Baker is a nurse. And Edith Baker had "a girlish passion" for you. I wonder.'

Someone was trying the door. He unlocked it, to find an inspector of police. 'I am Reginald Fortune,' he explained. 'Here's your case.'

'I've heard of you, sir,' said the inspector reverently. 'Bad business, isn't it? I'm sure it's very lucky you were here.'

'I wonder,' Reggie murmured.

'Could it be suicide, sir?'

Reggie shook his head. 'I wish it could. Not a nice murder. Not at all a nice murder. By the way, there's the knife. I picked it out of the fire.'

'Doctor's tool, isn't it, sir? Have you got any theory about it?' Reggie shook his head. 'There's the girl who gave the alarm: she's a nurse in the hospital, I'm told.'

'I don't know the girl,' said Reggie. 'You'd better see what you make of the room. I shall be downstairs.'

In the big hall the decorations and the Christmas tree with its ungiven presents glowed to emptiness and silence. Joan Amber came forward to meet him. He did not speak to her. He continued to stare at the ungiven presents on the Christmas tree. 'What do you want to do?' she said at last.

'This is the end of a perfect day,' said Mr Fortune. 'Poor kiddies.'

'The matron packed them all off to their dormitories.'

Mr Fortune laughed. 'Just as well to rub it in, isn't it?'

Miss Amber did not answer him for a moment. 'Do you know, you look rather terrible?' she said, and indeed his normally plump, fresh-coloured, cheery face had a certain ferocity.

'I feel like a fool, Joan. Where is everybody?'

'She sent everybody away too.'

'She would. Great organizer. No brain. My only aunt! A woman's murdered and every stranger who was in the place is hustled off before the police get to work. This isn't a crime, it's a nightmare.'

'Well, of course they were anxious to go.'

'They would be.'

'Reggie, who are you thinking of?'

'I can't think. There are no facts. Where's this matron now?'

The inspector came upon them as they were going to her room. 'I've finished upstairs, sir. Not much for me, is there? Plenty downstairs, though. I reckon I'll hear some queer stories before I've done. These homes are always full of gossip. People living too close together, wonderful what bad blood it makes. I—' He broke off and stared at Reggie. From the matron's room came the sound of sobbing. He opened the door without a knock.

The matron sat at her writing-table, coldly judicial. A girl in nurse's uniform was crying on the bosom of Lady Chantry, who caressed her and murmured in her ear.

'Sorry to interrupt, ma'am,' the inspector said, staring hard.

'You don't interrupt. This girl is Edith Baker, who seems to have been the last person who saw Dr Hall alive and was certainly the first person who saw her dead.'

'And who was very, very fond of her,' Lady Chantry said gently. 'Weren't you, dear?'

'I'll have to take her statement,' said the inspector. But the girl was torn with sobbing.

'Come, dear, come,' Lady Chantry strove with her.

'The Inspector only wants you to say how you left her and how you found her.'

'Edith, you must control yourself.' The matron lifted her voice.

'I hate you,' the girl cried, and tore herself away and rushed out of the room.

'She'll have to speak, you know, ma'am,' the inspector said.

'I am very sorry to say she has always had a passionate temperament,' said the matron.

'Poor child!' Lady Chantry rose. 'She was so fond of the doctor, you see. I'll go to her, matron, and see what I can do.'

'Does any one here know what the girl was up to this afternoon, ma'am?' said the inspector.

'I will try to find out for you,' said the matron, and rang her bell.

'Well, well,' said Reggie Fortune. 'Every little helps. You might find out what all the other people were doing this afternoon.'

The matron stared at him. 'Surely you're not thinking of the visitors, Mr Fortune?'

'I'm thinking of your children,' said Reggie, and she was the more amazed. 'Not a nice murder, you know, not at all a nice murder.'

And then he took Miss Amber home. She found him taciturn, which is his habit when he is angry. But she had never seen him angry before. She is a wise woman. When he was leaving her: 'Do you know what it is about you, sir?' she said. 'You're always just right.'

When the Hon. Sidney Lomas came to his room in Scotland Yard the next morning, Reggie Fortune was waiting for him. 'My dear fellow!' he protested. 'What is this? You're not really up, are you? It's not eleven. You're an hallucination.'

'Zeal, all zeal, Lomas. The orphanage murder is my trouble.'

'Have you come to give yourself up? I suspected you from the first, Fortune. Where is it? He took a copy of the *Daily Wire* from the rack. 'Yes. "Dr Reginald Fortune, the eminent surgeon, was attending the function and was able to give the police a first-hand account of the crime. Dr Fortune states that the weapon was a surgical knife." My dear fellow, the case looks black indeed.'

Reggie was not amused. 'Yes. I also was present. And several others,' he said. 'Do you know anything about any of us?'

Lomas put up his eyeglass. 'There's a certain bitterness about you, Fortune. This is unusual. What's the matter?'

'I don't like this murder,' said Reggie. 'It spoilt the children's party.'

'That would be a by-product,' Lomas agreed. 'You're getting very domestic in your emotions. Oh, I like it, my dear fellow. But it makes you a little irrelevant.'

'Domestic be damned. I'm highly relevant. It spoilt the children's party. Why did it happen at the children's party? Lots of other nice days to kill the resident medical officer.'

'You're suggesting it was one of the visitors?'

'No, no. It isn't the only day visitors visit. I'm suggesting "life is real, life is earnest"—and rather diabolical sometimes.'

'I'll call for the reports,' Lomas said, and did so. 'Good God! Reams! Barton's put in some heavy work.'

'I thought he would,' said Reggie, and went to read over Lomas's shoulder.

At the end Lomas lay back and looked up at him. 'Well? Barton's put his money on this young nurse, Edith Baker.'

'Yes. That's the matron's tip. I saw the matron. One of the world's organizers, Lomas. A place for everything and everything in its place.

[86]

And if you don't fit, God help you. Edith Baker didn't fit. Edith Baker has emotions. Therefore she does murders. QED.'

'Well, the matron ought to know the girl.'

'She ought,' Reggie agreed. 'And our case is, gentlemen, that the matron who ought to know girls says Edith Baker isn't a nice young person. Lomas dear, why do policemen always believe what they're told? What the matron don't like isn't evidence.'

'There is some evidence. The girl had one of these hysterical affections for the dead woman, passionately devoted and passionately jealous and so forth. The girl had access to the hospital instruments. All her time in the afternoon can't be accounted for, and she was the first to know of the murder.'

'It's not good enough, Lomas. Why did she give the alarm?'

Lomas shrugged. 'A murderer does now and then. Cunning or fright.'

'And why did she wait for the children's party to do the murder?'

'Something may have happened there to rouse her jealousy.'

'Something with one of the visitors?' Reggie suggested. 'I wonder.' And then he laughed. 'A party of the visitors went round the hospital, Lomas. They had access to surgical instruments.'

'And were suddenly seized with a desire for homicide? They also went to the gymnasium and the kitchen. Did any of them start boiling potatoes? My dear Fortune, you are not as plausible as usual.'

'It isn't plausible,' Reggie said. 'I know that. It's too dam' wicked.'

'Abnormal,' Lomas nodded. 'Of course the essence of the thing is that it's abnormal. Every once in a while we have these murders in an orphanage or school or some place where women and children are herded together. Nine times out of ten they are cases of hysteria. Your young friend Miss Baker seems to be a highly hysterical subject.'

'You know more than I do.'

'Why, that's in the evidence. And you saw her yourself half crazy with emotion after the murder.'

'Good Lord!' said Reggie. 'Lomas, old thing, you do run on. Pantin' time toils after you in vain. That girl wasn't crazy. She was the most natural of us all. You send a girl in her teens into the room where the woman she is keen on is sitting with her throat cut. She won't talk to you like a little lady. The evidence! Why do you believe what people tell you about people? They're always lying—by accident if not on purpose. This matron don't like the girl because she worshipped the lady doctor. Therefore the girl is called abnormal and jealous. Did you never hear of a girl in her teens worshipping a teacher? It's common form. Did you never hear of another teacher being vicious about it? That's just as common.'

'Do you mean the matron was jealous of them both?'

Reggie shrugged, 'It hits you in the eye.'

'Good Gad!' said Lomas. 'Do you suspect the matron?'

'I suspect the devil,' said Reggie gravely. 'Lomas, my child, whoever did that murder cut the woman's throat and then sat down in her easy chair and watched her die. I call that devilish.' And he told of the bloodstains and the turned cushions.

'Good Gad,' said Lomas once more, 'there's some hate in that.'

'Not a nice murder. Also it stopped the children's party.'

'You harp on that.' Lomas looked at him curiously. 'Are you thinking of the visitors?'

'I wonder,' Reggie murmured. 'I wonder.'

'Here's the list,' Lomas said, and Reggie came slowly to look. 'Sir George and Lady Bean, Lady Chantry, Mrs Carroway'—he ran his pencil down—'all well-known, blameless busybodies, full of good works. Nothing doing.'

'Crab Warnham,' said Reggie.

'Oh, Warnham: his wife took him, I suppose. She's a saint, and he eats out of her hand, they say. Well, he was a loose fish, of course, but murder! I don't see Warnham at that.'

'He has an eye for a woman.'

'Still? I dare say. But good Gad, he can't have known this lady doctor. Was she pretty?' Reggie nodded. 'Well, we might look for a link between them. Not likely, is it?'

'We're catching at straws,' said Reggie sombrely.

Lomas pushed the papers away. 'Confound it, it's another case without evidence. I suppose it can't be suicide like that Bigod affair?'

Reggie, who was lighting a cigar looked up and let the match burn his fingers. 'Not suicide. No,' he said. 'Was Bigod's?'

'Well, it was a deuced queer death by misadventure.'

'As you say.' Reggie nodded and wandered dreamily out.

This seems to have been the first time that anyone thought of comparing the Bigod case to the orphanage murder. When the inquest on the lady doctor was held the police had no more evidence to produce than you have heard, and the jury returned a verdict of murder by some person or persons unknown. Newspapers strove to enliven the dull calm of the holiday season by declaiming against the inefficiency of a police force which allowed murderers to remain anonymous, and hashed up the

Bigod case again to prove that the fall of Sir Humphrey Bigod into his chalk-pit, though called accidental, was just as mysterious as the cut throat of Dr Hall. And the Hon. Sidney Lomas cursed the man who invented printing.

These assaults certainly did not disturb Reggie Fortune, who has never cared what people say of him. With the help of Joan Amber he found a quiet, remote place for the unhappy girl suspected of the murder (Lady Chantry was pretty angry with Miss Amber about that, protesting that she wanted to look after Edith herself), and said he was only in the case as a philanthropist. After which he gave all his time to preparing his house and Miss Amber for married life. But the lady found him dreamy.

It was in fact while he was showing her how the new colours in the drawing-room looked under the new lighting that Dr Eden called him up. Dr Eden has a general practice in Kensington. Dr Eden wanted to consult him about a case: most urgent: 3 King William's Walk.

'But it's Mrs Warnham!' she cried.

'May I take the car?' said Reggie to Joan. 'He sounds rattled. You can go on home afterwards. It's not far from you either. I wonder who lives at 3 King William's Walk?'

'Oh, my aunt!' said Reggie Fortune; and said no more.

And Joan Amber did not call him out of his thoughts. She was as grave as he. Only when he was getting out of the car, 'Be good to her, dear,' she said gently. He kissed the hand on his arm.

The door was opened by a woman in evening-dress. 'It is Mr Fortune, isn't it? Please come in. It's so kind of you to come.' She turned to the maid in the background. 'Tell Dr Eden, Maggie. It's my little boy—and we are so anxious.'

'I'm very sorry, Mrs Warnham,' Reggie took her hand and found it cold. The face he remembered for its gentle calm, was sternly set. What is the trouble?'

'Gerald went to a party this afternoon. He came home gloriously happy and went to bed. He didn't go to sleep at once, he was rather excited, but he was quite well. Then he woke up crying with pain and was very sick. I sent for Dr Eden. It isn't like Gerald to cry, Mr Fortune. And—'

A hoarse voice said, 'Catherine, you oughtn't to be out there in the cold.' Reggie saw the gaunt face of Captain Warnham looking round a door at them.

'What does it matter?' she cried. 'Dr Eden doesn't want me to be with him, Mr Fortune. He is still in pain. And I don't think Dr Eden knows.'

[89]

Dr Eden came down in time to hear that. A large young man, he stood over them looking very awkward and uncomfortable.

'I'm sure Dr Eden has done everything that can be done,' said Reggie gently. 'I'll go up, please.' And they left the mother to her husband, that flushed, gaunt face peering round the corner as they kept step up the stairs.

'The child's seven years old,' said Eden. 'There's no history of any gastric trouble. Rather a good digestion. And then this—out of the blue!'

Reggie went into a nursery where a small boy lay huddled and restless with all the apparatus of sickness by his bed. He raised a pale face on which beads of sweat stood.

'Hallo, Gerald,' Reggie said quietly. 'Mother sent me up to make you all right again.' He took the child's hand and felt for the pulse. 'I'm Mr Fortune, your fortune, good fortune.' The child tried to smile and Reggie's hands moved over the uneasy body and all the while he murmured softly nonsense talk . . .

The child did not want him to go, but at last he went off with Eden into a corner of the room. 'Quite right to send for me,' he said gravely, and Eden put his hand to his head. 'I know. I know. It's horrible when it's a child. One of the irritant poisons. Probably arsenic. Have you given an emetic?'

'He's been very sick. And he's so weak.'

'I know. Have you got anything with you?'

'I sent home. But I didn't care to—'

'I'll do it. Sulphate of zinc. You go and send for a nurse. And find some safe milk. I wouldn't use the household stuff.'

'My God, Fortune! Surely it was at the party?'

'Not the household stuff,' Reggie repeated, and he went back to the child . . .

It was many hours afterwards that he came softly downstairs. In the hall husband and wife met him. It seemed to him that it was the man who had been crying. 'Are you going away?' Mrs Warnham said.

'There's no more pain. He is asleep.'

Her eyes darkened. 'You mean he's—dead?' the man gasped.

'I hope he'll live longer than any of us, Captain Warnham. But no one must disturb him. The nurse will be watching, you know. And I'm sure we all want to sleep sound—don't we?' He was gone. But he stayed a moment on the doorstep. He heard emotions within.

On the next afternoon Dr Eden came into his laboratory at St Saviour's. 'One moment. One moment.' Reggie was bent over a notebook. 'When I go to hell they'll set me doing sums.' He frowned at his figures. 'The third time is lucky. That's plausible if it isn't right. Well, how's our large patient?'

'He's doing well. Quite easy and cheerful.'

Reggie stood up. 'I think we might say, Thank God.'

'Yes, rather. I thought he was gone last night, Fortune. He would have been without you. It was wonderful how he bucked up in your hands. You ought to have been a children's specialist.'

'My dear chap! Oh, my dear chap! I'm the kind of fellow who would always ought to have been something else. And so I'm doing sums in a laboratory which God knows I'm not fit for.'

'Have you found out what it was?'

'Oh, arsenic, of course. Quite a fair dose he must have had. It's queer how they always will use arsenic.'

Eden stared at him. 'What are we to do?' he said in a low voice. 'Fortune, I suppose it couldn't have been accidental?'

'What is a child likely to eat in which he would find grains of accidental arsenic?'

'Yes, but then— I mean, who could want to kill that child?'

'That is the unknown quantity in the equation. But people do want to murder children, quite nice children.'

Eden grew pale. 'What do you mean? You know he's not Warnham's child. Warnham's his step-father.'

'Yes. Yes. Have you ever seen the two together?'

Eden hesitated. 'He—well he didn't seem to take to Warnham. But I'd have sworn Warnham was fond of him.'

'And that's all quite natural, isn't it? Well, well. I hope he's in.'

'What do you mean to do?'

'Tell Mrs Warnham—with her husband listening.'

Dr Eden followed him out like a man going to be hanged.

Mrs Warnham indeed met them in her hall. 'Mr Fortune'—she took his hand, she had won back her old calm, but her eyes grew dark as she looked at him—'Gerald has been asking for you. And I want to speak to you.'

'I shall be glad to talk over the case with you and Captain Warnham,' said Reggie gravely. 'I'll see the small boy first, if you don't mind.' And the small boy kept his Mr Fortune a long time.

Mrs Warnham had her husband with her when the doctors came down. 'I say, Fortune,' Captain Warnham started up, 'awfully good of you to take so much trouble. I mean to say'—he cleared his throat—'I feel it, you know. How is the little beggar?'

'There's no reason why he shouldn't do well,' Reggie said slowly. 'But it's a strange case, Captain Warnham. Yes, a strange case. You make take it, there is no doubt the child was poisoned.'

'Poisoned!' Warnham cried out in that queer hoarse voice.

'You mean it was something Gerald shouldn't have eaten?' Mrs Warnham said gently.

'It was arsenic, Captain Warnham. Not much more than an hour before the time he felt ill, perhaps less, he had swallowed enough arsenic to kill him.'

'I say, are you certain of all that? I mean to say, no doubt about anything?' Warnham was flushed. 'Arsenic—and the time—and the dose? It's pretty thick, you know.'

'There is no doubt. I have found arsenic. I can estimate the dose. And arsenic acts within that time.'

'But I can't believe it,' Mrs Warnham said. 'It would be too horribly cruel. Mr Fortune, couldn't it have been accident? Something in his food?'

'It was certainly in his food or drink. But not accident, Mrs Warnham. That is not possible.'

'I say, let's have it all out, Fortune,' Warnham growled. 'Do you suspect anyone?'

'That's rather for you, isn't it?' said Reggie.

'Who could want to poison Gerald?' Mrs Warnham cried.

'He says some one did,' Warnham growled. 'When do you suppose he took the stuff, Fortune? At the party or after he came home?'

'What did he have when he came home?'

Warnham looked at his wife. 'Only a little milk. He wouldn't eat anything,' she said. 'And I tasted his milk, I remember. It was quite nice.'

'That points to the party,' Eden said.

'But I can't believe it. Who could want to poison Gerald?'

'I've seen some of the people who were there,' Eden frowned. 'I don't believe there's another child ill. Only this one of the whole party.'

'Yes. Yes. A strange case,' said Reggie. 'Was there anyone there with a grudge against you, Mrs Warnham?'

'I don't think there's anyone with a grudge against me in the world.'

'I don't believe there is, Catherine,' her husband looked at her. 'But damn it, Fortune found the stuff in the child. I say, Fortune, what do you advise?'

[92]

'You're sure of your own household? There's nobody here jealous of the child?'

Mrs Warnham looked her distress. 'I couldn't, I couldn't doubt anybody. There isn't any reason. You know, it doesn't seem real.'

'And there it is,' Warnham growled.

'Yes. Well, I shouldn't talk about it, you know. When he's up again take him right away, somewhere quiet. You'll live with him yourself, of course. That's all safe. And I—well, I shan't forget the case. Goodbye.'

'Oh, Mr Fortune—' she started up and caught his hands.

'Yes, yes, good-bye,' said Reggie, and got away. But as Warnham let them out he felt Warnham's lean hand grip into his arm.

'A little homely comfort would be grateful,' Reggie murmured. 'Come and have tea at the Academies, Eden. They keep a pleasing muffin.' He sank down in his car at Eden's side with a happy sigh.

But Eden's brow was troubled. 'Do you think the child will be safe now, Fortune?' he said.

'Oh, I think so. If it was Warnham or Mrs Warnham who poisoned him—'

'Good Lord! You don't think that?'

'They are frightened,' said Reggie placidly. 'I frightened 'em quite a lot. And if it was somebody else—the child is going away and Mrs Warnham will be eating and drinking everything he eats and drinks. The small Gerald will be all right. There remains only the little problem, who was it?'

'It's a diabolical affair. Who could want to kill that child?'

'Diabolical is the word,' Reggie agreed. 'And a little simple food is what we need,' and they went into the club and through a long tea he talked to Eden of rock gardens and Chinese nursery rhymes.

But when Eden, somewhat dazed by his appetite and the variety of his conversation, was gone, he made for that corner of the club where Lomas sat drinking tea made in the Russian manner. He pointed a finger at the clear weak fluid. '"It was sad and bad and mad" and it was not even sweet,' he complained. 'Take care, Lomas. Think what's happened to Russia. You would never be happy as a Bolshevik.'

'I understand that the detective police force is the one institution which has survived in Russia.'

'Put down that repulsive concoction and come and take the air.'

Lomas stared at him in horror. 'Where's your young lady? I thought you were walking out. You're a faithless fellow, Fortune. Go and walk like a little gentleman.' But there was that in Reggie's eye which made him get up with a groan. 'You're the most ruthless man I know.'

The car moved away from the club and Reggie shrank under his rug as the January east wind met them. 'I hope you are cold,' said Lomas. 'What is it now?'

'It was nearly another anonymous murder,' and Reggie told him the story.

'Diabolical,' said Lomas.

'Yes, I believe in the devil,' Reggie nodded.

'Who stood to gain by the child's death? It's clear enough. There's only Warnham. Mrs Warnham was left a rich woman when her first husband died, old Staveleigh. Everyone knew that was why Warnham was after her. But the bulk of the fortune would go to the child. So he took the necessary action. Good Gad! We all knew Crab Warnham didn't stick at a trifle. But this—! Cold-blooded scoundrel. Can you make a case of it?'

'I like you, Lomas. You're so natural,' Reggie said. 'That's all quite clear. And it's all wrong. This case isn't natural, you see. It hath a devil.'

'Do you mean to say it wasn't Warnham?'

'It wasn't Warnham. I tried to frighten him. He was frightened. But not for himself. Because the child has an enemy and he doesn't know who it is.'

'Oh, my dear fellow! He's not a murderer because you like his face.'

'Who could like his face? No. The poison was given at the party where Warnham wasn't.'

'But why? What possible motive? Some homicidal lunatic goes to a Kensington children's party and picks out this one child to poison. Not very credible, is it?'

'No, it's diabolical. I didn't say a lunatic. When you tell me what lunacy is, we'll discuss whether the poisoner was sane. But the diabolical is getting a little too common, Lomas. There was Bigod: young, healthy, well off, just engaged to a jolly girl. He falls into a chalk-pit and the jury says it was misadventure. There was the lady doctor: young, clean living, not a ghost of a past, everybody liking her. She is murdered and a girl who was very fond of her nearly goes mad over it. Now there's the small Gerald: a dear kid, his mother worships him, his stepfather's mighty keen on him, everybody likes him. Somebody tries to poison him and nearly brings it off.'

'What are you arguing, Fortune? It's odd the cases should follow one another. It's deuced awkward we can't clean them up. But what then?

They're not really related. The people are unconnected. There's a different method of murder—if the Bigod case was murder. The only common feature is that the man who attempted murder is not known.'

'You think so? Well, well. What I want to know is, was there anyone at Mrs Lawley's party in Kensington who was also at the Home of Help party and also staying somewhere near the chalk-pit when Bigod fell into it. Put your men on to that.'

'Good Gad!' said Lomas. 'But the cases are not comparable—not in the same class. Different method—different kind of victim. What motive could any creature have for picking out just these three to kill?'

Reggie looked at him. 'Not nice murders, are they?' he said. 'I could guess—and I dare say we'll only guess in the end.'

That night he was taking Miss Amber, poor girl, to a state dinner of his relations. They had ten minutes together before the horrors of the ceremony began and she was benign to him about the recovery of the small Gerald. 'It was dear of you to ring up and tell me. I love Gerry. Poor Mrs Warnham! I just had to go round to her, and she was sweet. But she has been frightened. You're rather a wonderful person, sir. I didn't know you were a children's doctor—as well as a million other things. What was the matter? Mrs Warnham didn't tell us. It must—'

'Who are "us", Joan?'

'Why, Lady Chantry was with her. She didn't tell us what it really was. After we came away Lady Chantry asked me if I knew.'

'But I'm afraid you don't,' Reggie said. 'Joan, I don't want you to talk about the small Gerry? Do you mind?'

'My dear, of course not.' Her eyes grew bigger. 'But Reggie—the boy's going to be all right?'

'Yes. Yes. You're rather a dear, you know.'

And at the dinner-table which then received them his family found him of an unwonted solemnity. It was agreed, with surprise and reluctance, that his engagement had improved him: that there might be some merit in Miss Amber after all.

A week went by. He had been separated from Miss Amber for one long afternoon to give evidence in the case of the illegitimate Pekinese when she rang him up on the telephone. Lady Chantry, she said, had asked her to choose a day and bring Mr Fortune to dine. Lady Chantry did so want to know him.

'Does she, though?' said Mr Fortune.

'She was so nice about it,' said the telephone. 'And she really is a good sort, Reggie. She's always doing something kind.'

'Joan,' said Mr Fortune, 'you're not to go into her house.'

'Reggie!' said the telephone.

'That's that,' said Mr Fortune. 'I'll speak to Lady Chantry.'

Lady Chantry was at home. She sat in her austere pleasant drawing-room, toasting a foot at the fire, a small foot which brought out a pretty leg. Of course she was in black with some white about her neck, but the loose gown had grace. She smiled at him and tossed back her hair. Not a thread of white showed in its crisp brown, and it occurred to Reggie that he had never seen a woman of her age carry off bobbed hair so well. What was her age? Her eyes were as bright as a bird's and her clear pallor was unfurrowed.

'So good of you, Mr Fortune—'

'Miss Amber has just told me—'

They spoke together. She got the lead then. 'It was kind of her to let you know at once. But she's always kind, isn't she? I did so want you to come, and make friends with me before you're married, and it will be very soon now, won't it? Oh, but do let me give you some tea.'

'No tea, thank you.'

'Won't you? Well, please ring the bell. I don't know how men can exist without tea. But most of them don't now, do they? You're almost unique, you know. I suppose it's the penalty of greatness.'

'I came round to say that Miss Amber won't be able to dine with you, Lady Chantry.'

It was a moment before she answered. 'But that is too bad. She told me she was sure you could find a day.'

'She can't come,' said Reggie sharply.

'The man has spoken,' she laughed. 'Oh, of course, she mustn't go behind that.' He was given a keen mocking glance. 'And can't you come either, Mr Fortune?'

'I have a great deal of work, Lady Chantry. It's come rather unexpectedly.'

'Indeed, you do look worried. I'm so sorry. I'm sure you ought to take a rest, a long rest.' A servant came in. 'Won't you really have some tea?'

'No, thank you. Good-bye, Lady Chantry.'

He went home and rang up Lomas. Lomas, like the father of Baby Bunting, had gone a-hunting. Lomas was in Leicestershire. Superintendent Bell replied: Did Bell know if they had anything new about the unknown murderer?

'Inquiries are proceeding, sir,' said Superintendent Bell.

'Damn it, Bell, I'm not the House of Commons. Have you got anything?'

'Not what you'd call definite, sir, no.'

'You'll say that on the Day of Judgment,' said Reggie.

It was on the next day that he found a telegram waiting for him when he came home to dress for dinner:

Gerald ill again very anxious beg you will come sending car to meet evening trains.

Warnham
Fernhurst
Blackover.

He scrambled into the last carriage of the half-past six as it drew out of Waterloo.

Mrs Warnham had faithfully obeyed his orders to take Gerald to a quiet place. Blackover stands an equally uncomfortable distance from two main lines, one of which throws out towards it a feeble and spasmodic branch. After two changes Reggie arrived, cold and with a railway sandwich rattling in his emptiness, on the dimly lit platform of Blackover. The porter of all work who took his ticket thought there was a car outside.

In the dark station yard Reggie found only one: 'Do you come from Fernhurst?' he called, and the small chauffeur who was half inside the bonnet shut it up and touched his cap and ran round to his seat.

They dashed off into the night, climbing up by narrow winding roads through woodland. Nothing passed them, no house gave a gleam of light. The car stopped on the crest of a hill and Reggie looked out. He could see nothing but white frost and pines. The chauffeur was getting down.

'What's the trouble?' said Reggie, with his head out of the window: and slipped the catch and came out in a bundle.

The chauffeur's face was the face of Lady Chantry. He saw it in the flash of a pistol overhead as he closed with her. 'I will, I will,' she muttered and fought him fiercely. Another shot went into the pines. He wrenched her hand round. The third was fired into her face. The struggling body fell away from him, limp.

He carried it into the rays of the headlights and looked close. 'That's that,' he said with a shrug, and put it into the car.

He lit a cigar and listened. There was no sound anywhere but the sough of the wind in the pines. He climbed into the chauffeur's place and drove

[97]

away. At the next cross-roads he took that which led north and west, and so in a while came out on the Portsmouth road.

That night the frost gathered on a motor-car in a lane between Hindhead and Shottermill. Mr Fortune unobtrusively caught the last train from Haslemere.

When he came out from a *matinée* with Joan Amber next day, the newsboys were shouting 'Motor Car Mystery'. Mr Fortune did not buy a paper.

It was on the morning of the second day that Scotland Yard sent for him. Lomas was with Superintendent Bell. The two of them received him with solemnity and curious eyes. Mr Fortune was not pleased. 'Dear me, Lomas, can't you keep the peace for a week at a time?' he protested. 'What is the reason for your existence?'

'I had all that for breakfast,' said Lomas. 'Don't talk like the newspapers. Be original.'

'"Another Mysterious Murder,"' Reggie murmured, quoting headlines. '"Scotland Yard Baffled Again," "Police Mandarins." No, you haven't a "good Press," Lomas old thing.'

Lomas said something about the Press. 'Do you know who that woman chauffeur was, Fortune?'

'That wasn't in the papers, was it?'

'You haven't guessed?'

Again Reggie Fortune was aware of the grave curiosity in their eyes. 'Another of our mysterious murders,' he said dreamily. 'I wonder. Are you working out the series at last? I told you to look for someone who was always present.'

Lomas looked at Superintendent Bell. 'Lady Chantry was present at this one, Fortune,' he said. 'Lady Chantry took out her car the day before yesterday. Yesterday morning the car was found in a lane above Haslemere. Lady Chantry was inside. She wore chauffeur's uniform. She was shot through the head.'

'Well, well,' said Reggie Fortune.

'I want you to come down and look at the body.'

'Is the body the only evidence?'

'We know where she bought the coat and cap. Her own coat and hat were under the front seat. She told her servants she might not be back at night. No one knows what she went out for or where she went.'

'Yes. Yes. When a person is shot, it's generally with a gun. Have you found it?'

'She had an automatic pistol in her hand.'

Reggie Fortune rose. 'I had better see her,' he said sadly. 'A wearing world, Lomas. Come on. My car's outside.'

Two hours later he stood looking down at the slight body and the scorched wound in that pale face while a police surgeon demonstrated to him how the shot was fired. The pistol was gripped with the rigor of death in the woman's right hand, the bullet that was taken from the base of the skull fitted it, the muzzle—remark the stained, scorched flesh—must have been held close to her face when the shot was fired. And Reggie listened and nodded. 'Yes, yes. All very clear, isn't it? A straight case.' He drew the sheet over the body and paid compliments to the doctor as they went out.

Lomas was in a hurry to meet them. Reggie shook his head. 'There's nothing for me, Lomas. And nothing for you. The medical evidence is suicide. Scotland Yard is acquitted without a stain on its character.'

'No sort of doubt?' said Lomas.

'You can bring all the College of Surgeons to see her. You'll get nothing else.'

And so they climbed into the car again. 'Finis, thank God!' said Mr Fortune as the little town ran by.

Lomas looked at him curiously. 'Why did she commit suicide, Fortune?' he said.

'There are also other little questions,' Reggie murmured. 'Why did she murder Bigod? Why did she murder the lady doctor? Why did she try to murder the child?'

Lomas continued to stare at him. 'How do you know she did?' he said in a low voice. 'You're making very sure.'

'Great heavens! You might do some of the work. I know Scotland Yard isn't brilliant, but it might take pains. Who was present at all the murders? Who was the constant force? Haven't you found that out yet?'

'She was staying near Bigod's place. She was at the orphanage. She was at the child's party. And only she was at all three. It staggered me when I got the evidence complete. But what in heaven makes you think she is the murderer?'

Reggie moved uneasily. 'There was something malign about her.'

'Malign! But she was always doing philanthropic work.'

'Yes. It may be a saint who does that—or the other thing. Haven't you ever noticed—some of the people who are always busy about distress they rather like watching distress?'

'Why, yes. But murder! And what possible motive is there for killing

[99]

these different people? She might have hated one or another. But not all three.'

'Oh, there is a common factor. Don't you see? Each one had somebody to feel the deathlike torture—the girl Bigod was engaged to, the girl who was devoted to the lady doctor, the small Gerald's mother. There was always somebody to suffer horribly—and the person to be killed was always somebody who had a young good life to lose. Not at all nice murders, Lomas. Genus diabolical, species feminine. Say that Lady Chantry had a devilish passion for cruelty—and it ended that night in the motor-car.'

'But why commit suicide? Do you mean she was mad?'

'I wouldn't say that. That's for the Day of Judgment. When is cruelty madness? I don't know. Why did she—give herself away—in the end? Perhaps she found she had gone a little too far. Perhaps she knew you and I had begun to look after her. She never liked me much, I fancy. She was a little—odd—with me.'

'You're an uncanny fellow, Fortune.'

'My dear chap! Oh, my dear chap! I'm wholly normal. I'm the natural man,' said Reggie Fortune.

THE BUOY THAT DID NOT LIGHT

Edgar Wallace

Edgar Wallace (1872–1932) was a most prolific
writer of popular fiction with countless mystery
novels, short stories, plays, and non-fiction
articles to his name. 'The Buoy That Did Not
Light' was originally published in the *Grand*
(companion magazine to the *Strand*) in January
1923, and later appeared in his collection *The
Steward* (1932).

'W hat's that word that they use to describe an airplane that
can come down on the sea or the land? (It was the steward
inquiring.) Amphibian! That's it. It was the name our old
captain gave 'em. In the days when I was steward on board the old
Majestic—you remember how she killed a stoker every voyage—there
used to be a crowd that worked its way across twice a year—the only
crowd I ever knew that mixed it.

'Amphibians are rare. A man either works ships or he works towns. If
a ship's gang works a town at all, it is with people they've got to know on
board ship. Somebody said that a ship is like a prison, with a chance of
being drowned. It is certainly a bit too restricted for people who want to
sell gold bricks, or have had a lot of money left to them to distribute to
the poor, providing they can find the right kind of man to give it away.
The point I want to make is this: that the ship crowd and the land crowd
very seldom work together, and if the land people *do* travel by sea,
they've got to behave themselves, and not go butting in to any little game

that happens to be in progress in the smoke-room. The ship crowd naturally do not go to the captain or the purser and complain that there is an unauthorized gang on board eating into their profits. The case is settled out of court; and when you've real bad men travelling . . . Well, I've seen some curious things.

'There was a fellow, quite unknown to me except from hearsay, called Hoyle. He was a land man in a big way. Banks and bullion trains and post cars were his specialty, but there was hardly a piece of work he couldn't do if there was money to it.

'If he'd kept to land work, where by all accounts he was an artist, he'd have been lucky. You can't properly work both. I've had that from some of the biggest men that ever travelled the sea. What my old skippers called "The Barons of the Nimble Pack" work in a perfectly straightforward manner. All they need is a pair of hands, a pack of cards, a glib tongue and a nut. Sometimes they use more packs than one, but there is no fanciful apparatus, no plots and plannings, guns, masks or nitroglycerine. It's a profession like doctoring or lawyering—peaceful and, in a manner of speaking, inoffensive. When a land crowd comes barging into the smoke-room they're treated civilly so long as they're travelling for pleasure. Otherwise . . . Well, it's natural. If you're poaching a stream you don't want people throwing half-bricks into it. There's only one sensible way of being unlawful when you're poaching, and that is to poach.

'I've seen a bit of amphibian work and I'm telling you I don't want to see any more. In the year 19— we went out of Southampton with a full passenger list, the date being the 21st of December, and we carried to all appearance as nice a passenger list as you could wish to meet. Mostly Americans going home, though there was a fair sprinkling of British. We had a couple of genteel gangs on board—fellows who never played high or tried for big stakes, but managed to make a reasonable living. Tad Hesty of Pittsburg ran one, and a London fellow named Lew Isaacs managed the other. I think he was a Jew. A very nice, sensible fellow was Lew, polite and gentlemanly, and I've never heard a complaint against him, though I've travelled a score of voyages with him.

' "Felix," he said to me one day, "moderation in all things is my motto. Nobody was ever ruined by taking small profits. A man who loses a hundred dollars or twenty pounds doesn't squeal. Touch him for a thousand, and the pilot boat comes out looking like an excursion steamer, it's that full of bulls. A hundred dollars is speechless, Felix. It may give a tiny squeak, but it apologizes immediately afterwards. A thousand dollars has a steam siren, and ten thousand dollars makes a noise like a bomb in a powder plant.'

'He and his two friends used to share the same cabin. One was always dressed quiet and respectable, and never went into the smoke-room at all. He used to sit up on the deck, reading a book and getting acquainted with the serious-minded people from the Middle West, or the North of England mill-owners who think they're sporty because they own a couple of greyhounds that get into the second round of the Waterloo Cup.

'Lew was on very good terms with the Pittsburg crowd, and I've seen them drinking together and exchanging views about the slackness of trade and the income tax and things of that kind, without any ill word passing between them.

'A ship isn't out of port twenty-four hours before a steward knows the history of everybody on board; and the smoke-room steward told me that there was nobody else on board but the Pittsburg crowd and this man Lewis and his friends. In fact, it looked so much like being such a quiet voyage, that only the little cards warning passengers not to play with strangers were put up in the smoke-room. If the Flack gang had been travelling, we'd have put up the usual warning with four-inch type.

'I had eight state-rooms to look after. No 181 to 188, F Deck. A Chicago man had one, a Mr Mellish, who was a buyer at a St Louis store, was another, a young English officer—Captain Fairburn—attached to the British Embassy had another and the remainder were booked by Colonel Roger Markson for his party. There was the colonel, a tall, solemn-looking man, his wife, who was younger than him, and always seemed to be crying in her cabin, his son, a slick young fellow, generally dressed to kill, and there was Miss Colport.

'Personally, I don't take much notice of a passenger's personal appearance. I judge 'em by their hair-brushes. There's woodens, generally missionaries or fellows like reporters whose passage is paid by somebody else; there's ivory backs (the captain's was ivory) and silver backs and horn backs, with now and again a gold back. Gold backs are usually on their honeymoon. I can't remember whether this Miss Colport was an ivory or a silver. Maybe she was silver, for she was Markson's secretary and he'd got her in London, where she was stranded and anxious to get home. Not that she had any friends in New York. By all accounts she came from the west and went to London to take up a position as stenographer to an uncle, who first went broke in the rubber slump and then died.

[103]

'I knew she was a good-looker long before I saw the trouble she was making with the British Embassy. This captain used to be up hours before breakfast waiting for her on deck. Whether they knew or did not know one another before they came on board, I can't say. I should think not. On board ship you get an introduction from the after combing, as they say. The colonel and his son had breakfast in bed for the first day, for the *Beramic* is a cow of a ship, and she'd roll in a saucerful of milk.

'Anyway, somebody must have given them the word that their young lady secretary was getting acquainted with the British Army, for the second morning out young Markson (Julius by name) told me to call him at seven. And about five minutes after he'd climbed to the upper deck Miss came down, looking very pink in the face and not a bit pleased.

'Julius was mad about the girl. Used to follow her about like a tame cat or a wild tiger, whichever way you look at it. What first got me thinking was a bit of a conversation I heard between him and his father one afternoon when I was polishing the brasses in the alleyway.

' "I've got a few words to say to you, Julius," said the colonel. He had a growling, complaining voice at the best of times, but now it was like a file on granite. "If you get any pleasure out of making up to that girl, you're entitled to get it, so long as you're not too serious. I'll do all the serious stuff in that quarter."

' "She'll skip to Denver as soon as she lands," said Julius sulkily. And something in his voice told me that they were not father and son. I don't know what it was, but I jumped to that conclusion and I was right.

'I heard the colonel laugh, and it was the sort of laugh that has a bark to it.

' "Have I paid her passage to New York to have her skip anywhere?" he asked. "She's going to be very useful. Min's getting past her work. Colport is the woman I've been looking for . . ."

'That's all I heard, but I knew that "Min" was Mrs Roger Markson, because I'd heard him call her that lots of times. I had a good look at her after that. She was a woman just over 30, who used to make up a lot. I began to understand why her eyes were always red and why she was so scared looking when the colonel spoke to her. I knew, of course, that she was too young to be the mother of Julius. At first I thought that she was the colonel's second wife. Now I guessed that none of the three was related. It's a wicked world.

'The next day was Christmas Eve, and some queer things happened. It was in the morning that the deck steward met me and asked me to take Mrs Markson's wrap to her.

'I took it up and found them leaning against the rail opposite the smoke-room door. Julius was there, scowling at the captain and Miss Colport, who were sitting together, talking.

'Just as I was putting on the lady's wrap, Lew Isaacs came out of the smoke-room. I was standing behind the lady, looking over her shoulder, and I caught one glimpse of his face. His expression didn't exactly change as he looked at her. I don't know how I'd describe it . . . I think it must have been his eyes that lit, but he took no further notice and strolled down the deck with his hands in his pockets and his cap on the side of his head.

' "Good God!" said the colonel. "I didn't know he was on board."

'As I fixed the wrap I could feel Mrs Markson tremble.

' "He works this line," she said. "I told you in London . . ."

' "That will do, steward," said the colonel, and I had to go away at a moment when, as you might say, the story was getting interesting.

'It was a heavy day for me, and heavier than I expected, owing to Santa Claus.

'We always do our best to amuse passengers, and on this Christmas Eve a grand fancy-dress ball was arranged, which seemed to be passing off without anything unusual happening. Lew Isaacs spent the evening in the smoke-room playing bridge for a dollar a hundred, and the Pittsburg crowd had got hold of a man in the movie picture business, and was listening admiringly to all he was telling them about the way he won four thousand dollars from another fellow. This movie picture man was one of those kind of people you meet on board a ship, who are often sober.

'Well, the fancy-dress ball came off, and about eleven o'clock, when people were getting noisy, at what I call the streamer and confetti stage, a Santa Claus with a big sack on his back and a bundle of presents in his hand, went along all the alleyways, into every cabin he found open, and left a little cellular doll—celluloid, is it? You can buy them for a penny. A little doll without any clothes on except a bit of ribbon, with "A merry Christmas" printed on it. I saw him; lots of other stewards saw him; the purser saw him and wanted him to have a drink, but no, he said he had a lot to do, and he was right.

'Of course there was trouble in the morning. Nobody who has lost a pearl stick pin or a pair of ear-rings or a gold watch and chain or a cigarette case, is going to be satisfied with a two-cent doll in exchange. That old Santa Claus had cleared out every cabin of its valuables, and there were few people on board who enjoyed their Christmas dinner. The fortunate thing, from the stewards' point of view, was that everybody had seen this jolly old gentleman with white whiskers, and one or two had slapped him on the back. They were all anxious now to slap him almost any place, so long as they could lay hands on him. Every steward on board, all the ship's officers, and some of the engineering officers, spent Christmas Day making a thorough and systematic search of all the cabins. Naturally, the first people to be suspected were the stoke-hold staff. I say "naturally" because it is a popular idea among ships' officers that, if anything is pinched, it is a stoker that did it. Then the third-class saloons were searched, bags and boxes were opened; then finally—and it was the first place they should have looked—they had a tour of inspection of the first-class accommodation.

'One of the first persons they sent for was Mr Lew Isaacs.

'"Now, Isaacs," said the first purser, "you know what happened on the ship last night. I want you to help me. You needn't tell me that you and friends were playing cards in the smoke-room, and that all your crowd was there, because I know that. Who else is on board?"

'"If I never move from this carpet, Mr Cole," said Lew very earnestly, "I have no more idea who did this job than an unborn child. I am not saying," he went on, "that if there was a gentleman on board engaged in that kind of business, I should give you his name, because my motto is 'live and let live'. But it so happens that there isn't anybody that I know. When I heard about this you could have knocked me down with a feather,' he said. 'Naturally, it's not to my interest to make people suspicious and tighten up their wads, and I consider that, from my own point of view, the voyage has been spoilt, and every particle of enjoyment has been taken out of it."

'"That's all very well," said the purser, looking at him hard (I heard all this from Lacey, who does for the purser), "but there's been a complaint made, and your name has been mentioned by Colonel Markson. He says he knows that you are a card man and a dangerous character."

'Lew shook his head.

'"I don't know the colonel," he said, "except by sight. He's probably mistaken. It's easy to make mistakes. The first time I saw him I mistook him for a fellow named Hoyle that's wanted in London for the London and City Bank affair—they got away with twelve thousand pounds. Tell him that, will you, and apologize to him for my mind harbouring such libellous thoughts."

'On Christmas evening I saw the colonel talking to young Captain Fairburn at the door of Captain Fairburn's state-room. They were very friendly and they were both laughing.

'"I'm afraid I shall have to give you a cheque if I lose any more," said the captain.

'That was all. When he'd gone down to dinner I went into his cabin. He had been playing cards. How they got to be friendly I don't know. You can never keep tracks of things like that. You see a man and a girl pass without noticing one another the first day out. By the time the Irish coast is out of sight they are meeting on deck at daybreak and getting in the way of the watch that has to scrub down. Before they get to Sandy Hook they are receiving congratulations by wireless from their friends and relatives.

'Young Captain Fairburn came in after dinner to get some cigarettes.

'"Excuse me, Captain," I said, "but I shouldn't play cards in your state-room if I were you."

'"Why not, steward?" he asked, surprised. "Is it against the rules of the ship?"

'"No, sir," says I, "but it's dangerous."

'"Stuff!" said he. "I was only playing with Colonel Markson—you're not suggesting that he is a thief, are you?'

'"No, sir," I says. When people start asking me if I suggest that somebody is a thief, I resign.

'That is why stewards can't help passengers. Passengers know it all. They're men of the world, by gum!

'As soon as I had finished my eight state-rooms, I had to join one of the search parties that were hunting through the ship for the lost property. Our purser was still certain that matter must occupy space, and we searched space from the crow's-nest to the bunkers. I didn't see or hear anything of what happened in the smoke-room, and I never knew till the next morning that the colonel and Julius had played cut-throat poker with young Fairburn in full view of the smoke-room, and that the Captain had lost a lot more than he could afford. In fact, the cheque he gave was for four figures. The deck steward told me that when they came out on the promenade, he heard the colonel say to Julius: "That settles our young friend's matrimonial plans—if he had any."

'At this moment I was on the boat deck having my second pipe. I was naturally lying doggo—in other words, invisible—not wishing to be seen by any of the ship's officers or the master at arms, and the night being cold, I was wedged between the second officer's cabin and the wireless house. From where I sat I had a limited view, and if the couple hadn't stopped right opposite to where I was, I'd have missed everything. But I always have been lucky that way. All that I could hear at first was a woman crying, and somehow I guessed it was "Mrs Markson". Perhaps it was because she was the only woman I had seen crying since the voyage started.

'But when I heard the man's voice, why, I nearly jumped. It was Lew Isaacs.

'"Oh, Lew, I've treated you badly. I don't deserve anything . . ."

'I saw him put his arm round her shoulder, and I knew by the way her sobs were stifled that she was crying on to his chest.

'"I bear no ill will, Minnie," he said. "I've always said that if you liked Hoyle better than me, you were entitled to marry him, old girl."

'There was a long silence, and then she said:

'"I'm not married, Lew."

'He said nothing for a minute, and when he did speak, he seemed to have turned the subject.

'"He told the purser that I was in that Father Christmas job. That's the kind of swine Hoyle is. Where's the stuff, Min . . .? You needn't tell me. It is in the calcium canister of one of these life-buoys. Had it ready planted and painted and substituted it one dark night, eh? It's an old trick of Hoyle's."

'My hair almost stood up. Round all the promenade decks are life-buoys hooked to the rail. Attached are cans containing a chemical to light up the moment it touches water. The lid of the canister is jerked off automatically as the life-buoy is thrown. It was the simplest idea in the world. Hoyle had a duplicate life-buoy in his cabin baggage. One dark night—probably the first night out—he'd carry it up to the boat deck and put it in the place of another that he'd throw overboard after cutting the cord that opened the calcium tin. He wouldn't have a chance of doing it on the promenade, but the boat deck was dark and was easily reached.

'They were talking in low tones and I could only catch an occasional word. Then, just as they were turning to go, I heard her whisper:

'"There he is!"

'It was the colonel. I caught a whiff of his cigar before I saw him.

'"Hullo! That's Lew Isaacs, isn't it? Meeting old friends, eh, Min?"

'"Hoyle, I've got a word or two to say to you. The first is business. You've been breaking into our game to-night with that young officer. Tad is pretty mad about it."

'"Got a franchise to work the Western Ocean, Lew? What do I have to do—get a written permission before I work a ship?"

'"That's one thing," said Lew. "Here's another, and that is business too. You told the purser that I was in your Santa Claus game."

'"He knew all about you," said the colonel, and I saw the red end of his cigar gleaming and fading. "It did you no harm, and testified to my respectability—that's right, eh, Lew? Anything more?"

'Lew struck a match to light his cigarette, and I saw his face. Saw the woman's too—just for a fraction of a second.

'"You've got a young girl in your outfit—secretary or something. What's the great idea?"

'The colonel laughed softly.

'"Min's been talking, eh? Jealous. Well, Lew, it's like this: Men grow old and it doesn't matter. Looks are not my asset. They are in the case of Min. There's no sense in seeing these things sentimentally. When a card man loses his fingers he's finished, isn't he? When Min loses her looks . . . Well, be sensible. I can't work with a plain woman. She's got to hook first time, Lew. Isn't that common sense? It's tough on Min, but I'm going to play fair. She's got a big roll coming to her—'

'"What about the girl? She's a decent woman and a countrywoman of mine," said Lew.

'Hoyle laughed again.

'"I didn't know that a Jew had a country, but we won't argue. She's a mighty nice girl, and when she's a little wiser than she is at present . . . Anyway, we're not going to quarrel."

'I saw the dark figure of Lew. He was leaning back with both his elbows on the rail.

'"I never quarrel with a man who keeps his gun in his hand all the time," he said, and I think that one struck home, for the colonel moved kind of startled.

'"Besides," said Lew, "I'm not actually in this. Off you go, Min, I want a chat about this Father Christmas notion."

'He took the arm of the colonel, and they went for'ard, and I followed Mrs Markson down the deck. The first person I went to see was the chief purser. I don't want to say anything against the chief pursers of the "Starcuna" Line, but all I can say is that if there's one with the brain of a Napoleon, I've never sailed with him. Our chief purser at the time was a man who thought in about fifty phrases, one of which I've told you. "Do nothing precipitate" was another. "Dereliction of duty" was also a great favourite. I don't know what it means and I'll bet he didn't either.

'"It's an extraordinary story," he said, "and I'll report the matter to the captain first thing in the morning. We must do nothing precipitate. But what were you doing on the boat deck, Jenks, smoking? That was a dereliction of duty, surely! However, we'll wait until the morning. I was certain the missing property would be found. Matter must occupy space.''

'I was so agitated and put out that I went out to the promenade deck and helped the steward on duty stack up the chairs and collect the rugs and the library books. It was getting late, and I spotted Miss Colport and the captain very close together and looking over the rail. I suppose the sea was vaster than ever that night, for if they weren't holding hands then I'm inexperienced. I can tell hand-holders a mile off.

'Farther along the deck was Mrs Markson and Julius. They were talking together, too, but not so friendly.

'It was late, and some of the bulkhead lights were out. I saw the second officer coming along the deck in his heavy overcoat and sea boots, and at that minute something flashed past the rail.

'I heard the shriek, and then the second officer yelled:

' ''*Man overboard!*''

'He sprang to the rail, lifted up a buoy, and flung it as the *Beramic* heeled over to port and the engines rang astern.

' ''The calcium light's not burning,'' shouted the second, and, racing along the deck, he flung over a second buoy. It hardly touched the water before it burst into a green flame.

' ''That works all right—what in hell was wrong with the other?'' asked the second officer.

'The *Beramic* was moving in a slow circle, and the watch had the fore lifeboat into the water in double quick time. The deck was crowded now. The passengers had flocked out of the saloon and the smoke-room, and were crowding up the companionway in their dressing-gowns. I think it was the ''man boat'' signal on the siren that roused 'em. The boat pulled round and reached the second buoy, but the first they never found, nor the man either.

' ''What is it, steward?''

'I looked round and saw Mr Lew Isaacs. He was in his pyjamas and dressing-gown.

' ''A man overboard, sir,'' I said; ''and they threw him a buoy that had no calcium tank. I think it was Colonel Markson.''

' ''How extraordinary!'' said Mr Lew Isaacs.

'The captain had an inquiry next morning, and I told all that I'd heard. Mr Isaacs said he had never been on the boat deck, and so did Mrs Markson. All the life-buoys were examined, but none were found that had jewellery in the canister.

'After the inquiry was over the captain had a talk with me.

'"Two against one, Jenks," he said. "This had better be an accident or a suicide, or anything you like. We don't want this yarn of yours to get into the newspaper, do you understand?"

'"Yes, sir," I said.

'"And don't smoke on the boat deck, steward. If you want to smoke, come and have a pipe with me on the bridge."

'A very sarcastic person was the skipper of the *Beramic*.

'I don't think Captain Fairburn was as poor as Markson thought— even though his cheque was never presented.

'The reason why I think this is because, when he came back to the *Beramic* about six months later, he had the honeymoon suite, and Mrs Fairburn (Miss Colport, that was) had the dandiest set of gold back brushes I've ever seen.'

A CHRISTMAS TRAGEDY

Agatha Christie

Agatha Christie (1890–1976), the most popular
crime novelist of all time, is equally celebrated
for her two best-known creations, Hercule
Poirot and Jane Marple. The elderly (but
ageless) Miss Marple, the most famous spinster
sleuth in detective fiction, is featured in this
early story, taken from *The Thirteen Problems*
(1932).

'I have a complaint to make,' said Sir Henry Clithering.

His eyes twinkled gently as he looked round at the assembled
company. Colonel Bantry, his legs stretched out, was frowning at
the mantelpiece as though it were a delinquent soldier on parade, his wife
was surreptitiously glancing at a catalogue of bulbs which had come by
the late post, Dr Lloyd was gazing with frank admiration at Jane Helier,
and that beautiful young actress herself was thoughtfully regarding her
pink polished nails. Only that elderly spinster lady, Miss Marple, was
sitting bolt upright, and her faded blue eyes met Sir Henry's with an
answering twinkle.

'A complaint?' she murmured.

'A very serious complaint. We are a company of six, three representatives of each sex, and I protest on behalf of the down-trodden males.
We have had three stories told tonight—and told by the three men! I
protest that the ladies have not done their fair share.'

'Oh!' said Mrs Bantry with indignation. 'I'm sure we have. We've listened with the most intelligent appreciation. We've displayed the true womanly attitude—not wishing to thrust ourselves into the limelight!'

'It's an excellent excuse,' said Sir Henry; 'but it won't do. And there's a very good precedent in the Arabian Nights! So, forward, Scheherazade.'

'Meaning me?' said Mrs Bantry. 'But I don't know anything to tell. I've never been surrounded by blood or mystery.'

'I don't absolutely insist upon blood,' said Sir Henry. 'But I'm sure one of you three ladies has got a pet mystery. Come now, Miss Marple— the "Curious Coincidence of the Charwoman" or the "Mystery of the Mothers' Meeting." Don't disappoint me in St Mary Mead.'

Miss Marple shook her head.

'Nothing that would interest you, Sir Henry. We have our little mysteries, of course—there was that gill of picked shrimps that disappeared so incomprehensibly; but that wouldn't interest you because it all turned out to be so trivial, though throwing a considerable light on human nature.'

'You have taught me to dote on human nature,' said Sir Henry solemnly.

'What about you, Miss Helier?' asked Colonel Bantry. 'You must have had some interesting experiences.'

'Yes, indeed,' said Dr Lloyd.

'Me?' said Jane. 'You mean—you want me to tell you something that happened to me?'

'Or to one of your friends,' amended Sir Henry.

'Oh!' said Jane vaguely. 'I don't think anything has ever happened to me—I mean not that kind of thing. Flowers, of course, and queer messages—but that's just men, isn't it? I don't think'—she paused and appeared lost in thought.

'I see we shall have to have that epic of the shrimps,' said Sir Henry. 'Now then, Miss Marple.'

'You're so fond of your joke, Sir Henry. The shrimps are only nonsense; but now I come to think of it, I *do* remember one incident— at least not exactly an incident, something very much more serious—a tragedy. And I was, in a way, mixed up in it; and for what I did, I have never had any regrets—no, no regrets at all. But it didn't happen in St Mary Mead.'

'That disappoints me,' said Sir Henry. 'But I will endeavour to bear up. I knew we should not rely upon you in vain.'

He settled himself in the attitude of a listener. Miss Marple grew slightly pink.

'I hope I shall be able to tell it properly,' she said anxiously. 'I fear I am very inclined to become *rambling*. One wanders from the point—altogether without knowing that one is doing so. And it is so hard to remember each fact in its proper order. You must all bear with me if I tell my story badly. It happened a very long time ago now.

'As I say it was not connected with St Mary Mead. As a matter of fact, it had to do with a Hydro—'

'Do you mean a seaplane?' asked Jane with wide eyes.

'You wouldn't know, dear,' said Mrs Bantry, and explained. Her husband added his quota:

'Beastly places—absolutely beastly! Got to get up early and drink filthy-tasting water. Lot of old women sitting about. Ill-natured tittle tattle. God, when I think—'

'Now, Arthur,' said Mrs Bantry placidly. 'You know it did you all the good in the world.'

'Lot of old women sitting round talking scandal,' grunted Colonel Bantry.

'That, I am afraid, is true,' said Miss Marple. 'I myself—'

'My dear Miss Marple,' cried the colonel, horrified. 'I didn't mean for one moment—'

With pink cheeks and a little gesture of the hand, Miss Marple stopped him.

'But it is *true*, Colonel Bantry. Only I should like to say this. Let me recollect my thoughts. Yes. Talking scandal, as you say—well it *is* done a good deal. And people are very down on it—especially young people. My nephew, who writes books—and very clever ones, I believe—has said some most *scathing* things about taking people's characters away without any kind of proof—and how wicked it is, and all that. But what I say is that none of these young people ever stop to *think*. They really don't examine the facts. Surely the whole crux of the matter is this. *How often is tittle tattle*, as you call it, *true*! And I think if, as I say, they really examined the facts they would find that it was true nine times out of ten! That's really just what makes people so annoyed about it.'

'The inspired guess,' said Sir Henry.

'No, not that, not that at all! It's really a matter of practice and experience. An Egyptologist, so I've heard, if you show him one of those curious little beetles, can tell you by the look and the feel of the thing what date BC it is, or if it's a Birmingham imitation. And he can't always

[114]

give a definite rule for doing so. He just *knows*. His life has been spent handling such things.

'And that's what I'm trying to say (very badly, I know). What my nephew calls 'superfluous women' have a lot of time on their hands, and their chief interest is usually *people*. And so, you see, they get to be what one might call *experts*. Now young people nowadays—they talk very freely about things that weren't mentioned in my young days, but on the other hand their minds are terribly innocent. They believe in everyone and everything. And if one tries to warn them, ever so gently, they tell one that one has a Victorian mind—and that, they say, is like a *sink*.'

'After all,' said Sir Henry, 'what is wrong with a *sink*?'

'Exactly,' said Miss Marple eagerly. 'It's the most necessary thing in any house; but, of course, not romantic. Now I must confess that I have my *feelings*, like everyone else, and I have sometimes been cruelly hurt by unthinking remarks. I know gentlemen are not interested in domestic matters, but I must just mention my maid Ethel—a very good-looking girl and obliging in every way. Now I realized as soon as I saw her that she was the same type as Annie Webb and poor Mrs Bruitt's girl. If the opportunity arose *mine and thine* would mean nothing to her. So I let her go at the month and I gave her a written reference saying she was honest and sober, but privately I warned old Mrs Edwards against taking her; and my nephew, Raymond, was exceedingly angry and said he had never heard of anything so wicked—yes, *wicked*. Well, she went to Lady Ashton, whom I felt no obligation to warn—and what happened? All the lace cut off her underclothes and two diamond brooches taken—and the girl departed in the middle of the night and never heard of since!'

Miss Marple paused, drew a long breath, and then went on.

'You'll be saying this has nothing to do with what went on at Keston Spa Hydro—but it has in a way. It explains why I felt no doubt in my mind the first moment I saw the Sanders together that he meant to do away with her.'

'Eh?' said Sir Henry, leaning forward.

Miss Marple turned a placid face to him.

'As I say, Sir Henry, I felt no doubt in my own mind. Mr Sanders was a big, good-looking, florid-faced man, very hearty in his manner and popular with all. And nobody could have been pleasanter to his wife than he was. But I knew! He meant to make away with her.'

'My dear Miss Marple—'

'Yes, I know. That's what my nephew Raymond West, would say. He'd tell me I hadn't a shadow of proof. But I remember Walter Hones, who kept the Green Man. Walking home with his wife one night she fell into the river—and *he* collected the insurance money! And one or two other people that are walking about scot free to this day—one indeed in our own class of life. Went to Switzerland for a summer holiday climbing with his wife. I warned her not to go—the poor dear didn't get angry with me as she might have done—she only laughed. It seemed to her funny that a queer old thing like me should say such things about her Harry. Well, well, there was an accident—and Harry is married to another woman now. But what could I *do*? I *knew*, but there was no proof.'

'Oh! Miss Marple,' cried Mrs Bantry. 'You don't really mean—'

'My dear, these things are very common—very common indeed. And gentlemen are especially tempted, being so much the stronger. So easy if a thing looks like an accident. As I say, I knew at once with the Sanders. It was on a tram. It was full inside and I had had to go on top. We all three got up to get off and Mr Sanders lost his balance and fell right against his wife, sending her headfirst down the stairs. Fortunately the conductor was a very strong young man and caught her.'

'But surely that must have been an accident.'

'Of course it was an accident—nothing could have looked more accidental. But Mr Sanders had been in the Merchant Service, so he told me, and a man who can keep his balance on a nasty tilting boat doesn't lose it on top of a tram if an old woman like me doesn't. Don't tell me!'

'At any rate we can take it that you made up your mind, Miss Marple,' said Sir Henry. 'Made it up then and there.'

The old lady nodded.

'I was sure enough, and another incident in crossing the street not long afterwards made me surer still. Now I ask you, what could I do, Sir Henry? Here was a nice contented happy little married woman shortly going to be murdered.'

'My dear lady, you take my breath away.'

'That's because, like most people nowadays, you won't face facts. You prefer to think such a thing couldn't be. But it was so, and I knew it. But one is so sadly handicapped! I couldn't, for instance, go to the police. And to warn the young woman would, I could see, be useless. She was devoted to the man. I just made it my business to find out as much as I could about them. One has a lot of opportunities doing one's needlework round the fire. Mrs Sanders (Gladys, her name was) was only too willing to talk. It seems they had not been married very long. Her husband had some property that was coming to him, but for the moment they were very badly off. In fact, they were living on her little income. One has heard that tale before. She bemoaned the fact that she could not touch the capital. It seems that somebody had had some sense somewhere! But the money was hers to will away—I found that out. And she and her husband had made wills in favour of each other directly after their marriage. Very touching. Of course, when Jack's affairs came right—That was the burden all day long, and in the meantime they were very hard up indeed—actually had a room on the top floor, all among the servants—and so dangerous in case of fire, though, as it happened, there was a fire escape just outside their window. I inquired carefully if there was a balcony—dangerous things, balconies. One push—you know!

'I made her promise not to go out on the balcony; I said I'd had a dream. That impressed her—one can do a lot with superstition sometimes. She was a fair girl, rather washed-out complexion, and an untidy roll of hair on her neck. Very credulous. She repeated what I had said to her husband, and I noticed him looking at me in a curious way once or twice. *He* wasn't credulous; and he knew I'd been on that tram.

'But I was very worried—terribly worried—because I couldn't see how to circumvent him. I could prevent anything happening at the Hydro, just by saying a few words to show him I suspected. But that only meant his putting off his plan till later. No, I began to believe that the only policy was a bold one—somehow or other to lay a trap for him. If I could induce him to attempt her life in a way of my own choosing— well, then he would be unmasked, and she would be forced to face the truth however much of a shock it was to her.'

'You take my breath away,' said Dr Lloyd. 'What conceivable plan could you adopt?'

'I'd have found one—never fear,' said Miss Marple. 'But the man was too clever for me. He didn't wait. He thought I might suspect, and so he struck before I could be sure. He knew I would suspect an accident. So he made it murder.'

A little gasp went round the circle. Miss Marple nodded and set her lips grimly together.

'I'm afraid I've put that rather abruptly. I must try and tell you exactly what occurred. I've always felt very bitterly about it—it seems to me that I ought, somehow, to have prevented it. But doubtless Providence knew best. I did what I could at all events.

'There was what I can only describe as a curiously eerie feeling in the air. There seemed to be something weighing on us all. A feeling of misfortune. To begin with, there was George, the hall porter. Had been there for years and knew everybody. Bronchitis and pneumonia, and passed away on the fourth day. Terribly sad. A real blow to everybody. And four days before Christmas too. And then one of the housemaids—such a nice girl—a septic finger, actually died in twenty-four hours.

'I was in the drawing room with Miss Trollope and old Mrs Carpenter, and Mrs Carpenter was being positively ghoulish—relishing it all, you know.

' "Mark my words," she said. "*This isn't the end.* You know the saying? *Never two without three.* I've proved it true time and again. There'll be another death. Not a doubt of it. And we shan't have long to wait. *Never two without three.*"

'As she said the last words, nodding her head and clicking her knitting needles, I just chanced to look up and there was Mr Sanders standing in the doorway. Just for a minute he was off guard, and I saw the look in his face as plain as plain. I shall believe till my dying day that it was that ghoulish Mrs Carpenter's words that put the whole thing into his head. I saw his mind working.

'He came forward into the room smiling in his genial way.

' "Any Christmas shopping I can do for you ladies?" he asked. "I'm going down to Keston presently."

'He stayed a minute or two, laughing and talking, and then went out. As I tell you I was troubled, and I said straight away:

' "Where's Mrs Sanders? Does anyone know?"

'Mrs Trollope said she'd gone out to some friends of hers, the Mortimers, to play Bridge, and that eased my mind for the moment. But I was still very worried and most uncertain as to what to do. About half an hour later I went up to my room. I met Dr Coles, my doctor, there, coming down the stairs as I was going up, and as I happened to want to consult him about my rheumatism, I took him into my room with me then and there. He mentioned to me then (in confidence, he said) about the death of the poor girl Mary. The manager didn't want the news to get about, he said, so would I keep it to myself. Of course I didn't tell him that we'd all been discussing nothing else for the last hour—ever since the poor girl breathed her last. These things are always known at once, and a man of his experience should know that well enough; but Dr Coles always was a simple unsuspicious fellow who believed what he wanted to believe and that's just what alarmed me a minute later. He said as he was leaving that Sanders had asked him to have a look at his wife. It seemed she'd been seedy of late—indigestion, etc.

'Now that very self-same day Gladys Sanders had said to me that she'd got a wonderful digestion and was thankful for it.

'You see? All my suspicions of that man came back a hundredfold. He was preparing the way—for what? Dr Coles left before I could make up my mind whether to speak to him or not—though really if I had spoken I shouldn't have known what to say. As I came out of my room, the man himself—Sanders—came down the stairs from the floor above. He was dressed to go out and he asked me again if he could do anything for me in town. It was all I could do to be civil to the man! I went straight into the lounge and ordered tea. It was just on half-past five, I remember.

'Now I'm very anxious to put clearly what happened next. I was still in the lounge at a quarter to seven when Mr Sanders came in. There were two gentlemen with him and all three of them were inclined to be a little on the lively side. Mr Sanders left his two friends and came right over to where I was sitting with Miss Trollope. He explained that he wanted our advice about a Christmas present he was giving his wife. It was an evening bag.

'"And you see, ladies," he said. "I'm only a rough sailor-man. What do I know about such things? I've had three sent to me on approval and I want an expert opinion on them."

'We said, of course, that we would be delighted to help him, and he asked if we'd mind coming upstairs, as his wife might come in any minute if he brought the things down. So we went up with him. I shall never forget what happened next—I can feel my little fingers tingling now.

'Mr Sanders opened the door of the bedroom and switched on the light. I don't know which of us saw it first . . .

'*Mrs Sanders was lying on the floor, face downwards—dead.*

'I got to her first. I knelt down and took her hand and felt for the pulse, but it was useless, the arm itself was cold and stiff. Just by her head was a stocking filled with sand—the weapon she had been struck down with. Miss Trollope, silly creature, was moaning and moaning by the door and holding her head. Sanders gave a great cry of "My wife, my wife," and rushed to her. I stopped him touching her. You see, I was sure at the moment that he had done it, and there might have been something that he wanted to take away or hide.

'"Nothing must be touched," I said. "Pull yourself together, Mr Sanders. Miss Trollope, please go down and fetch the manager."

'I stayed there, kneeling by the body. I wasn't going to leave Sanders alone with it. And yet I was forced to admit that if the man was acting, he was acting marvellously. He looked dazed and bewildered and scared out of his wits.

'The manager was with us in no time. He made a quick inspection of the room then turned us all out and locked the door, the key of which he took. Then he went off and telephoned to the police. It seemed a positive age before they came (we learnt afterwards that the line was out of order). The manager had to send a messenger to the police station, and the Hydro is right out of the town, up on the edge of the moor; and Mrs Carpenter tried us all very severely. She was so pleased at her prophecy of "Never two without three" coming true so quickly. Sanders, I hear, wandered out into the grounds, clutching his head and groaning and displaying every sign of grief.

'However, the police came at last. They went upstairs with the manager and Mr Sanders. Later, they sent down for me. I went up. The inspector was there, sitting at a table writing. He was an intelligent-looking man and I liked him.

' "Miss Jane Marple?" he said.

' "Yes."

' "I understand, Madam, that you were present when the body of the deceased was found?"

'I said I was and I described exactly what had occurred. I think it was a relief to the poor man to find someone who could answer his questions coherently, having previously had to deal with Sanders and Emily Trollope, who, I gather, was completely demoralized—she would be, the silly creature! I remember my dear mother teaching me that a gentle-woman should always be able to control herself in public, however much she may give way in private.'

'An admirable maxim,' said Sir Henry gravely.

'When I had finished the inspector said:

' "Thank you, Madam. Now I'm afraid I must ask you just to look at the body once more. Is that exactly the position in which it was lying when you entered the room? It hasn't been moved in any way?"

'I explained that I had prevented Mr Sanders from doing so, and the inspector nodded approval.

' "The gentleman seems terribly upset," he remarked.

' "He seems so—yes," I replied.

'I don't think I put any special emphasis on the "seems", but the inspector looked at me rather keenly.

' "So we can take it that the body is exactly as it was when found?" he said.

' "Except for the hat, yes," I replied.

'The inspector looked up sharply.

' "What do you mean—the hat?"

[120]

'I explained that the hat had been on poor Gladys' head, whereas now it was lying beside her. I thought, of course, that the police had done this. The inspector, however, denied it emphatically. Nothing had, as yet, been moved or touched. He stood looking down at that poor prone figure with a puzzled frown. Gladys was dressed in her outdoor clothes— a big dark-red tweed coat with a grey fur collar. The hat, a cheap affair of red felt, lay just by her head.

'The inspector stood for some minutes in silence, frowning to himself. Then an idea struck him.

'"Can you, by any chance, remember, Madam, whether there were ear-rings in the ears, or whether the deceased habitually wore ear-rings?"

'Now fortunately I am in the habit of observing closely. I remembered that there had been a glint of pearls just below the hat brim, though I had paid no particular notice to it at the time. I was able to answer his first question in the affirmative.

'"Then that settles it. The lady's jewel case was rifled—not that she had anything much of value, I understand—and the rings were taken from her fingers. The murderer must have forgotten the ear-rings, and come back for them after the murder was discovered. A cool customer! Or perhaps—" He stared round the room and said slowly. "He may have been concealed here in this room—all the time."

'But I negatived that idea. I myself, I explained, had looked under the bed. And the manager had opened the doors of the wardrobe. There was nowhere else where a man could hide. It is true the hat cupboard was locked in the middle of the wardrobe, but as that was only a shallow affair with shelves, no one could have been concealed there.

'The inspector nodded his head slowly whilst I explained all this.

'"I'll take your word for it, Madam," he said. "In that case, as I said before, he must have come back. A very cool customer."

'"But the manager locked the door and took the key!"

'"That's nothing. The balcony and the fire escape—that's the way the thief came. Why, as likely as not, you actually disturbed him at work. He slips out of the window, and when you've all gone, back he comes and goes on with his business."

'"You are sure," I said, "that there *was* a thief?"

'He said dryly:

'"Well, it looks like it, doesn't it?"

'But something in his tone satisfied me. I felt that he wouldn't take Mr Sanders in the rôle of the bereaved widower too seriously.

'You see, I admit it frankly, I was absolutely under the opinion of what

I believe our neighbours, the French, call the *idée fixe*. I knew that that man, Sanders, intended his wife to die. What I didn't allow for was that strange and fantastic thing, coincidence. My views about Mr Sanders were—I was sure of it—absolutely right and *true*. The man was a scoundrel. But although his hypocritical assumptions of grief didn't deceive me for a minute, I do remember feeling at the time that his *surprise* and *bewilderment* were marvellously well done. They seemed absolutely *natural*—if you know what I mean. I must admit that after my conversation with the inspector, a curious feeling of doubt crept over me. Because if Sanders had done this dreadful thing, I couldn't imagine any conceivable reason why he should creep back by means of the fire escape and take the ear-rings from his wife's ears. It wouldn't have been a *sensible* thing to do, and Sanders was such a very sensible man—that's just why I always felt he was so dangerous.'

Miss Marple looked round at her audience.

'You see, perhaps, what I am coming to? It is, so often, the unexpected that happens in this world. I was so *sure*, and that, I think, was what blinded me. The result came as a shock to me. *For it was proved, beyond any possible doubt, that Mr Sanders could not possibly have committed the crime . . .*'

A surprised gasp came from Mrs Bantry. Miss Marple turned to her.

'I know, my dear, that isn't what you expected when I began this story. It wasn't what I expected either. But facts are facts, and if one is proved to be wrong, one must just be humble about it and start again. That Mr Sanders was a murderer at heart I knew—and nothing ever occurred to upset that firm conviction of mine.

'And now, I expect, you would like to hear the actual facts themselves. Mrs Sanders, as you know, spent the afternoon playing bridge with some friends, the Mortimers. She left them at about a quarter past six. From her friends' house to the Hydro was about a quarter of an hour's walk—less if one hurried. She must have come in then, about six-thirty. No one saw her come in, so she must have entered by the side door and hurried straight up to her room. There she changed (the fawn coat and skirt she wore to the bridge party were hanging up in the cupboard) and was evidently preparing to go out again, when the blow fell. Quite possibly, they say, she never even knew who struck her. The sandbag, I understand, is a very efficient weapon. That looks as though the attackers were concealed in the room, possibly in one of the big wardrobe cupboards—the one she didn't open.

'Now as to the movements of Mr Sanders. He went out, as I have said, at about five-thirty—or a little after. He did some shopping at a couple of shops and at about six o'clock he entered the Grand Spa Hotel where he encountered two friends—the same with whom he returned to the Hydro later. They played billiards and, I gather, had a good many whiskies and sodas together. These two men (Hitchcock and Spender, their names were) were actually with him the whole time from six o'clock onwards. They walked back to the Hydro with him and he only left them to come across to me and Miss Trollope. That, as I told you, was about a quarter to seven—at which time his wife must have been already dead.

'I must tell you that I talked myself to these two friends of his. I did not like them. They were neither pleasant nor gentlemanly men, but I was quite certain of one thing, that they were speaking the absolute truth when they said that Sanders had been the whole time in their company.

'There was just one other little point that came up. It seems that while bridge was going on Mrs Sanders was called to the telephone. A Mr Littleworth wanted to speak to her. She seemed both excited and pleased about something—and incidentally made one or two bad mistakes. She left rather earlier than they had expected her to do.

'Mr Sanders was asked whether he knew the name of Littleworth as being one of his wife's friends, but he declared he had never heard of anyone of that name. And to me that seems borne out by his wife's attitude—she too, did not seem to know the name of Littleworth. Nevertheless she came back from the telephone smiling and blushing, so it looks as though whoever it was did not give his real name, and that in itself has a suspicious aspect, does it not?

'Anyway, that is the problem that was left. The burglar story, which seems unlikely—or the alternative theory that Mrs Sanders was preparing to go out and meet somebody. Did that somebody come to her room by means of the fire escape? Was there a quarrel? Or did he treacherously attack her?'

Miss Marple stopped.

'Well?' said Sir Henry. 'What is the answer?'

'I wondered if any of you could guess.'

'I'm never good at guessing,' said Mrs Bantry. 'It seems a pity that Sanders had such a wonderful alibi; but if it satisfied you it must have been all right.'

Jane Helier moved her beautiful head and asked a question.

'Why,' she said, 'was the hat cupboard locked?'

'How very clever of you, my dear,' said Miss Marple, beaming. 'That's just what I wondered myself. Though the explanation was quite simple.

In it were a pair of embroidered slippers and some pocket handkerchiefs that the poor girl was embroidering for her husband for Christmas. That's why she locked the cupboard. The key was found in her handbag.'

'Oh!' said Jane. 'Then it isn't very interesting after all.'

'Oh! but it is,' said Miss Marple. 'It's just the one really interesting thing—the thing that made all the murderer's plans go wrong.'

Everyone stared at the old lady.

'I didn't see it myself for two days,' said Miss Marple. 'I puzzled and puzzled—and then suddenly there it was, all clear. I went to the inspector and asked him to try something and he did.'

'What did you ask him to try?'

'I asked him to fit that hat on the poor girl's head—and of course he couldn't. It wouldn't go on. It wasn't her hat, you see.'

Mrs Bantry stared.

'But it was on her head to begin with?'

'Not on her head—'

Miss Marple stopped a moment to let her words sink in, and then went on.

'We took it for granted that it was poor Gladys's body there; but we never looked at the face. She was face downwards, remember, and the hat hid everything.'

'But she was killed?'

'Yes, later. At the moment that we were telephoning to the police, Gladys Sanders was alive and well.'

'You mean it was someone pretending to be her? But surely when you touched her—'

'It was a dead body, right enough,' said Miss Marple gravely.

'But, dash it all,' said Colonel Bantry, 'you can't get hold of dead bodies right and left. What did they do with the—the first corpse afterwards?'

'He put it back,' said Miss Marple. 'It was a wicked idea—but a very clever one. It was our talk in the drawing room that put it into his head. The body of poor Mary, the housemaid—why not use it? Remember, the Sanders' room was up amongst the servants' quarters. Mary's room was two doors off. The undertakers wouldn't come till after dark—he counted on that. He carried the body along the balcony (it was dark at five), dressed it in one of his wife's dresses and her big red coat. And then he found the hat cupboard locked! There was only one thing to be done, he fetched one of the poor girl's own hats. No one would notice. He put the sandbag down beside her. Then he went off to establish his alibi.

'He telephoned to his wife—calling himself Mr Littleworth. I don't know what he said to her—she was a credulous girl, as I said just now. But he got her to leave the bridge party early and not to go back to the Hydro, and arranged with her to meet him in the grounds of the Hydro near the fire escape at seven o'clock. He probably told her he had some surprise for her.

'He returns to the Hydro with his friends and arranges that Miss Trollope and I shall discover the crime with him. He even pretends to turn the body over—and I stop him! Then the police are sent for, and he staggers out into the grounds.

'Nobody asked him for an alibi *after* the crime. He meets his wife, takes her up the fire escape, they enter their room. Perhaps he has already told her some story about the body. She stoops over it, and he picks up his sandbag and strikes . . . Oh, dear! it makes me sick to think of, even now! Then quickly he strips off her coat and skirt, hangs them up, and dresses her in the clothes from the other body.

'*But the hat won't go on.* Mary's head is shingled—Gladys Sanders, as I say, had a great bun of hair. He is forced to leave it beside the body and hope no one will notice. Then he carries poor Mary's body back to her own room and arranges it decorously once more.'

'It seems incredible,' said Dr Lloyd. 'The risks he took. The police might have arrived too soon.'

'You remember the line was out of order,' said Miss Marple. 'That was a piece of *his* work. He couldn't afford to have the police on the spot too soon. When they did come, they spent some time in the manager's office before going up to the bedroom. That was the weakest point—the chance that someone might notice the difference between a body that had been dead two hours and one that had been dead just over half an hour; but he counted on the fact that the people who first discovered the crime would have no expert knowledge.'

Dr Lloyd nodded.

'The crime would be supposed to have been committed about a quarter to seven or thereabouts, I suppose,' he said. 'It was actually committed at seven or a few minutes later. When the police surgeon examined the body it would be about half-past seven at earliest. He couldn't possibly tell.'

'I am the person who should have known,' said Miss Marple. 'I felt the poor girl's hand and it was icy cold. Yet a short time later the inspector spoke as though the murder must have been committed just before we arrived—and I saw nothing!'

'I think you saw a good deal, Miss Marple,' said Sir Henry. 'The case was before my time. I don't even remember hearing of it. What happened?'

'Sanders was hanged,' said Miss Marple crisply. 'And a good job too. I have never regretted my part in bringing that man to justice. I've no patience with modern humanitarian scruples about capital punishment.'

Her stern face softened.

'But I have often reproached myself bitterly with failing to save the life of that poor girl. But who would have listened to an old woman jumping to conclusions? Well, well—who knows? Perhaps it was better for her to die while life was still happy than it would have been for her to live on, unhappy and disillusioned, in a world that would have seemed suddenly horrible. She loved that scoundrel and trusted him. She never found him out.'

'Well, then,' said Jane Helier, 'she was all right. Quite all right. I wish—' she stopped.

Miss Marple looked at the famous, the beautiful, the successful Jane Helier and nodded her head gently.

'I see, my dear,' she said very gently. 'I see.'

THE GHOST'S TOUCH

Fergus Hume

Shortly before Conan Doyle achieved fame with
A Study in Scarlet and Sherlock Holmes, *The
Mystery of a Hansom Cab* (1886) was fast
becoming the best-selling detective novel of the
nineteenth century, with sales passing the half-
million mark. Its author was Fergus Hume
(1859–1932), who went on to write over a
hundred more crime and detective novels. 'The
Ghost's Touch' is one of Hume's best short
mystery stories, taken from his rare collection
The Dancer in Red (1906).

I shall never forget the terrible Christmas I spent at Ringshaw Grange
in the year '93. As an army doctor I have met with strange
adventures in far lands, and have seen some gruesome sights in the
little wars which are constantly being waged on the frontiers of our
empire; but it was reserved for an old country house in Hants to be the
scene of the most noteworthy episode in my life. The experience was a
painful one, and I hope it may never be repeated; but indeed so ghastly
an event is not likely to occur again. If my story reads more like fiction
than truth, I can only quote the well-worn saying, of the latter being
stranger than the former. Many a time in my wandering life have I proved
the truth of this proverb.

The whole affair rose out of the invitation which Frank Ringan sent me
to spend Christmas with himself and his cousin Percy at the family seat
near Christchurch. At that time I was home on leave from India; and

shortly after my arrival I chanced to meet with Percy Ringan in Piccadilly. He was an Australian with whom I had been intimate some years before in Melbourne: a dapper little man with sleek fair hair and a transparent complexion, looking as fragile as a Dresden china image, yet with plenty of pluck and spirits. He suffered from heart disease, and was liable to faint on occasions; yet he fought against his mortal weakness with silent courage, and with certain precautions against over-excitement, he managed to enjoy life fairly well.

Notwithstanding his pronounced effeminacy, and somewhat truckling subserviency to rank and high birth, I liked the little man very well for his many good qualities. On the present occasion I was glad to see him, and expressed my pleasure.

'Although I did not expect to see you in England,' said I, after the first greetings had passed.

'I have been in London these nine months, my dear Lascelles,' he said, in his usual mincing way, 'partly by way of a change and partly to see my cousin Frank—who indeed invited me to come over from Australia.'

'Is that the rich cousin you were always speaking about in Melbourne?'

'Yes. But Frank is not rich. I am the wealthy Ringan, but he is the head of the family. You see, Doctor,' continued Percy, taking my arm and pursuing the subject in a conversational manner, 'my father, being a younger son, emigrated to Melbourne in the gold-digging days, and made his fortune out there. His brother remained at home on the estates, with very little money to keep up the dignity of the family; so my father helped the head of his house from time to time. Five years ago both my uncle and father died, leaving Frank and me as heirs, the one to the family estate, the other to the Australian wealth. So—'

'So you assist your cousin to keep up the dignity of the family as your father did before you.'

'Well, yes, I do,' admitted Percy, frankly. 'You see, we Ringans think a great deal of our birth and position. So much so, that we have made our wills in one another's favour.'

'How do you mean?'

'Well, if I die Frank inherits my money; and if he dies, I become heir to the Ringan estates. It seems strange that I should tell you all this, Lascelles; but you were so intimate with me in the old days that you can understand my apparent rashness.'

I could not forbear a chuckle at the reason assigned by Percy for his confidence, especially as it was such a weak one. The little man had a tongue like a town-crier, and could no more keep his private affairs to himself than a woman could guard a secret. Besides I saw very well that with his inherent snobbishness he desired to impress me with the position and antiquity of his family, and with the fact—undoubtedly true—that it ranked amongst the landed gentry of the kingdom.

However, the weakness, though in bad taste, was harmless enough, and I had no scorn for the confession of it. Still, I felt a trifle bored, as I took little interest in the chronicling of such small beer, and shortly parted from Percy after promising to dine with him the following week.

At this dinner, which took place at the Athenian Club, I met with the head of the Ringan family; or, to put it plainer, with Percy's cousin Frank. Like the Australian he was small and neat, but enjoyed much better health and lacked the effeminacy of the other. Yet on the whole I liked Percy the best, as there was a sly cast about Frank's countenance which I did not relish; and he patronized his colonial cousin in rather an offensive manner.

The latter looked up to his English kinsman with all deference, and would, I am sure, have willingly given his gold to regild the somewhat tarnished escutcheon of the Ringans. Outwardly, the two cousins were so alike as to remind one of Tweedledum and Tweedledee; but after due consideration I decided that Percy was the better-natured and more honourable of the two.

For some reason Frank Ringan seemed desirous of cultivating my acquaintance; and in one way and another I saw a good deal of him during my stay in London. Finally, when I was departing on a visit to some relatives in Norfolk he invited me to spend Christmas at Ringshaw Grange—not, as it afterwards appeared, without an ulterior motive.

'I can take no refusal,' said he, with a heartiness which sat ill on him. 'Percy, as an old friend of yours, has set his heart on my having you down; and—if I may say so—I have set my heart on the same thing.'

'Oh, you really must come, Lascelles,' cried Percy, eagerly. 'We are going to keep Christmas in the real old English fashion. Washington Irving's style, you know: holly, wassail-bowl, games, and mistletoe.'

'And perhaps a ghost or so,' finished Frank, laughing, yet with a side glance at his eager little cousin.

'Ah,' said I. 'So your Grange is haunted.'

'I should think so,' said Percy, before his cousin could speak, 'and with a good old Queen Anne ghost. Come down, Doctor, and Frank shall put you in the haunted chamber.'

'No!' cried Frank, with a sharpness which rather surprised me, 'I'll put no one in the Blue Room; the consequences might be fatal. You smile, Lascelles, but I assure you our ghoest has been proved to exist!'

'That's a paradox; a ghost can't exist. But the story of your ghost—'

'Is too long to tell now,' said Frank, laughing. 'Come down to the Grange and you'll hear it.'

'Very good,' I replied, rather attracted by the idea of a haunted house, 'you can count upon me for Christmas. But I warn you, Ringan, that I don't believe in spirits. Ghosts went out with gas.'

'Then they must have come in again with electric light,' retorted Frank Ringan, 'for Lady Joan undoubtedly haunts the Grange. I don't mind; as it adds distinction to the house.'

'All old families have a ghost,' said Percy, importantly. 'It is very natural when one has ancestors.'

There was no more said on the subject for the time being, but the upshot of this conversation was that I presented myself at Ringshaw Grange two or three days before Christmas. To speak the truth, I came more on Percy's account than my own, as I knew the little man suffered from heart disease, and a sudden shock might prove fatal. If, in the unhealthy atmosphere of an old house, the inmates got talking of ghosts and goblins, it might be that the consequences would be dangerous to so highly strung and delicate a man as Percy Ringan.

For this reason, joined to a sneaking desire to see the ghost, I found myself a guest at Ringshaw Grange. In one way I regret the visit; yet in another I regard it as providential that I was on the spot. Had I been absent the catastrophe might have been greater, although it could scarcely have been more terrible.

Ringshaw Grange was a quaint Elizabethan house, all gables and diamond casements, and oriel windows, and quaint terraces, looking like an illustration out of an old Christmas number. It was embowered in a large park, the trees of which came up almost to the doors, and when I saw it first in the moonlight—for it was by a late train that I came from London—it struck me as the very place for a ghost.

Here was a haunted house of the right quality if ever there was one, and I only hoped when I crossed the threshold that the local spectre would be worthy of its environment. In such an interesting house I did not think to pass a dull Christmas; but—God help me—I did not anticipate so tragic a Yuletide as I spent.

As our host was a bachelor and had no female relative to do the honours of his house the guests were all of the masculine gender. It is true that there was a housekeeper—a distant cousin I understood—who was rather elderly but very juvenile as to dress and manner. She went by the name of Miss Laura, but no one saw much of her as, otherwise than attending to her duties, she remained mostly in her own rooms.

So our party was composed of young men—none save myself being over the age of thirty, and few being gifted with much intelligence. The talk was mostly of sport, of horse-racing, big game shooting and yacht-sailing: so that I grew tired at times of these subjects and retired to the library to read and write. The day after I arrived Frank showed me over the house.

It was a wonderful old barrack of a place, with broad passages, twisting interminably like the labyrinth of Daedalus; small bedrooms furnished in an old-fashioned manner, and vast reception apartments with polished floors and painted ceilings. Also there were the customary number of family portraits frowning from the walls; suits of tarnished armour; and ancient tapestries embroidered with grim and ghastly legends of the past.

The old house was crammed with treasures, rare enough to drive an antiquarian crazy; and filled with the flotsam and jetsam of many centuries, mellowed by time into one soft hue, which put them all in keeping with one another. I must say that I was charmed with Ringshaw Grange, and no longer wondered at the pride taken by Percy Ringan in his family and their past glories.

'That's all very well,' said Frank, to whom I remarked as much; 'Percy is rich, and had he this place could keep it up in proper style; but I am as poor as a rat, and unless I can make a rich marriage, or inherit a comfortable legacy, house and furniture, park and timber may all come to the hammer.'

He looked gloomy as he spoke; and, feeling that I had touched on a somewhat delicate matter, I hastened to change the subject, by asking to be shown the famous Blue Chamber, which was said to be haunted. This was the true Mecca of my pilgrimage into Hants.

'It is along this passage,' said Frank, leading the way, 'and not very far from your own quarters. There is nothing in its looks likely to hint at the ghost—at all events by day—but it is haunted for all that.'

Thus speaking he led me into a large room with a low ceiling, and a broad casement looking out on to the untrimmed park, where the woodland was most sylvan. The walls were hung with blue cloth embroidered with grotesque figures in black braid or thread, I know not which. There was a large old-fashioned bed with tester and figured curtains and a quantity of cumbersome furniture of the early Georgian

[131]

epoch. Not having been inhabited for many years the room had a desolate and silent look—if one may use such an expression—and to my mind looked gruesome enough to conjure up a battalion of ghosts, let alone one.

'I don't agree with you!' said I, in reply to my host's remark. 'To my mind this is the very model of a haunted chamber. What is the legend?'

'I'll tell it to you on Christmas Eve,' replied Ringan, as we left the room. 'It is rather a blood-curdling tale.'

'Do you believe it?' said I, struck by the solemn air of the speaker.

'I have had evidence to make me credulous,' he replied dryly, and closed the subject for the time being.

It was renewed on Christmas Eve when all our company were gathered round a huge wood fire in the library. Outside, the snow lay thick on the ground, and the gaunt trees stood up black and leafless out of the white expanse. The sky was of a frosty blue with sharply twinkling stars, and a hard-looking moon. On the snow the shadows of interlacing boughs were traced blackly as in Indian ink, and the cold was of Arctic severity.

But seated in the holly-decked apartment before a noble fire which roared bravely up the wide chimney we cared nothing for the frozen world out of doors. We laughed and talked, sang songs and recalled adventures, until somewhere about ten o'clock we fell into a ghostly vein quite in keeping with the goblin-haunted season. It was then that Frank Ringan was called upon to chill our blood with his local legend. This he did without much pressing.

'In the reign of the good Queen Anne,' said he, with a gravity befitting the subject, 'my ancestor Hugh Ringan was the owner of this house. He was a silent misanthropic man, having been soured early in life by the treachery of a woman. Mistrusting the sex he refused to marry for many years; and it was not until he was fifty years of age that he was beguiled by the arts of a pretty girl into the toils of matrimony. The lady was Joan Challoner, the daughter of the Earl of Branscourt; and she was esteemed one of the beauties of Queen Anne's court.

'It was in London that Hugh met her, and thinking from her innocent and child-like appearance that she would make him a true-hearted wife, he married her after a six months' courtship and brought her with all honour to Ringshaw Grange. After his marriage he became more cheerful and less distrustful of his fellow-creatures. Lady Joan was all to him that a wife could be, and seemed devoted to her husband and child—for she early became a mother—when one Christmas Eve all this happiness came to an end.'

'Oh!' said I, rather cynically. 'So Lady Joan proved to be no better than the rest of her sex.'

'So Hugh Ringan thought, Doctor; but he was as mistaken as you are. Lady Joan occupied the Blue Room, which I showed you the other day; and on Christmas Eve, when riding home late, Hugh saw a man descend from the window. Thunderstruck by the sight, he galloped after the man and caught him before he could mount a horse which was waiting for him. The cavalier was a handsome young fellow of twenty-five, who refused to answer Hugh's questions. Thinking, naturally enough, that he had to do with a lover of his wife's, Hugh fought a duel with the stranger and killed him after a hard fight.

'Leaving him dead on the snow he rode back to the Grange, and burst in on his wife to accuse her of perfidy. It was in vain that Lady Joan tried to defend herself by stating that the visitor was her brother, who was engaged in plots for the restoration of James II, and on that account wished to keep secret the fact of his presence in England. Hugh did not believe her, and told her plainly that he had killed her lover; whereupon Lady Joan burst out into a volley of reproaches and cursed her husband. Furious at what he deemed was her boldness Hugh at first attempted to kill her, but not thinking the punishment sufficient, he cut off her right hand.'

'Why?' asked everyone, quite unprepared for this information.

'Because in the first place Lady Joan was very proud of her beautiful white hands, and in the second Hugh had seen the stranger kiss her hand—her right hand—before he descended from the window. For these reasons he mutilated her thus terribly.'

'And she died.'

'Yes, a week after her hand was cut off. And she swore that she would come back to touch all those in the Blue Room—that is who slept in it—who were foredoomed to death. She kept her promise, for many people who have slept in that fatal room have been touched by the dead hand of Lady Joan, and have subsequently died.'

'Did Hugh find out that his wife was innocent?'

'He did,' replied Ringan, 'and within a month after her death. The stranger was really her brother, plotting for James II, as she had stated. Hugh was not punished by man for his crime, but within a year he slept in the Blue Chamber and was found dead next morning with the mark of three fingers on his right wrist. It was thought that in his remorse he had courted death by sleeping in the room cursed by his wife.'

'And there was a mark on him?'

[133]

'On his right wrist red marks like a burn; the impression of three fingers. Since that time the room has been haunted.'

'Does everyone who sleeps in it die?' I asked.

'No. Many people have risen well and hearty in the morning. Only those who are doomed to an early death are thus touched!'

'When did the last case occur?'

'Three years ago,' was Frank's unexpected reply. 'A friend of mine called Herbert Spencer would sleep in that room. He saw the ghost and was touched. He showed me the marks next morning—three red finger marks.'

'Did the omen hold good?'

'Yes. Spencer died three months afterwards. He was thrown from his horse.'

I was about to put further questions in a sceptical vein, when we heard shouts outside, and we all sprang to our feet as the door was thrown open to admit Miss Laura in a state of excitement.

'Fire! Fire!' she cried, almost distracted. 'Oh! Mr Ringan,' addressing herself to Percy, 'your room is on fire! I—'

We waited to hear no more, but in a body rushed up to Percy's room. Volumes of smoke were rolling out of the door, and flames were flashing within. Frank Ringan, however, was prompt and cool-headed. He had the alarm bell rung, summoned the servants, grooms, and stable hands, and in twenty minutes the fire was extinguished.

On asking how the fire had started, Miss Laura, with much hysterical sobbing, stated that she had gone into Percy's room to see that all was ready and comfortable for the night. Unfortunately the wind wafted one of the bed-curtains towards the candle she was carrying, and in a moment the room was in a blaze. After pacifying Miss Laura, who could not help the accident, Frank turned to his cousin. By this time we were back again in the library.

'My dear fellow,' he said, 'your room is swimming in water, and is charred with fire. I'm afraid you can't stay there tonight; but I don't know where to put you unless you take the Blue Room.'

'The Blue Room!' we all cried. 'What! The haunted chamber?'

'Yes; all the other rooms are full. Still, if Percy is afraid—'

'Afraid!' cried Percy indignantly. 'I'm not afraid at all. I'll sleep in the Blue Room with the greatest of pleasure.'

'But the ghost—'

'I don't care for the ghost,' interrupted the Australian, with a nervous laugh. 'We have no ghosts in our part of the world, and as I have not seen one, I do not believe there is such a thing.'

We all tried to dissuade him from sleeping in the haunted room, and several of us offered to give up our apartments for the night—Frank among the number. But Percy's dignity was touched, and he was resolute to keep his word. He had plenty of pluck, as I said before, and the fancy that we might think him a coward spurred him on to resist our entreaties.

The end of it was that shortly before midnight he went off to the Blue Room, and declared his intention of sleeping in it. There was nothing more to be said in the face of such obstinacy, so one by one we retired, quite unaware of the events to happen before the morning. So on that Christmas Eve the Blue Room had an unexpected tenant.

On going to my bedroom I could not sleep. The tale told by Frank Ringan haunted my fancy, and the idea of Percy sleeping in that ill-omened room made me nervous. I did not believe in ghosts myself, nor, so far as I knew, did Percy, but the little man suffered from heart disease—he was strung up to a high nervous pitch by our ghost stories—and if anything out of the common—even from natural causes—happened in that room, the shock might be fatal to its occupant.

I knew well enough that Percy, out of pride, would refuse to give up the room, yet I was determined that he should not sleep in it; so, failing persuasion, I employed stratagem. I had my medicine chest with me, and taking it from my portmanteau I prepared a powerful narcotic. I left this on the table and went along to the Blue Room, which, as I have said before, was not very far from mine.

A knock brought Percy to the door, clothed in pyjamas, and at a glance I could see that the ghostly atmosphere of the place was already telling on his nerves. He looked pale and disturbed, but his mouth was firmly set with an obstinate expression likely to resist my proposals. However, out of diplomacy, I made none, but blandly stated my errand, with more roughness, indeed, than was necessary.

'Come to my room, Percy,' I said, when he appeared, 'and let me give you something to calm your nerves.'

'I'm not afraid!' he said, defiantly.

'Who said you were?' I rejoined, tartly. 'You believe in ghosts no more than I do, so why should you be afraid? But after the alarm of fire your nerves are upset, and I want to give you something to put them right. Otherwise, you'll get no sleep.'

'I shouldn't mind a composing draught, certainly,' said the little man. 'Have you it here?'

[135]

'No, it's in my room, a few yards off. Come along.'

Quite deluded by my speech and manner, Percy followed me into my bedroom, and obediently enough swallowed the medicine. Then I made him sit down in a comfortable armchair, on the plea that he must not walk immediately after the draught. The result of my experiment was justified, for in less than ten minutes the poor little man was fast asleep under the influence of the narcotic. When thus helpless, I placed him on my bed, quite satisfied that he would not awaken until late the next day. My task accomplished, I extinguished the light, and went off myself to the Blue Room, intending to remain there for the night.

It may be asked why I did so, as I could easily have taken my rest on the sofa in my own room; but the fact is, I was anxious to sleep in a haunted chamber. I did not believe in ghosts, as I had never seen one, but as there was a chance of meeting here with an authentic phantom I did not wish to lose the opportunity.

Therefore when I saw that Percy was safe for the night, I took up my quarters in the ghostly territory, with much curiosity, but—as I can safely aver—no fear. All the same, in case of practical jokes on the part of the feather-headed young men in the house, I took my revolver with me. Thus prepared, I locked the door of the Blue Room and slipped into bed, leaving the light burning. The revolver I kept under my pillow ready to my hand in case of necessity.

'Now,' said I grimly, as I made myself comfortable, 'I'm ready for ghosts, or goblins, or practical jokers.'

I lay awake for a long time, staring at the queer figures on the blue draperies of the apartment. In the pale flame of the candle they looked ghostly enough to disturb the nerves of anyone: and when the draught fluttered the tapestries the figures seemed to move as though alive. For this sight alone I was glad that Percy had not slept in that room. I could fancy the poor man lying in that vast bed with blanched face and beating heart, listening to every creak, and watching the fantastic embroideries waving on the walls. Brave as he was, I am sure the sounds and sights of that room would have shaken his nerves, I did not feel very comfortable myself, sceptic as I was.

When the candle had burned down pretty low I fell asleep. How long I slumbered I know not: but I woke up with the impression that something or someone was in the room. The candle had wasted nearly to the socket and the flame was flickering and leaping fitfully, so as to display the room one moment and leave it almost in darkness the next. I heard a soft step crossing the room, and as it drew near a sudden spurt of flame from the candle showed me a little woman standing by the side of the bed. She was dressed in a gown of flowered brocade, and wore the towering head dress of the Queen Anne epoch. Her face I could scarcely see, as the flash of flame was only momentary: but I felt what the Scotch call a deadly grue as I realized that this was the veritable phantom of Lady Joan.

For the moment the natural dread of the supernatural quite overpowered me, and with my hands and arms lying outside the counterpane I rested inert and chilled with fear. This sensation of helplessness in the presence of evil, was like what one experiences in a nightmare of the worst kind.

When again the flame of the expiring candle shot up, I beheld the ghost close at hand, and—as I felt rather than saw—knew that it was bending over me. A faint odour of musk was in the air, and I heard the soft rustle of the brocaded skirts echo through the semi-darkness. The next moment I felt my right wrist gripped in a burning grasp, and the sudden pain roused my nerves from their paralysis.

With a yell I rolled over, away from the ghost, wrenching my wrist from that horrible clasp, and, almost mad with pain I groped with my left hand for the revolver. As I seized it the candle flared up for the last time, and I saw the ghost gliding back towards the tapestries. In a second I raised the revolver and fired. The next moment there was a wild cry of terror and agony, the fall of a heavy body on the floor, and almost before I knew where I was I found myself outside the door of the haunted room. To attract attention I fired another shot from my revolver, while the Thing on the floor moaned in the darkness most horribly.

In a few moments guests and servants, all in various stages of undress, came rushing along the passage bearing lights. A babel of voices arose, and I managed to babble some incoherent explanation, and led the way into the room. There on the floor lay the ghost, and we lowered the candles to look at its face. I sprang up with a cry on recognizing who it was.

'Frank Ringan!'

It was indeed Frank Ringan disguised as a woman in wig and brocades. He looked at me with a ghostly face, his mouth working nervously. With an effort he raised himself on his hands and tried to speak—whether in confession or exculpation, I know not. But the attempt was too much for him, a choking cry escaped his lips, a jet of blood burst from his mouth, and he fell back dead.

Over the rest of the events of that terrible night I draw a veil. There are

[137]

some things it is as well not to speak of. Only I may state that all through the horror and confusion Percy Ringan, thanks to my strong sleeping draught, slumbered as peacefully as a child, thereby saving his life.

With the morning's light came discoveries and explanations. We found one of the panels behind the tapestry of the Blue Room open, and it gave admittance into a passage which on examination proved to lead into Frank Ringan's bedroom. On the floor we discovered a delicate hand formed of steel, and which bore marks of having been in the fire. On my right wrist were three distinct burns, which I have no hesitation in declaring, were caused by the mechanical hand which we picked up near the dead man. And the explanation of these things came from Miss Laura, who was wild with terror at the death of her master, and said in her first outburst of grief and fear, what I am sure she regretted in her calmer moments.

'It's all Frank's fault,' she wept. 'He was poor and wished to be rich. He got Percy to make his will in his favour, and wanted to kill him by a shock. He knew that Percy had heart disease and that a shock might prove fatal; so he contrived that his cousin should sleep in the Blue Room on Christmas Eve; and he himself played the ghost of Lady Joan with the burning hand. It was a steel hand, which he heated in his own room so as to mark with a scar those it touched.'

'Whose idea was this?' I asked, horrified by the devilish ingenuity of the scheme.

'Frank's!' said Miss Laura, candidly. 'He promised to marry me if I helped him to get the money by Percy's death. We found that there was a secret passage leading to the Blue Room; so some years ago we invented the story that it was haunted.'

'Why, in God's name?'

'Because Frank was always poor. He knew that his cousin in Australia had heart disease, and invited him home to kill him with fright. To make things safe he was always talking about the haunted room and telling the story so that everything should be ready for Percy on his arrival. Our plans were all carried out. Percy arrived and Frank got him to make the will in his favour. Then he was told the story of Lady Joan and her hand, and by setting fire to Percy's room last night I got him to sleep in the Blue Chamber without any suspicion being aroused.'

'You wicked woman!' I cried. 'Did you fire Percy's room on purpose?'

'Yes. Frank promised to marry me if I helped him. We had to get Percy to sleep in the Blue Chamber, and I managed it by setting fire to his bedroom. He would have died with fright when Frank, as Lady Joan, touched him with the steel hand, and no one would have been the wiser. Your sleeping in that haunted room saved Percy's life, Dr Lascelles: yet Frank invited you down as part of his scheme, that you might examine the body: and declare the death to be a natural one.'

'Was it Frank who burnt the wrist of Herbert Spencer some years ago?' I asked.

'Yes!' replied Miss Laura, wiping her red eyes. 'We thought if the ghost appeared to a few other people, that Percy's death might seem more natural. It was a mere coincidence that Mr Spencer died three months after the ghost touched him.'

'Do you know you are a very wicked woman, Miss Laura?'

'I am a very unhappy one,' she retorted. 'I have lost the only man I ever loved; and his miserable cousin survives to step into his shoes as the master of Ringshaw Grange.'

That was the sole conversation I had with the wretched woman, for shortly afterwards she disappeared, and I fancy must have gone abroad, as she was never more heard of. At the inquest held on the body of Frank the whole strange story came out, and was reported at full length by the London press to the dismay of ghost-seers: for the fame of Ringshaw Grange as a haunted mansion had been great in the land.

I was afraid lest the jury should bring in a verdict of manslaughter against me, but the peculiar features of the case being taken into consideration I was acquitted of blame, and shortly afterwards returned to India with an unblemished character. Percy Ringan was terribly distressed on hearing of his cousin's death, and shocked by the discovery of his treachery. However, he was consoled by becoming the head of the family, and as he lives a quiet life at Ringshaw Grange there is not much chance of his early death from heart disease—at all events from a ghostly point of view.

The Blue Chamber is shut up, for it is haunted now by a worse spectre than that of Lady Joan, whose legend (purely fictitious) was so ingeniously set forth by Frank. It is haunted by the ghost of the cold-blooded scoundrel who fell into his own trap; and who met with his death in the very moment he was contriving that of another man. As to myself, I have given up ghost-hunting and sleeping in haunted rooms. Nothing will ever tempt me to experiment in that way again. One adventure of that sort is enough to last me a lifetime.

THE GROTTO

Pamela Sewell

Pamela Sewell (b. 1966) has contributed several
fine short stories to magazines and anthologies.
The following seasonal tale is published here for
the first time.

I t had been a shock to everyone: and everyone agreed that it was a
thoroughly nasty affair. Mr Jones of accounts was the last person
they'd have expected to do that sort of thing. He'd worked for
Debridge's department store for nearly thirty years, starting as a clerk
when he left school, and gradually becoming head of accounts. Everyone
thought of the gentle, mild-mannered man as the rock of the firm, the last
person to see it cheated . . .

It had been old Debridge's nephew, Matthew, who'd discovered it.
Old Debridge was a crusty old so-and-so, it was rumoured—hardly
anyone had seen him. The younger members of the firm occasionally
wondered if he even existed. But he certainly did: his nephew was living
proof of that.

Old Debridge was one of the old school, believing that you should
start from the bottom and work your way up. Which was precisely what
young Matthew Debridge had done. First as office junior, sorting the
post and making tea; then into accounts, finally becoming Mr Jones's
assistant.

Matthew had been working with Jones for nearly ten months when it
happened. And had he not discovered the discrepancies himself, figures

shifted craftily from various accounts to one steadily increasing one, the finger might have been pointed at him, too.

All in all, the whole affair left a nasty taste in the mouth. Matthew had been embarrassed, not wanting to be there when his uncle called Jones into his office, but knowing that his duty was to the firm. Jones had broken down when he'd been confronted, said that it wasn't true, that he would never cheat his employer. But the facts were against him. Entries made in his own handwriting, the bank clerk's description of the slight, greying man . . . What else could Jones do but resign? The fact that he'd hanged himself three weeks later, on Christmas Eve, made it somewhat worse.

Everyone had felt uncomfortable at the store. It simply didn't feel right. The first year for twenty years that Jones hadn't been Father Christmas. Of course, young Matthew was as helpful as ever, ready to do anything for the firm. Just like old Mr Debridge was, so some said. He simply stepped into the breach, said that he'd be Father Christmas that year. *You couldn't disappoint all the kiddies, could you?* was his answer, when the perfume salesgirls declared that they couldn't step into Mr Jones's place, not if old Debridge paid them double.

Matthew had risen steadily through the ranks since then. In fact, he wasn't far from taking Mr Jones's place: old Debridge was beginning to reward his nephew's hard work. And it was Matthew's third time as Father Christmas: most began to think of him as the traditional Santa, rather than Mr Jones.

It has to be said that some had their doubts about Matthew. At times, there was a certain look in his eyes, as if he had some secret . . . But then he'd smile in his charming way, and the doubts would dissolve. Of course not. Young Debridge, as he was beginning to be known, was always a model of perfect behaviour. Even checked round the store, last thing at night, before he went home, the way his uncle had once done . . .

Matthew hummed to himself as he walked through the grotto. Things were going well. Since the Jones business, he could do no wrong. Especially in his uncle's eyes. He began to smile. Matthew's various bank accounts were beginning to look decidedly healthy. Even more so than Jeannie, the girl in the bank who'd described old Jones, dared dream. Or the various other girls, whose existence Jeannie never even suspected, but who kept Matthew pleasurably occupied when Jeannie wasn't available.

It had been his master stroke, setting up old Jones. Matthew had always been good at drawing, had easily managed to copy the old man's writing. That, and his knowledge of the accounts, had made it all too easy to transfer money into other accounts. Most of which didn't link up: just the ones he used for Jones, when he thought the old man was on to him. Jeannie was devoted to Matthew; she had agreed to describe Jones, when asked about the mystery account-holder, thinking that it would win her Matthew's love.

Matthew had felt slightly guilty when Jones hanged himself. He hadn't expected that. But it wasn't his fault that the old man had been unbalanced, was it?

He swallowed. The grotto made him feel uneasy. Still, he had his duty to perform, until he'd amassed enough to keep him for the rest of his life. Probably another year or two. Then he'd arrange his disappearance. France, Spain, somewhere where he couldn't be traced. Somewhere warm, where he and Jeannie could spend the money the old man had been too mean to give him, the money he'd earned with his brilliant schemes.

He shivered. It shouldn't be this cold in the grotto. Not this early in the evening. And his sense of unease had grown. He felt as if someone were watching him from the shadows. Almost superstitiously, he switched the lights full on. Nothing. Just the empty grotto, Matthew, and the red suit. He was being stupid. Of course nothing was wrong. Everything was going according to plan, wasn't it?

Shrugging, he picked up the Father Christmas costume and slipped it on. Luckily it fitted him exactly: he was about the same size as Jones had been, all those years ago, when his sister first made the costume. The red material was wearing thin; he noticed that his jacket showed through in places. And the beard was growing tatty; he walked over to the mirror, stared at himself. His face showed far too much. He made a mental note to speak to his uncle about it, and turned away.

As he walked down the grotto, he began to feel dizzy. The beard was suddenly far too heavy, too much. He reached to pull it off, breathe more air, and found to his horror that he couldn't remove it. It was stuck fast. His arms flailed as he tried desperately to breathe. The thing was choking him, smothering him—almost in the way that Jones had choked to his death on the end of a rope . . .

The doctor shook his head. 'A good twenty-four hours, I should think.'

Mrs Bates stared at him. 'It's impossible. He was here this morning, in the costume. I spoke to him myself, asked him if he was feeling all right— he had the flu last week, and I thought he didn't look too well.'

'Are you sure?'

She glared at him, stiffening. The cheek of doctors nowadays. Daring to doubt her word, almost calling her a liar. Her voice was frosty. 'I can tell you, doctor, he was here. Had a whole line of kiddies, today: didn't even stop for lunch. His voice was muffled a bit by the beard, but he was adamant. *Can't let the kiddies down*, he said.' Her face twisted. 'He sounded just like old Mr Jones, the way he would always be Father Christmas, even the year he had the flu. He liked to see their happy little faces. Funny, Matthew's eyes looked almost like his, the way they'd glow before he gave the first child its present.'

The doctor spread his hands. 'I can't say the exact time of death, but I'd swear on oath it was long before this morning.'

Mrs Bates sighed. 'I don't know. I mean—heart attack, you said?'

The doctor nodded. 'Classic case. Nasty time, too, Christmas Eve. Not exactly the best Christmas present for his family.' He looked at the young man lying on the carpet, the red costume still by his side. The beard, twisted by his hand, seemed almost to be smiling, as if it knew better.

THE SHOW MUST NOT GO ON

David G. Rowlands

David G. Rowlands (b. 1941) is one of the best
short story writers working today. This new
(hitherto unpublished) story features the
Schneiderman & Murray Investigation Agency,
and is also an affectionate pastiche of H.C.
Bailey's 'Reggie Fortune' stories. Lady Chantry
(see 'The Unknown Murderer' elsewhere in this
anthology) is also mentioned in this story.

In affectionate memory of Mr H.C. Bailey, whose 'Reggie Fortune' still forms
part of my favourite reading.

'For the Dead travel fast'—*Dracula*

I t was the opinion of Mr Fortune afterward, that the case afforded
the best example of the use of disease in the world. The Hon. Sidney
Lomas, Head of the CID, retorted that without Mr Fortune's
incredibly diffuse knowledge and acquaintance, the case would never
have become complex. Superintendent Bell was content to observe that
it was just another example of Mr Fortune's uncanny feel for a case.
However all that was afterward.

The suburb of Westhampton is complacent and smug and would

certainly not welcome notoriety. Yet for a brief spell, one Christmastide in the 1920s, it attracted sensational attention.

It began when Mrs Elizabeth Folsom of the Westhampton Players went downstairs in the early hours of the morning to see what had delayed her husband—and fell over his body. Judging from the marks on the floor, he had crawled from the study to the foot of the stairs. Her shrieks aroused servants and neighbours who drew the constable on the beat. He reported by telephone to his station sergeant, who in turn called the local doctor, Mr Fortune Senior.

It happened that Fortune Senior, together with Reggie's mother, was away for Christmas and had reluctantly left the practice in the irresponsible hands of his son and heir. Reggie had given up local practice for Wimpole Street and was complacently ecstatic, having married Miss Jane Brown, otherwise Joan Amber, after a long engagement. A late dinner at his father's house saw him later to bed, hoping fervently that no night calls would disturb him.

Indeed he looked so cherubic and innocent asleep that Gorton—his father's factotum—hesitated to wake him. The housekeeper, Mrs Wix, was of sterner stuff however, despite a fondness for her 'young master' of three decades.

Arriving at the Folsom's villa, Reggie was met by Inspector Mordan, in those days still with the Westhampton Force.

'Blest if I can see what killed him, Mr Fortune. But he's dead all right.'

'Is he though?' purred Reggie. 'Well, that's one little fact at any rate.'

He busied himself about the body, peering into the eyes, smelling at the mouth. Then, on his knees, but keeping out of the direct line of the man's travel, he followed back the scuff marks on the carpet into the study.

The chair at the desk had tipped over backward . . . a typescript lay on the floor and, twisting his head, Reggie read the title: UNDEAD.

'Hmm,' he grunted, 'not very appropriate here, at any rate. Playing locally, Mordan?'

'What's that, sir?' asked the Inspector, who had followed on Reggie's heels.

'Is that the play the Westhampton Players are doing? The Undead?'

'Yes, at the Community Centre, I believe. Always popular at Christmas, Mr Folsom's plays. Evening thriller for the adults and pantomime matinée for the kids. I took the family to an Edgar Wallace last year: lots of secret passages and revolving bookcases . . . that sort of thing.'

[145]

Reggie looked around the study, at the objects on the desk.

'Well, no revolving bookcases here,' he sighed.

He went to the window, which was closed.

'No sign of an entrance, Mordan?'

'None, Mr Folsom always locked up early, according to his wife.'

Reggie returned to the body, just as other police were arriving. He asked the photographer to pay attention to certain details. Then he sat back on his heels.

'Dead about an hour, Mordan. No signs of violence. Interestin' case— his eyes . . . well, have a word with the Coroner. I'd like to have a look at the body in the mortuary, if it won't upset any of your officials.'

Inspector Mordan grinned, recalling his earliest encounter with the ebullient young doctor.

'I'll make the necessary arrangements, Mr Fortune.'

Two days later Reggie strolled into the Scotland Yard rooms of the Hon. Sidney Lomas, who was heavily jocular.

'Damme, Fortune, is your old man's practice too busy for you? Had to reduce it by creating a corpse or two, eh?'

Reggie surveyed him gloomily. 'Those he wishes to confound, he first makes foolish. Prime example bein' the Head of the CID.

'Nothing organically wrong with the corpse, Lomas. No failures, no seizures. Apparently in perfect health.' He flopped down into a chair squirming on the base of his spine. 'Yet the man's dead. No sign of any other presence on the scene.'

'There you are, then. Natural Causes. Trouble with you, Fortune, you look for mystery where there is none.'

Reggie became plaintive. 'Not me. Not so's you'd notice. I believe in evidence. What about this then? Facts unknown to the Hon. Lomas and the CID. Two other members of the Westhampton Players died that night: man and woman, two miles apart. In both cases, no apparent cause . . . like Folsom. One of 'em, man living on his own, had tried to struggle out of bed, but succumbed to whatever it was: no violence. The second, a maiden lady living with her sister. Survivin' sister not a member of theatre company. In that case, sister woke thinking she heard a cry . . . went to the actress's room and found her on the floor, same as Folsom. She expired just as the lady got to her, sayin' something like "red-eye". Far as I can judge they all died within the same hour, probably within minutes of each other!'

Lomas whistled in mock concern. 'Red-eye, eh? There you are,

Fortune, done by Whisky Bill.' He sobered a little. 'It's deuced odd, though, I grant you. Three dead, same time, three miles apart. Your Daddy is not going to be pleased. You are supposed to look after his practice, not decimate it!' He shrugged. 'Well, I suppose the play will not go on now; that's something Westhampton is spared.'

Reggie had been glaring at him from the depths of his chair, but suddenly sat up.

'That bein' so,' he said, 'you might give Mordan some help. Put your people on to these dead persons . . . what they have in common beside the Players; do something to justify your existence!'

Lomas stared. 'What have you in your mind, Reginald? I know that look of yours.' He stopped and held up a hand. 'No, on second thoughts, I don't want to know about it.' He reached for the phone as Reggie went out to lunch.

Normally Reggie did not talk 'shop' or crime with his wife, but after discussing the Christmas concerts and his marionette theatre and the latest soufflé Elise, he asked her about the Westhampton players.

'A good little repertory company, I believe,' she said. 'Ted Folsom was noted for his adaptations, though not always scrupulous about rights and licences. His dramatizations were more to avoid legal charges of plagiarism than they were good theatre.'

Mr Fortune left her to dress for a tea visit and went to his laboratory, where he busied himself with the grim business of Esmee the stoat.

He had intended to visit the widowed Mrs Folsom, but she came to the surgery one evening. 'Oh, Dr Fortune,' she gulped, when ushered into the consulting room. She was very pleasant to look at and he patted her hand, then began to ask questions. How many actors were there? Several in minor parts but only four principals of whom three died the same night. Of course the theatre had closed . . . all those children disappointed of their pantomime . . . and at Christmas too!

Reggie leaned forward. 'Who was the fourth?'

Oh, Willy Rattu: a professional actor who had fallen on hard times. She chose her words carefully, to imply that he was often the worse for drink and self-pity.

Did they get on? Yes, reasonably well. Billy always thought that he knew it all. There were lots of arguments during rehearsals. They were at loggerheads over the play they had currently been doing, *The Undead*. (She coloured slightly.) It derived from a 'shilling shocker', *The Vampire*. The author was long dead, some sort of relation of Willy's. Indeed Willy had suggested the play, hoping that some performance fees might come to him. But of course being a rep company, they were unable to pay such fees. Ted 'derived' a similar story to avoid having to pay anything to the author's, Samuel Broker's, estate.

'You will see I am being frank, Dr Fortune.'

There was little more information to be gained, so Reggie prescribed for her and promised a visit shortly. After the housekeeper had seen her out, he sank deeper into his chair, reflecting.

'Queer lot the Old Fellow's got here.'

He and Joan were to join his sister—the one who married the Treasury official—on Christmas Day, and before departing he went round to visit William Rattu.

The actor inhabited a rather down-at-heel house for Westhampton. The door was opened by an indolent manservant who winked when asked for his master.

'Yessir. I'll see if he's awake. But after Christmas Eve . . . well, you know,' (again the wink) 'he likes to lay in.'

Rattu was a cadaverous individual, garbed in a creased, stained dressing gown, and with all the symptoms of insobriety. Reggie took his hand, felt the pulse and looked into the man's eyes, holding up the lids; all of which Rattu bore indifferently.

He agreed that he had drunk himself silly on the evening of the deaths after an argument with Folsom over the play.

'S'not right, Fortune, story was written by my Uncle Samuel, gaw bless him, pinched by Teddie Folsom and we're not gettin' a penny.' He giggled. 'I went and told Uncle Samuel, too.'

Reggie sat up from lolling on his spine. 'He's alive then?'

'Ha, ha! Not he! Buried in the churchyard,' he leered knowingly, like a caricature of his valet, 'suffered from the clap he did and they wanted to cremate his body. But the fambly refused . . . and so I went to tell him: how Folsom was cheatin' the fambly.' He sighed, passing a hand over his unshaven face. 'I must have fallen asleep there, for next thing I knew my man Morton had brought me home.'

On his way out, Reggie spoke to Morton.

'That's right, Mr Fortune. The sexton of the church phoned me—in a rare taking he was—said it was real spooky up there: dogs howlin' and all, and the master asleep among the tombs and he not able to wake him. I took the car and sure enough, there he was, lyin' across a mound, dead drunk and all a-twitch. As I carried him off, there was a biggish bat a-flappin' round me, for all it's winter time and freezin' cold.'

Reggie touched his shoulder. 'Look to yourself too, Morton. We must get Mr Rattu into the Cottage Hospital. I'll arrange the ambulance. He has meningitis. You may need to call my father in future, but I'll leave him notes.'

'Thank you, sir.'

A call from Sergeant Underwood came through just as Reggie was leaving to join Joan.

'Nothing, Mr Fortune. All clean so far as we can tell. Nothing to connect the people together, other than the play-acting.'

'Sorry, young fellow,' said Reggie. 'I could have saved you the bother if I'd thought this through a little more quickly.'

'Never mind, sir; you see more than we do—always. Oh, Mr Lomas says "Happy Christmas" to Mrs Fortune.'

[Interpolation by Mrs Sheila Murray of the Schneiderman & Murray Investigation Agency, from notes in her casebook.]

I arrived downstairs one morning a few days after Christmas to find my husband in conference with a friend who rose to greet me. He was short and innocent-looking—almost cherubic—with an engagingly shy and childlike expression, belied by a pair of eyes that looked dreamily enough through half-closed lids, yet I was conscious of being shrewdly studied and analysed. Another of them!

'Sheila, my dear. Let me introduce Reginald Fortune, one of my brighter Oxford students, now active in the same criminal investigations as ourselves, but on the more factual plane; in fact, a surgeon and consultant to the CID.

'Reginald. This is my wife and partner.'

We shook hands and Mr Fortune waited for me to sit down.

'Reginald is married to Miss Joan Amber: you will remember her Rosalind as the definitive performance.'

Mr Fortune bowed modestly, blushing slightly.

'Reginald has an interesting problem involving simultaneous, unexplained deaths in his father's practice. Since he is supposedly looking after it, he wants us to probe via Nat Schneiderman. I have appraised him of our techniques and since we conducted a number of psychic experiments together at Oxford he wishes to partake in the inquiry. Please take notes as usual.

'Reggie has a theory that he is holding out on me, but he has forgotten his old tutor's aptitudes and I think I can link up the chain myself.' (Mr Fortune smiled broadly at this.)

'Briefly the details are these.' (He recounted the sequence with which the

reader is already familiar.) 'I guess he wants to know how Rattu effected the killings without leaving any traces or clues, eh?' My husband turned to his pupil who nodded.

In accordance with our practice, I darkened the room for the seance and placed cushions for Arthur to relax. It seemed only a few moments before he sat up in the character of Nat Schneiderman, a dead Pinkerton Detective Agency operative, who was his 'guide' in the psychic realm.

Mr Fortune took it very calmly and shook hands when Arthur spoke in a heavy drawl and stuck out a hand. I began my transcription.

'Glad to meet you, Mr Fortune. I admired your work with Lady Chantry, last Christmas sir. Just great! It's not often we see summary justice. Say, would you care to speak with the lady?'

Mr Fortune held up his hand with a grimace.

'Ah, well, just a thought.' Arthur shook his head.

'This Westhampton stunt then. You ain't quite got it right. Ole Nat can still show you sumpin', eh? You have a vampire here, sir, and quite a potent one. You spotted actor Rattu had contracted syphilitic meningitis . . . good. There's your proof he was used by his uncle. Old Sam's earthbound spirit was mad at the cheatin' over income from his book. He got into William's drunken mind, just as I use Art here, and killed the other three principals, includin' the actor–manager–playwright.'

'How did he do it?' asked Reginald.

'Takin' the vital force from them: spirit, not blood—that's vampirism. The dead 'uns are right here now; guess they're jest too flimsy in spirit to get through to you. OK. We got work to do—or you have, I guess. Unless old Sam is stopped, he'll spread that disease around. He's gotten in quite a lot of living force. Get him exhumed and cremated.'

Reginald leaned forward. 'That explains a lot and I don't know how you found out . . .'

Arthur laughed. 'Like you, Mr Fortune . . . intuition.'

'But, look here . . . there's no justice I can achieve except to ease Rattu's suffering, eh? Surely you aren't goin' to tell me I shall find the uncle's coffin full of blood and him floatin' in it? The murderer is already dead and buried.'

'No, siree,' came back emphatically. 'He's undead. Oh, yeah, he had to get into Rattu first, but now he's sucked in life force from three others. He'll sure try to get around and spread that pox. You want an epidemic?'

Mr Fortune rose in the dark. 'Brer Lomas is going to love this! There never was a more perfect official. Ought to have married my sister! Well, that seems to be that Mr Schneiderman, Mrs Murray. Except for one thing . . .?'

'Yep?'

[150]

'How did Uncle Sam manage to kill all three so quickly and at more or less the same time? That seems even more incredible than the rest of this astoundin' business!'

'Heck, don't call him "Uncle Sam", Fortune! An' have you never heard? The dead travel fast!'

'I assume you are joking, Fortune?' Lomas crossed one elegantly socked and trousered leg across the other and leaned back in his chair. 'I can't apply for exhumation of a 20-year old grave on the basis of this moonshine you're spinning. Be reasonable, man! Why, there's not even a shred of tangible evidence against Rattu himself.'

'You might credit me with some common sense,' said Reggie, 'same like I can't do for you. No, the CID prefer a few more corpses to justify making a decision. Prevention of crime not in the police vocabulary.'

'Now, be fair, Mr Fortune,' said Superintendent Bell heavily. 'We can't go outside the rules.'

'No, you're safe there,' hooted Reggie. 'Take no chances!'

'Why not try the traditional remedies,' sneered Lomas. 'A sprig of garlic or a stoup of holy water. Haven't you a crucifix at home?'

'The method that commends itself to me, Lomas,' shrilled Reggie, 'is that of cutting off the head and putting an apple in the mouth. I could do that to you. If it was fashionable to stop wearing hats, you'd have no further use for your head!' He stamped out in a bad temper.

'Dammit, Bell,' said Lomas, 'we'd be crucified putting up a story like that as reason for exhumation.'

'I know, sir. But you can't get away from it: he's usually right.'

'Yes, damn him,' snapped Lomas, turning to his in-tray.

At Westhampton Cottage Hospital, the matron received Mr Fortune portentously with hushed whispers and a crackling of starched uniform.

'Sir Daniel Ferrers is here, Mr Fortune.'

'Good-o,' said he, pushing open the door of the isolation room, 'I thought I recognized the Bentley outside.' He shook hands with the eminent physician.

'You'll not save him now, Fortune,' said he, indicating Rattu who was twitching and shivering in the bed.

'Grateful to have your confirmation, Sir Daniel,' replied Reggie meekly. 'I may as well give him some morphine to ease the pain.'

'Yes, indeed. Can do no harm now. You must excuse me: I have clients waiting.' And Sir Daniel took his leave.

[151]

Next morning Lomas answered the phone.

'Fortune here. Rattu's dead. No near kinfolk ... have sold family lawyer on rapid cremation and burial in family grave.'

'What family grave?'

'Whose d'you think? Uncle Samuel's of course.'

After a dinner which was a paean of praise by Elise, his cook, and at which Reggie discoursed on claret and the growing of strawberries, he indicated to Mordan that it was time to be moving and ordered the car.

'You aren't driving, are you sir?' said Mordan, alarmed, for Mr Fortune's driving is a wonder of miraculous escapes.

'No, be at peace, Mordan. Anxiety is bad for digesting the mullet. Gorton is driving us to the churchyard.'

'The churchyard? At this time of night?'

'Yes, we're meeting Hanbury the sexton there.'

The church and graveyard were in darkness lit only by a gaslight at the street corner. A bitter north wind gave promise of snow to come, and as the two men got out of the car, a short, sturdy figure emerged from the darkness of the lich-gate.

'Ah, Mr Hanbury,' said Reggie. 'Good man. Have you got the stuff?'

'Yessir. I left it round by the grave what I opened up this arternoon. I'll put the barrer away termorrer, sir. Thankee, sir.' There came a clinking of silver coin and the good man lit his cycle lamps and pedalled off homeward.

Reggie next produced rubber gloves and hospital masks which, after some protest, he persuaded Mordan to put on. So accoutred, they entered the churchyard.

Mordan's torch helped them follow the gravel path through the rows of gravestones to where a tarpaulin, a barrow and a mound of earth disfigured the winter grass.

'Hold the torch on the hole, Mordan.' Reggie pulled away the tarpaulin to reveal the remains of a damp and mould-stained coffin, its walls and top badly warped now they were released from the confining earth mould.

'Uncle Sam, Mordan. Although there will be only ashes of Rattu to put here, I got Hanbury to dig down to the box.'

There was a dull sound as he wrenched away the crumbling lid, and Mordan directed his torch on to the occupant.

'Strewth!' he nearly dropped the torch.

In the torchlight, shaken by his trembling hand, the yellowy bones and sinews, covered by a tight-shrunken membraneous skin, were seen to be protruding through the soiled remains of clothing. Hair was still matted around the head and cheekbones.

Mr Fortune turned swiftly to the barrow and unscrewed the top from a can. He sloshed liquid liberally over the coffin and its contents, ignoring Mordan's protests, and taking care not to spill any liquid outside the grave. A heavy smell of petroleum penetrated their masks.

'Back now.' He shoved Mordan so hard that he stumbled, and while he righted himself, Reggie produced a phial from his pocket. 'Potassium chlorate, sugar and sulphuric acid,' he commented. 'When the inner tube breaks, up she goes.' So saying, he tossed the phial lightly into the grave.

There came a chinking, cracking sound and a flash of flame shot skyward, throwing the churchyard into an instant of light.

For an instant, too, the simulacrum of a tall, bearded figure, its hands outstretched in rage or agony, reached out of the flame, as if to seize them . . . and was as instantly gone. They were left to the feeble glow of the torch.

Reggie approached the edge of the grave and carefully placed a few shovelfuls of earth from the mound within the hole.

'Once we have buried Mr Rattu there tomorrow, that will be the end of it,' said he.

Mordan was shaking his head as they made their way back to the car.

'I wouldn't have thought it of you, Mr Fortune; making me an accessory . . .'

'Accessory to what, Mordan? No crime . . . no sacrilege. Purification and release, same as Ayesha and Kallikrates. In any case I needed official presence in case the fire was seen.'

'Who? Do you really believe that?'

'Whom, you mean. Never mind. Yes, I do believe it as a matter of fact.'

Inspector Mordan sniffed suspiciously. 'Coincidence Mr Rattu dying like that. You'd never have got an exhumation order to dig out the grave otherwise.' He peered at his young companion as they got into the car. 'Almost providential.'

'Don't press it, Mordan,' sighed Reggie, leaning back. 'You'll catch me out one day.'

'But what do I tell the CID of this?' gasped the Inspector.

'Nothing at all, if you've any sense,' said Reggie. 'Home Gorton!'

RED LILY

Dick Donovan

'Dick Donovan' was the pseudonym and *alter
ego* of J.E.P. Muddock (1843–1934), author of
more than fifty mystery and detective
volumes—many starring Donovan himself—and
a frequent contributor to the *Strand* and most
other popular magazines of the period. 'Red
Lily' is taken from Donovan's rare collection,
Tales of Terror (1899).

O
n one of the wildest nights for which the Bay of Biscay is
notorious, the sailing ship *Sirocco* was ploughing her way under
close-reefed topsails across that stormy sea. The *Sirocco* was a
large, full-rigged vessel, bound from Bombay towards England, her
destination being London. She had a mixed cargo, though a large
percentage of it was composed of jute. Four months had passed since she
cleared from her port of lading, and was towed out of the beautiful
harbour of Bombay in a dead calm. For many days after the tug left her
the *Sirocco* did nothing but drift with the current. She was as 'a painted
ship upon a painted ocean.' No breath came out of the sultry heavens to
waft her towards her haven in far away England. It was a bad beginning
to the voyage. The time was about the middle of August, and all on board
were anxiously looking forward to reaching their destination in time to
spend Christmas at home. But as August wore out and September came
in, and still the horrid calms continued, pleasant anticipations gave place
to despair, for many a thousand leagues of watery wastes had to be sailed

before the white cliffs of Albion would gladden the eyes of the wanderers.

The crew of the vessel numbered sixty hands all told, and in addition there were twenty saloon passengers. With two of these passengers we have now to deal. The one is a fair young girl, slender, tall, and delicate. She is exceedingly pretty. Her features are regular and delicately chiselled. Her hair is a soft, wavy, golden brown and her brown eyes are as liquid and gentle as a fawn's. The pure whiteness of her neck and temples is contrasted by the most exquisite tinge of rose colour in the cheeks, which puts, as it were, a finish upon a perfect picture. The whiteness of her skin, the delicate flush in the face, the brown, flossy hair, the tall, slender, graceful figure were all so suggestive of the purest of flowers that her friends for many years had called her 'Red Lily'. Her name was Lily Hetherington, and she yet wanted some months to the completion of her twenty-first birthday. Lily was the daughter of an officer of the Hon. East India Company's Service—his only daughter, and by him worshipped. For many years he had been stationed in India, and at last, seeing no chance of returning to his wife and family, which consisted of two sons in addition to the girl, he requested them to join him in the East. This request was quickly and gladly complied with, and Mrs Hetherington and her children started on their journey. Mr Hetherington at that time was well off, for he had invested all his savings in the Agra and Masterman Bank, and held shares to a large amount in the concern, the stability of which, at that period, no one would have dared to have doubted. Indian officers throughout India swore by it, and they congratulated themselves, as they entrusted their hard-won money to the Bank, that they were making splendid provision for their wives and children when those wives and children should become widows and orphans.

As Mr Hetherington possessed considerable influence he had no difficulty in quickly procuring his sons suitable appointments. Fond as he was of his lads, who were aged respectively twenty-two and twenty-four, his love for them was as nothing when compared with that he bore for his beautiful daughter, his 'Bonnie Red Lily', as he called her. Nor was Lily less fond of her father. She was a mere child when he left England, but she had never forgotten him, and never a mail left but it bore from Lily a long and loving epistle to the lonely officer, who was bravely doing his duty in the distant eastern land.

One day, soon after her arrival, Mr Hetherington said to his daughter as they sat in the verandah of the bungalow, 'Lily, my pet, I have got a little surprise for you.'

'Have you, pa dear; and pray what is it?' she answered. 'You are such a dear, good kind papa that you are always giving me pleasant surprises.'

'Well, yes, of course, I like to give you pleasant surprises, but this one is different from any of the others,' he returned with a smile, at the same time stroking her soft brown hair, and looking proudly into her beautiful face.

'Oh, do tell me what it is,' she exclaimed, as he paused in a tantalizing way; 'do you hear, pa? Don't keep me in suspense.'

'Restrain that woman's curiosity of yours, my darling, and don't be impatient.'

'I declare you are awfully wicked, papa,' she returned, with a pretty pout of her red lips. 'Tell me instantly what it is. I demand to know.'

'And so you shall,' he answered, as he kissed her fondly and patted her head. 'Tomorrow, then, I have a visitor coming to stay with us for a week or two.'

'Indeed. Is it a lady or gentleman?'

'A gentleman.'

'Oh, do tell me what he's like.'

'Well, well, you are a little Miss Curious,' Mr Hetherington laughed heartily as he blew a cloud of blue smoke from his cigar into the stagnant air. 'Not to keep you in suspense any longer, then, the name of my visitor is Dick Fenton, Richard Cronmire Joyce Fenton, to give him his full name. He is a year or two your senior, and a fine, handsome, manly young fellow to boot.'

'Indeed,' muttered Lily, thoughtfully, as she fancied that her father's words had a hidden meaning.

'Yes. His father was a very old friend of mine, and we saw long service together. He died some four or five years ago, but before dying he made me promise I would look after his boy, who was an only child and motherless. Of course, I gladly gave this promise, and have sacredly carried it out.'

'Ah, what a good, kind, generous man you are,' Lily said, as she nestled closer to him, and tightened her little white fingers round his brown, hairy hand.

'I saw there was stuff in the lad, and I took to him almost as if he had been my own son. Unfortunately, my good friend Fenton died poor, and was only enabled to leave three thousand pounds, for which he had insured his life, for his son's education. I succeeded in getting Dick into one of the Company's training establishments, and the marked ability he displayed very soon pushed him forward, and having gone through his cadetship with honour and credit, he was appointed a year ago to what in time will be a most lucrative post. I have watched the lad closely, and seen with pride the many noble qualities he possesses, and I have no doubt at all he will distinguish himself. During the years that he has been my protégé I have constantly said to myself, "If my Lily should like Dick, and Dick should like my Lily, they shall be man and wife."'

'Oh, papa!' exclaimed Lily, as the beautiful tinge in her face deepened to scarlet, that spread to her neck and temples.

'Why, my darling, why do you blush so? It is surely every honest woman's desire to become a wife, and I am very anxious to see you comfortably married before I die. Men go off very suddenly in this treacherous country, and I am well worn with service, and cannot hope to last much longer. But, understand me, Lily, pet, your own will and womanly instincts must guide you in this matter. I shall not seek to influence you in any way, and if you have already given your heart to another, if he is an honest and worthy man, even though he be poor as a church mouse, I shall not offer the slightest opposition to your wishes. It is your future happiness I study, and I am not selfish enough to attempt to coerce you into an objectionable union.'

Lily rose and twined her arms round her father's neck, and pressing her soft, white face to his bronzed cheeks, said:

'My dear, dear father, I have not given my heart to anyone, and your wishes are mine.'

On the morrow Fenton duly arrived at Mr Hetherington's bungalow. He had travelled by dak from a station near Calcutta; and when he had refreshed himself with a bath, and made himself presentable, Hetherington took him on one side, and said:

'Dick, lad, I have repeatedly spoken to you about my daughter, and before I introduce you to her, let me say that I shall be proud to have you as a son-in-law, providing that there is the most perfect reciprocal feeling between you and my Lily. I am not a man of many words, and I will content myself with remarking that your father was the very soul of honour. Never disgrace him, and never betray the confidence I repose in you.'

'Do not doubt me, sir,' said Dick. 'I am indebted to you for everything, and I should be base if I did anything that could inflict pain upon you or yours.'

'Bravely said, my boy. God prosper you. Win Lily if you can; but win her as a man should.'

Hetherington had previously made known his wishes to his wife, and she had readily acquiesced in them.

Fenton was, as his guardian had described him, a fine, manly, handsome young fellow. His frank, open bearing was well calculated to find favour with women, even if he had not been possessed of good looks.

Hetherington and his wife watched the young people narrowly, and they soon saw that a mutual liking for each other was springing up, and before Dick's leave of two months had expired he and Lily were betrothed, while the bond between them was that of the most perfect love.

Dick returned to his station, and Mr and Mrs Hetherington congratulated themselves on having, so far as they were able, provided for their daughter's future, a future that seemed likely to be one of unclouded happiness. 'L'homme propose, et Dieu dispose' says the French proverb, and never was the proverb more fully borne out than in this case. Within six months of Dick's return to his duties, all civilized India was shocked to its inmost heart by a terrific commercial convulsion—for so only can it be described. Through the length and breadth of the land, the fearful rumour spread on the wings of the wind that the great bank of Agra and Masterman had broken. Men stood aghast, and women paled with fright, for, to hundreds and thousands of households in all parts of the world, it meant utter ruin, as many and many a one at the present day knows to his bitter cost. Many a widow living in poverty now might have reposed in the lap of luxury, and many a young man and woman, now in ignorance and want, might have been otherwise but for this cruel collapse of the great banking firm. It was so essentially an Indian bank, a depository for the earnings of Indian servants of the Company, that it affected a class of people who for the most part had been tenderly nurtured and led to believe that they occupied, and were destined to occupy so long as they might live, a good position in life, and to take their stand among the great middle class of society.

At first men doubted the rumour, but soon the awful truth became too apparent to be longer questioned, and those who had grown grey and feeble beneath the burning Indian sun saw now that their few remaining days must be passed in poverty and misery. It was bitter, very bitter, but it was fate, and could not be averted.

[158]

Amongst the greatest sufferers was Mr Hetherington. He had invested, one way and another, nearly one hundred thousand pounds in that bank, and now every penny piece was gone. The shock came upon him with great severity. His health had long been failing, and he had looked forward with great eagerness to retiring from the service in another year and 'going home' with his family. But that was never to be now. For a time he was stunned. He tried to bear up against the blow, but he was only human; his brain gave way, and in a moment of temporary aberration he shot himself.

This new grief almost crushed the unhappy widow and her family. Fortunately 'the boys' had good appointments that held out every promise of improvement, but their incomes at that time were scarcely sufficient for their own needs, though they generously curtailed their expenses in every way in order to contribute towards the support of their sister and mother.

The shock of her father's death threw Lily into a dangerous illness, and for some time her life was threatened; but there was one who never lost an opportunity of cheering her with his love, and that was Dick Fenton.

When she was convalescent she one day said to him:

'Dick, I have something to say to you.'

'Nothing very serious, darling,' he answered, laughingly.

'Yes, very serious. When I was first engaged to you my father was considered to be a wealthy man, and I understand that he promised you that my dowry should be something handsome. That is all changed now. We are ruined, and my dear father is in his grave. Under these circumstances I can no longer hold you to your engagement, and therefore release you from every promise. You must give me up and seek for someone better suited for you than I am.'

She fairly broke down here, and burst into violent weeping. Dick's arm stole around her waist, he pressed her head to his breast, and, whispering softly to her said, with deep earnestness:

'Lily, there is one thing, and only one thing, that shall break our engagement.'

'What is that?' she stammered between her sobs.

'The death of one of us!' he answered, with strong emphasis.

She needed no further assurance. There was that in his manner and tone that convinced more than words could possibly have done. And so, save for the shadow which hung over the little household, she would have been perfectly happy.

A year went by and Mrs Hetherington still lingered in India, for she did not like to leave her sons; but failing health at length rendered it necessary that she should return to England. At this time Dick had just been granted two years' leave of absence, and he urged Lily to become his wife before they left India, as he too was going home. She had asked him, however, to postpone the event, and made a solemn promise that the wedding should take place on Christmas Day, adding:

'It is not long to wait, dear. It is now the middle of July, and, as we sail in a fortnight, the vessel is sure to be home by that time. Besides, I am so fond of Christmas. It is so full of solemn and purifying associations, and a fitting season for a man and woman to take upon themselves the responsibility of the marriage state. A wedding on Christmas Day brings good luck. Of course you will say this is stupid superstition. So it may be, but I am a woman, and you must let me have my way.'

Pressing his lips to hers, he made answer:

'And so you shall, my own Red Lily; but, remember, come what may, you'll be my wife on Christmas Day.'

'Come what may, I will be your wife on Christmas Day,' she returned solemnly.

August arrived, and Dick, Lily, and Mrs Hetherington were passengers on board the good ship *Sirocco*. Their fellow-passengers were a miscellaneous lot, and included several Indian officers, a planter or two, a clergyman, and some merchants, who, having amassed fortunes, were going home to end their days.

The second officer of the *Sirocco* was a young man, of about eight or nine-and-twenty, Alfred Cornell. He was a wild, reckless, daring fellow, with a splendid physique. His hair was almost black, his eyes the very darkest shade of brown, and small, keen, and piercing as a hawk's. In those eyes the character of the man was written. For somehow they seemed to suggest a vain, heartless, selfish, vindictive nature, and the firm lips told of an iron will. He was every inch a sailor, bold as a lion, and a magnificent swimmer. The crew, however, hated him, for he was the hardest of taskmasters, but was an especial favourite with the captain, as such men generally are, for he was perfect in every department of his profession, and the sailors under his control were kept to their duties with an iron hand.

About this man—Alfred Cornell—there was something that amounted almost to weirdness. The strange, keen eyes exercised a sort of fascination over some people. This was especially the case with women. In fact, he made a boast that he had never yet seen the woman he could not subdue. From the moment that he and Dick Fenton stood face to face a mutual dislike sprang up in their hearts for each other. Dick could not exactly tell why he did not take to the man, but he had an instinctive dislike for him. The fact was there, the cause was not easy to determine, but instincts are seldom wrong. The moment that Alfred Cornell and Lily Hetherington met each other a shadow fell upon her, and a devil came into his heart. She had an instinctive dread of him, and yet felt fascinated. He thought to himself:

'By heavens, that's a splendid girl, and I'll win her if I die for it.'

For the first week or two he paid her no more than the most ordinary attentions, and the dread she at first felt for him began to wear off; she could not help admitting to herself that he was certainly handsome and attractive. The pet name by which she was known amongst her family— the Red Lily—soon leaked out on board, as such things will, and the passengers with whom she was most intimate frequently addressed her in this style by way of compliment, for she was a favourite with them all, and her beauty was a theme of admiration amongst the men, even the ladies could not help but admit that she *was* 'good looking', though they said spiteful things about her, as women will say of each other. Alfred Cornell had never addressed her in any other way but as 'Miss Hetherington'; but one morning, when the ship was in the tropics, she had gone on deck very early to see the sun rise. The heat in the cabins was so great that she could not sleep, and as the sailors had just finished holy-stoning and washing down she had thrown a loose robe over her shoulders and gone quietly on to the poop. It was Cornell's watch, but in all probability she did not know that at the time. It was a very long poop, and save for the man at the wheel not a soul was to be seen. The sea was oily in its calmness, and the sky was aflame with the most gorgeous colours, such colours as can be nowhere seen save in the tropics, and only then when the sun with regal pomp and splendour commences to rise. The sails hung in heavy folds against the masts, and there was a rhythmical kind of motion in the ship as she rose and fell ever so gently to the light swell which even in the calmest ocean is never absent. Lily leaned pensively against the mizzen rigging, gazing thought-fully across the sleeping sea to where the gold, and amethyst, and purples, and scarlets were blended together in one blaze of dazzling colour. Suddenly she was startled by a voice speaking in a subdued tone close to her ear, and which said:

'The Red Lily is up early this morning.'

She recognized the voice as that of Cornell, and turning quickly round said, with much dignity:

'Excuse me, sir, I am Miss Hetherington to you.'

'Miss Hetherington,' he answered, strongly emphasizing the words. 'I beg your pardon, but the pretty name so fits you that I made bold to use it. I trust I have not offended you.'

'Oh, no,' she said, as she averted her gaze from his piercing eyes, for she felt like a bird before the fabled basilisk. She would have rushed away, but was spellbound. The strange man held her in a thrall.

'How charming you look this morning,' he remarked. 'Why, you put even the glory of the sunrise to shame.'

'Really, Mr Cornell,' she exclaimed indignantly, and blushing to the very roots of her hair, 'you insult me by such extravagant and stupid compliments. I don't like men who talk nonsense, and think that all a girl wants is to be flattered. Of course plenty of empty-headed girls do, but I'm not one of them.'

'Don't be angry with me, please; I am sincere. Can the wretched moth that flutters into the flame of the candle help itself? Not a bit of it. You would pity the moth; why not pity me?'

'This is audacity, Mr Cornell, and I will complain to the captain about you,' she exclaimed as she made a movement to go. But ever so lightly, and without any effort, he touched her hand. What was the fearful magic of that touch that she should thrill so? What was the power in his voice that held her in a spell? She did not go, but stood there. Her left hand resting on one of the ratlings of the rigging, her right hand hanging down by her side, his large powerful fingers touching hers, her head averted, for she felt as if she dare not look at him.

'It is not in your nature to be cruel, Miss Hetherington'—he spoke low, so that there should be no possibility of the man at the wheel catching his words, though he was so far off there was not much fear of that—'why, then, should you be cruel with me?'

'I am not cruel, but you are rude, very rude,' she answered with a voice that trembled from suppressed emotion.

'I am *not* rude, and you *are* cruel,' he returned, dwelling deliberately on every word. 'You are a beautiful young woman, and I am a man. Surely I should be less than a man if I failed to admire you? Do you not admire the beauty of the sky there? Why, then, should I do less than you, though in your face I find more to admire than in those glowing colours.'

'If you do not instantly leave me I will call out for assistance,' she said. She felt faint and powerless, and as though she would certainly fall down on the deck if she let go her hold of the rigging.

'No, you must not do that,' he answered coolly. 'How can I possibly help feeling for you what I do feel. I am not a stone statue, but a man with a heart, and though a bolt from heaven should strike me into the sea for speaking the words, I tell you now, though I never utter another syllable to you, *that I love you.*'

He had never taken his fingers from hers, and now he pressed her hand. The sea seemed to be going round and round before her eyes. The wonderful colours in the sky were all blended in one confused mass. The ship appeared to be sinking beneath her feet, and yet she managed to murmur in a low, weak voice:

'For God's sake leave me!'

Without another word he walked away, and then she seemed to breathe more freely, and in a few minutes had quite recovered herself. She turned and went towards the companion way, and as she did so she saw Cornell talking to the captain, who had just come on deck. The captain bade her good morning, but Cornell was as immovable and impassive as a piece of sculpture.

Oh! what a sense of relief she experienced when she got down to her cabin. The spell seemed to be lifted at last, and, closing the door, she threw herself into the bunk and wept passionately. When the hysterical fit had passed she was relieved, and she determined to tell her mother what had happened, but this determination only lasted for a few minutes, as on reflection she thought that it could but lead to unpleasantness, and in a little floating world such as a ship is the slightest things are looked upon as legitimate food for scandal to batten upon. Therefore, her second thoughts were to keep the matter to herself. Still she was very unhappy, and Dick noticed it. He naturally asked her the cause, but she made an excuse by saying that she was a little out of sorts. She was strongly tempted to tell him all, but was restrained by a fear that it might lead to a quarrel between him and the second mate.

For several days after the unpleasant incident with Cornell she studiously avoided going on deck alone for fear of meeting him, but whenever he had occasion to pass her she would shudder, for his strange eyes seemed to exercise a power over her which was simply marvellous. She felt, in fact, when he was looking at her that she could grovel at his feet at his mere bidding. It was a dreadful feeling, and her health naturally suffered. Her mother and lover were both concerned about her, but she endeavoured to remove any anxiety they might have had by saying that her indisposition was of a very trivial character. One evening she had been sitting on the poop with Fenton. The weather was fine, but a strong breeze was blowing, and the vessel was tearing through the water. The daylight had almost faded out, and it was impossible to distinguish people who were standing or sitting only a few yards away. Fenton left her for a few minutes to go down to his cabin for some cigars, and scarcely had he disappeared when she was startled by the sudden appearance of Cornell. It seemed almost as though he had risen up out of the deck. She was seated on a camp stool, and he bent his head low until she could feel his hot breath on her cheek. He whispered to her in a voice that could not possibly have been heard by anyone else, however near they might have been; but she heard every word, every syllable, as it was poured into her ear, and it seemed to burn into her brain.

'Lily, you are cruel,' he said; 'I love you madly, and yet you avoid me. You must give me some encouragement, or I will drown myself; and if you breathe a word of what I have said to you to any living soul, I tell you in God's name that I will throw myself overboard, and my death will lie at your door. Remember what I say. I am a determined man, and nothing on earth will stop me carrying out my will.'

Once again his fingers touched her hand; then in a moment he was gone as suddenly as he had appeared. He seemed to fade away into the darkness like a spectre, but almost immediately afterwards she heard him bawling some orders in stentorian tones to the watch.

When Fenton came back she was trembling and faint, and though she struggled hard to conceal from him that she was agitated, he could not fail to observe it, and in a tone of alarm asked the cause.

'Oh, nothing dear—nothing,' she answered; 'at least, nothing of any consequence. A slight feeling of faintness has come over me; but really it is not worth bothering about.'

Oh, how she longed to tell him all; but the words of the strange man who was exercising such a powerful influence over her were still ringing in her ears, and she was silent.

Fenton did not make any further remark then on the subject, but he felt uneasy. He was convinced that there was some mystery, but what it was he could not for the life of him determine. The thought did flash through his brain that she was deceiving him, but instantly he put it away as unworthy of him. It seemed so preposterous to associate deceit with the Red Lily, who was as pure as the beautiful flower after which she was called.

When he escorted her down to the cabin a little later, he said:

'Darling, I am uneasy about you. Something is wrong, I am sure, but your gentle heart prompts you to keep it from me for fear of giving me pain. Do be good to yourself for my sake. Why don't you take your mother into your confidence, and tell her if you have any trouble, since you do not apparently care to confide it to me.'

'Do not be uneasy,' she answered. 'Believe me, oh, do believe me, when I say that my indisposition is of a very trifling character. I have nothing to tell my mother, and you know perfectly well, Dick, you have my full confidence.'

She felt a little guilty as she said this, for she knew that she ought to have told him at once of Cornell's conduct. But, firstly, the strange fascination he exercised over her kept her silent; and, secondly, she was really afraid of causing a scene between the two men. Besides, she comforted herself with the thought that the voyage would soon be over, and once clear of the ship it would be goodbye to Cornell for ever. She regarded him as a vain, presumptuous fellow, who imagined that every girl he looked at must be in love with him.

As soon as her lover had left her, and she had been to wish her mother goodnight, the Red Lily once again gave unrestrained vent to her feelings, and wept passionately. She could not help it. She felt almost as if she would die if she did not weep, and weep she did bitterly until she fretted herself to sleep.

The following morning she was weak and pale, and did not put in an appearance at breakfast. The beautiful pink had faded from her face, and she had the look of one who was jaded and unhappy. Mrs Hetherington visited her daughter, and naturally felt alarmed. There was a doctor on board, and Mrs Hetherington expressed a determination to consult him; but Lily pleaded with such earnestness, and at last expressed such a strong determination not to see him, that her mother yielded, and Lily kept in her cabin all that day.

On the following day she was better. Cornell's influence had passed away, and she had to a considerable extent regained her spirits.

The weather was now very chilly, and unfortunately the wind was unfavourable, so that the ship had to sail on long and short tacks. It was worse than tantalizing to those who had looked forward so eagerly to spending Christmas with their friends in the dear old country. The hope of doing that was now past, for the distance was too great to cover in the time that intervened between them and the great Christian Festival. Well wrapped in rugs, Lily was once more seated on deck in company with Dick. She had been doing some fancy needlework, and he had been sketching a large vessel that had been in company with them two or three days. Presently he laid down his sketching block on the deck, and looking up into the fair face of his companion, he said:

[165]

'Lily, pet, do you remember the promise you made to me before we left India?'

What was that, Dick?' she asked.

'That you would become my wife on Christmas Day.'

'Oh, yes,' she said quickly, and with some slight agitation; 'but we shall not be home by that time.'

'That is true; but it need not affect your promise.'

'I don't understand you,' she answered.

'You are surely aware, Lily, that a marriage on board of a ship is perfectly legal. Even a captain has the power to marry people; but it fortunately happens, as you know, that we have a Church of England clergyman amongst us, and therefore I claim the fulfilment of your promise.'

'Oh, Dick, it cannot be.'

'Cannot be!' he echoed in some astonishment. 'Were your words, then, *only* words after all?'

'Ah, love, do not be harsh with me. I should so much prefer that our wedding took place in the regular way on shore, and it is to be hoped that we shall arrive in England by the New Year.'

'I am far from being harsh with you, Lily,' answered Dick, a little sadly; 'but you yourself expressed a wish to be married on the Christmas morning, even saying that you were superstitious about it. Although there is every prospect now that we shall be at sea on that day, there is no reason at all why we should not be married on board; and if you like we will go through the ceremony again when we reach England. The mere circumstance of being married in or out of a church cannot possibly affect our union, and I am sure you have too much good sense to be influenced by the stupid idea which possesses some small-brained people—that a marraige performed out of a church cannot be sanctified.'

'I have no such idea,' she said. 'I should be ashamed of myself if I had.'

'Very well, then, Lily, say that you will be my wife on Christmas morning, even though we are at sea.'

'How long does it want to Christmas, Dick?'

'Three weeks exactly.'

'Then I promise you that if mamma offers no objection I will gratify your wish.'

'I am perfectly satisfied that your mother will willingly let us have our own way, so on Christmas Day we will become man and wife, if we are both living.'

'On Christmas Day we will become man and wife if we are both living,' she repeated solemnly, but the words had scarcely left her lips when she almost uttered a scream, for close beside her stood Cornell. He had his sextant in his hand, and had come up the companion way (near which Dick and Lily were sitting) with the captain to take the sun.

'Make eight bells,' said the captain, 'we shall get no sun today.'

'Eight bells,' roared out Cornell.

'Come, dear, let us go down to luncheon,' said Dick as he rose, gathered up the wraps, and offered his arm to his fiancée.

She had to pass Cornell to reach the companion way, and she saw his hawk-like eyes fixed upon her, although he pretended to be examining the figures on his sextant. Those eyes burned into her soul, as it were, and the strange hysterical feeling came back again so that she felt as if she must weep, but by a powerful effort she controlled herself, and Dick did not notice how she was affected.

The question of the marriage being put to Mrs Hetherington, that lady said that she should offer no objection to the wishes of the young people. Consequently it was soon understood that the monotony of the voyage would be relieved by a wedding on Christmas morning. In which case there would be a double occasion for rejoicing and festivities.

Christmas at sea is always a festive time, but this particular one on board the *Sirocco* promised to be unusually lively. The captain gave orders to the steward that he was to reserve a good supply of his best champagne for the occasion, and the cook was ordered to make plenty of cakes and fancy things; while the butcher was instructed to kill the fattest geese of the few that remained, and the last pig was to be slaughtered in order to add to the feast. The lady and gentlemen passengers rummaged amongst their boxes to try and fish out suitable little presents to give to the young couple, and there was much fun and laughter as all sorts of odd suggestions were made; while the ladies further busied themselves in improvising suitable decorations for the saloon. In fact, this coming marriage was looked upon as a blessing almost, for the voyage had been so long and tedious, that the little excitement caused by the prospective union of the Red Lily and Dick Fenton was most welcome.

As the second mate seemed to purposely avoid Lily now, she recovered her spirits; in fact, several days passed without her seeing him, and she began to laugh at her stupidity in allowing him to have such an influence over her. Dick could not fail to notice the change, and, attributing it to the pleasure she anticipated at the near prospect of their union, he was delighted also.

Christmas Day was now anxiously looked forward to by all the passengers, and as it only wanted eight days to the time great preparations were going on, and ladies busied themselves in stoning raisins and performing other incidental necessaries in connection with the concoction of those mysteries—Christmas puddings. The gentlemen found occupation in dressing the saloon with flags, and decorations ingeniously constructed by the fair sex out of the most likely and unlikely things. No one who has not been a long voyage in a passenger ship can imagine with what avidity every little incident calculated to relieve the monotony of life at sea—if it can truthfully be said to be monotonous—is seized upon. Therefore, Christmastide and a marriage in the bargain were such important events, that the little floating world which the *Sirocco* represented was agitated to its very centre, and the excitement rose to fever heat.

Life at sea, however, is influenced by laws which do not affect it on land. Changes in the weather; changes from calm to rough weather have a marked effect on a floating community, and a few hours often produce the most extraordinary transformations. An oily sea may become raging mountains of water, and the steadiness of a ship is turned into violent pitching and tossing that renders walking to all but the most experienced a matter of great difficulty. At such times soup plates will perform somersaults into your lap, and joints of meat evince a decided objection to remain in their proper positions. While, as for poultry, wine bottles, and so on, they suddenly acquire an agility for flying through the air, so that what with dodging these missiles, and holding on like grim death to the table or the back of the settee, one's life at meal time on board of a ship in stormy weather is by no means as comfortable as it might be in a well appointed dining-room on shore.

Within a week of Christmas it became manifest that the *Sirocco* was destined to encounter some bad weather. There had been sullen calms succeeded by fitful bursts of storm, but the good ship had crept on and on until she had reached the verge of the Bay of Biscay. The bay, although it bears such a bad character, is suggestive of nearing home to those who come from afar, and consequently the passengers were high-spirited, notwithstanding that it was pretty certain that a good deal of knocking about was in store for them.

One night during the middle watch a furious squall suddenly burst upon the vessel, and as she had all sail set she heeled over almost on to her beam ends. Several sails were rent to fragments by the force of the wind, and the long strips flying out in the tempest made a tremendous cracking like the cracking of stock whips. 'All hands' were called on deck, and there were all the noise, and shouting, and uproar incidental to a sudden squall in the dead of night. To the timid and the inexperienced this is particularly alarming, for as the ship flies along on her side the waters hiss in a strange manner, the shouting and tramp of the sailors, the orders given hastily and in stentorian tones, the cracker-like reports of the torn sails, the groaning and creaking of the rudder chains, the indescribable howling of the wind, and the extreme angle of the vessel, are sufficiently alarming to produce nervousness even in those whose acquaintance with the sea is not of recent date. And this is more particularly the case when such a squall occurs at night; then the sky is inky in its blackness, and nothing can be seen save the spectral-like outlines of the rigging and the masts, and such objects as are immediately near the spectator. When this particular squall struck the ship it happened that the Red Lily's cabin was on the weather side, and so suddenly did the ship heel over that Lily narrowly escaped being thrown from her bunk. Although this was not her first experience of a squall at night she felt unusually alarmed, for the vessel was lying over at such an unusual angle, and there was so much noise on deck.

Hastily throwing on a few articles of clothing, and covering them with a dressing-gown, she encased her feet in slippers, and rushed over to her mother's cabin, which was on the lee side. Undisturbed by the shock Mrs Hetherington was sleeping soundly, and so, not wishing to wake her, the first impression of alarm having passed away, Lily closed the cabin door gently, and then went up the companion way and peeped out into the darkness. The white waters were flying past, and the vessel was lying over almost to her lee scuppers. Lily stepped on to the deck, holding on to the handle of the companion way door. There was a babel of mingled sounds, and the wind was blowing a perfect hurricane. She had stood there but a few minutes when suddenly she became aware that Cornell was standing beside her. He was superintending the stowing of the mizzen to' gallant sail. He was evidently surprised to see her there. She was about to descend again, for his presence brought back all her old fears, when he caught her arm, and with gentle force restrained her.

'This is fortunate,' he said. 'The opportunity I have longed for this squall has at last given me.'

'Let me go,' she exclaimed, 'or I will scream.' She was trembling with fear and excitement, but he still held her.

'You dare not,' he answered in a strange tone. Then, after a pause, he added, 'You have been cruel to me, but you must be so no longer or I shall die. I cannot live without you.'

'Are you mad?' she said with a shudder.

'Perhaps I am. If I am you have made me so.' He passed his arm round her waist and held her closely.

She struggled to free herself, but she was powerless in his strong grasp. The mysterious influence he exercised over her now kept her tongue tied so that she could not scream, could not cry out. He bent low and pressed his lips to hers, and yet that did not break the spell which bound her.

'You are to be married on Christmas Day,' he said in a whisper. 'I hope before then *he* or I will be dead. If I live you shall become *my* wife. Do you hear? my wife. You may think I am talking mere words, but you will see.'

He released her and she found herself in her cabin. How she got down she did not know. She was burning with indignation and shame. His polluting lips had touched hers, and she shivered as she thought of it. She rubbed her lips with her handkerchief as though he had left some stain which she was trying to wipe away. She yearned to go at once to Fenton's cabin and tell him all, but a deadly fear of Cornell withheld her, the spell of his extraordinary power was upon her, and she felt that she *dare not* open her mouth to tell aught of what had occurred. The man's influence, whatever it was, was paramount. She feared and hated him, and yet dare not denounce him. Of course she was weak, but then he was no ordinary man. His strength of will was enormous, and subdued her.

During the rest of the night she could not sleep, and she longed for Christmas Day to come, so that, as Dick's wife, she might be free from the persecutions of the mysterious Cornell.

When the morning broke the storm had died away, leaving a gentle wind that wafted the ship along at about eight knots an hour.

'We shall have steady weather now,' the captain observed at breakfast time, as he examined the barometer that swung over the cabin table.

His prognostication proved correct. The wind increased day by day until it was blowing a strong gale, but as it was favourable a large spread of canvas was carried upon the ship.

The day preceding Christmas Day arrived; the *Sirocco* was in the Bay of Biscay, off the inhospitable Cape Finisterre. By Christmas Eve the wind had increased very much, so that the ship was 'snugged down'. Extra look-outs were kept, for a great number of outward and homeward bound vessels were in the Bay. The night promised to be a very 'dirty one', but there was merriment on board, and many a toast to 'Sweethearts and Wives' was drunk, both in the cabin and in the forecastle, for a liberal allowance of grog had been served out to the crew.

The preparations for the wedding were all complete. The saloon was gaily decorated, and it was arranged that the marriage ceremony was to be performed at eleven o'clock in the morning. But before eleven o'clock strange things were to happen.

The night waned, and as eight bells sounded Dick Fenton went on deck to smoke a cigar before turning in. The ladies had all retired, and only a single night lamp burned in the saloon. The wind had drawn ahead a good deal, and the vessel could only carry close-reefed main-top-sail and fore-topsail, so that she was making very little way, simply 'forging', as sailors say, at the rate of about two knots an hour. A favourite seat with Dick when he went on deck to smoke his cigar was on the rail near the mizzen shrouds. There he was under the shelter of the captain's gig, which was slung outside on davits, and his feet rested on a hen coop that ran along the poop. Sitting there now pensively dreaming of his Red Lily, and the happiness that awaited him on the morrow when she would become his wife, he had no thought of danger. There was music in the rush of the wild waters and the screaming sweep of the wind. The vessel had that short, jerky motion which a ship has in a rough sea when under reefed topsails.

Suddenly there rose up before Dick's vision the dark figure of a man.

'Hallo! is that you, captain?' exclaimed Dick.

'No,' was the answer, and in the gruff voice Dick recognized the second mate.

'Oh, it's you, Cornell,' he said. 'This is a wild night. Do you think the wind will free at all before the morning?'

'It may, and may not,' was the somewhat surly answer, and in the husky tones Cornell betrayed that he was the worse for liquor. 'I suppose you were thinking of the Red Lily,' he remarked.

'Really, Mr Cornell, you are a little familiar,' Dick said, not unkindly, for he was willing to make every allowance at such a time.

'Bah, why am I familiar?' sneered the second mate. 'I suppose the night before his marriage every man thinks of the woman who is to be his wife.'

'I suppose he does,' Dick answered curtly, for he was not anxious to prolong the conversation seeing the strange humour Cornell was in.

'You have quite made up your mind that she is to be your wife?' asked Cornell.

'Well, please God that nothing happens between now and the morning, Miss Hetherington will certainly become Mrs Fenton.'

'But it is destined that *something* shall happen,' Cornell exclaimed, 'and you will never see the morrow.'

The words were spoken rapidly, and with a lightning-like movement he threw the whole weight of his body against Dick, who, unprepared for such an assault, was pressed backwards, and falling between the boat and the side of the vessel was lost in the dark, hissing waters.

'A man overboard!' cried the second mate with all the power of his lusty lungs, and instantly the dreadful cry was taken up, and the watch came rushing aft. The captain, who was in his cabin, tore on deck, and in a moment all was confusion.

'Who is it, who is it?' exclaimed the captain.

'Mr Fenton, I think, for I saw him sitting on the rail a few minutes before,' said Cornell.

'Clear away the boat, men, quick!' cried the captain. Then he and Cornell cut away life buoys and cast them into the sea.

'I will try and save him, sir,' said Cornell, as he divested himself of his heavy sea boots and his oil skins.

Divining his motives the captain laid hold of his arm and said:

'Are you mad, man? It is enough that one life should be sacrificed.' But Cornell, making no reply, shook himself free, mounted the rail, and dived headlong into the black waters.

The excitement was now intense. Everyone on board knew what had happened, but everyone did not know that it was Dick who had gone. The Red Lily was in this state of blissful ignorance, though she with the other ladies crowded up the companion way, and waited in breathless and painful anxiety.

The boat was manned and lowered. Lamps were brought and held up so as to throw a light as far as possible over the sea. The boat was away about an hour. It was a fearful agony of suspense that hour. The ship was hove to, and everything done that could be done. The searchers returned at last, bringing with them the second mate in an exhausted condition, but not Dick; he had gone, and as nothing more could be done, sail was again set, and the Sirocco went upon her way with one soul less.

Christmas morning dawned. The gaiety was changed to sorrow, and the marriage decorations were taken down and signs of mourning appeared.

Tenderly and gently the sad news was broken to the Red Lily, and those who told her did not fail to tell how 'nobly' the second mate had risked his life to try and save that of her lover. Tenderly as the news was broken, the shock stunned her, and for days she lay in a state of partial coma. But there were loving hands to tend, and loving voices to soothe, and gradually she came round. All the sunshine, however, seemed to have gone out of her nature, and she was a crushed woman.

For the first time for many days she went on deck, and was propped with pillows in a sofa-chair, and for the first time since that terrible night she saw Cornell. All her feeling of revulsion for him had changed, and, stretching forth her white hand to him, she said in her loving, sweet voice:

'Mr Cornell, I have been unjust to you. You must forgive me. You are a brave and generous man.'

He took her hand and answered:

'I grieve with you, Miss Hetherington. I did my best to save him, but it was not to be. No man can prevent his fate. It is not for me to say why, at such a moment, your lover should have met his doom. It was Destiny; but, though I battled with the waves and the darkness of the night, it was not my destiny to drown.'

Lily shuddered. The man spoke so strangely. There was such a weird appearance about him, and his influence over her was as strong as ever. And yet a fearful thought came to her. Was it not probable that Cornell had hurled her lover into the sea, and then, seized with sudden remorse, had dived after him?

Oh, how that dreadful thought troubled and pained her! She struggled with it for days, and wept and wept and wept again. At one moment she resolved to take her mother into her confidence, and tell her all. But whenever this feeling came upon her the mysterious Cornell seemed to be at her side, and then all her will power went again. She felt that she hated him one moment, but the next she could and would have grovelled at his feet, overcome by a curious fascination, mingled with a sort of admiration, for the daring, reckless, wicked, iron-willed fellow.

A week later the ship was in the London docks.

Lily and her mother went on shore at Gravesend. The poor girl was bowed with sorrow, and she felt as though she would never again hold up her head. Before she left the ship Cornell begged hard to be allowed to call upon her. She wanted to refuse him, but could not, and, with the consent of her mother, she gave him permission to do so, for the mother felt she was indebted to him.

Lily and Mrs Hetherington went to reside in the West End of London, and Cornell, availing himself of their permission, was almost a daily visitor. He announced his intention of not going to sea again for some time, and the old fascination he had exercised over Lily was exerted now to a greater degree; and though she was sure she possessed no love for him, she felt drawn towards him in a strange manner. One day, four months after their arrival home, he pressed her to become his wife, and she reluctantly gave her consent. She would have said 'No' if she could, but she was powerless; and believing that she had previously misjudged him and done him a wrong, she said:

'I will be a dutiful and faithful wife to you, but you must never hope to win my love. *That* is buried in the cruel sea.'

It was arranged that the wedding was to take place in a few months' time. He objected to the delay, but she was firm on the point, for she felt that it would not be respectful to her dead love to marry so soon after the calamity. Many a girl who knew Lily and her lover envied her. Cornell was so 'handsome', so 'fascinating', so 'manly', 'such a splendid type of a sailor'; but when her friends congratulated her she only sighed. She felt as if she were sacrificing herself; but then her affianced husband had so nobly risked his life for her lover's sake, notwithstanding his previous strange conduct, and on that account alone she was going to give him her hand. She little dreamed that his jumping overboard was only part of his diabolical plan, and was meant to avert suspicion—which it did most effectually. So far as the risk to himself was concerned, it was reduced to a minimum, for he was a magnificent and powerful swimmer, and before he took the leap he was careful to see that plenty of life buoys had been dropped over, and that the boat was all ready for lowering.

In the course of the next few months Mrs Hetherington and her daughter removed to the village of Bowness, on the banks of Winder-mere, as they had friends living there; and it was arranged that the marriage should take place in the parish church of that place.

The wedding day came. It was a glorious summer's morning, and the air was filled with the music of birds and the scent of flowers. The wedding was to be very quiet, and but few guests had been invited. Those who knew Lily well said that the 'Red Lily had drooped.' All the brightness was out of her life, for she felt that her heart was beneath the waves of the Bay of Biscay.

The wedding party had assembled in the church, and the ceremony had commenced. When the grey-haired clergyman asked if anyone knew any just cause or impediment why the man and woman should not be joined together in the bonds of holy matrimony, there rose up a man in the body of the church, and in a loud and steady voice exclaimed:

'I forbid this marriage.'

Had a thunderbolt fallen through the roof the consternation and confusion could not have been greater. With a great cry the Red Lily threw up her arms, and then fell forward on her face in a swoon. For a few moments Cornell stood as if petrified. His face was ghastly pale. By this time the man had come forward to the altar rails, and then Cornell found tongue.

'Good God!' he exclaimed, 'is it possible that the dead can come to life?'

'No; but the living can thwart the machinations of a villain, and I am here to do that,' said Dick Fenton, for he it was. 'This man,' continued Dick, addressing the astonished spectators, 'attempted to murder me.'

No one moved. They were dumb with amazement, for they naturally thought a madman was amongst them. Dick himself stooped and lifted up the inanimate form of the Lily, and bore her into the vestry. Taking advantage of the confusion—for everyone seemed bewildered—Cornell stole from the church, got clear away, and was never heard of more.

It was some time before Lily recovered consciousness. It is better to leave the reunion of the lovers to the imagination of the reader, for words always fail to convey anything like an adequate notion of such a scene. The news of the affair had rapidly spread over the village; an enormous crowd had gathered about the church, and the uproar was immense. The wedding party had to wait a considerable time before they could get back to their homes; then explanations were given.

On that dreadful night in the Bay of Biscay Dick had escaped death almost by a miracle, as it were. He was a good swimmer, but was a little stunned by striking his head against the side of the vessel in his descent. He had a recollection, however, of making a powerful effort to swim, and in a little while he felt something touch his hand, and found it was a life buoy. On this he supported himself for a long time—it seemed to him two or three hours. Then he saw the outlines of a vessel, which he took to be the *Sirocco*, and he shouted with all his might, and presently had the satisfaction to hear the plash of oars. He had only a faint recollection of hearing a human voice, and feeling the grasp of hands about him. Then ensued a blank. When next he opened his eyes he found himself in a comfortable cabin, and he soon learnt that it was not the *Sirocco* that had picked him up, but an outward bound ship, called the *Golden Fleece*. She was bound for the Cape, and so Dick was mortified to find that he must accompany her there, unless a homeward bounder should be fallen in with, and he could get on board. This chance did not occur, and so to the Cape he went, but the vessel made a long voyage. As soon after arrival as possible he took ship for England, and on reaching there he soon discovered to his amazement that the Red Lily was on the eve of being married to Cornell. He hurried down to the Lake district, and was there a whole week determining not to declare himself until the last moment, so that the discomfiture of his enemy might be the more complete.

For some months after this strange and startling incident Lily remained in such delicate health that grave fears were at one time entertained. Sudden joy is almost as bad as great sorrow at times, and the unexpected return of her lost lover had been too great a shock. Care, attention, and change of air, however, gradually restored her, and again she made preparations for her marriage, which was to take place on Christmas Day, twelve months after the terrible scene in the Bay of Biscay, when Dick was hurled into the sea.

The day came at last—cold, crisp, and bright. The earth was wrapped in a robe of spotless white, and the church was decorated with holly and winter flowers. As the bells pealed forth merrily, and the winter sun shone out from the dull sky, Dick Fenton led his bride down the pathway to the carriage that waited them at the gate, and the crowd of villagers that had gathered in the old churchyard declared that no bonnier bride had ever been seen than the Red Lily.

THE BLACK BAG
LEFT ON
A DOORSTEP

C.L. Pirkis

The amazing and worldwide success of Sherlock
Holmes quickly brought a large number of
detectives in his wake, solving numerous crimes
in the pages of popular monthly magazines,
which were often reprinted in book form. One
of the best—the earliest—female detectives was
Loveday Brooke, whose exploits were described
by novelist Mrs Catherine Louisa Pirkis
(1841–1910) in the *Ludgate* magazine during
1893 and collected as *The Experiences of Loveday
Brooke: Lady Detective* (Hutchinson, 1894). Mrs
Pirkis was an enthusiastic humanitarian and
antivivisectionist, and one of the founders of the
National Canine Defence League in Britain.

'It's a big thing,' said Loveday Brooke, addressing Ebenezer Dyer, chief of the well-known detective agency in Lynch Court, Fleet Street; 'Lady Cathrow has lost £30,000 worth of jewellery, if the newspaper accounts are to be trusted.'

'They are fairly accurate this time. The robbery differs in few respects from the usual run of country-house robberies. The time chosen, of course, was the dinner-hour, when the family and guests were at table and the servants not on duty were amusing themselves in their own quarters. The fact of its being Christmas Eve would also of necessity add to the busyness and consequent distraction of the household. The entry to the house, however, in this case was not effected in the usual manner by a ladder to the dressing-room window, but through the window of a room on the ground floor—a small room with one window and two doors, one of which opens into the hall, and the other into a passage that leads by the back stairs to the bedroom floor. It is used, I believe, as a sort of hat and coat room by the gentlemen of the house.'

'It was, I suppose, the weak point of the house?'

'Quite so. A very weak point indeed. Craigen Court, the residence of Sir George and Lady Cathrow, is an oddly built old place, jutting out in all directions, and as this window looked out upon a blank wall, it was filled in with stained glass, kept fastened by a strong brass catch, and never opened, day or night, ventilation being obtained by means of a glass ventilator fitted in the upper panes. It seems absurd to think that this window, being only about four feet from the ground, should have had neither iron bars nor shutters added to it; such, however, was the case. On the night of the robbery, someone within the house must have deliberately, and of intention, unfastened its only protection, the brass catch, and thus given the thieves easy entrance to the house.'

'Your suspicions, I suppose, centre upon the servants?'

'Undoubtedly; and it is in the servants' hall that your services will be required. The thieves, whoever they were, were perfectly cognizant of the ways of the house. Lady Cathrow's jewellery was kept in a safe in her dressing-room, and as the dressing-room was over the dining-room, Sir George was in the habit of saying that it was the "safest" room in the house. (Note the pun, please, Sir George is rather proud of it.) By his orders the window of the dining-room immediately under the dressing-room window was always left unshuttered and without blind during dinner, and as a full stream of light thus fell through it on to the outside terrace, it would have been impossible for anyone to have placed a ladder there unseen.'

'I see from the newspapers that it was Sir George's invariable custom to fill his house and give a large dinner on Christmas Eve.'

'Yes. Sir George and Lady Cathrow are elderly people, with no family and few relatives, and have consequently a large amount of time to spend on their friends.'

'I suppose the key of the safe was frequently left in the possession of Lady Cathrow's maid?'

'Yes. She is a young French girl, Stephanie Delcroix by name. It was her duty to clear the dressing-room directly after her mistress left it: put away any jewellery that might be lying about, lock the safe, and keep the key till her mistress came up to bed. On the night of the robbery, however, she admits that, instead of so doing, directly her mistress left the dressing-room, she ran down to the housekeeper's room to see if any letters had come for her, and remained chatting with the other servants for some time—she could not say for how long. It was by the half-past-seven post that her letters generally arrived from St Omer, where her home is.'

'Oh, then, she was in the habit of thus running down to enquire for her letters, no doubt, and the thieves, who appear to be so thoroughly cognizant of the house, would know this also.'

'Perhaps; though at the present moment I must say things look very black against the girl. Her manner, too, when questioned, is not calculated to remove suspicion. She goes from one fit of hysterics into another; contradicts herself nearly every time she opens her mouth, then lays it to the charge of her ignorance of our language; breaks into voluble French; becomes theatrical in action, and then goes off into hysterics once more.'

'All that is quite Français, you know,' said Loveday. 'Do the authorities at Scotland Yard lay much stress on the safe being left unlocked that night?'

'They do, and they are instituting a keen enquiry as to the possible lovers the girl may have. For this purpose they have sent Bates down to stay in the village and collect all the information he can outside the house. But they want someone within the walls to hob-nob with the maids generally, and to find out if she has taken any of them into her confidence respecting her lovers. So they sent to me to know if I would send down for this purpose one of the shrewdest and most clear-headed of my female detectives. I, in my turn, Miss Brooke, have sent for you— you may take it as a compliment if you like. So please now get out your notebook, and I'll give you sailing orders.'

Loveday Brooke, at this period of her career, was a little over thirty years of age, and could be best described in a series of negations.

She was not tall, she was not short; she was not dark, she was not fair; she was neither handsome nor ugly. Her features were altogether nondescript; her one noticeable trait was a habit she had, when absorbed in thought, of dropping her eyelids over her eyes till only a line of eyeball showed, and she appeared to be looking out at the world through a slit, instead of through a window.

Her dress was invariably black, and was almost Quaker-like in its neat primness.

Some five or six years previously, by a jerk of Fortune's wheel, Loveday had been thrown upon the world penniless and all but friendless. Marketable accomplishments she had found she had none, so she had forthwith defied convention, and had chosen for herself a career that had cut her off sharply from her former associates and her position in society. For five or six years she drudged away patiently in the lower walks of her profession; then chance, or, to speak more precisely, an intricate criminal case, threw her in the way of the experienced head of the flourishing detective agency in Lynch Court. He quickly enough found out the stuff she was made of, and threw her in the way of better-class work—work, indeed, that brought increase of pay and of reputation alike to him and to Loveday.

Ebenezer Dyer was not, as a rule, given to enthusiasm; but he would at times wax eloquent over Miss Brooke's qualifications for the profession she had chosen.

'Too much of a lady, do you say?' he would say to anyone who chanced to call in question those qualifications. 'I don't care two-pence-halfpenny whether she is or is not a lady. I only know she is the most sensible and practical woman I ever met. In the first place, she has the faculty—so rare among women—of carrying out orders to the very letter; in the second place, she has a clear, shrewd brain, unhampered by any hard-and-fast theories; thirdly, and most important item of all, she has so much common sense that it amounts to genius—positively to genius, sir.'

But although Loveday and her chief as a rule worked together upon an easy and friendly footing, there were occasions on which they were wont, so to speak, to snarl at each other.

Such an occasion was at hand now.

Loveday showed no disposition to take out her notebook and receive her 'sailing orders'.

'I want to know,' she said, 'if what I saw in one newspaper is true—that one of the thieves before leaving, took the trouble to close the safe door, and to write across it in chalk: 'To be let, unfurnished?'

'Perfectly true; but I do not see that stress need be laid on the fact. The scoundrels often do that sort of thing out of insolence or bravado. In that robbery at Reigate, the other day, they went to a lady's Davenport, took a sheet of her notepaper, and wrote their thanks on it for her kindness in not having had the lock of her safe repaired. Now, if you will get out your note-book—'

'Don't be in such a hurry,' said Loveday calmly; 'I want to know if you have seen this?' She leaned across the writing table at which they sat, one either side, and handed to him a newspaper cutting which she took from her letter-case.

Mr Dyer was a tall, powerfully built man with a large head, benevolent bald forehead and a genial smile. That smile, however, often proved a trap to the unwary, for he owned a temper so irritable that a child with a chance word might ruffle it.

The genial smile vanished as he took the newspaper cutting from Loveday's hand.

'I would have you to remember, Miss Brooke,' he said severely, 'that although I am in the habit of using despatch in my business, I am never known to be in a hurry; hurry in affairs I take to be the especial mark of the slovenly and unpunctual.'

Then, as if still further to give contradiction to her words, he very deliberately unfolded her slip of newspaper and slowly, accentuating each word and syllable, read as follows:—

'Singular Discovery.

'A black leather bag, or portmanteau, was found early yesterday morning by one of Smith's newspaper boys on the doorstep of a house in the road running between Easterbrook and Wreford, and inhabited by an elderly spinster lady. The contents of the bag include a clerical collar and necktie, a Church Service, a book of sermons, a copy of the works of Virgil, a facsimile of Magna Carta, with translations, a pair of black kid gloves, a brush and comb, some newspapers, and several small articles suggesting clerical ownership. On the top of the bag the following extraordinary letter, written in pencil on a long slip of paper, was found: "The fatal day has arrived. I can exist no longer. I go hence and shall be no more seen. But I would have Coroner and Jury know that I am a sane man, and a verdict of temporary insanity in my case would be an error most gross after this intimation. I care not if it is *felo de se*, as I shall have passed all suffering. Search diligently for my poor lifeless body in the immediate neighbourhood—on the cold heath, the rail, or the river by yonder bridge—a few moments will decide how I shall depart. If I had walked aright I might have been a power in the Church of which I am now an unworthy member and priest; but the damnable sin of gambling got hold on me, and betting has been my ruin, as it has been the ruin of thousands who have preceded me. Young man, shun the bookmaker and the racecourse as you would shun the devil and hell. Farewell, chums of Magdalen. Farewell, and take warning. Though I can claim relationship

[181]

with a Duke, a Marquess, and a Bishop, and though I am the son of a noble woman, yet am I a tramp and an outcast, verily and indeed. Sweet death, I greet thee. I dare not sign my name. To one and all, farewell. O, my poor Marchioness mother, a dying kiss to thee. RIP."

'The police and some of the railway officials have made a "diligent search" in the neighbourhood of the railway station, but no "poor lifeless body" has been found. The police authorities are inclined to the belief that the letter is a hoax, though they are still investigating the matter.'

In the same deliberate fashion as he had opened and read the cutting, Mr Dyer folded and returned it to Loveday.

'May I ask,' he said sarcastically, 'what you see in that silly hoax to waste your and my valuable time over?'

'I wanted to know,' said Loveday, in the same level tones as before, 'if you saw anything in it that might in some way connect this discovery with the robbery at Craigen Court?'

Mr Dyer stared at her in utter, blank astonishment.

'When I was a boy,' he said sarcastically as before, 'I used to play at a game called "what is my thought like?" Someone would think of something absurd—say the top of the monument—and someone else would hazard a guess that his thought might be—say the toe of his left boot, and that unfortunate individual would have to show the connection between the toe of his left boot and the top of the monument. Miss Brooke, I have no wish to repeat the silly game this evening for your benefit and mine.'

'Oh, very well,' said Loveday, calmly; 'I fancied you might like to talk it over, that was all. Give me my "sailing orders", as you call them, and I'll endeavour to concentrate my attention on the little French maid and her various lovers.'

Mr Dyer grew amiable again.

'That's the point on which I wish you to fix your thoughts,' he said, 'you had better start for Craigen Court by the first train tomorrow—it's about sixty miles down the Great Eastern line. Huxwell is the station you must land at. There one of the grooms from the Court will meet you, and drive you to the house. I have arranged with the housekeeper there—Mrs Williams, a very worthy and discreet person—that you shall pass in the house for a niece of hers, on a visit to recruit, after severe study in order to pass board-school teachers' exams. Naturally you have injured your eyes as well as your health with overwork; and so you can wear your blue spectacles. Your name, by the way, will be Jane Smith—better write it down. All your work will lie among the servants of the establishment, and there will be no necessity for you to see either Sir George or Lady Cathrow—in fact, neither of them have been appraised of your intended visit—the fewer we take into our confidence the better. I've no doubt, however, that Bates will hear from Scotland Yard that you are in the house, and will make a point of seeing you.'

'Has Bates unearthed anything of importance?'

'Not as yet. He has discovered one of the girl's lovers, a young farmer of the name of Holt; but as he seems to be an honest, respectable young fellow, and entirely above suspicion, the discovery does not count for much.'

'I think there's nothing else to ask,' said Loveday, rising to take her departure. 'Of course, I'll telegraph, should the need arise, in our usual cipher.'

The first train that left Bishopsgate for Huxwell on the following morning included, among its passengers, Loveday Brooke, dressed in the neat black supposed to be appropriate to servants of the upper class. The only literature with which she had provided herself in order to beguile the tedium of her journey was a small volume bound in paper boards, and entitled, 'The Reciter's Treasury'. It was published at the low price of one shilling, and seemed specially designed to meet the requirements of third-rate amateur reciters at penny readings.

Miss Brooke appeared to be all-absorbed in the contents of this book during the first half of her journey. During the second, she lay back in the carriage with closed eyes, and motionless as if asleep or lost in deep thought.

The stopping of the train at Huxwell aroused her, and set her collecting together her wraps.

It was easy to single out the trim groom from Craigen Court from among the country loafers on the platform. Someone else beside the trim groom at the same moment caught her eye—Bates, from Scotland Yard got up in the style of a commercial traveller, and carrying the orthodox 'commercial bag' in his hand. He was a small, wiry man, with red hair and whiskers, and an eager, hungry expression of countenance.

'I am half-frozen with cold,' said Loveday, addressing Sir George's groom; 'if you'll kindly take charge of my portmanteau, I'd prefer walking to driving to the Court.'

The man gave her a few directions as to the road she was to follow, and then drove off with her box, leaving her free to indulge Mr Bates' evident wish for a walk and confidential talk along the country road.

Bates seemed to be in a happy frame of mind that morning.

'Quite a simple affair, this, Miss Brooke,' he said; 'a walk over the course, I take it, with you working inside the castle walls and I unearthing without. No complications as yet have arisen, and if that girl does not find herself in jail before another week is over her head, my name is not Jeremiah Bates.'

'You mean the French maid?'

'Why, yes, of course. I take it there's little doubt but what she performed the double duty of unlocking the safe and the window too. You see I look at it this way, Miss Brooke: all girls have lovers, I say to myself, but a pretty girl like that French maid, is bound to have double the number of lovers than the plain ones. Now, of course, the greater the number of lovers, the greater chance there is of a criminal being found among them. That's plain as a pikestaff, isn't it?'

'Just as plain.'

Bates felt encouraged to proceed.

'Well, then arguing on the same lines, I say to myself, this girl is only a pretty, silly thing, not an accomplished criminal, or she wouldn't have admitted leaving open the safe door; give her rope enough and she'll hang herself. In a day or two, if we let her alone, she'll be bolting off to join the fellow whose nest she has helped to feather, and we shall catch the pair of them 'twixt here and Dover Straits, and also possibly get a clue that will bring us on the traces of their accomplices. Eh, Miss Brooke, that'll be a thing worth doing?'

'Undoubtedly. Who is this coming along in this buggy at such a good pace?'

The question was added as the sound of wheels behind them made her look round.

Bates turned also. 'Oh, this is young Holt; his father farms land about a couple of miles from here. He is one of Stephanie's lovers, and I should imagine about the best of the lot. But he does not appear to be first favourite; from what I hear someone else must have made the running on the sly. Ever since the robbery I'm told the young woman has given him the cold shoulder.'

As the young man came nearer in his buggy he slackened his pace, and Loveday could not but admire his frank, honest expression of countenance.

'Room for one—can I give you a lift?' he said, as he came alongside of them.

And to the ineffable disgust of Bates, who had counted upon at least an hour's confidential talk with her, Miss Brooke accepted the young farmer's offer, and mounted beside him in his buggy.

As they went swiftly along the country road, Loveday explained to the young man that her destination was Craigen Court, and that as she was a stranger to the place, she must trust to him to put her down at the nearest point to it that he would pass.

At the mention of Craigen Court his face clouded.

'They're in trouble there, and their trouble has brought trouble on others,' he said a little bitterly.

'I know,' said Loveday sympathetically; 'it is often so. In such circumstances as these suspicion frequently fastens on an entirely innocent person.'

'That's it! that's it!' he cried excitedly; 'if you go into that house you'll hear all sorts of wicked things said of her, and see everything setting in dead against her. But she's innocent. I swear to you she is as innocent as you or I are.'

His voice rang out above the clatter of his horse's hoofs. He seemed to forget that he had mentioned no name, and that Loveday, as a stranger, might be at a loss to know to whom he referred.

'Who is guilty Heaven only knows,' he went on after a moment's pause; 'it isn't for me to give an ill name to anyone in that house; but I only say she is innocent, and that I'll stake my life on.'

'She is a lucky girl to have found one to believe in her, and trust her as you do,' said Loveday, even more sympathetically than before.

'Is she? I wish she'd take advantage of her luck, then,' he answered bitterly. 'Most girls in her position would be glad to have a man to stand by them through thick and thin. But not she! Ever since the night of that accursed robbery she has refused to see me—won't answer my letters— won't even send me a message. And, great Heavens! I'd marry her tomorrow, if I had the chance, and dare the world to say a word against her.'

He whipped up his pony. The hedges seemed to fly on either side of them, and before Loveday realized that half her drive was over, he had drawn rein, and was helping her to alight at the servants' entrance to Craigen Court.

'You'll tell her what I've said to you, if you get the opportunity, and beg her to see me, if only for five minutes?' he petitioned before he remounted his buggy. And Loveday, as she thanked the young man for his kind attention, promised to make an opportunity to give his message to the girl.

Mrs Williams, the housekeeper, welcomed Loveday in the servants' hall, and then took her to her own room to pull off her wraps. Mrs Williams was the widow of a London tradesman, and a little beyond the average housekeeper in speech and manner.

She was a genial, pleasant woman, and readily entered into conversation with Loveday. Tea was brought in, and each seemed to feel at home with the other. Loveday in the course of this easy, pleasant talk, elicited from her the whole history of the events of the day of the robbery, the number and names of the guests who sat down to dinner that night, together with some other apparently trivial details.

The housekeeper made no attempt to disguise the painful position in which she and every one of the servants of the house felt themselves to be at the present moment.

'We are none of us at our ease with each other now,' she said, as she poured out hot tea for Loveday, and piled up a blazing fire. 'Everyone fancies that everyone else is suspecting him or her, and trying to rake up past words or deeds to bring in as evidence. The whole house seems under a cloud. And at this time of year, too; just when everything as a rule is at its merriest!' and here she gave a doleful glance to the big bunch of holly and mistletoe hanging from the ceiling.

'I suppose you are generally very merry downstairs at Christmas time?' said Loveday. 'Servants' balls, theatricals, and all that sort of thing?'

'I should think we were! When I think of this time last year and the fun we all had, I can scarcely believe it is the same house. Our ball always follows my lady's ball, and we have permission to ask our friends to it, and we keep it up as late as ever we please. We begin our evening meal with a concert and recitations in character, then we have a supper and then we dance right on till morning; but this year!'—she broke off, giving a long, melancholy shake of her head that spoke volumes.

'I suppose,' said Loveday, 'some of your friends are very clever as musicians or reciters?'

'Very clever indeed. Sir George and my lady are always present during the early part of the evening, and I should like you to have seen Sir George last year laughing fit to kill himself at Harry Emmett dressed in prison dress with a bit of oakum in his hand, reciting the "Noble Convict!" Sir George said if the young man had gone on the stage, he would have been bound to make his fortune.'

'Half a cup, please,' said Loveday, presenting her cup. 'Who was this Harry Emmett then—a sweetheart of one of the maids?'

'Oh, he would flirt with them all, but he was sweetheart to none. He was footman to Colonel James, who is a great friend of Sir George's, and Harry was constantly backwards and forwards bringing messages from his master. His father, I think, drove a cab in London, and Harry for a time did so also; then he took it into his head to be a gentleman's servant, and great satisfaction he gave as such. He was always such a bright, handsome young fellow and so full of fun, that everyone liked him. But I shall tire you with all this; and you, of course, want to talk about something so different;' and the housekeeper sighed again, as the thought of the dreadful robbery entered her brain once more.

'Not at all. I am greatly interested in you and your festivities. Is Emmett still in the neighbourhood? I should amazingly like to hear him recite myself.'

'I'm sorry to say he left Colonel James about six months ago. We all missed him very much at first. He was a good, kind-hearted young man, and I remember he told me he was going away to look after his dear old grandmother, who had a sweetstuff shop somewhere or other, but where I can't remember.'

Loveday was leaning back in her chair now, with eyelids drooped so low that she literally looked out through 'slits' instead of eyes.

Suddenly and abruptly she changed the conversation.

'When will it be convenient for me to see Lady Cathrow's dressing-room?' she asked.

The housekeeper looked at her watch. 'Now, at once,' she answered; 'it's a quarter to five now and my lady sometimes goes up to her room to rest for half an hour before she dresses for dinner.'

'Is Stephanie still in attendance on Lady Cathrow?' Miss Brooke asked as she followed the housekeeper up the back stairs to the bedroom floor.

'Yes, Sir George and my lady have been goodness itself to us through this trying time, and they say we are all innocent till we are proved guilty, and will have it that none of our duties are to be in any way altered.'

'Stephanie is scarcely fit to perform hers, I should imagine?'

'Scarcely. She was in hysterics nearly from morning till night for the first two or three days after the detectives came down, but now she has grown sullen, eats nothing and never speaks a word to any of us except when she is obliged. This is my lady's dressing-room, walk in please.'

Loveday entered a large, luxuriously furnished room, and naturally

[187]

made her way straight to the chief point of attraction in it—the iron safe fitted into the wall that separated the dressing-room from the bedroom.

It was a safe of the ordinary description, fitted with a strong iron door and Chubb lock. And across this door was written with chalk in characters that seemed defiant in their size and boldness, the words: 'To be let, unfurnished.'

Loveday spent about five minutes in front of this safe, all her attention concentrated upon the big, bold writing.

She took from her pocket-book a narrow strip of tracing paper and compared the writing on it, letter by letter, with that on the safe door. This done she turned to Mrs Williams and professed herself ready to follow her to the room below.

Mrs Williams looked surprised. Her opinion of Miss Brooke's professional capabilities suffered considerable diminution.

'The gentlemen detectives,' she said, 'spent over an hour in this room; they paced the floor, they measured the candles, they—'

'Mrs Williams,' interrupted Loveday, 'I am quite ready to look at the room below.' Her manner had changed from gossiping friendliness to that of the business woman hard at work at her profession.

Without another word, Mrs Williams led the way to the little room which had proved itself to be the 'weak point' of the house.

They entered it by the door which opened into a passage leading to the back-stairs of the house. Loveday found the room exactly what it had been described to her by Mr Dyer. It needed no second glance at the window to see the ease with which anyone could open it from the outside, and swing themselves into the room, when once the brass catch had been unfastened.

Loveday wasted no time here. In fact, much to Mrs Williams's surprise and disappointment, she merely walked across the room, in at one door and out at the opposite one, which opened into the large inner hall of the house.

Here, however, she paused to ask a question:

'Is that chair always placed exactly in that position?' she said, pointing to an oak chair that stood immediately outside the room they had just quitted.

The housekeeper answered in the affirmative. It was a warm corner. 'My lady' was particular that everyone who came to the house on messages should have a comfortable place to wait in.

'I shall be glad if you will show me to my room now,' said Loveday, a

[188]

little abruptly; 'and will you kindly send up to me a county trade directory, if, that is, you have such a thing in the house?'

Mrs Williams, with an air of offended dignity, led the way to the bedroom quarters once more. The worthy housekeeper felt as if her own dignity had, in some sort, been injured by the want of interest Miss Brooke had evinced in the rooms which, at the present moment, she considered the 'show' rooms of the house.

'Shall I send someone to help you unpack?' she asked, a little stiffly, at the door of Loveday's room.

'No, thank you; there will not be much unpacking to do. I must leave here by the first up-train tomorrow morning.'

'Tomorrow morning! Why, I have told everyone you will be here at least a fortnight!'

'Ah, then you must explain that I have been suddenly summoned home by telegram. I'm sure I can trust you to make excuses for me. Do not, however, make them before supper time. I shall like to sit down to that meal with you. I suppose I shall see Stephanie then?'

The housekeeper answered in the affirmative, and went her way, wondering over the strange manners of the lady whom, at first, she had been disposed to consider 'such a nice, pleasant, conversable person!'

At supper time, however, when the upper-servants assembled at what was to them, the pleasantest meal of the day, a great surprise was to greet them.

Stephanie did not take her usual place at table, and a fellow-servant, sent to her room to summon her, returned, saying that the room was empty, and Stephanie was nowhere to be found.

Loveday and Mrs Williams together went to the girl's bedroom. It bore its usual appearance: no packing had been done in it, and, beyond her hat and jacket, the girl appeared to have taken nothing away with her.

On enquiry, it transpired that Stephanie had, as usual, assisted Lady Cathrow to dress for dinner; but after that not a soul in the house appeared to have seen her.

Mrs Williams thought the matter of sufficient importance to be at once reported to her master and mistress; and Sir George, in his turn, promptly despatched a messenger to Mr Bates, at the 'King's Head', to summon him to an immediate consultation.

Loveday despatched a messenger in another direction—to young Mr Holt, at his farm, giving him particulars of the girl's disappearance.

Mr Bates had a brief interview with Sir George in his study, from which he emerged radiant. He made a point of seeing Loveday before he left the Court, sending a special request to her that she would speak to him for a minute in the outside drive.

Loveday put her hat on, and went out to him. She found him almost dancing for glee.

'Told you so! told you so! told you so! Now, didn't I, Miss Brooke?' he exclaimed. 'We'll come upon her traces before morning, never fear. I'm quite prepared. I knew what was in her mind all along. I said to myself, when that girl bolts it will be after she has dressed my lady for dinner—when she has two good clear hours all to herself, and her absence from the house won't be noticed, and when, without much difficulty, she can catch a train leaving Huxwell for Wreford. Well, she'll get to Wreford safe enough; but from Wreford she'll be followed every step of the way she goes. Only yesterday I set a man on there—a keen fellow at this sort of thing—and gave him full directions; and he'll hunt her down to her hole properly. Taken nothing with her, do you say? What does that matter? She thinks she'll find all she wants where she's going—"the feathered nest"? I spoke to you about this morning. Ha! ha! Well, instead of stepping into it, as she fancies she will, she'll walk straight into a detective's arms, and land her pal there into the bargain. There'll be two of them netted before another forty-eight hours are over our heads, or my name's not Jeremiah Bates.'

'What are you going to do now?' asked Loveday, as the man finished his long speech.

'Now! I'm back to the "King's Head" to wait for a telegram from my colleague at Wreford. Once he's got her in front of him he'll give me instructions at what point to meet him. You see, Huxwell being such an out-of-the-way place, and only one train leaving between 7.30 and 10.15, makes us really positive that Wreford must be the girl's destination and relieves my mind from all anxiety on the matter.'

'Does it?' answered Loveday gravely. 'I can see another possible destination for the girl—the stream that runs through the wood we drove past this morning. Good night, Mr Bates, it's cold out here. Of course so soon as you have any news you'll send it up to Sir George.'

The household sat up late that night, but no news was received of Stephanie from any quarter. Mr Bates had impressed upon Sir George the ill-advisability of setting up a hue and cry after the girl that might possibly reach her ears and scare her from joining the person whom he was pleased to designate as her 'pal'.

'We want to follow her silently, Sir George, silently as the shadow follows the man,' he had said grandiloquently, 'and then we shall come upon the two, and I trust upon their booty also.' Sir George in his turn had impressed Mr Bates's wishes upon his household, and if it had not been for Loveday's message, despatched early in the evening to young Holt, not a soul outside the house would have known of Stephanie's disappearance.

Loveday was stirring early the next morning, and the eight o'clock train for Wreford numbered her among its passengers. Before starting, she despatched a telegram to her chief in Lynch Court. It read rather oddly, as follows:—

'Cracker fired. Am just starting for Wreford. Will wire to you from there. L.B.'

Oddly though it might read, Mr Dyer did not need to refer to his cipher book to interpret it. 'Cracker fired' was the easily remembered equivalent for 'clue found' in the detective phraseology of the office.

'Well, she has been quick enough about it this time!' he soliloquised as he speculated in his own mind over what the purport of the next telegram might be.

Half an hour later there came to him a constable from Scotland Yard to tell him of Stephanie's disappearance and the conjectures that were rife on the matter, and he then, not unnaturally, read Loveday's telegram by the light of this information, and concluded that the clue in her hands related to the discovery of Stephanie's whereabouts as well as to that of her guilt.

A telegram received a little later on, however, was to turn this theory upside down. It was, like the former one, worded in the enigmatic language current in the Lynch Court establishment, but as it was a lengthier and more intricate message, it sent Mr Dyer at once to his cipher book.

'Wonderful! She has cut them all out this time!' was Mr Dyer's exclamation as he read and interpreted the final word.

In another ten minutes he had given over his office to the charge of his head clerk for the day, and was rattling along the streets in a hansom in the direction of Bishopsgate Station.

There he was lucky enough to catch a train just starting for Wreford.

'The event of the day,' he muttered, as he settled himself comfortably in a corner seat, 'will be the return journey when she tells me, bit by bit, how she has worked it all out.'

It was not until close upon three o'clock in the afternoon that he arrived at the old-fashioned market town of Wreford. It chanced to be cattle-market day, and the station was crowded with drovers and farmers. Outside the station Loveday was waiting for him, as she had told him in her telegram that she would, in a four-wheeler.

'It's all right,' she said to him as he got in; 'he can't get away, even if he had an idea that we were after him. Two of the local police are waiting outside the house door with a warrant for his arrest, signed by a magistrate. I did not, however, see why the Lynch Court office should not have the credit of the thing, and so telegraphed to you to conduct the arrest.'

They drove through the High Street to the outskirts of the town, where the shops became intermixed with private houses let out in offices. The cab pulled up outside one of these, and two policemen in plain clothes came forward, and touched their hats to Mr Dyer.

'He's in there now, sir, doing his office work,' said one of the men pointing to a door, just within the entrance, on which was painted in black letters, 'The United Kingdom Cab-drivers' Beneficent Association'. 'I hear, however, that this is the last time he will be found there, as a week ago he gave notice to leave.'

As the man finished speaking, a man, evidently of the cab-driving fraternity, came up the steps. He stared curiously at the little group just within the entrance, and then chinking his money in his hand, passed on to the office as if to pay his subscription.

'Will you be good enough to tell Mr Emmett in there,' said Mr Dyer, addressing the man, 'that a gentleman outside wishes to speak with him.'

The man nodded and passed into the office. As the door opened, it disclosed to view an old gentleman seated at a desk apparently writing receipts for money. A little in his rear at his right hand, sat a young and decidedly good-looking man, at a table on which were placed various little piles of silver and pence. The get-up of this young man was gentleman-like, and his manner was affable and pleasant as he responded, with a nod and a smile, to the cab-driver's message.

'I shan't be a minute,' he said to his colleague at the other desk, as he rose and crossed the room towards the door.

But once outside that door it was closed firmly behind him, and he found himself in the centre of three stalwart individuals, one of whom informed him that he held in his hand a warrant for the arrest of Harry Emmett on the charge of complicity in the Craigen Court robbery, and that he had 'better come along quietly, for resistance would be useless.'

Emmett seemed convinced of the latter fact. He grew deadly white for a moment, then recovered himself.

'Will someone have the kindness to fetch my hat and coat,' he said in a lofty manner. 'I don't see why I should be made to catch my death of cold because some other people have seen fit to make asses of themselves.'

His hat and coat were fetched, and he was handed into the cab between the two officials.

'Let me give you a word of warning, young man,' said Mr Dyer, closing the cab door and looking in for a moment through the window at Emmett. 'I don't suppose it's a punishable offence to leave a black bag on an old maid's doorstep, but let me tell you, if it had not been for that black bag you might have got clean off with your spoil.'

Emmett, the irrepressible, had his answer ready. He lifted his hat ironically to Mr Dyer; 'You might have put it more neatly, guv'nor,' he said; 'if I had been in your place I would have said: "Young man, you are being justly punished for your misdeeds; you have been taking off your fellow-creatures all your life long, and now they are taking off you."'

Mr Dyer's duty that day did not end with the depositing of Harry Emmett in the local jail. The search through Emmett's lodgings and effects had to be made, and at this he was naturally present. About a third of the lost jewellery was found there, and from this it was consequently concluded that his accomplices in the crime had considered that he had borne a third of the risk and of the danger of it.

Letters and various memoranda discovered in the rooms, eventually led to the detection of those accomplices, and although Lady Cathrow was doomed to lose the greater part of her valuable property, she had ultimately the satisfaction of knowing that each one of the thieves received a sentence proportionate to his crime.

It was not until close upon midnight that Mr Dyer found himself seated in the train, facing Miss Brooke, and had leisure to ask for the links in the chain of reasoning that had led her in so remarkable a manner to connect the finding of a black bag, with insignificant contents, with an extensive robbery of valuable jewellery.

Loveday explained the whole thing, easily, naturally, step by step in her usual methodical manner.

'I read,' she said, 'as I dare say a great many other people did, the account of the two things in the same newspaper, on the same day, and I detected, as I dare say a great many other people did not, a sense of fun in the principal actor in each incident. I notice while all people are agreed as to the variety of motives that instigate crime, very few allow sufficient margin for variety of character in the criminal. We are apt to imagine that he stalks about the world with a bundle of deadly motives under his arm, and cannot picture him at his work with a twinkle in his eye and a keen sense of fun, such as honest folk have sometimes when at work at their calling.'

Here Mr Dyer gave a little grunt; it might have been either of assent or dissent.

Loveday went on:

'Of course, the ludicrousness of the diction of the letter found in the bag would be apparent to the most casual reader; to me the high falutin' sentences sounded in addition strangely familiar; I had heard or read them somewhere I felt sure, although where I could not at first remember. They rang in my ears, and it was not altogether out of idle curiosity that I went to Scotland Yard to see the bag and its contents, and to copy, with a slip of tracing paper, a line or two of the letter. When I found that the handwriting of this letter was not identical with that of the translations found in the bag, I was confirmed in my impression that the owner of the bag was not the writer of the letter; that possibly the bag and its contents had been appropriated from some railway station for some distinct purpose; and, that purpose accomplished, the appropriator no longer wished to be burdened with it, and disposed of it in the readiest fashion that suggested itself. The letter, it seemed to me, had been begun with the intention of throwing the police off the scent, but the irrepressible spirit of fun that had induced the writer to deposit his clerical adjuncts upon the old maid's doorstep had proved too strong for him here, and had carried him away, and the letter that was intended to be pathetic ended in being comic.'

'Very ingenious, so far,' murmured Mr Dyer: 'I've no doubt when the contents of the bag are widely made known through advertisements a claimant will come forward, and your theory be found correct.'

'When I returned from Scotland Yard,' Loveday continued, 'I found your note, asking me to go round and see you respecting the big jewel robbery. Before I did so I thought it best to read once more the newspaper account of the case, so that I might be well up in its details. When I came to the words that the thief had written across the door of the safe, "To be Let, Unfurnished", they at once connected themselves in my mind with the "dying kiss to my Marchioness Mother", and the solemn warning against the racecourse and the bookmaker, of the black-bag letter-writer. Then, all in a flash, the whole thing became clear to me. Some two or three years back my professional duties necessitated my frequent attendance at certain low class penny-readings, given in the South London slums. At these penny-readings young shop assistants, and others of their class, glad of an opportunity for exhibiting their accomplishments, declaim with great vigour; and, as a rule, select pieces which their very mixed audience might be supposed to appreciate. During my attendance at these meetings, it seemed to me that one book of selected readings was a great favourite among the reciters, and I took the trouble to buy it. Here it is.'

Here Loveday took from her cloakpocket 'The Reciter's Treasury', and handed it to her companion.

'Now,' she said, 'if you will run your eye down the index column you will find the titles of those pieces to which I wish to draw your attention. The first is "The Suicide's Farewell"; the second, "the Noble Convict"; the third, "To be Let, Unfurnished".'

'By Jove! so it is!' ejaculated Mr Dyer.

'In the first of these pieces, "The Suicide's Farewell", occur the expressions with which the black-bag letter begins—"The fatal day has arrived", etc., the warnings against gambling, and the allusions to the "poor lifeless body". In the second, "The Noble Convict", occur the allusions to the aristocratic relations and the dying kiss to the marchioness mother. The third piece, "To be Let, Unfurnished", is a foolish little poem enough, although I dare say it has often raised a laugh in a not too-discriminating audience. It tells how a bachelor, calling at a house to enquire after rooms to be let unfurnished, falls in love with the daughter of the house, and offers her his heart, which, he says, is to be let unfurnished. She declines his offer, and retorts that she thinks his head must be to let unfurnished too. With these three pieces before me, it was not difficult to see a thread of connection between the writer of the black-bag letter and the thief who wrote across the empty safe at Craigen Court. Following this thread, I unearthed the story of Harry Emmett— footman, reciter, general lover and scamp. Subsequently I compared the writing on my tracing paper with that on the safe door and, allowing for the difference between a bit of chalk and a steel nib, came to the conclusion that there could be but little doubt but what both were written by the same hand. Before that, however, I had obtained another, and what I consider the most important, link in my chain of evidence— how Emmett brought his clerical dress into use.'

'Ah, how did you find out that now?' asked Mr Dyer, leaning forward with his elbows on his knees.

'In the course of conversation with Mrs Williams, whom I found to be a most communicative person, I elicited the names of the guests who had sat down to dinner on Christmas Eve. They were all people of undoubted respectability in the neighbourhood. Just before dinner was announced, she said, a young clergyman had presented himself at the front door, asking to speak with the Rector of the parish. The Rector, it seems, always dines at Craigen Court on Christmas Eve. The young clergyman's story was that he had been told by a certain clergyman, whose name he mentioned, that a curate was wanted in the parish, and he had travelled down from London to offer his services. He had been, he said, to the Rectory and had been told by the servants where the Rector was dining, and fearing to lose his chance of the curacy, had followed him to the Court. Now the Rector had been wanting a curate and had filled the vacancy only the previous week; he was a little inclined to be irate at this interruption to the evening's festivities, and told the young man that he didn't want a curate. When, however, he saw how disappointed the poor young fellow looked—I believe he shed a tear or two—his heart softened; he told him to sit down and rest in the hall before he attempted the walk back to the station, and said he would ask Sir George to send him out a glass of wine. The young man sat down in a chair immediately outside the room by which the thieves entered. Now I need not tell you who that young man was, nor suggest to your mind, I am sure, the idea that while the servant went to fetch him his wine, or indeed, so soon as he saw the coast clear, he slipped into that little room and pulled back the catch of the window that admitted his confederates, who, no doubt, at that very moment were in hiding in the grounds. The housekeeper did not know whether this meek young curate had a black bag with him. Personally I have no doubt of the fact, nor that it contained the cap, cuffs, collar, and outer garments of Harry Emmett, which were most likely re-donned before he returned to his lodgings at Wreford, where I should say he repacked the bag with its clerical contents, and wrote his serio-comic letter. This bag, I suppose, he must have deposited in the very early morning, before anyone was stirring, on the doorstep of the house in the Easterbrook Road.'

Mr Dyer drew a long breath. In his heart was unmitigated admiration for his colleague's skill, which seemed to him to fall little short of inspiration. By-and-by, no doubt, he would sing her praises to the first person who came along with a hearty good will; he had not, however, the slightest intention of so singing them in her own ears—excessive praise was apt to have a bad effect on the rising practitioner.

So he contented himself with saying:

'Yes, very satisfactory. Now tell me how you hunted the fellow down to his diggings?'

'Oh, that was mere A B C work,' answered Loveday. 'Mrs Williams told me he had left his place at Colonel James's about six months previously, and had told her he was going to look after his dear old grandmother, who kept a sweetstuff-shop; but where she could not remember. Having heard that Emmett's father was a cab-driver, my thoughts at once flew to the cabman's vernacular—you know something of it, no doubt—in which their provident association is designated by the phrase, "the dear old grandmother", and the office where they make and receive their payments is styled "the sweetstuff-shop".'

'Ha, ha, ha! And good Mrs Williams took it all literally, no doubt?'

'She did; and thought what a dear kind-hearted fellow the young man was. Naturally I supposed there would be a branch of the association in the nearest market-town, and a local trades' directory confirmed my supposition that there was one at Wreford. Bearing in mind where the black bag was found, it was not difficult to believe that young Emmett, possibly through his father's influence and his own prepossessing manners and appearance, had attained to some position of trust in the Wreford branch. I must confess I scarcely expected to find him as I did, on reaching the place, installed as receiver of the weekly moneys. Of course, I immediately put myself in communication with the police there, and the rest I think you know.'

Mr Dyer's enthusiasm refused to be longer restrained.

'It's capital, from first to last,' he cried; 'you've surpassed yourself this time!'

'The only thing that saddens me,' said Loveday, 'is the thought of the possible fate of that poor little Stephanie.'

Loveday's anxieties on Stephanie's behalf were, however, to be put to flight before another twenty-four hours had passed. The first post on the following morning brought a letter from Mrs Williams telling how the girl had been found before the night was over, half dead with cold and fright, on the verge of the stream running through Craigen Wood—'found too'—wrote the housekeeper, 'by the very person who ought to have found her, young Holt, who was, and is so desperately in love with her. Thank goodness! at the last moment her courage failed her, and instead of throwing herself into the stream, she sank down, half-fainting, beside it. Holt took her straight home to his mother, and there, at the farm, she is now, being taken care of and petted generally by everyone.'

THE GRAVE BY
THE HANDPOST

Thomas Hardy

Thomas Hardy (1840–1928), author of many
classic novels including *Tess of the D'Urbervilles*
and *The Mayor of Casterbridge*, wrote several
atmospheric short tales dealing with crime,
mystery and superstition, often written specially
for publication at Christmas. 'The Grave by the
Handpost' first appeared in the Christmas
Number of *St James's Budget*, December 1897.

I never pass through Chalk-Newton without turning to regard the
neighbouring upland, at a point where a lane crosses the lone
straight highway dividing this from the next parish; a sight which
does not fail to recall the event that once happened there; and, though it
may seem superfluous, at this date, to disinter more memories of village
history, the whispers of that spot may claim to be preserved.

It was on a dark, yet mild and exceptionally dry evening at Christmas
time (according to the testimony of William Dewy of Mellstock,
Michael Mail, and others), that the choir of Chalk-Newton—a large
parish situate about half-way between the towns of Ivell and Casterbridge, and now a railway station—left their homes just before midnight
to repeat their annual harmonies under the windows of the local
population. The band of instrumentalists and singers was one of the
largest in the county; and, unlike the smaller and finer Mellstock string-
band, which eschewed all but the catgut, it included brass and reed

performers at full Sunday services, and reached all across the west gallery.

On this night there were two or three violins, two 'cellos, a tenor viol, double bass, hautboy, clarionets, serpent, and seven singers. It was, however, not the choir's labours, but what its members chanced to witness, that particularly marked the occasion.

They had pursued their rounds for many years without meeting with any incident of an unusual kind, but tonight, according to the assertions of several, there prevailed, to begin with, an exceptionally solemn and thoughtful mood among two or three of the oldest in the band, as if they were thinking they might be joined by the phantoms of dead friends who had been of their number in earlier years, and now were mute in the churchyard under flattening mounds—friends who had shown greater zest for melody in their time than was shown in this; or that some past voice of a semi-transparent figure might quaver from some bedroom window its acknowledgment of their nocturnal greeting, instead of a familiar living neighbour. Whether this were fact or fancy, the younger members of the choir met together with their customary thoughtlessness and buoyancy. When they had gathered by the stone stump of the cross in the middle of the village, near the White Horse Inn, which they made their starting point, some one observed that they were full early, that it was not yet twelve o'clock. The local waits of those days mostly refrained from sounding a note before Christmas morning had astronomically arrived, and not caring to return to their beer, they decided to begin with some outlying cottages in Sidlinch Lane, where the people had no clocks, and would not know whether it were night or morning. In that direction they accordingly went; and as they ascended to higher ground their attention was attracted by a light beyond the houses, quite at the top of the lane.

The road from Chalk-Newton to Broad Sidlinch is about two miles long and in the middle of its course, where it passes over the ridge dividing the two villages, it crosses at right angles, as has been stated, the lonely monotonous old highway known as Long Ash Lane, which runs, straight as a surveyor's line, many miles north and south of this spot, on the foundation of a Roman road, and has often been mentioned in these narratives. Though now quite deserted and grass-grown, at the beginning of the century it was well kept and frequented by traffic. The glimmering light appeared to come from the precise point where the roads intersected.

'I think I know what that mid mean!' one of the group remarked.

[199]

They stood a few moments, discussing the probability of the light having origin in an event of which rumours had reached them, and resolved to go up the hill.

Approaching the high land their conjectures were strengthened. Long Ash Lane cut athwart them, right and left; and they saw that at the junction of the four ways, under the handpost, a grave was dug, into which, as the choir drew nigh, a corpse had just been thrown by the four Sidlinch men employed for the purpose. The cart and horse which had brought the body thither stood silently by.

The singers and musicians from Chalk-Newton halted, and looked on while the gravediggers shovelled in and trod down the earth, till, the hole being filled, the latter threw their spades into the cart, and prepared to depart.

'Who mid ye be a-burying there?' asked Lot Swanhills in a raised voice. 'Not the sergeant?'

The Sidlinch men had been so deeply engrossed in their task that they had not noticed the lanterns of the Chalk-Newton choir till now.

'What—be you the Newton carol singers?' returned the representatives of Sidlinch.

'Ay, sure. Can it be that it is old Sergeant Holway you've a-buried there?'

''Tis so. You've heard about it, then?'

The choir knew no particulars—only that he had shot himself in his apple closet on the previous Sunday. 'Nobody seem'th to know what 'a did it for, 'a b'lieve? Leastwise, we don't know at Chalk-Newton,' continued Lot.

'O yes. It all came out at the inquest.'

The singers drew close, and the Sidlinch men, pausing to rest after their labours, told the story. 'It was all owing to that son of his, poor man. It broke his heart.'

'But the son is a soldier, surely; now with his regiment in the East Indies?'

'Ay. And it have been rough with the army over there lately. 'Twas a pity his father persuaded him to go. But Luke shouldn't have twyted the sergeant o't, since 'a did it for the best.'

The circumstances, in brief, were these: The sergeant who had come to this lamentable end, father of the young soldier who had gone with his regiment to the East, had been singularly comfortable in his military experiences, these having ended long before the outbreak of the great war with France. On his discharge, after duly serving his time, he had returned to his native village, and married, and taken kindly to domestic life. But the war in which England next involved herself had cost him many frettings that age and infirmity prevented him from being ever again an active unit of the army. When his only son grew to young manhood, and the question arose of his going out in life, the lad expressed his wish to be a mechanic. But his father advised enthusiastically for the army.

'Trade is coming to nothing in these days,' he said. 'And if the war with the French lasts, as it will, trade will be still worse. The army, Luke— that's the thing for 'ee. 'Twas the making of me, and 'twill be the making of you. I hadn't half such a chance as you'll have in these splendid hotter times.'

Luke demurred, for he was a home-keeping, peace-loving youth. But, putting respectful trust in his father's judgment, he at length gave way, and enlisted in the —d Foot. In the course of a few weeks he was sent out to India to his regiment, which had distinguished itself in the East under General Wellesley.

But Luke was unlucky. News came home indirectly that he lay sick out there; and then on one recent day when his father was out walking, the old man had received tidings that a letter awaited him at Casterbridge. The sergeant sent a special messenger the whole nine miles, and the letter was paid for and brought home; but though, as he had guessed, it came from Luke, its contents were of an unexpected tenor.

The letter had been written during a time of deep depression. Luke said that his life was a burden and a slavery, and bitterly reproached his father for advising him to embark on a career for which he felt unsuited. He found himself suffering fatigues and illnesses without gaining glory, and engaged in a cause which he did not understand or appreciate. If it had not been for his father's bad advice he, Luke, would now have been working comfortably at a trade in the village that he had never wished to leave.

After reading the letter the sergeant advanced a few steps till he was quite out of sight of everybody, and then sat down on the bank by the wayside.

When he arose half an hour later he looked withered and broken, and from that day his natural spirits left him. Wounded to the quick by his son's sarcastic stings, he indulged in liquor more and more frequently. His wife had died some years before this date, and the sergeant lived alone in the house which had been hers. One morning in the December under notice the report of a gun had been heard on his premises, and on entering the neighbours found him in a dying state. He had shot himself with an old firelock that he used for scaring birds; and from what he had said the day before, and the arrangements he had made for his decease, there was no doubt that his end had been deliberately planned, as a consequence of the despondency into which he had been thrown by his son's letter. The coroner's jury returned a verdict of *felo de se*.

'Here's his son's letter,' said one of the Sidlinch men. ''Twas found in his father's pocket. You can see by the state o't how many times he read it over. Howsomever, the Lord's will be done, since it must, whether or no.'

The grave was filled up and levelled, no mound being shaped over it. The Sidlinch men then bade the Chalk-Newton choir goodnight, and departed with the cart in which they had brought the sergeant's body to the hill. When their tread had died away from the ear, and the wind swept over the isolated grave with its customary siffle of indifference, Lot Swanhills turned and spoke to old Richard Toller, the hautboy player.

''Tis hard upon a man, and he a wold sojer, to serve en so, Richard. Not that the sergeant was ever in a battle bigger than would go into a half-acre paddock, that's true. Still, his soul ought to hae as good a chance as another man's, all the same, hey?'

Richard replied that he was quite of the same opinion. 'What d'ye say to lifting up a carrel over his grave, as 'tis Christmas, and no hurry to begin down in parish, and 'twouldn't take up ten minutes, and not a soul up here to say us nay, or know anything about it?'

Lot nodded assent. 'The man ought to hae his chances,' he repeated.

'Ye may as well spet upon his grave, for all the good we shall do en by what we lift up, now he's got so far,' said Notton, the clarinet man and professed sceptic of the choir. 'But I'm agreed if the rest be.'

They thereupon placed themselves in a semicircle by the newly stirred earth, and roused the dull air with the well-known Number Sixteen of their collection, which Lot gave out as being the one he thought best suited to the occasion and the mood:—

> He comes' the pri'–soners to' re–lease',
> In Sa'–tan's bon'–dage held'.

'Jown it—we've never played to a dead man afore,' said Ezra Cattstock, when, having concluded the last verse, they stood reflecting for a breath or two. 'But it do seem more merciful than to go away and leave en, as they t'other fellers have done.'

'Now backalong to Newton, and by the time we get overright the pa'son's 'twill be half after twelve,' said the leader.

They had not, however, done more than gather up their instruments when the wind brought to their notice the noise of a vehicle rapidly driven up the same lane from Sidlinch which the gravediggers had lately retraced. To avoid being run over when moving on, they waited till the benighted traveller, whoever he might be, should pass them where they stood in the wider area of the Cross.

In half a minute the light of the lanterns fell upon a hired fly, drawn by a steaming and jaded horse. It reached the handpost, when a voice from the inside cried, 'Stop here!' The driver pulled rein. The carriage door was opened from within, and there leapt out a private soldier in the uniform of some line regiment. He looked around, and was apparently surprised to see the musicians standing there.

'Have you buried a man here?' he asked.

'No. We bain't Sidlinch folk, thank God; we be Newton choir. Though a man is just buried here, that's true; and we've raised a carrel over the poor mortal's natomy. What—do my eyes see before me young Luke Holway, that went wi' his regiment to the East Indies, or do I see his spirit straight from the battlefield? Be you the son that wrote the letter—'

'Don't—don't ask me. The funeral is over, then?'

'There wer no funeral, in a Christen manner of speaking. But's buried, sure enough. You must have met the men going back in the empty cart.'

'Like a dog in a ditch, and all through me!'

He remained silent, looking at the grave, and they could not help pitying him. 'My friends,' he said, 'I understand better now. You have, I suppose, in neighbourly charity sung peace to his soul? I thank you, from my heart, for your kind pity. Yes; I am Sergeant Holway's miserable son—I'm the son who has brought about his father's death, as truly as if I had done it with my own hand!'

'No, no. Don't yet take on so, young man. He'd been naturally low for a good while, off and on, so we hear.'

'We were out in the East when I wrote to him. Everything had seemed to go wrong with me. Just after my letter had gone we were ordered home. That's how it is you see me here. As soon as we got into barracks at Casterbridge I heard o' this—. . . Damn me! I'll dare to follow my father, and make away with myself, too. It is the only thing left to do!'

'Don't ye be rash, Luke Holway, I say again; but try to make amends by your future life. And maybe your father will smile a smile down from heaven upon 'ee for 't.'

He shook his head. 'I don't know about that!' he answered bitterly.

'Try and be worthy of your father at his best. 'Tis not too late.'

'D' ye think not? I fancy it is! . . . Well, I'll turn it over. Thank you for your good counsel. I'll live for one thing, at any rate. I'll move father's body to a decent Christian churchyard, if I do it with my own hands. I can't save his life, but I can give him an honourable grave. He shan't lie in this accursed place!'

'Ay, as our pa'son, says, 'tis a barbarous custom they keep up at Sidlinch, and ought to be done away wi'. The man a' old soldier, too. You see, our pa'son is not like yours at Sidlinch.'

'He says it is barbarous, does he? So it is!' cried the soldier. 'Now hearken, my friends.' Then he proceeded to inquire if they would increase his indebtedness to them by undertaking the removal, privately, of the body of the suicide to the churchyard, not of Sidlinch, a parish he now hated, but of Chalk-Newton. He would give them all he possessed to do it.

Lot asked Ezra Cattstock what he thought of it.

Cattstock, the 'cello player, who was also the sexton, demurred, and advised the young soldier to sound the rector about it first. 'Mid be he would object, and yet 'a midn't. The pa'son o' Sidlinch is a hard man, I own ye, and 'a said if folk will kill theirselves in hot blood they must take the consequences. But ours don't think like that at all, and might allow it.'

'What's his name?'

'The honourable and reverent Mr Oldham, brother to Lord Wessex. But you needn't be afeard o' en on that account. He'll talk to 'ee like a common man, if so be you haven't had enough drink to gie 'ee bad breath.'

'O, the same as formerly. I'll ask him. Thank you. And that duty done—'

'What then?'

'There's war in Spain. I hear our next move is there. I'll try to show myself to be what my father wished me. I don't suppose I shall—but I'll try in my feeble way. That much I swear—here over his body. So help me God.'

Luke smacked his palm against the white handpost with such force that it shook. 'Yes, there's war in Spain; and another chance for me to be worthy of father.'

So the matter ended that night. That the private acted in one thing as he had vowed to do soon became apparent, for during the Christmas week the rector came into the churchyard when Cattstock was there, and asked him to find a spot that would be suitable for the purpose of such an interment, adding that he had slightly known the late sergeant, and was not aware of any law which forbade him to assent to the removal, the letter of the rule having been observed. But as he did not wish to seem moved by opposition to his neighbour at Sidlinch, he had stipulated that the act of charity should be carried out at night, and as privately as possible, and that the grave should be in an obscure part of the enclosure. 'You had better see the young man about it at once,' added the rector.

But before Ezra had done anything Luke came down to his house. His furlough had been cut short, owing to new developments of the war in the Peninsula, and being obliged to go back to his regiment immediately, he was compelled to leave the exhumation and reinterment to his friends. Everything was paid for, and he implored them all to see it carried out forthwith.

With this the soldier left. The next day Ezra, on thinking the matter over, again went across to the rectory, struck with sudden misgiving. He had remembered that the sergeant had been buried without a coffin, and he was not sure that a stake had not been driven through him. The business would be more troublesome than they had at first supposed.

'Yes, indeed!' murmured the rector. 'I am afraid it is not feasible after all.'

The next event was the arrival of a headstone by carrier from the nearest town; to be left at Mr Ezra Cattstock's; all expenses paid. The sexton and the carrier deposited the stone in the former's outhouse; and Ezra, left alone, put on his spectacles and read the brief and simple inscription:—

HERE LYETH THE BODY OF SAMUEL HOLWAY, LATE SERGEANT IN HIS MAJESTY'S ——D REGIMENT OF FOOT, WHO DEPARTED THIS LIFE DECEMBER THE 20TH, 180-. ERECTED BY L. H.
'I AM NOT WORTHY TO BE CALLED THY SON.'

Ezra again called at the riverside rectory. 'The stone is come, sir. But I'm afeard we can't do it nohow.'

'I should like to oblige him,' said the gentlemanly old incumbent. 'And I would forgo all fees willingly. Still, if you and the others don't think you can carry it out, I am in doubt what to say.'

'Well, sir; I've made inquiry of a Sidlinch woman as to his burial, and what I thought seems true. They buried en wi' a new six-foot hurdle-saul drough's body, from the sheep-pen up in North Ewelease, though they won't own to it now. And the question is, Is the moving worth while, considering the awkwardness?'

'Have you heard anything more of the young man?'

Ezra had only heard that he had embarked that week for Spain with the rest of the regiment. 'And if he's as desperate as 'a seemed, we shall never see him here in England again.'

'It is an awkward case,' said the rector.

Ezra talked it over with the choir; one of whom suggested that the stone might be erected at the crossroads. This was regarded as impracticable. Another said that it might be set up in the churchyard without removing the body; but this was seen to be dishonest. So nothing was done.

The headstone remained in Ezra's outhouse till, growing tired of seeing it there, he put it away among the bushes at the bottom of his garden. The subject was sometimes revived among them, but it always ended with: 'Considering how 'a was buried, we can hardly make a job o't.'

There was always the consciousness that Luke would never come back, an impression strengthened by the disasters which were rumoured to have befallen the army in Spain. This tended to make their inertness permanent. The headstone grew green as it lay on its back under Ezra's bushes; then a tree by the river was blown down, and, falling across the stone, cracked it in three pieces. Ultimately the pieces became buried in the leaves and mould.

Luke had not been born a Chalk-Newton man, and he had no relations left in Sidlinch, so that no tidings of him reached either village throughout the war. But after Waterloo and the fall of Napoleon there arrived at Sidlinch one day an English sergeant-major covered with stripes and, as it turned out, rich in glory. Foreign service had so totally changed Luke Holway that it was not until he told his name that the inhabitants recognized him as the sergeant's only son.

He had served with unswerving effectiveness through the Peninsular campaigns under Wellington; had fought at Busaco, Fuentes d'Onore, Ciudad Rodrigo, Badajoz, Salamanca, Vittoria, Quatre Bras, and Waterloo; and had now returned to enjoy a more than earned pension and repose in his native district.

He hardly stayed in Sidlinch longer than to take a meal on his arrival. The same evening he started on foot over the hill to Chalk-Newton, passing the handpost, and saying as he glanced at the spot, 'Thank God: he's not there!' Nightfall was approaching when he reached the latter village; but he made straight for the churchyard. On his entering it there remained light enough to discern the headstones by, and these he narrowly scanned. But though he searched the front part by the road, and the back part by the river, what he sought he could not find—the grave of Sergeant Holway, and a memorial bearing the inscription: 'I AM NOT WORTHY TO BE CALLED THY SON.'

He left the churchyard and made inquiries. The honourable and reverend old rector was dead, and so were many of the choir; but by degrees the sergeant-major learnt that his father still lay at the cross-roads in Long Ash lane.

Luke pursued his way moodily homewards, to do which, in the natural course, he would be compelled to repass the spot, there being no other road between the two villages. But he could not now go by that place, vociferous with reproaches in his father's tones; and he got over the hedge and wandered deviously through the ploughed fields to avoid the scene. Through many a fight and fatigue Luke had been sustained by the thought that he was restoring the family honour and making noble amends. Yet his father lay still in degradation. It was rather a sentiment than a fact that his father's body had been made to suffer for his own misdeeds; but to his super-sensitiveness it seemed that his efforts to retrieve his character and to propitiate the shade of the insulted one had ended in failure.

He endeavoured, however, to shake off his lethargy, and, not liking the associations of Sidlinch, hired a small cottage at Chalk-Newton which had long been empty. Here he lived alone, becoming quite a hermit, and allowing no woman to enter the house.

The Christmas after taking up his abode herein he was sitting in the chimney corner by himself, when he heard faint notes in the distance, and soon a melody burst forth immediately outside his own window. It came from the carol singers, as usual; and though many of the old hands, Ezra and Lot included had gone to their rest, the same old carols were still played out of the same old books. There resounded through the sergeant-major's window shutters the familiar lines that the deceased choir had rendered over his father's grave:—

He comes' the pri'–soners to' re–lease',
In Sa'–tan's bon'–dage held'.

[207]

When they had finished they went on to another house, leaving him to silence and loneliness as before.

The candle wanted snuffing, but he did not snuff it, and he sat on till it had burnt down into the socket and made waves of shadow on the ceiling.

The Christmas cheerfulness of next morning was broken at breakfast time by tragic intelligence which went down the village like wind. Sergeant-Major Holway had been found shot through the head by his own hand at the crossroads in Long Ash Lane where his father lay buried.

On the table in the cottage he had left a piece of paper, on which he had written his wish that he might be buried at the Cross beside his father. But the paper was accidentally swept to the floor, and overlooked till after his funeral, which took place in the ordinary way in the churchyard.

MR WRAY'S
CASH BOX
OR THE MASK
AND THE
MYSTERY—
A CHRISTMAS
SKETCH

Wilkie Collins

The celebrated Wilkie Collins, author of *The
Moonstone* and *The Woman in White*, wrote
several mystery stories, some in collaboration
with his friend Charles Dickens. *Mr Wray's Cash
Box*, one of his early novellas, was written for
Christmas 1852 and was published on its own
as a small book in an identical format to *A
Christmas Carol* and Dickens's other Christmas
books. Unlike these, Wilkie Collins's story was
never reissued, and this is its first appearance in
nearly 140 years.

I

I should be insulting the intelligence of readers generally, if I thought
it at all necessary to describe to them that widely-celebrated town,
Tidbury-on-the-Marsh. As a genteel provincial residence, who is
unacquainted with it? The magnificent new hotel that has grown on to

the side of the old inn; the extensive library, to which, not satisfied with only adding new books, they are now adding a new entrance as well; the projected crescent of palatial abodes in the Grecian style, on the top of the hill, to rival the completed crescent of castellated abodes, in the Gothic style, at the bottom of the hill—are not such local objects as these perfectly well known to any intelligent Englishman? Of course they are! The question is superfluous. Let us get on at once, without wasting more time, from Tidbury in general to the High Street in particular, and to our present destination there—the commercial establishment of Messrs Dunball and Dark.

Looking merely at the coloured liquids, the miniature statue of a horse, the corn plasters, the oil-skin bags, the pots of cosmetics, and the cut-glass saucers full of lozenges in the shop window, you might at first imagine that Dunball and Dark were only chemists. Looking carefully through the entrance, towards an inner apartment, an inscription; a large, upright, mahogany receptacle, or box, with a hole in it; brass rails protecting the hole; a green curtain ready to draw over the hole; and a man with a copper money shovel in his hand, partially visible behind the hole; would be sufficient to inform you that Dunball and Dark were not chemists only, but 'Branch Bankers' as well.

It is a rough squally morning at the end of November. Mr Dunball (in the absence of Mr Dark, who has gone to make a speech at the vestry meeting) has got into the mahogany box, and has assumed the whole business and direction of the branch bank. He is a very fat man, and looks absurdly over-large for his sphere of action. Not a single customer has, as yet, applied for money—nobody has come even to gossip with the branch banker through the brass rails of his commercial prison house. There he sits, staring calmly through the chemical part of the shop into the street—his gold in one drawer, his notes in another, his elbows on his ledgers, his copper shovel under his thumb; the picture of monied loneliness; the hermit of British finance.

In the outer shop is the young assistant, ready to drug the public at a moment's notice. But Tidbury-on-the-Marsh is an unprofitably healthy place; and no public appears. By the time the young assistant has ascertained from the shop clock that it is a quarter past ten, and from the weather-cock opposite that the wind is 'Sou'-sou'-west', he has exhausted all external sources of amusement, and is reduced to occupying himself by first sharpening his penknife, and then cutting his nails. He has completed his left hand, and has just begun on the right hand thumb, when a customer actually darkens the shop door at last!

Mr Dunball starts, and grasps the copper shovel: the young assistant shuts up his penknife in a hurry, and makes a bow. The customer is a young girl, and she has come for a pot of lip salve.

She is very neatly and quietly dressed; looks about eighteen or nineteen years of age; and has something in her face which I can only characterize by the epithet—lovable. There is a beauty of innocence and purity about her forehead, brow, and eyes—a calm, kind, happy expression as she looks as you—and a curious home-sound in her clear utterance when she speaks, which, altogether, make you fancy, stranger as you are, that you must have known her and loved her long ago, and somehow or other ungratefully forgotten her in the lapse of time. Mixed up, however, with the girlish gentleness and innocence which form her more prominent charm, there is a look of firmness—especially noticeable about the expression of her lips—that gives a certain character and originality to her face. Her figure—

I stop at her figure. Not by any means for want of phrases to describe it; but from a disheartening conviction of the powerlessness of any description of her at all to produce the right effect on the minds of others. If I were asked in what particular efforts of literature the poverty of literary material most remarkably appears. I should answer, in personal descriptions of heroines. We have all read these by the hundred—some of them so carefully and finely finished, that we are not only informed about the lady's eyes, eyebrows, nose, cheeks, complexion, mouth, teeth, neck, ears, head, hair, and the way it was dressed; but are also made acquainted with the particular manner in which the sentiments below made the bosom above heave or swell; besides the exact position of head in which her eyelashes were just long enough to cast a shadow on her cheeks. We have read all this attentively and admiringly, as it deserves; and have yet risen from the reading, without the remotest approach to a realization in our own minds of what sort of a woman the heroine really was. We vaguely knew she was beautiful, at the beginning of the description; and we know just as much—just as vaguely—at the end.

Penetrated with the conviction above-mentioned, I prefer leaving the reader to form his own realization of the personal appearance of the customer at Messrs Dunball and Dark's. Eschewing the magnificent beauties of his acquaintance, let him imagine her to be like any pretty intelligent girl whom he knows—any of those pleasant little fire-side angels, who can charm us even in a merino morning gown, darning an old pair of socks. Let this be the sort of female reality in the reader's mind; and neither author, nor heroine, need have any reason to complain.

Well; our young lady came to the counter, and asked for lip salve. The assistant, vanquished at once by the potent charm of her presence, paid her the first little tribute of politeness in his power, by asking permission to send the gallipot home for her.

'I beg your pardon, miss,' said he; 'but I think you live lower down, at No. 12. I was passing; and I think I saw you going in there, yesterday, with an old gentleman, and another gentleman—I think I did, miss?'

'Yes: we lodge at No. 12,' said the young girl; 'but I will take the lip salve home with me, if you please. I have a favour, however, to ask of you before I go,' she continued very modestly, but without the slightest appearance of embarrassment; 'if you have room to hang this up in your window, my grandfather, Mr Wray, would feel much obliged by your kindness.'

And here, to the utter astonishment of the young assistant, she handed him a piece of cardboard, with a string to hang it up by, on which appeared the following inscription, neatly written:—

Mr Reuben Wray, pupil of the late celebrated John Kemble, Esquire, begs respectfully to inform his friends and the public that he gives lessons in elocution, delivery, and reading aloud, price two-and-sixpence the lesson of an hour. Pupils prepared for the stage, or private theatricals, on a principle combining intelligent interpretation of the text, with the action of the arms and legs adopted by the late illustrious Roscius of the English stage, J. Kemble, Esquire; and attentively studied from close observation of Mr J.K. by Mr R.W. Orators and clergymen improved (with the strictest secrecy), at three-and-sixpence the lesson of an hour. Impediments and hesitation of utterance combated and removed. Young ladies taught the graces of delivery, and young gentlemen the proprieties of diction. A discount allowed to schools and large classes. Please to address, Mr Reuben Wray (late of the Theatre Royal, Drury Lane), 12, High Street, Tidbury-on-the-Marsh.

No Babylonian inscription that ever was cut, no manuscript on papyrus that ever was penned, could possibly have puzzled the young assistant more than this remarkable advertisement. He read it all through in a state of stupefaction; and then observed, with a bewildered look at the young girl on the other side of the counter:—

'Very nicely written, miss; and very nicely composed indeed! I suppose—in fact, I'm sure Mr Dunball'— Here a creaking was heard, as of some strong wooden construction being gradually rent asunder. It was

Mr Dunball himself, squeezing his way out of the branch bank box, and coming to examine the advertisement.

He read it all through very attentively, following each line with his forefinger; and then cautiously and gently laid the cardboard down on the counter. When I state that neither Mr Dunball nor his assistant were quite certain what a 'Roscius of the English stage' meant, or what precise branch of human attainment Mr Wray designed to teach in teaching 'Elocution', I do no injustice either to master or man.

'So you want this hung up in the window, my—in the window, miss?' asked Mr Dunball. He was about to say, 'my dear'; but something in the girl's look and manner stopped him.

'If you could hang it up without inconvenience, sir.'

'May I ask what's your name? and where you come from?'

'My name is Annie Wray; and the last place we came from was Stratford-upon-Avon.'

'Ah! indeed—and Mr Wray teaches, does he?—elocution for half-a-crown—eh?'

'My grandfather only desires to let the inhabitants of this place know that he can teach those who wish it, to speak or read with a good delivery and a proper pronunciation.'

Mr Dunball felt rather puzzled by the straightforward, self-possessed manner in which he—a branch banker, a chemist, and a municipal authority—was answered by little Annie Wray. He took up the advertisement again; and walked away to read it a second time in the solemn monetary seclusion of the back shop.

The young assistant followed. 'I think they're respectable people, sir,' said he, in a whisper; 'I was passing when the old gentleman went into No. 12, yesterday. The wind blew his cloak on one side, and I saw him carrying a large cash box under it—I did indeed, sir; and it seemed a heavy one.'

'Cash box!' cried Mr Dunball. 'What does a man with a cash box want with elocution, and two-and-sixpence an hour? Suppose he should be a swindler!'

'He can't be, sir: look at the young lady! Besides, the people at No. 12 told me he gave a reference, and paid a week's rent in advance.'

'He did—did he? I say, are you sure it was a cash box?'

'Certain, sir. I suppose it had money in it, of course?'

'What's the use of a cash box, without cash?' said the branch banker, contemptuously. 'It looks rather odd, though! Stop! maybe it's a wager. I've heard of gentlemen doing queer things for wagers. Or, maybe, he's cracked! Well, she's a nice girl; and hanging up this thing can't do any harm. I'll make enquiries about them, though, for all that.'

Frowning portentously as he uttered this last cautious resolve, Mr Dunball leisurely returned into the chemist's shop. He was, however, nothing like so ill-natured a man as he imagined himself to be; and, in spite of his dignity and his suspicions, he smiled far more cordially than he at all intended, as he now addressed little Annie Wray.

'It's out of our line, miss,' said he; 'but we'll hang the thing up to oblige you. Of course, if I want a reference, you can give it? Yes, yes! of course. There! there's the card in the window for you—a nice prominent place (look at it as you go out)—just between the string of corn plasters and the dried poppy-heads! I wish Mr Wray success; though I rather think Tidbury is not quite the sort of place to come to for what you call elocution—eh?'

'Thank you, sir; and good morning,' said little Annie. And she left the shop just as composedly as she had entered it.

'Cool little girl, that!' said Mr Dunball, watching her progress down the street to No. 12.

'Pretty little girl, too!' thought the assistant, trying to watch, like his master, from the window.

'I should like to know who Mr Wray is,' said Mr Dunball, turning back into the shop, as Annie disappeared. 'And I'd give something to find out what Mr Wray keeps in his cash box,' continued the banker–chemist, as he thoughtfully re-entered the mahogany money chest in the back premises.

You are a wise man, Mr Dunball; but you won't solve those two mysteries in a hurry, sitting alone in that branch bank sentry-box of yours!—Can anybody solve them? I can.

Who is Mr Wray? and what has he got in his cash box?—Come to No. 12, and see!

II

Before we go boldly into Mr Wray's lodgings, I must first speak a word or two about him, behind his back—but by no means slanderously. I will take his advertisement, now hanging up in the shop window of Messrs Dunball and Dark, as the text of my discourse.

Mr Reuben Wray became, as he phrased it, a 'pupil of the late celebrated John Kemble, Esquire' in this manner. He began life by being apprenticed for three years to a statuary. Whether the occupation of taking casts and clipping stones proved of too sedentary a nature to suit his temperament, or whether an evil counsellor within him, whose name was VANITY, whispered:—'Seek public admiration, and be certain of public applause,'—I know not; but the fact is, that, as soon as his time was out, he left his master and his native place to join a company of strolling players; or, as he himself more magniloquently expressed it, he went on the stage.

Nature had gifted him with good lungs, large eyes, and a hook nose; his success before barn audiences was consequently brilliant. His professional exertions, it must be owned, barely sufficed to feed and clothe him; but then he had a triumph on the London stage, always present in the far perspective to console him. While waiting this desirable event, he indulged himself in a little intermediate luxury, much in favour as a profitable resource for young men in extreme difficulties—he married; married at the age of nineteen, or thereabouts, the charming Columbine of the company.

And he got a good wife. Many people, I know, will refuse to believe this,—it is a truth, nevertheless. The one redeeming success of the vast social failure which his whole existence was doomed to represent, was this very marriage of his with a strolling Columbine. She, poor girl, toiled as hard and as cheerfully to get her own bread after marriage, as before; trudged many a weary mile by his side from town to town, and never uttered a complaint; praised his acting; partook his hopes; patched his clothes; pardoned his ill-humour; paid court for him to his manager; made up his squabbles;—in a word, and in the best and highest sense of that word, loved him. May I be allowed to add, that she only brought him one child—a girl? And, considering the state of his pecuniary resources, am I justified in ranking this circumstance as a strong additional proof of her excellent qualities as a married woman?

After much perseverance and many disappointments, Reuben at last succeeded in attaching himself to a regular provincial company—Tate Wilkinson's at York. He had to descend low enough from his original dramatic pedestal before he succeeded in subduing the manager. From the leading business in Tragedy and Melodrama, he sank at once, in the established provincial company, to a 'minor utility'—words of theatrical slang signifying an actor who is put to the smaller dramatic uses which the necessities of the stage require. Still, in spite of this, he persisted in hoping for the chance that was never to come; and still poor Columbine faithfully hoped with him to the last.

[215]

Time passed—years of it; and this chance never arrived; and he and Columbine found themselves one day in London, forlorn and starving. Their life at this period would make a romance of itself, if I had time and space to write it; but I must get on, as fast as may be, to later dates; and the reader must be contented merely to know that, at the last gasp—the last of hope; almost the last of life—Reuben got employment, as an actor of the lower degree, at Drury Lane.

Behold him, then, now—still a young man, but crushed in his young man's ambition for ever—receiving the lowest theatrical wages for the lowest theatrical work; appearing on the stage as soldier, waiter, footman, and so on; with not a line in the play to speak; just showing his poverty-shrunken carcase to the audience, clothed in the frowsiest habiliments of the old Drury Lane wardrobe, for a minute or two at a time, at something like a shilling a night—a miserable being, in a miserable world; the World behind the Scenes!

John Philip Kemble is now acting at the theatre: and his fame is rising to its climax. How the roar of applause follows him almost every time he leaves the scene! How majestically he stalks away into the Green Room, abstractedly inhaling his huge pinches of snuff as he goes! How the poor inferior brethren of the buskin, as they stand at the wing and stare upon him reverently, long for his notice; and how few of them can possibly get it! There is, nevertheless, one among this tribe of unfortunates whom he has really remarked, though he has not yet spoken to him. He has detected this man, shabby and solitary, constantly studying his acting from any vantage-ground the poor wretch could get amid the dust, dirt, draughts, and confusion behind the scenes. Mr Kemble also observes, that whenever a play of Shakespeare's is being acted, this stranger has a tattered old book in his hands; and appears to be following the performance closely from the text, instead of huddling into warm corners over a pint of small beer, with the rest of his supernumerary brethren. Remarking these things, Mr Kemble over and over again intends to speak to the man, and find out who he is; and over and over again utterly forgets it. But, at last, a day comes when the long-deferred personal communication really takes place; and it happens thus:—

A new Tragedy is to be produced—a pre-eminently bad one, by-the-by, even in those days of pre-eminently bad Tragedy-writing. The scene is laid in Scotland; and Mr Kemble is determined to play his part in a Highland dress. The idea of acting a drama in the appropriate costume of the period which that drama illustrates, is considered so dangerous an innovation, that no one else dare follow his example; and he, of all the characters, is actually about to wear the only Highland dress in a Highland play. This does not at all daunt him. He has acted Othello, a night or two before, in the uniform of a British General Officer, and is so conscious of the enormous absurdity of the thing, that he is determined to persevere, and start the reform in stage costume, which he was afterwards destined so thoroughly to carry out.

The night comes; the play begins. Just as the stage waits for Mr Kemble, Mr Kemble discovers that his goatskin purse—one of the most striking peculiarities of the Highland dress—is not on him. There is no time to seek it—all is lost for the cause of costume!—he must go on the stage exposed to public view as only half a Highlander! No! Not yet! While everybody else hurries frantically hither and thither in vain, one man quickly straps something about Mr Kemble's waist, just in the nick of time. It is the lost purse! and Roscius after all steps on the stage, a Highlander complete from top to toe!

On his first exit, Mr Kemble inquires for the man who found the purse. It is that very poor player whom he has already remarked. The great actor had actually been carrying the purse about in his own hands before the performance; and, in a moment of abstraction, had put it down on a chair, in a dark place behind the prompter's box. The humble admirer, noticing everything he did, noticed this; and so found the missing goatskin in time, when nobody else could.

'Sir, I am infinitely obliged to you,' says Mr Kemble, courteously, to the confused, blushing man before him—'You have saved me from appearing incomplete, and therefore ridiculous, before a Drury Lane audience. I have marked you, sir, before; reading, while waiting for your call, our divine Shakespeare—the poetic bond that unites all men, however professional distances may separate them. Accept, sir, this offered pinch—this pinch of snuff.'

When the penniless player went home that night, what wonderful news he had for his wife! And how proud and happy poor Columbine was, when she heard that Reuben Wray had been offered a pinch of snuff out of Mr Kemble's own box!

But the kind-hearted tragedian did not stop merely at a fine speech and a social condescension. Reuben read Shakespeare, when none of his comrades would have cared to look into the book at all; and that of itself was enough to make him interesting to Mr Kemble. Besides, he was a young man; and might have capacities which only wanted encouragement.

'I beg you to recite to me, sir,' said the great John Philip, one night;

desirous of seeing what his humble admirer really could do. The result of the recitation was unequivocal: poor Wray could do nothing that hundreds of his brethren could not have equalled. In him, the yearning to become a great actor was only the ambition without the power.

Still, Reuben gained something by the goatskin purse. A timely word from his new protector raised him two or three degrees higher in the company, and increased his salary in proportion. He got parts now with some lines to speak in them; and—condescension on condescension!—Mr Kemble actually declaimed them for his instruction at rehearsal, and solemnly showed him (oftener, I am afraid, in jest than earnest) how a patriotic Roman soldier, or a bereaved father's faithful footman, should tread the stage.

These instructions were always received by the grateful Wray in the most perfect good faith; and it was precisely in virtue of his lessons thus derived—numbering about half-a-dozen, and lasting about two minutes each—that he afterwards advertised himself, as teacher of elocution and pupil of John Kemble. Many a great man has blazed away famously before the public eye, as pupil of some other great man, from no larger a supply of original educational fuel than belonged to Mr Reuben Wray.

Having fairly traced our friend to his connection with Mr Kemble, I may dismiss the rest of his advertisement more briefly. All, I suppose, that you now want further explained, is:—How he came to teach elocution, and how he got on by teaching it.

Well: Reuben stuck fast to Drury Lane theatre through rivalries, and quarrels, and disasters, and fluctuations in public taste, which overthrew more important interests than his own. The theatre was rebuilt, and burnt, and rebuilt again; and still Old Wray (as he now began to be called) was part and parcel of the establishment, however others might desert it. During this long lapse of monotonous years, affliction and death preyed cruelly on the poor actor's home. First, his kind, patient Columbine died; then, after a long interval, Columbine's only child married early;—and woe is me!—married a sad rascal, who first ill-treated and then deserted her. She soon followed her mother to the grave, leaving one girl—the little Annie of this story—to Reuben's care. One of the first things her grandfather taught the child was to call herself Annie *Wray*. He never could endure hearing her dissolute father's name pronounced by anybody; and was resolved that she should always bear his own.

Ah! what woeful times were those for the poor player! How many a night he sat in the darkest corner behind the scenes, with his tattered

Shakespeare—the only thing about him he had never pawned—in his hand, and the tears rolling down his hollow, painted cheeks, as he thought on the dear lost Columbine, and Columbine's child! How often those tears still stood thick in his eyes when he marched across the stage at the head of a mock army, or hobbled up to deliver the one eternal letter to the one eternal dandy hero of high Comedy!—Comedy, indeed! If the people before the lamps, who were roaring with laughter at the fun of the mercurial fine gentleman of the play, had only seen what was tugging at the heart of the miserable old stage footman who brought him his chocolate and newspapers, all the wit in the world would not have saved the comedy from being wept over as the most affecting tragedy that was ever written.

But the time was to come—long after this, however—when Reuben's connection with the theatre was to cease. As if fate had ironically bound up together the stage destinies of the great actor and the small, the year of Mr Kemble's retirement from the boards, was the year of Mr Wray's dismissal from them.

He had been, for some time past, getting too old to be useful—then, the theatrical world in which he had been bred was altering, and he could not alter with it. A little man with fiery black eyes, whose name was Edmund Kean, had come up from the country and blazed like a comet through the thick old conventional mists of the English stage. From that time, the new school began to rise, and the old school to sink; and Reuben went down, with other insignificant atoms, in the vortex. At the end of the season, he was informed that his services were no longer required.

It was then, when he found himself once more forlorn in the world—almost as forlorn as when he had first come to London with poor Columbine—that the notion of trying elocution struck him. He had a little sum of money to begin with, subscribed for him by his richer brethren when he left the theatre. Why might he not get on as a teacher of elocution in the country, just as some of his superior fellow-players got on in the same vocation in London? Necessity whispered, Doubt not, but try. He had a grandchild to support—so he did try.

His method of teaching was exceedingly simple. He had one remedy for the deficiencies of every class whom he addressed—the Kemble remedy: he had watched Mr Kemble year by year, till he knew every inch of him; and, so to speak, had learnt him by heart. Did a pupil want to walk the stage properly?—teach him Mr Kemble's walk. Did a rising politician want to become impressive as an orator?—teach him Mr

Kemble's gesticulations in Brutus. So again, with regard to strictly vocal necessities. Did gentleman number one, wish to learn the art of reading aloud?—let him learn the Kemble cadences. Did gentleman number two, feel weak in his pronunciation?—let him sound vowels, consonants, and crack-jaw syllables, just as Mr Kemble sounded them on the stage. And, out of what book were they to be taught?—from what manual were the clergymen and orators, the aspirants for dramatic fame, the young ladies whose delivery was ungraceful, and the young gentlemen whose diction was improper, to be all alike improved! From Shakespeare—every one of them from Shakespeare! He had no idea of anything else: literature meant Shakespeare to *him*. It was his great glory and triumph, that he had Shakespeare by heart. All that he knew, every tender and lovable recollection, every small honour he had gained in his own poor blank sphere, was somehow sure to be associated with William Shakespeare!

And why not? What is Shakespeare but a great sun that shines upon humanity—the large heads and the little, alike? Have not the rays of that mighty light penetrated into many poor and lowly places for good? What marvel then that they should fall, pleasant and invigorating, even upon Reuben Wray?

So—right or wrong—with Shakespeare for his textbook, and Mr Kemble for his model, our friend in his old age bravely invaded provincial England as a teacher of elocution, with all its supplementary accomplishments. And, wonderful to relate, though occasionally enduring dreadful privations, he just managed to make elocution—or what passed instead of it with his patrons—keep his grandchild and himself!

I cannot say that any orators or clergymen anxiously demanded secret improvement from him (see advertisement) at three-and-sixpence an hour; or that young ladies sought the graces of delivery, and young gentlemen the proprieties of diction (see advertisement again) from his experienced tongue. But he got on in other ways, nevertheless. Sometimes he was hired to drill the boys on a speech day at a country school. Sometimes he was engaged to prevent provincial amateur actors from murdering the dialogue outright, and incessantly jostling each other on the stage. In this last capacity, he occasionally got good employment, especially with regular amateur societies, who found his terms cheap enough, and his knowledge of theatrical discipline inestimably useful.

But chances like these were as nothing to the chances he got when he was occasionally employed to superintend all the toilsome part of the business in arranging private theatricals at country houses. Here, he met with greater generosity than he had ever dared to expect: here, the letter from Mr Kemble, vouching for his honesty and general stage-knowledge—the great actor's legacy of kindness to him, which he carried about everywhere—was sure to produce prodigious effect. He and little Annie, and a third member of the family whom I shall hereafter introduce, lived for months together on the proceeds of such a windfall as a private theatrical party—for the young people, in the midst of their amusement, found leisure to pity the poor old ex-player, and to admire his pretty granddaughter; and liberally paid him for his services full five times as much as he would ever have ventured to ask.

Thus, wandering about from town to town, sometimes miserably unsuccessful, sometimes re-animated by a little prosperity, he had come from Stratford-upon-Avon, while the present century was some twenty-five years younger than it is now, to try his luck at elocution with the people of Tidbury-on-the-Marsh—to teach the graces of delivery at seventy years of age, with half his teeth gone! Will he succeed? I, for one, hope so. There is something in the spectacle of this poor old man, sorely battered by the world, yet still struggling for life and for the grandchild whom he loves better than life—struggling hard, himself a remnant of a bygone age, to keep up with a new age which has already got past him, and will hardly hear his feeble voice of other times, except to laugh at it—there is surely something in this which forbids all thought of ridicule, and bids fair with everybody for compassion and goodwill.

But we have had talk enough, by this time, about Mr Reuben Wray. Let us now go at once and make acquaintance with him—not forgetting his mysterious cash box—at No. 12.

III

The breakfast things are laid in the little drawing-room at Reuben's lodgings. This drawing-room, observe, has not been hired by our friend; he never possessed such a domestic luxury in his life. The apartment, not being taken, has only been lent to him by his landlady, who is hugely impressed by the tragic suavity of her new tenant's manner and 'delivery'. The breakfast things, I say again, are laid. Three cups, a loaf, half-a-pound of salt butter, some moist sugar in a saucer, and a black earthenware tea-pot, with a broken spout; such are the sumptuous preparations which tempt Mr Wray and his family to come down at nine o'clock in the morning, and yet nobody appears!

Hark! there is a sound of creaking boots, descending, apparently, from some loft at the top of the house, so distant is the noise they make at first. This sound, coming heavily nearer and nearer, only stops at the drawing-room door, and heralds the entry of—

Mr Wray, of course? No!—no such luck: my belief is, that we shall never succeed in getting to Mr Wray personally. The individual in question is not even any relation of his; but he is a member of the family, for all that; and as the first to come downstairs, he certainly merits the reward of immediate notice.

He is nearly six feet high, proportionately strong and stout, and looks about thirty years of age. His gait is as awkward as it well can be; his features are large and ill-proportioned, his face is pitted with the small-pox, and what hair he has on his head—not much—seems to be growing in all sorts of contrary directions at once. I know nothing about him, personally, that I can praise, but his expression; and that is so thoroughly good-humoured, so candid, so innocent even, that it really makes amends for everything else. Honesty and kindliness look out so brightly from his eyes, as to dazzle your observation of his clumsy nose, and lumpy mouth and chin, until you hardly know whether they are ugly or not. Some men, in a certain sense, are ugly with the lineaments of the Apollo Belvedere; and others handsome, with features that might sit for a caricature. Our new acquaintance was of the latter order.

Allow me to introduce him to you:—THE GENTLE READER—JULIUS CAESAR. Stop! start not at those classic syllables; I will explain all.

The history of Mr Martin Blunt, alias 'Julius Caesar', is a good deal like the history of Mr Reuben Wray. Like him, Blunt began life with strolling players—not, however, as an actor, but as stage-carpenter, candle-snuffer, door-keeper, and general errand-boy. On one occasion, when the company were ambitiously bent on the horrible profanation of performing Shakespeare's *Julius Caesar*, the actor who was to personate the emperor fell ill. Nobody was left to supply his place—every other available member of the company was engaged in the play; so, in despair, they resorted to Martin Blunt. He was big enough for a Roman hero; and that was all they looked to.

They first cut out as much of his part as they could, and then half crammed the rest into his reluctant brains; they clapped a white sheet about the poor lad's body for a toga, stuck a truncheon into his hand, and a short beard on his chin; and remorselessly pushed him on the stage. His performance was received with shouts of laughter; but he went through it; was duly assassinated; and fell with a thump that shook the

[222]

surrounding scenery to its centre, and got him a complete round of applause all to himself.

He never forgot this. It was his first and last appearance; and, in the innocence of his heart, he boasted of it on every occasion, as the great distinction of his life. When he found his way to London; and as a really skilful carpenter, procured employment at Drury Lane, his fellow-workmen managed to get the story of his first performance out of him directly, and made a standing joke of it. He was elected a general butt, and nicknamed 'Julius Caesar', by universal acclamation. Everybody conferred on him that classic title; and I only follow the general fashion in these pages. If you don't like the name, call him any other you please: he is too good-humoured to be offended with you, do what you will.

He was thus introduced to old Wray:—

At the time when Reuben was closing his career at Drury Lane, our stout young carpenter had just begun to work there. One night, about a week before the performance of a new Pantomime, some of the heavy machinery tottered just as Wray was passing by it; and would have fallen on him, but for 'Julius Caesar' (I really can't call him Blunt!), who, at the risk of his own limbs, caught the tumbling mass; and by a tremendous exertion of main strength arrested it in its fall, till the old man had hobbled out of harm's way. This led to gratitude, friendship, intimacy. Wray and his preserver, in spite of the difference in their characters and ages, seemed to suit each other, somehow. In fine, when Reuben started to teach elocution in the country, the carpenter followed him, as protector, assistant, servant, or whatever you please.

'Julius Caesar' had one special motive for attaching himself to old Wray's fortunes, which will speedily appear, when little Annie enters the drawing-room. Awkward as he might be, he was certainly no encumbrance. He made himself useful and profitable in fifty different ways. He took round handbills soliciting patronage; constructed the scenery when Mr Wray got private theatrical engagements; worked as journeyman–carpenter when other resources failed; and was, in fact, ready for anything, from dunning for a bad debt, to cleaning a pair of boots. His master might at times be as fretful as he pleased, and treat him like an infant during occasional fits of crossness—he never replied, and never looked sulky. The only things he could not be got to do, were to abstain from inadvertently knocking everything down that came in his reach, and to improve the action of his arms and legs on the principle of the late Mr Kemble.

Let us return to the drawing-room, and the breakfast-things. 'Julius

Caesar', of the creaking boots, came into the room with a small work-box (which he had been secretly engaged in making for some time past) in one hand, and a new muslin cravat in the other. It was Annie's birthday. The box was a present; the cravat, what the French would call, a homage to the occasion.

His first proceeding was to drop the work-box, and pick it up again in a great hurry; his second, to go to the looking glass (no such piece of furniture ornamented his loft bedroom), and try to put on the new cravat. He had only half tied it, and was hesitating, utterly helpless, over the bow, when a light step sounded on the floor-cloth outside. Annie came in.

'Julius Caesar at the looking-glass! Oh, good gracious, what *can* have come to him!' exclaimed the little girl with a merry laugh.

How fresh, and blooming, and pretty she looked, as she ran up the next moment; and telling him to stoop, tied his cravat directly—standing on tiptoe. 'There,' she cried, 'now that's done, what have you got to say to me, sir, on my birthday!'

'I've got a box; and I'm so glad it's your birthday,' says Julius Caesar, too confused by the suddenness of the cravat-tying to know exactly what he is talking about.

'Oh, what a splendid work-box! how kind of you, to be sure! what care I shall take of it! Come, sir, I suppose I must tell you to give me a kiss after that,' and, standing on tiptoe again, she held up her fresh rosy cheek to be kissed, with such a pretty mixture of bashfulness, gratitude, and arch enjoyment in her look, that 'Julius Caesar', I regret to say, felt inclined then and there to go down upon both his knees and worship her outright.

Before the decorous reader has time to consider all this very improper, I had better, perhaps, interpose a word, and explain that Annie Wray had promised Martin Blunt, (I give his real name again here, because this is serious business,) yes; had actually promised him that one day she would be his wife. She kept all her promises; but I can tell you she was especially determined to keep this.

Impossible! exclaims the lady reader. With her good looks she might aspire many degrees above a poor carpenter; besides, how could she possibly care about a great lumpish, awkward fellow, who *is* ugly, say what you will about his expression?

I might reply, madam, that our little Annie had looked rather deeper than the skin in choosing her husband; and had found out certain qualities of heart and disposition about this poor carpenter, which made her love—aye, and respect and admire him too. But I prefer asking you a question, by way of answer. Did you never meet with any individuals of your own sex, lovely, romantic, magnificent young women, who have fairly stupefied the whole circle of their relatives and friends by marrying particularly short, scrubby, matter-of-fact, middle-aged men, showing, too, every symptom of fondness for them into the bargain? I fancy you must have seen such cases as I have mentioned; and, when you can explain them to *my* satisfaction, I shall be happy to explain the anomalous engagement of little Annie to *yours*.

In the meantime it may be well to relate, that this odd love affair was only once hinted at to Mr Wray. The old man flew into a frantic passion directly; and threatened dire extremities if the thing was ever thought of more. Lonely, and bereaved of all other ties, as he was, he had, in regard to his granddaughter, that jealousy of other people loving her, which is of all weaknesses, in such cases as his, the most pardonable and the most pure. If a duke had asked for Annie in marriage, I doubt very much whether Mr Wray would have let him have her, except upon the understanding that they were all to live together.

Under these circumstances, the engagement was never hinted at again. Annie told her lover they must wait, and be patient, and remain as brother and sister to one another, till better chances and better times came. And 'Julius Caesar' listened, and strictly obeyed. He was a good deal like a large, faithful dog to his little betrothed: he loved her, watched over her, guarded her, with his whole heart and strength; only asking in return, the privilege of fulfilling her slightest wish.

Well; this kiss, about which I have been digressing so long, was fortunately just over, when another footstep sounded outside; the door opened; and—yes! we have got him at last, in his own proper person! Enter Mr Reuben Wray!

Age has given him a stoop, which he tries to conceal, but cannot. His cheeks are hollow; his face is seamed with wrinkles, the work not only of time, but of trial, too. Still, there is vitality of mind, courage of heart about the old man, even yet. His look has not lost all its animation, nor his smile its warmth. *There* is the true Kemble walk, and the true Kemble carriage of the head for you, if you like!—*there* is the second-hand tragic grandeur and propriety, which the unfortunate 'Julius Caesar' daily contemplates, yet cannot even faintly copy! Look at his dress, again. Threadbare as it is (patched, I am afraid, in some places), there is not a speck of dust on it, and what little hair is left on his bald head is as carefully brushed as if he rejoiced in the love-locks of Absalom himself. No! though misfortune, and disappointment, and grief, and heavy-handed penury have all been assailing him ruthlessly enough for more than half a century, they have not got the brave old fellow down yet! At seventy years of age he is still on his legs in the prize-ring of Life; badly punished all over (as the pugilists say), but determined to win the fight to the last!

'Many happy reurns of the day, my love,' says old Reuben, going up to Annie, and kissing her. 'This is the twentieth birthday of yours I've lived to see. Thank God for that!'

'Look at my present, grandfather,' cries the little girl, proudly showing her work-box. 'Can you guess who made it?'

'You are a good fellow, Julius Caesar!' exclaims Mr Wray, guessing directly. 'Good morning; shake hands.'—(Then, in a lower voice to Annie)—'Has he broken anything in particular, since he's been up?' 'No!' 'I'm very glad to hear it. Julius Caesar, let me offer you a pinch of snuff,' and here he pulled out his box quite in the Kemble style. He had his natural manner, and his Kemble manner. The first only appeared when anything greatly pleased or affected him—the second was for those ordinary occasions when he had time to remember that he was a teacher of elocution, and a pupil of the English Roscius.

'Thank ye, kindly, sir,' said the gratified carpenter, cautiously advancing his huge finger and thumb towards the offered box.

'Stop!' cried old Wray, suddenly withdrawing it. He always lectured to Julius Caesar on elocution when he had nobody else to teach, just to keep his hand in. 'Stop! that won't do. In the first place, "Thank ye, kindly, sir", though good-humoured, is grossly inelegant. "Sir, I am obliged to you", is the proper phrase—mind you sound the *i* in obliged—never say *obleeged*, as some people do; and remember, what I am now telling *you*, Mr Kemble once said to the Prince Regent! The next hint I have to give is this—never take your pinch of snuff with your right hand finger and thumb; it should be always the left. Perhaps you would like to know why?'

'Yes, please, sir,' says the admiring disciple, very humbly.

'"Yes, *if* you please, sir," would have been better; but let that pass as a small error.—And now, I will tell you why, in an anecdote. Matthews was one day mimicking Mr Kemble to his face, in *Penruddock*—the great scene where he stops to take a pinch of snuff. "Very good, Matthews; very like me," says Mr Kemble complacently, when Matthews had done; "but you have made one great mistake." "What's that?" cries Matthews sharply. "My friend, you have not represented me taking snuff like a gentleman: now, I always do. You took your pinch, in imitating my

Penruddock, with your right hand: I use my *left*—a gentleman invariably does, because then he has his right hand always clean from tobacco to give to his friend!"—There! remember that: and now you may take your pinch.'

Mr Wray next turned round to speak to Annie; but his voice was instantly drowned in a perfect explosion of sneezes, absolutely screamed out by the unhappy 'Julius Caesar', whose nasal nerves were convulsed by the snuff. Mentally determining never to offer his box to his faithful follower again, old Reuben gave up making his proposed remark, until they were all quietly seated round the breakfast table: then, he returned to the charge with renewed determination.

'Annie, my dear,' said he, 'you and I have read a great deal together of our divine Shakespeare, as Mr Kemble always called him. You are my regular pupil, you know, and ought to be able to quote by this time almost as much as I can. I am going to try you with something quite new—suppose I had offered *you* the pinch of snuff (Mr Julius Caesar shall never have another, I can promise him); what would you have said from Shakespeare applicable to *that*? Just think now!'

'But, grandfather, snuff wasn't invented in Shakespeare's time—was it?' said Annie.

'That's of no consequence,' retorted the old man: 'Shakespeare was for *all* time: you can quote him for everything in the world, as long as the world lasts. Can't you quote him for snuff? I can. Now, listen. You say to me, "I offer you a pinch of snuff?" I answer from Cymbeline (Act iv, scene 2): "Pisanio! I'll now taste of thy drug." There! won't that do? What's snuff but a drug for the nose? It just fits—everything of the divine Shakespeare's does, when you know him by heart, as I do—eh, little Annie? And now give me some more sugar; I wish it was lump for *your* sake, dear; but I'm afraid we can only afford moist. Anybody called about the advertisement? a new pupil this morning—eh?'

No! no pupils at all: not a man, woman, or child in the town, to teach elocution to yet! Mr Wray was not at all despondent about this; he had made up his mind that a pupil must come in the course of the day; and that was enough for him. His little quibbling from Shakespeare about the snuff had put him in the best of good humours. He went on making quotations, talking elocution, and eating bread and butter, as brisk and happy, as if all Tidbury had combined to form one mighty class for him, and resolved to pay ready money for every lesson.

But after breakfast, when the things were taken away, the old man seemed suddenly to recollect something which changed his manner altogether. He grew first embarrassed; then silent; then pulled out his Shakespeare, and began to read with ostentatious assiduity, as if he were especially desirous that nobody should speak to him.

At the same time, a close observer might have detected Mr 'Julius Caesar' making various uncouth signs and grimaces to Annie, which the little girl apparently understood, but did not know how to answer. At last, with an effort, as if she were summoning extraordinary resolution, she said:—

'Grandfather—you have not forgotten your promise?'

No answer from Mr Wray. Probably, he was too much absorbed over Shakespeare to hear.

'Grandfather,' repeated Annie, in a louder tone; 'you promised to explain a certain mystery to us, on my birthday.'

Mr Wray was obliged to hear this time. He looked up with a very perplexed face.

'Yes, dear,' said he; 'I did promise; but I almost wish I had not. It's rather a dangerous mystery to explain, little Annie, I can tell you! Why should you be so very curious to know about it?'

'I'm sure, grandfather,' pleaded Annie, 'you can't say I am over-curious, or Julius Caesar either, in wanting to know it. Just recollect—we had been only three days at Stratford-upon-Avon, when you came in, looking so dreadfully frightened, and said we must go away directly. And you made us pack up; and we all went off in a hurry, more like prisoners escaping, than honest people.'

'We did!' groaned old Reuben, beginning to look like a culprit already.

'Well,' continued Annie; 'and you wouldn't tell us a word of what it was all for, beg as hard as we might. And then, when we asked why you never let that old cash box (which I used to keep my odds and ends in) out of your own hands, after we left Stratford—you wouldn't tell us that, either, and ordered us never to mention the thing again. It was only in one of your particular good humours, that I just got you to promise you would tell us all about it on my next birthday—to celebrate the day, you said. I'm sure we are to be trusted with any secrets; and I don't think it's being very curious to want to know this.'

'Very well,' said Mr Wray, rising, with a sort of desperate calmness; 'I've promised, and, come what may, I'll keep my promise. Wait here; I'll be back directly.' And he left the room, in a great hurry.

He returned immediately, with the cash box. A very battered, shabby affair, to make such a mystery about! thought Annie, as he put the box on the table, and solemnly laid his hands across it.

'Now, then,' said old Wray, in his deepest tragedy tones, and with very serious looks; 'Promise me, on your word of honour—both of you—that you'll never say a word of what I'm going to tell, to anybody, on any account whatever—I don't care what happens—*on any account whatever!*'

Annie and her lover gave their promises directly, and very seriously. They were getting a little agitated by all these elaborate preparations for the coming disclosure.

'Shut the door!' said Mr Wray, in a stage whisper. 'Now sit close and listen; I'm ready to explain the mystery.'

IV

'I suppose,' said old Reuben, 'you have neither of you forgotten that, on the second day of our visit to Stratford, I went out in the afternoon to dine with an intimate friend of mine, whom I'd known from a boy, and who lived at some little distance from the town—'

'Forget that!' cried Annie! 'I don't think we ever shall—I was frightened about you, all the time you were gone.'

'Frightened about what?' asked Mr Wray sharply. 'Do you mean to tell me, Annie, you suspected—'

'I don't know what I suspected, grandfather; but I thought your going away by yourself, to sleep at your friend's house (as you told us), and not to come back till the next morning, something very extraordinary. It was the first time we had ever slept under different roofs—only think of that!'

'I'm ashamed to say, my dear'—rejoined Mr Wray, suddenly beginning to look and speak very uneasily—'that I turned hypocrite, and something worse, too, on that occasion. I deceived you. I had no friend to go and dine with; and I didn't pass that night in any house at all.'

'Grandfather!'—cried Annie, jumping up in a fright—'What *can* you mean!'

'Beg pardon, sir,' added 'Julius Caesar', turning very red, and slowly clenching both his enormous fists as he spoke—'Beg pardon; but if you was put upon, or made fun of by any chaps that night, I wish you'd just please tell me where I could find 'em.'

'Nobody ill-used me,' said the old man, in steady, and even solemn tones. 'I passed that night by the grave of William Shakespeare, in Stratford-upon-Avon Church!'

Annie sank back into her seat, and lost all her pretty complexion in a moment. The worthy carpenter gave such a start, that he broke the back rail of his chair. It was a variation on his usual performances of this sort, which were generally confined to cups, saucers, and wine-glasses.

Mr Wray took no notice of the accident. This was of itself enough to show that he was strongly agitated by something. After a momentary silence, he spoke again, completely forgetting the Kemble manner and the Kemble elocution, as he went on.

'I say again, I passed all that night in Stratford Church; and you shall know for what. You went with me, Annie, in the morning—it was Tuesday: yes, Tuesday morning—to see Shakespeare's bust in the church. You looked at it, like other people, just as a curiosity—I looked at it, as the greatest treasure in the world; the only true likeness of Shakespeare! It's been done from a mask, taken from his own face, after death—I know it: I don't care what people say, I know it. Well, when we went home, I felt as if I'd seen Shakespeare himself, risen from the dead! Strangers would laugh if I told them so; but it's true—I did feel it. And this thought came across me, quick, like the shooting of a sudden pain:— I must make that face of Shakespeare mine; my possession, my companion, my great treasure that no money can pay for! And I've got it!—Here!—the only cast in the world from the Stratford bust is locked up in this old cash box!'

He paused a moment. Astonishment kept both his auditors silent.

'You both know,' he continued, 'that I was bred apprentice to a statuary. Among other things, he taught me to take casts: it was part of our business—the easiest part. I knew I could take a mould off the Stratford bust, if I had the courage; and the courage came to me: on the Tuesday, it came. I went and bought some plaster, some soft soap, and a quart basin—those were my materials—and tied them up together in an old canvas bag. Water was all I wanted besides; and that I saw in the church vestry, in the morning—a jug of it, left I suppose since Sunday, where it had been put for the clergyman's use. I could carry my bag under my cloak quite comfortably, you understand. The only thing that troubled me now was how to get into the church again, without being suspected. While I was thinking, I passed the inn door. Some people were on the steps, talking to some other people in the street: they were making an appointment to go all together, and see Shakespeare's bust and grave that very afternoon. This was enough for me: I determined to go into the church with them.'

'What! and stop there all night, grandfather?'

'And stop there all night, Annie. Taking a mould, you know, is not a

very long business; but I wanted to take mine unobserved; and the early
morning, before anybody was up, was the only time to do that safely in
the church. Besides, I wanted plenty of leisure, because I wasn't sure I
should succeed at first, after being out of practice so long in making casts.
But you shall hear how I did it, when the time comes. Well, I made up
the story about dining and sleeping at my friend's, because I didn't know
what might happen, and because—because, in short, I didn't like to tell
you what I was going to do. So I went out secretly, near the church; and
waited for the party coming. They were late—late in the afternoon,
before they came. We all went in together; I with my bag, you know, hid
under my cloak. The man who showed us over the church in the
morning, luckily for me, wasn't there: an old woman took his duty for
him in the afternoon. I waited till the visitors were all congregated round
Shakespeare's grave, bothering the poor woman with foolish questions
about him. I knew that was my time, and slipped off into the vestry, and
opened the cupboard, and hid myself among the surplices, as quiet as a
mouse. After a while, I heard one of the strangers in the church (they
were very rude, boisterous people) asking the other, what had become of
the 'old fogey with the cloak?' and the other answered that he must have
gone out, like a wise man, and that they had all better go after him, for
it was precious cold and dull in the church. They went away: I heard the
doors shut, and knew I was locked in for the night.'

'All night in a church! Oh, grandfather, how frightened you must have
been!'

'Well, Annie, I was a little frightened; but more at what I was going to
do, than at being alone in the church. Let me get on with my story
though. Being autumn weather, it grew too dark after the people went,
for me to do anything then; so I screwed my courage up to wait for the
morning. The first thing I did was to go and look quietly, all by myself,
at the bust; and I made up my mind that I could take the mould in about
three or four pieces. All I wanted was what they call a *mask*: that means
just a forehead and face, without the head. It's an easy thing to take a
mask off a bust—I knew I could do it; but, somehow, I didn't feel quite
comfortable just then. The bust began to look very awful to me, in the
fading light, all alone in the church. It was almost like looking at the ghost
of Shakespeare, in that place, and at that time. If the door hadn't been
locked, I think I should have run out of the church; but I couldn't do
that; so I knelt down and kissed the grave-stone—a curious fancy coming
over me as I did so, that it was like wishing Shakespeare good night—and
then I groped my way back to the vestry. When I got in, and had shut the

[231]

door between me and the grave, I grew bolder, I can tell you; and thought to myself—I'm doing no harm; I'm not going to hurt the bust; I only want what an Englishman and an old actor may fairly covet, a copy of Shakespeare's face; why shouldn't I eat my bit of supper here, and say my prayers as usual, and get my nap into the bargain, if I can? Just as I thought that—BANG went the clock, striking the hour! It almost knocked me down, bold as I felt the moment before. I was obliged to wait till it was all still again, before I could pull the bit of bread and cheese I had got with me out of my pocket. And when I did, I couldn't eat: I was too impatient for the morning; so I sat down in the parson's armchair; and tried, next, whether I could sleep at all.'

'And could you, grandfather?'

'No—I couldn't sleep either; at least, not at first. It was quite dark now; and I began to feel cold and awe-struck again. The only thing I could think of to keep up my spirits at all, was first saying my prayers, and then quoting Shakespeare. I went at it, Annie, like a dragon; play after play— except the tragedies; I was afraid of *them*, in a church at night, all by myself. Well: I think I had got half through the *Midsummer Night's Dream*, whispering over bit after bit of it; when I whispered myself into a doze. Then I fell into a queer sleep; and then I had such a dream! I dreamt that the church was full of moonlight—brighter moonlight than ever I saw awake. I walked out of the vestry; and there were the fairies of the *Midsummer Night's Dream*—all creatures like sparks of silver light— dancing round the Shakespeare bust! The moment they caught sight of me, they all called out in their sweet nightingale voices:—'Come along, Reuben! sly old Reuben! we know what you're here for, and we don't mind you a bit! You love Shakespeare, and so do we—dance, Reuben, and be happy! Shakespeare likes an old actor; he was an actor himself— nobody sees us! we're out for the night! foot it, old Reuben—foot it away!' And we all danced like mad: now, up in the air; now, down on the pavement; and now, all round the bust five hundred thousand times at least without stopping, till—BANG went the clock! and I woke up in the dark, in a cold perspiration.'

'I'm in one too!' gasped 'Julius Caesar', dabbing his brow vehemently with a ragged cotton pocket handkerchief.

'Well, after that dream I fell to reciting again; and got another doze; and had another dream—a terrible one, about ghosts and witches, that I don't recollect so well as the other. I woke up once more, cold, and in a great fright that I'd slept away all the precious morning daylight. No! all dark still! I went into the church again, and then back to the vestry, not being able to stay there. I suppose I did this a dozen times without knowing why. At last, never going to sleep again, I got somehow through the night—the night that seemed never to be done. Soon after daybreak, I began to walk up and down the church briskly, to get myself warm, keeping at it for a long time. Then, just as I saw through the windows that the sun was rising, I opened my bag at last, and got ready for work. I can tell you my hand trembled and my sight grew dim—I think the tears were in my eyes; but I don't know why—as I first soaped the bust all over to prevent the plaster I was going to put on it from sticking. Then I mixed up the plaster and water in my quart basin, taking care to leave no lumps, and finding it come as natural to me as if I had only left the statuary's shop yesterday; then—but it's no use telling you, little Annie, about what you don't understand; I'd better say shortly I made the mould, in four pieces, as I thought I should—two for the upper part of the face, and two for the lower. Then, having put on the outer plaster case to hold the mould, I pulled all off clean together, and looked, and knew that I had got a mask of Shakespeare from the Stratford bust!'

'Oh, grandfather, how glad you must have been then!'

'No, that was the odd part of it. At first, I felt as if I had robbed the bank, or the King's jewels, or had set fire to a train of gunpowder to blow up all London; it seemed such a thing to have done! Such a tremendously daring, desperate thing! But, a little while after, a frantic sort of joy came over me: I could hardly prevent myself from shouting and singing at the top of my voice. Then I felt a perfect fever of impatience to cast the mould directly; and see whether the mask would come out without a flaw. The keeping down that impatience was the hardest thing I had had to do since I first got into the church.'

'But, please, sir, whenever did you get out at last? Do pray tell us that!' asked 'Julius Caesar'.

'Not till after the clock had struck twelve, and I'd eaten all my bread and cheese,' said Mr Wray, rather piteously. 'I was glad enough when I heard the church door open at last, from the vestry where I had popped in but a moment before. It was the same woman came in who had shown the bust in the afternoon. I waited my time; and then slipped into the church; but she turned round sharply, just as I'd got half way out, and came up to me. I never was frightened by an old woman before; but I can tell you, *she* frightened me. "Oh! there are you again!" says she: "Come, I say! this won't do. You sneaked out yesterday afternoon without paying anything; and you sneak in again after me, as soon as I open the door this morning—ain't you ashamed of being so shabby as that, at your age?—

[233]

ain't you?" I never paid money in my life, Annie, with pleasure, till I gave that old woman some to stop her mouth! And I don't recollect either that I'd ever tried to run since leaving the stage (where we had a good deal of running, first and last, in the battle scenes); but I ran as soon as I got well away from the church, I can promise you—ran almost the whole way home.'

'That's what made you look so tired when you came in, grandfather,' said Annie; 'we couldn't think what was the matter with you at the time.'

'Well,' continued the old man, 'as soon as I could possibly get away from you, after coming back, I went and locked myself into my bedroom, pulled the mould in a great hurry out of the canvas bag, and took the cast at once—a beautiful cast! a perfect cast! I never produced a better when I was in good practice, Annie! When I sat down on the side of the bed, and looked at Shakespeare—*my* Shakespeare—got with so much danger, and made with my own hands—so white and pure and beautiful, just out of the mould! Old as I am, it was all I could do to keep myself from dancing for joy!'

'And yet, grandfather,' said Annie reproachfully, 'you could keep all that joy to yourself: you could keep it from *me*!'

'It was wrong my love, wrong on my part not to trust you—I'm sorry for it now. But the joy, after all, lasted a very little while—only from the afternoon to the evening. In the evening, if you remember, I went out to the butcher's to buy something for my own supper; something I could fancy, to make me comfortable before I went to bed (you little thought how I wanted my bed that night!). Well, when I got into the shop, several people were there; and what do you think they were all talking about? It makes me shudder even to remember it now! They were talking about a cast having been taken—*feloniously* taken, just fancy that, from the Stratford bust!'

Annie looked pale again instantly at this part of the story. As for 'Julius Caesar', though he said nothing, he was evidently suffering from a second attack of the sympathetic cold perspiration which had already troubled him. He used the cotton handkerchief more copiously than ever just at this moment.

'The butcher was speaking when I came in,' pursued Mr Wray. '"Who's been and took it," says the fellow, (his grammar and elocution were awful, Annie!) "nobody don't know yet; but the Town Council will know by to-morrow, and then he'll be took himself." "Ah," says a dirty little man in black, "he'll be cast into prison, for taking a cast—eh?" They laughed, actually laughed at this vile pun. Then another man asked how it had been found out. "Some says," answered the butcher, "he was seen a doin' of it, through the window, by some chap looking in accidental like: some says, nobody don't know but the churchwardens, and *they* won't tell till they've got him." "Well," says a woman, waiting with a basket to be served, "but how will they get him?—(two chops, please, when you're quite ready)—that's the thing: how will they get him?" "Quite easy; take my word for it;" says the man who made the bad pun. "In the first place, they've posted up handbills, offering a reward for him; in the second place, they're going to examine the people who show the church; in the third place—" "Bother your places!" cried the woman, "I wish I could get my chops." "There you are Mum," says the butcher, cutting off the chops, "and if you want my opinion about this business, it's this here: they'll transport him right away, in no time." "They can't," cries the dirty man, "they can only imprison him." "For life—eh?" says the woman, going off with the chops. "Be so kind as to let me have a couple of kidneys," said I; for my knees knocked together, and I could stand it no longer.'

'Then you thought, grandfather, that they suspected you?'

'I thought everything that was horrible, Annie. However, I got my kidneys, and went out unhindered, leaving them still talking about it. On my way home I saw the handbill—the handbill itself! Ten pounds reward for apprehending the man who had taken the cast! I read it twice through, in a sort of trance of terror. My mask taken away, and myself put in prison, if not transported—that was the prospect I had to give me an appetite for the kidneys. There was only one thing to be done: to get away from Stratford while I had the chance. The night-coach went that very evening, straight through to this place, which was far enough off for safety. We had some money, you know, left, after that last private-theatrical party, where they treated us so generously. In short, I made you pack up, Annie, as you said just now, and got you both off by the coach, in time, not daring to speak a word about my secret, and as miserable as I could be the whole journey. But let us say no more about that—here we are, safe and sound! and here's my face of Shakespeare— my diamond above all price—safe and sound, too! You shall see it; you shall look at the mask, both of you, and then, I hope, you'll acknowledge that you know as much as I do about the mystery!'

'But the mould,' cried Annie; 'haven't you got the mould with you, too?'

'Lord bless my soul!' exclaimed Mr Wray, slapping both hands, in desperation, on the lid of the cash box. 'Between the fright and the hurry of getting away, I quite forgot it—it's left at Stratford!'

'Left at Stratford!' echoed Annie, with a vague feeling of dismay, that she could not account for.

'Yes: rolled up in the canvas bag, and poked behind the landlord's volumes of the *Annual Register*, on the top shelf of the cupboard, in my bedroom. Between thinking of how to take care of the mask, and how to take care of myself, I quite forgot it. Don't look so frightened, Annie! The people at the lodgings are not likely to find it; and if they did, they wouldn't know what it was, and would throw it away. I've got the mask; and that's all I want—the mould is of no consequence to *me*, now—it's the mask that's everything—everything in the world!'

'I can't help feeling frightened, grandfather; and I can't help wishing you had brought away the mould, though I don't know why.'

'You're frightened, Annie, about the Stratford people coming after me here—that's what you're frightened about. But, if you and Julius Caesar keep the secret from everybody—and I know you will—there is no fear at all. They won't catch me back at Stratford again, or you either; and if the churchwardens themselves found the mould, *that* wouldn't tell them where I was gone, would it? Look up, you silly little Annie! We're quite safe here. Look up, and see the great sight I'm going to show you—a sight that nobody in England can show, but me;—the mask! the mask of Shakespeare!'

His cheeks flushed, his fingers trembled, as he took the key out of his pocket and put it into the lock of the old cash box. 'Julius Caesar', breathless with wonder and suspense, clapped both his hands behind him, to make sure of breaking nothing this time. Even Annie caught the infection of the old man's triumph and delight, and breathed quicker than usual when she heard the click of the opening lock.

'There!' cried Mr Wray, throwing back the lid; 'there is the face of William Shakespeare! there is the treasure which the greatest lord in this land doesn't possess—a copy of the Stratford bust! Look at the forehead! Who's got such a forehead now? Look at his eyes; look at his nose. He was not only the greatest man that ever lived, but the handsomest, too! Who says this isn't just what his face was; his face taken after death? Who's bold enough to say so? Just look at the mouth, dropped and open—that's one proof? Look at the cheek, under the right eye; don't you see a little paralytic gathering up of the muscle, not visible on the other side?—that's another proof! Oh, Annie, Annie! there's the very face that once looked out, alive and beaming, on this poor old world of ours! There's the man who's comforted me, informed me, made me what I am! There's the "counterfeit presentment", the precious earthly relic of that great spirit who is now with the angels in Heaven, and singing among the sweetest of them!'

His voice grew faint, and his eyes moistened. He stood looking at the mask, with a rapture and a triumph which no speech could express. At such moments as those, even through that poor, meagre face, the immortal spirit within could still shine out in the beauty which never dies!—even in that frail old earthly tenement, could still vindicate outwardly the divine destiny of all mankind!

They were yet gathered silently round the Shakespeare cast, when a loud knock sounded at the room door. Instantly, old Reuben banged down the lid of the cash box, and locked it; and *as* instantly, without waiting for permission to enter, a stranger walked in.

He was dressed in a long greatcoat, wore a red comforter round his neck, and carried a very old and ill-looking cat-skin cap in his hand. His face was uncommonly dirty; his eyes uncommonly inquisitive; his whiskers uncommonly plentiful; and his voice most uncommonly and determinately gruff, in spite of his efforts to dulcify it for the occasion.

'Miss, and gentlemen both, beggin' all your pardons,' said this new arrival, 'vich *is* Mr Wray?' As he spoke, his eyes travelled all round the room, seeing everything and everybody in it; and then glancing sharply at the cash box.

'I am Mr Wray, sir,' exclaimed our old friend, considerably startled, but recovering the Kemble manner and the Kemble elocution as if by magic.

'Wery good,' said the stranger. 'Then beggin' your pardon again, sir, in pertickler, could you be so kind as to 'blige me with a card o' terms? It's for a young gentleman as wants you, Mr Wray,' he continued in a whisper, approaching the old man, and quite abstractedly leaning one hand on the cash box.

'Take your hand off that box, sir,' cried Mr Wray, in a very fierce manner, but with a very trembling voice. At the same moment 'Julius Caesar' advanced a step or two, partially doubling his fist. The man with the cat-skin cap had probably never before been so nearly knocked down in his life. Perhaps he suspected as much; for he took his hand off the box in a great hurry.

'It was inadwertent, sir,' he remarked in explanation—'a little inadwertency of mine, that's all. But *could* you 'blige me with that card o' terms? The young gentleman as wants it has heerd of your advertisement;

[237]

and, bein' d'awful shaky in his pronounciashun, as vell as 'scruciatin' bad at readin' aloud, he's 'ard up for improvement—the sort o' secret thing you gives, you know, to the oraytors and the clujjymen, at three-and-six an hour. You'll heer from him in secret, Mr Wray, sir; and precious vork you'll 'ave to git him to rights; but do just 'blige me 'vith the card o' terms and the number of the 'ouse; 'cos I promised to git 'em for him today.'

'There is a card, sir, and I will engage to improve his delivery be it ever so bad,' said Mr Wray, considerably relieved at hearing the real nature of the stranger's errand.

'Miss, and gentlemen both, good mornin',' said the man, putting on his cat-skin cap, 'you'll heer from the young gentleman today; and wotever you do, sir, mind you keep the h'applicashun a secret—mind that!' He winked; and went out.

'I declare,' muttered Mr Wray, as the door closed, 'I thought he was a thief-taker from Stratford. Think of his being only a messenger from a new pupil! I told you we should have a pupil today. I told you so.'

'A very strange-looking messenger, grandfather, for a young gentle-man to choose!' said Annie.

'He can't help his looks, my dear; and I'm sure we shan't mind them, if he brings us money. Have you seen enough of the mask? if you hav'nt I'll open the box again.'

'Enough for today, I think, grandfather. But, tell me, why do you keep the mask in that old cash box?'

'Because I've nothing else, Annie, that will hold it, and lock up too. I was sorry, my dear, to disturb your "odds and ends", as you call them; but really there was nothing else to take. Stop! I've a thought! Julius Caesar shall make me a new box for the mask, and then you shall have your old one back again.'

'I don't want it, grandfather! I'd rather we none of us had it. Carrying a cash box like that about with us, might make some people think we had money in it.'

'Money! People think I have any money! Come, come, Annie! that really won't do! That's much too good a joke, you sly little puss, you!' And the old man laughed heartily, as he hurried off, to deposit the precious mask in his bedroom.

'You'll make that new box, Julius Caesar, won't you?' said Annie earnestly, as soon as her grandfather left the room.

'I'll get some wood, this very day,' answered the carpenter, 'and turn out such a box, by tomorrow, as—as—' He was weak at comparisons; so he stopped at the second 'as'.

'Make it quick, dear, make it quick,' said the little girl, anxiously; 'and then we'll give away the old cash box. If grandfather had only told us what he was going to do, at first, he need never have used it; for you could have made him a new box beforehand. But, never mind! make it quick, now!'

Oh, 'Julius Caesar!' strictly obey your little betrothed in this, as in all other injunctions! You know not how soon that new box may be needed, or how much evil it may yet prevent!

V

Perhaps, by this time, you are getting tired of three such simple, homely characters as Mr and Miss Wray, and Mr 'Julius Caesar', the carpenter. I strongly suspect you, indeed, of being downright anxious to have a little literary stimulant provided in the shape of a villain. You shall taste this stimulant—double distilled; for I have *two* villains all ready for you in the present chapter.

But, take my word for it, when you know your new company, you will be only too glad to get back again to Mr Wray and his family.

About three miles from Tidbury-on-the-Marsh, there is a village called Little London; sometimes, popularly entitled, in allusion to the characters frequenting it, 'Hell-End'. It is a dirty, ruinous-looking collection of some dozen cottages, and an ale-house. Ruffianly men, squalid women, filthy children, are its inhabitants. The chief support of this pleasant population is currently supposed to be derived from their connection with the poaching and petty larcenous interests of their native soil. In a word, Little London looks bad, smells bad, and *is* bad; a fouler blot of a village, in the midst of a prettier surrounding landscape, is not to be found in all England.

Our principal business is with the ale-house. The 'Jolly Ploughboys' is the sign; and Judith Grimes, widow, is the proprietor. The less said about Mrs Grimes's character, the better; it is not quite adapted to bear discussion in these pages. Mrs Grimes's mother (who is now bordering on eighty) may be also dismissed to merciful oblivion; for, at her daughter's age, she was—if possible—rather the worse of the two. Towards her son, Mr Benjamin Grimes (as one of the rougher sex), I feel less inclined to be compassionate. When I assert that he was in every respect a complete specimen of a provincial scoundrel, I am guilty, according to a profound and reasonable maxim of our law, of uttering a great libel, because I am repeating a great truth.

You know the sort of man well. You have seen the great, hulking, heavy-browed, sallow-complexioned fellow often enough, lounging at village corners, with a straw in his mouth and a bludgeon in his hand. Perhaps you have asked your way of him; and have been answered by a growl and a petition for money; or, you have heard of him in connection with a cowardly assault on your rural policeman; or a murderous fight with your friend's gamekeeper; or a bad case for your other friend, the magistrate, at petty sessions. Anybody who has ever been in the country, knows the man—the ineradicable plague-spot of his whole neighbour-hood—as well as I do.

About eight o'clock in the evening, and on the same day which had been signalized by Mr Wray's disclosures, Mrs Grimes, senior—or, as she was generally called, 'Mother Grimes'—sat in her armchair in the private parlour of The Jolly Ploughboys, just making up her mind to go to bed. Her ideas on this subject rather wanted acceleration; and they got it from her dutiful son, Mr Benjamin Grimes.

'Coom, old 'ooman, why doesn't thee trot up stairs?' demanded this provincial worthy.

'I'm a-going, Ben,—gently, Judith!—I'm a-going!' mumbled the old woman, as Mrs Grimes, junior, entered the room, and very unceremon-iously led her mother off.

'Mind thee doesn't let nobody in here tonight,' bawled Benjamin, as his sister went out. 'Chummy Dick's going to coom,' he added, in a mysterious whisper.

Left to himself to await the arrival of Chummy Dick, Mr Grimes found time hung rather heavy on his hands. He first looked out of the window. The view commanded a few cottages and fields, with a wood beyond on the rising ground,—a homely scene enough in itself; but the heavenly purity of the shining moonlight gave it, just now, a beauty not its own. This beauty was not apparently to the taste of Mr Grimes, for he quickly looked away from the window back into the room. Staring dreamily, his sunken sinister grey eyes fixed upon the opposite wall, encountering there nothing but four coloured prints, representing the career of the prodigal son. He had seen them hundreds of times before; but he looked at them again from mere habit.

In the first of the series, the prodigal son was clothed in a bright red dress coat, and was just getting on horseback (the wrong side); while his father, in a bright blue coat, helped him on with one hand, and pointed disconsolately with the other to a cheese-coloured road, leading straight from the horse's fore-feet to a distant city in the horizon, entirely composed of towers. In the second plate, master prodigal was feasting between two genteel ladies, holding gold wine glasses in their hands; while a debauched companion sprawled on the ground by his side, in a state of cataleptic drunkenness. In the third, he lay on his back; his red coat torn, and showing his purple skin; one of his stockings off; a thunderstorm raging over his head, and two white sows standing on either side of him—one of them apparently feeding off the calf of his leg. In the fourth—

Just as Mr Grimes had got to the fourth print he heard somebody whistling a tune outside, and turned to the window. It was Chummy Dick; or, in other words, the man with the cat-skin cap, who had honoured Mr Wray with a morning call.

Chummy Dick's conduct on entering the parlour had the merit of originality as an exhibition of manners. He took no more notice of Mr Grimes than if he had not been in the room; drew his chair to the fire-place; put one foot on each of the hobs; pulled a little card out of his greatcoat pocket; read it; and then indulged himself in a long, steady, unctuous fit of laughter, cautiously pitched in what musicians would call the 'minor key'.

'What dost thee laugh about like that?' asked Grimes.

'Git us a glass of 'ot grog fust—two lumps o' sugar, mind!—and then, Benjamin, you'll know in no time!' said Chummy Dick, maintaining an undercurrent of laughter all the while he spoke.

While Benjamin is gone for the grog, there is time enough for a word or two of explanation.

Possibly you may remember that the young assistant at Messrs Dunball and Dark's happened to see Mr Wray carrying his cash box into No. 12. The same gust of wind which, by blowing aside old Reuben's cloak, betrayed what he had got under it to this assistant, exposed the same thing, at the same time, to the observation of Mr Grimes, who happened to be lounging about the High Street on the occasion in question. Knowing nothing about either the mask or the mystery connected with it, it was only natural that Benjamin should consider the cash box to be a receptacle for cash; and it was, furthermore, not at all out of character that he should ardently long to be possessed of that same cash, and should communicate his desire to Chummy Dick.

And for this reason. With all the ambition to be a rascal of first-rate ability, Mr Grimes did not possess the necessary cunning and capacity, and had not received the early London education requisite to fit him for so exalted a position. Stealing poultry out of a farmyard, for instance, was quite in Benjamin's line; but stealing a cash box out of a barred and bolted-up house, standing in the middle of a large town, was an achievement above his powers—an achievement that but one man in his circle of acquaintance was mighty enough to compass—and that man was Chummy Dick, the great London housebreaker. Certain recent passages in the life of this illustrious personage had rendered London and its neighbourhood very insecure, in his case, for purposes of residence, so he had retired to a safe distance in the provinces; and had selected Tidbury and the adjacent country as a suitable field for action, and a very pretty refuge from the Bow Street Runners into the bargain.

'Wery good, Benjamin; and not too sveet,' remarked Chummy Dick, tasting the grog which Grimes had brought him. He was not, by any means, one of your ferocious housebreakers, except under strong provocation. There was more of oil than of aqua fortis in the mixture of his temperament. His robberies were marvels of skill, cunning, and cool determination. In short, he stole plate or money out of dwelling houses, as cats steal cream off breakfast tables—by biding his time, and never making a noise.

'Hast thee seen the cash box?' asked Grimes, in an eager whisper.

'Look at my 'and, Benjamin,' was the serenely triumphant answer. 'It's bin on the cash box! You're all right: the swag's ready for us.'

'Swag! Wot be that?'

'That's swag!' said Chummy Dick, pulling half-a-crown out of his pocket, and solemnly holding it up for Benjamin's inspection. 'I haven't got a fi' pun' note, or a christenin' mug about me; but notes and silver's swag, too. Now, young Grimes, you knows swag; and you'll *have* your swag before long, if you looks out sharp. If it ain't quite so fine a night tomorrer—if there ain't quite so much of that moonshine as there is now to let gratis for nothin'—why, we'll 'ave the cash box!'

'Half on it for *me*! Thee knows't that, Chummy Dick!'

'Check that 'ere talky-talky tongue of your'n; and you'll 'ave your 'alf. I've bin to see the old man; and he's gived me his wisitin' card, with the number of the 'ouse. Ho! ho! ho! think of his givin' his card to *me*! It's as good as inwitin' one to break into the 'ouse—it is, every bit!' And, with another explosion of laughter, Chummy Dick triumphantly threw Mr Wray's card into the fire.

'But that ain't the *pint*,' he resumed, when he had recovered his breath. 'We'll stick to the pint—the pint's the cash box.' And, to do him justice, he *did* stick to the point, never straying away from it, by so much as a hair's breadth, for a full half-hour.

The upshot of the long harangue to which he now treated Mr Benjamin Grimes, was briefly this: he had invented a plan, after reading the old man's advertisement first, for getting into Mr Wray's lodgings unsuspected; he had seen the cash box with his own eyes, and was satisfied, from certain indications, that there was money in it—he held the owner of this property to be a miser, whose gains were all hoarded up in his cash box, stray shillings and stray sovereigns together—he had next found out who were the inmates of the house; and had discovered that the only formidable person sleeping at No. 12 was our friend the carpenter—he had then examined the premises; and had seen that they were easily accessible by the back drawing-room window, which looked out on the wash-house roof—finally, he had ascertained that the two watchmen appointed to guard the town, performed that duty by going to bed regularly at eleven o'clock, and leaving the town to guard itself; the whole affair was perfectly easy—too easy in fact for anybody but a young beginner.

'Now, Benjamin,' said Chummy Dick, in conclusion—'mind this: no wiolence! Take your swag quiet, and you takes it safe. Wiolence is sometimes as bad as knockin' up a whole street—wiolence is the downy cracksman's last kick-out when he's caught in a fix. Fust and foremost, you've got your mask,' (here he pulled out a shabby domino mask,) 'wery good; nobody can't swear to you in that. Then, you've got your barker,' (he produced a pistol,) 'just to keep 'em quiet with the look of it, and if that won't do, there's your gag and bit o' rope' (he drew them forth,) 'for their mouths and 'ands. Never pull your trigger, till you see another man ready to pull his. Then you *must* make your row; and then you make it to some purpose. The nobs in our business—remember this, young Grimes!—always takes the swag easy; and when they can't take it easy, they takes it as easy as they can. That's visdom—the visdom of life!'

'Why thee bean't a-going, man?' asked Benjamin in astonishment, as the philosophical housebreaker abruptly moved towards the door.

'Me and you must'nt be seen together, tomorrer,' said Chummy Dick, in a whisper. 'You let me alone: I've got business to do tonight—never mind wot! At eleven tomorrer night, you be at the cross roads that meets on the top of the common. Look out sharp; and you'll see *me*.'

'But if so be it do keep moonshiny,' suggested Grimes.

'On second thoughts, Benjamin,' said the housebreaker, after a moment's reflection, 'we'll risk all the moonshine as ever shone—High

Street, Tidbury, ain't Bow Street, London!—we may risk it safe. Moon, or no moon, young Grimes! tomorrer night's *our* night!'

By this time he had walked out of the house. They separated at the door. The radiant moonlight falling lovely on all things, fell lovely even on *them*. How pure it was! how doubly pure, to shine on Benjamin Grimes and Chummy Dick, and not be soiled by the contact!

VI

During the whole remainder of Annie's birthday, Mr Wray sat at home, anxiously expecting the promised communication from the mysterious new pupil whose elocution wanted so much setting to rights. Though he never came, and never wrote, old Reuben still persisted in expecting him forthwith; and still waited for him as patiently the next morning, as he had waited the day before.

Annie sat in the room with her grandfather, occupied in making lace. She had learnt this art, so as to render herself, if possible, of some little use in contributing to the general support; and, sometimes, her manufacture actually poured a few extra shillings into the scantily filled family coffer. Her lace was not at all the sort of thing that your fine people would care to look at twice—it was just simple and pretty, like herself; and only sold (when it *did* sell, and that alas! was not often!) among ladies whose purses were very little better furnished than her own.

'Julius Caesar' was downstairs, in the back kitchen, making the all-important box—or, as the landlady irritably phrased it, 'making a mess about the house'. She was not partial to sawdust and shavings, and almost lost her temper when the glue pot invaded the kitchen fire. But work away, honest carpenter! work away, and never mind her! Get the mask of Shakespeare out of the old box, and into the new, before night comes; and you will have done the best day's work you ever completed in your life!

Annie and her grandfather had a great deal of talk about the Shakespeare cast, while they were sitting together in the drawing-room. If I were to report all old Reuben's rhapsodies and quotations during that period, I might fill the whole remaining space accorded to me in this little book. It was only once that the conversation varied at all. Annie just asked, by way of changing the subject a little, how a plaster cast was taken from the mould; and Mr Wray instantly went off at a tangent, in the midst of a new quotation, to tell her. He was still describing, for the second time, how the plaster and water were to be mixed, how the mixture was to be left to 'set', and how the mould was to be pulled off it, when the landlady, looking very hot and important, bustled into the room, exclaiming:—

'Mr Wray, sir! Mr Wray! Here's Squire Colebatch, of Cropley Court, coming upstairs to see you!' She then added, in a whisper: 'He's very hot-tempered and odd, sir, but the best gentleman in the world—'

'That will do, ma'am! that will do!' interrupted a hearty voice, outside the door. 'I can introduce myself; an old playwriter and an old play-actor don't want much introduction, I fancy! How are you, Mr Wray? I've come to make your acquaintance: how do you do, sir!'

Before the Squire came in, Mr Wray's first idea was that the young gentleman pupil had arrived at last—but when the Squire appeared, he discovered that he was mistaken. Mr Colebatch was an old gentleman with a very rosy face, with bright black eyes that twinkled incessantly, and with perfectly white hair, growing straight up from his head in a complete forest of venerable bristles. Moreover, his elocution wanted no improvement at all; and his 'delivery' proclaimed itself at once, as the delivery of a gentleman—a very eccentric one, but a gentleman still.

'Now, Mr Wray,' said the Squire, sitting down, and throwing open his greatcoat, with the air of an old friend; 'I've a habit of speaking to the point, because I hate ceremony and botheration. My name's Matthew Colebatch; I live at Cropley Court, just outside the town; and I come to see you, because I've had an argument about your character with the Reverend Daubeny Daker, the Rector here!'

Astonishment bereft Mr Wray of all power of speech, while he listened to this introductory address.

'I'll tell you how it was, sir,' continued the Squire. 'In the first place, Daubeny Daker's a canting sneak—a sort of fellow who goes into poor people's cottages, asking what they've got for dinner, and when they tell him, he takes the cover off the saucepan and sniffs at it, to make sure that they've spoken the truth. That's what *he* calls doing his duty to the poor, and what *I* call being a canting sneak! Well, Daubeny Daker saw your advertisement in Dunball's shop window. I must tell you, by-the-by, that he calls theatres the devil's houses, and actors the devil's missionaries; I heard him say that in a sermon, and have never been into his church since! Well, sir, he read your advertisement; and when he came to that part about improving clergymen at three-and-sixpence an hour (it would be damned cheap to improve Daubeny Daker at that price!) he falls into one of his nasty, cold-blooded, sneering rages, goes into the shop, and insists on having the thing taken down, as an insult offered by a vagabond actor to the clerical character—don't lose your temper, Mr Wray, don't, for God's sake—I trounced him about it handsomely, I can promise you! And now, what do you think that fat jackass Dunball did, when he heard what the parson said? Took your card down!—took it out of the window directly, as if Daubeny Daker was King of Tidbury, and it was death to disobey him!'

'My character, sir!' interposed Mr Wray.

'Stop, Mr Wray! I beg your pardon; but I *must* tell you how I trounced him. Half an hour after the thing had been taken down, I dropped into the shop. Dunball, smiling like a fool, tells me about the business. "Put it up again, directly!" said I; "I won't have any man's character bowled down like that by people who don't know him!" Dunball makes a wry face and hesitates. I pull out my watch, and say to him, "I give you a minute to decide between *my* custom and interest, and Daubeny Daker's." I happen to be what's called a rich man, Mr Wray; so Dunball decided in about two seconds, and up went your advertisement again, just where it was before!'

'I have no words, sir, to thank you for your kindness,' said poor old Reuben.

'Hear how I trounced Daubeny Daker, sir—hear that! I met him out at dinner, the same night. He was talking about you, and what he'd done— as proud as a peacock! "In fact," says he, at the end of his speech, "I considered it my duty, as a clergyman, to have the advertisement taken down." "And I considered it my duty, as a gentleman," said I, "to have it put up again." *Then*, we began the argument (he hates me, because I once wrote a play—I know he does). I won't tell you what he said, because it would distress you. But it ended, after we'd been at it, hammer and tongs, for about an hour, by my saying that his conduct in setting you down as a disreputable character, without making a single enquiry about you, showed a want of Christianity, justice, and common sense. "I can bear with your infirmities of temper, Mr Colebatch," says he, in his nasty, sneering way; "but allow me to ask, do *you*, who defend Mr Wray so warmly, know any more of him than I do?" He thought this was a settler; but I was at him again, quick as lightning. "No, sir; but I'll set you a proper example, by going tomorrow morning, and judging of the man from the man himself!" That was a settler for *him*: and now, here I am this morning, to do what I said.'

'I will show you, Mr Colebatch, that I have deserved the honour of being defended by you,' said Mr Wray, with a mixture of artless dignity and manly gratitude in his manner, which became him wonderfully; 'I have a letter, sir, from the late Mr Kemble—'

'What, my old friend, John Philip!' cried the Squire; 'let's see it instantly! He, Mr Wray, was "the noblest Roman of them all", as Shakespeare says.'

Here was an inestimable friend indeed! He knew Mr Kemble and quoted Shakespeare. Old Reuben could actually have embraced the Squire at that moment; but he contented himself with producing the great Kemble letter.

Mr Colebatch read it, and instantly declared that, as a certificate of character, it beat all other certificates that ever were written completely out of the field; and established Mr Wray's reputation as above the reach of all calumny. 'It's the most tremendous crusher for Daubeny Daker that ever was composed, sir!' Just as the old gentleman said this, his eyes encountered little Annie, who had been sitting quietly in the corner of the room, going on with her lace. He had hardly allowed himself leisure enough to look at her, in the first heat of his introductory address, but he made up for lost time now, with characteristic celerity.

'Who's that pretty little girl?' said he; and his bright eyes twinkled more than ever as he spoke.

'My granddaughter, Annie,' answered Mr Wray, proudly.

'Nice little thing! how pretty and quiet she sits making her lace!' cried Mr Colebatch, enthusiastically. 'Don't move, Annie; don't go away! I like to look at you! You won't mind a queer old bachelor, like me—will you? You'll let me look at you—won't you? Go on with your lace, my dear, and Mr Wray and I will go on with our chat.'

This 'chat' completed what the Kemble letter had begun. Encouraged by the Squire, old Reuben artlessly told the little story of his life, as if to an intimate friend; and told it with all the matchless pathos of simplicity and truth. What time Mr Colebatch could spare from looking at Annie—and that was not much—he devoted to anathematising his implacable enemy, Daubeny Daker, in a series of violent expletives; and anticipating, with immense glee, the sort of consummate 'trouncing' he should now be able to inflict on that reverend gentleman, the next time he met with him. Mr Wray only wanted to take one step more after this in the Squire's estimation, to be considered the phoenix of all professors of elocution, past, present, and future: and he took it. He actually recollected the production of Mr Colebatch's play—a tragedy all bombast and bloodshed—at Drury Lane Theatre; and, more than that, he had himself performed one of the minor characters in it!

The Squire seized his hand immmediately. This play (in virtue of which he considered himself a dramatic author,) was his weak point. It had enjoyed a very interrupted 'run' of one night; and had never been heard of after. Mr Colebatch attributed this circumstance entirely to public misappreciation; and, in his old age, boasted of his tragedy wherever he went, utterly regardless of the reception it had met with. It has often been asserted that the parents of sickly children are the parents who love their children best. This remark is sometimes, and only sometimes, true. Transfer it, however, to the sickly children of literature, and it directly becomes a rule which the experience of the whole world is powerless to confute by a single exception!

'My dear sir!' cried Mr Colebatch, 'your remembrance of my play is a new bond between us! It was entitled—of course you recollect—*The Mysterious Murderess*. Gad, sir, do you happen to call to mind the last four lines of the guilty Lindamira's death scene? It ran thus, Mr Wray:—

'Murder and midnight hail! Come all ye horrors!
My soul's congenial darkness quite defies ye!
I'm sick with guilt!—What is to cure me?—This! (*Stabs herself*)
Ha! ha! I'm better now—(*smiles faintly*)—I'm comfortable!' (*Dies*)

'If that's not pretty strong writing, sir, my name's not Matthew Colebatch! and yet the besotted audience failed to appreciate it! Bless my soul!' (pulling out his watch) 'one o'clock, already! I ought to be at home! I must go directly. Goodbye, Mr Wray. I'm so glad to have seen you, that I could almost thank Daubeny Daker for putting me in the towering passion that sent me here. You remind me of my young days, when I used to go behind the scenes, and sup with Kemble and Matthews. Goodbye, little Annie! I'm a wicked old fellow, and I mean to kiss you some day! Not a step further, Mr Wray; not a step, by George, sir; or I'll never come again. I mean to make the Tidbury people employ your talents; they're the most infernal set of asses under the canopy of heaven; but they *shall* employ them! I engage you to read my play, if nothing else will do, at the Mechanics' Institution. We'll make their flesh creep, sir; and their hair stand on end, with a little tragedy of the good old school. Goodbye, till I see you again, and God bless you!' And away the talkative old Squire went, in a mighty hurry, just as he had come in.

'Oh, grandfather! what a nice old gentleman!' exclaimed Annie, looking up for the first time from her lace cushion.

'What unexampled kindness to *me*! What perfect taste in everything! Did you hear him quote Shakespeare?' cried old Reuben, in an ecstasy. They went on alternately, in this way, with raptures about Mr Colebatch, for something like an hour. After that time, Annie left her work, and walked to the window.

'It's raining—raining fast,' she said. 'Oh, dear me! we can't have our walk today!'

'Hark! there's the wind moaning,' said the old man. 'It's getting colder, too. Annie! we are going to have a stormy night.'

Four o'clock! And the carpenter still at his work in the back kitchen. Faster, 'Julius Caesar'; faster. Let us have that mask of Shakespeare out of Mr Wray's cash box, and snugly ensconced in your neat wooden casket, before anybody goes to bed tonight. Faster, man!—Faster!

VII

For some household reason not worth mentioning, they dined later that day than usual at No. 12. It was five o'clock before they sat down to table. The conversation all turned on the visitor of the morning; no terms in Mr Wray's own vocabulary being anything like choice enough to characterize the eccentric old squire, he helped himself to Shakespeare, even more largely than usual, every time he spoke of Mr Colebatch. He managed to discover some striking resemblance to that excellent gentleman (now in one particular, and now in another), in every noble and venerable character, throughout the whole series of the plays—not forgetting either, on one or two occasions, to trace the corresponding likeness between the more disreputable and intriguing personages, and that vindictive enemy to all plays, players, and playhouses, the Reverend Daubeny Daker. Never did any professed commentator on Shakespeare (and the assertion is a bold one) wrest the poet's mighty meaning more dexterously into harmony with his own microscopic ideas, than Mr Wray now wrested it, to furnish him with eulogies on the goodness and generosity of Mr Matthew Colebatch, of Cropley Court.

Meanwhile, the weather got worse and worse, as the evening advanced. The wind freshened almost to a gale; and dashed the fast-falling rain against the window, from time to time, with startling violence. It promised to be one of the wildest, wettest, darkest nights they had had at Tidbury since the winter began.

Shortly after the table was cleared, having pretty well exhausted himself on the subject of Mr Colebatch, for the present, old Reuben fell asleep in his chair. This was rather an unusual indulgence for him, and was probably produced by the especial lateness of the dinner. Mr Wray generally took that meal at two o'clock, and set off for his walk afterwards, reckless of all the ceremonial observances of digestion. He was a poor man, and could not afford the luxurious distinction of being dyspeptic.

The behaviour of Mr 'Julius Caesar', the carpenter, when he appeared from the back kitchen to take his place at dinner, was rather perplexing. He knocked down a salt-cellar; spurted some gravy over his shirt; and spilt a potato, in trying to transport it a distance of about four inches, from the dish to Annie's plate. This, to begin with, was rather above the general average of his number of table accidents at one meal. Then, when dinner was over, he announced his intention of returning to the back kitchen for the rest of the evening, in tones of such unwonted mystery, that Annie's curiosity was aroused, and she began to question him. Had he not done the new box yet? No! Why, he might have made such a box in an hour, surely? Yes, he might. And why had he not? 'Wait a bit, Annie, and you'll see!' And having said that, he laid his large finger mysteriously against the side of his large nose, and walked out of the room forthwith.

In half-an-hour afterwards he came in again, looking very sheepish and discomposed, and trying, unsuccessfully, to hide an enormous poultice—a perfect loaf of warm bread and water—which decorated the palm of his right hand. This time, Annie insisted on an explanation.

It appeared that he had conceived the idea of ornamenting the lid of the new box with some uncouth carvings of his own, in compliment to Mr Wray and the mask of Shakespeare. Being utterly unpractised in the difficult handiwork he proposed to perform, he had run a splinter into the palm of his hand. And there the box was now in the back kitchen, waiting for lock and hinges, while the only person in the house who could put them on, was not likely to handle a hammer again for days to come. Miserable 'Julius Caesar!' Never was well-meant attention more fatally misdirected than this attention of yours! Of all the multifarious accidents of your essentially accidental life, this special casualty, which has hindered you from finishing the new box tonight, is the most ill-timed and the most irreparable!

When the tea came in Mr Wray woke up; and as it usually happens with people who seldom indulge in the innocent sensuality of an after-dinner nap, changed at once, from a state of extreme somnolence to a state of extreme wakefulness. By this time the night was at its blackest; the rain fell fierce and thick, and the wild wind walked abroad in the darkness, in all its might and glory. The storm began to affect Annie's spirits a little, and she hinted as much to her grandfather, when he awoke. Old Reuben's extraordinary vivacity immediately suggested a remedy for this. He proposed to read a play of Shakespeare's as the surest mode of diverting attention from the weather; and, without allowing a moment for the consideration of his offer, he threw open the book, and began *Macbeth*.

As he not only treated his hearers to every one of the Kemble pauses, and every infinitesimal inflection of the Kemble elocution, throughout the reading; but also exhibited a serious parody of Mrs Siddons' effects in Lady Macbeth's sleep-walking scene, with the aid of a white pocket-handkerchief, tied under his chin, and a japanned bedroom candlestick in his hand—and as, in addition to these special and strictly dramatic delays, he further hindered the progress of his occupation by vigilantly keeping his eye on 'Julius Caesar', and unmercifully waking up that ill-starred carpenter every time he went to sleep, (which, by the way, was once in every ten minutes,) nobody can be surprised to hear that *Macbeth* was not finished before eleven o'clock. The hour was striking from Tidbury Church, as Mr Wray solemnly declaimed the last lines of the tragedy, and shut up the book.

'There!' said old Reuben, 'I think I've put the weather out of your head, Annie, by this time! You look sleepy, my dear; go to bed. I had a few remarks to make, about the right reading of Macbeth's dagger-scene, but I can make them tomorrow morning, just as well. I won't keep you up any longer. Good night, love!'

Was Mr Wray not going to bed, too? No: he never felt more awake in his life; he would sit up a little, and have a good 'warm' over the fire. Should Annie bear him company? By no means! he would not keep poor Annie from her bed, on any account. Should 'Julius Caesar'?—Certainly not! he was sure to go to sleep immediately; and to hear him snore, Mr Wray said, was worse than hearing him sneeze. So the two young people wished the old man goodnight, and left him to have his 'warm', as he desired. This was the way in which he prepared himself to undergo that luxurious process:—

He drew his armchair in front of the fire, then put a chair on either side of it, then unlocked the cupboard, and took out the cash box that contained the mask of Shakespeare. This he deposited upon one of the side chairs; and upon the other he put his copy of the Plays, and the candle. Finally, he sat down in the middle—cosy beyond all description—and slowly inhaled a copious pinch of snuff.

'How it blows, outside!' said old Reuben, 'and how snug I am, in here!'

He unlocked the cash box, and taking it on his knee, looked down on the mask that lay inside. Gradually, the pride and pleasure at first appearing in his eyes, gave place to a dreamy fixed expression. He gently closed the lid, and reclined back in his chair; but he did not shut up the cash box for the night, for he never turned the key in the lock.

Old recollections were crowding on him, revived by his conversation of the morning with Mr Colebatch; and now evoked by many a Shakespeare association of his own, always connected with the treasured, the inestimable mask. Tender remembrances spoke piteously and solemnly within him. Poor Columbine—lost, but never forgotten—moved loveliest and holiest of all those memory shadows, through the dim world of his waking visions. How little the grave can hide of us! The love that began before it, lasts after it. The sunlight to which our eyes looked, while it shone on earth, changes but to the star that guides our memories when it passes to heaven!

Hark! the church clock chimes the quarters; each stroke sounds with the ghostly wildness of all bell-tones, when heard amid the tumult of a storm, but fails to startle old Reuben now. He is far away in other scenes; living again in other times. Twelve strikes; and then, when the clock bell rings its long midnight peal, he rouses—he hears that.

The fire has died down to one, dull, red spot: he feels chilled; and sitting up in his chair, yawning, tries to summon resolution enough to rise and go upstairs to bed. His expression is just beginning to grow utterly listless and weary, when it suddenly alters. His eyes look eager again; his lips close firmly; his cheeks get pale all at once—he is listening.

He fancies that, when the wind blows in the loudest gusts, or when the rain dashes heaviest against the window, he hears a very faint, curious sound—sometimes like a scraping noise, sometimes like a tapping noise. But in what part of the house—or even whether outside or in—he cannot tell. In the calmer moments of the storm, he listens with especial attention to find this out; but it is always at that very time that he hears nothing.

It must be imagination. And yet, that imagination is so like a reality that it has made him shudder all over twice in the last minute.

Surely he hears that strange noise now! Why not get up, and go to the window, and listen if the faint tapping comes by any chance from outside, in front of the house? Something seems to keep him in his chair, perfectly motionless—something makes him afraid to turn his head, for fear of seeing a sight of horror close at his side—

Hush! it sounds again, plainer and plainer. And now it changes to a cracking noise—close by—at the shutter of the back drawing-room window.

What is that, sliding along the crack between the folding doors and the floor?—a light!—a light in that empty room which nobody uses. And now, a whisper—footsteps—the handle on the lock of the door moves—

'Help! Help! for God's sake!—Murder! Mur—'

Just as that cry for help passed the old man's lips, the two robbers, masked and armed, appeared in the room; and the next instant, Chummy Dick's gag was fast over his mouth.

He had the cash box clasped tight to his breast. Mad with terror, his eyes glared like a dead man's, while he struggled in the powerful arms that held him.

Grimes, unused to such scenes, was so petrified by astonishment at finding the old man out of bed, and the room lit up, that he stood with his pistol extended, staring helplessly through the eyeholes of his mask. Not so with his experienced leader. Chummy Dick's ears and eyes were as quick as his hands—the first informed him that Reuben's cry for help (skilfully as he had stifled it with the gag) had aroused some one in the house: the second instantly detected the cash box, as Mr Wray clasped it to his breast.

'Put up your pop-gun, you precious yokel, you!' whispered the housebreaker fiercely. 'Look alive; and pull it out of his arms. Damn you! do it quick! they're awake, up stairs!'

It was not easy to 'do it quick'. Weak as he was, Reuben actually held his treasure with the convulsive strength of despair, against the athletic ruffian who was struggling to get it away. Furious at the resistance, Grimes exerted his whole force, and tore the box so savagely from the old man's grasp, that the mask of Shakespeare flew several feet away, through the open lid, before it fell, shattered into fragments on the floor.

For an instant, Grimes stood aghast at the sight of what the contents of the cash box really were. Then, frantic with the savage passions produced by the discovery, he rushed up to the fragments, and, with a horrible oath, stamped his heavy boot upon them, as if the very plaster could feel his vengeance. 'I'll kill him, if I swing for it!' cried the villain, turning on Mr Wray the next moment, and raising his horse-pistol by the barrel over the old man's head.

But, exactly at the same time, brave as his heroic namesake, 'Julius Caesar' burst into the room. In the heat of the moment, he struck at Grimes with his wounded hand. Dealt even under that disadvantage, the blow was heavy enough to hurl the fellow right across the room, till he dropped down against the opposite wall. But the triumph of the stout carpenter was a short one. Hardly a second after his adversary had fallen, he himself lay stunned on the floor by the pistol-butt of Chummy Dick.

Even the nerve of the London housebreaker deserted him, at the first discovery of the astounding self-deception of which he and his companion had been the victims. He only recovered his characteristic coolness and self-possession when the carpenter attacked Grimes. Then, true to his system of never making unnecessary noise, or wasting unnecessary powder, he hit 'Julius Caesar' just behind the ear, with unerring dexterity. The blow made no sound, and seemed to be inflicted by a mere turn of the wrist; but it was decisive—he had thoroughly stunned his man.

And now, the piercing screams of the landlady, from the bedroom floor poured quicker and quicker into the street, through the opened window. They were mingled with the fainter cries of Annie, whom the good woman forcibly detained from going into danger down stairs. The female servant (the only other inmate of the house) rivalled her mistress in shrieking madly and incessantly for help, from the window of the garret above.

'The whole street will be up in a crack!' cried Chummy Dick, swearing at every third word he uttered, and hauling the partially-recovered Grimes into an erect position again, 'there's no swag to be got here! step out quick, young yokel, or you'll be nabbed!'

He pushed Grimes into the back drawing-room; hustled him over the window-sill on to the wash-house roof, leaving him to find his own way, how he could, to the ground; and then followed, with Mr Wray's watch and purse, and a brooch of Annie's that had been left on the chimney-piece, all gathered into his capacious greatcoat pocket in a moment. They were not worth much as spoils; but the dexterity with which they were taken instantly with one hand, while he had Grimes to hold with the other; and the strength, coolness, and skill he displayed in managing the retreat, were worthy even of the reputation of Chummy Dick. Long before the two Tidbury watchmen had begun to think of a pursuit, the housebreaker and his companion were out of reach—even though the Bow Street Runners themselves had been on the spot to give chase.

How long the old man has kept in that one position!—crouching down there in the corner of the room, without stirring a limb or uttering a word. He dropped on his knees at that place, when the robbers left him; and nothing has moved him from it since.

When Annie broke away from the landlady, and ran down stairs—he never stirred. When the long wail of agony burst from her lips, as she saw the dead look of the brave man lying stunned on the floor—he never spoke. When the street door was opened; and the crowd of terrified, half-dressed neighbours all rushed together into the house, shouting and trampling about, half panic-stricken at the news they heard—he never noticed a single soul. When the doctor was sent for; and, amid an awful hush of expectation, proceeded to restore the carpenter to his senses— even at that enthralling moment, he never looked up. It was only when the room was cleared again—when his granddaughter came to his side, and, putting her arm round his neck, laid her cold cheek close to his— that he seemed to live at all. Then, he just heaved a heavy sigh; his head dropped down lower on his breast; and he shivered throughout his whole frame, as if some icy influence was freezing him to the heart.

All that long, long time he had been looking on one sight—the fragments of the mask of Shakespeare lying beneath him. And there he kept now—when they tried in their various methods to coax him away— still crouching over them; just in the same position; just with the same hard, frightful look about his face that they had seen from the first.

Annie went and fetched the cash box; and tremblingly put it down before him. The instant he saw it, his eyes began to flash. He pounced in a fury of haste upon the fragments of the mask, and huddled them all together into the box, with shaking hands, and quick panting breath. He picked up the least chip of plaster that the robber had ground under his boot; and strained his eyes to look for more, when not an atom more was left. At last, he locked the box, and caught it up tight to his breast; and then he let them raise him up, and lead him gently away from the place.

He never quitted hold of his box, while they got him into bed. Annie, and her lover, and the landlady, all sat up together in his room; and all, in different degrees, felt the same horrible foreboding about him, and shrank from communicating it to one another. Occasionally, they heard him beating his hands strangely on the lid of the box; but he never spoke; and, as far as they could discover, never slept.

The doctor had said he would be better when the daylight came.—Did the doctor really know what was the matter with him?—and had the doctor any suspicion that something precious had been badly injured that night, besides the mask of Shakespeare?

VIII

By the next morning the news of the burglary had not only spread all through Tidbury, but all through the adjacent villages as well. The very first person who called at No. 12, to see how they did after the fright of the night before, was Mr Colebatch. The old gentleman's voice was heard louder than ever, as he ascended the stairs with the landlady. He declared he would have both the Tidbury watchmen turned off, as totally unfit to take care of the town. He swore that, if it cost him a hundred pounds, he would fetch the Bow Street Runners down from London, and procure the catching, trying, convicting, and hanging of 'those two infernal housebreakers' before Christmas came. Invoking vengeance and retribution in this way, at every fresh stair, the Squire's temperament was up at 'bloodheat', by the time he got into the drawing-room. It fell directly, however, to 'temperate' again, when he found nobody there; and it sank twenty degrees lower still, at the sight of little Annie's face, when she came down to see him.

'Cheer up, Annie!' said the old gentleman with a last faint attempt at joviality. 'It's all over now, you know: how's grandfather? Very much frightened still—eh?'

'Oh, sir! frightened, I'm afraid out of his mind!' and unable to control herself any longer, poor Annie fairly burst into tears.

'Don't cry, Annie! no crying! I can't stand it—you mustn't really!' said the Squire in anything but steady tones, 'I'll talk him back into his mind; I will, as sure as my name's Matthew Colebatch—Stop!' (here he pulled out his voluminous India pocket handkerchief, and began very gently and caressingly to wipe away her tears, as if she had been a little child, and his own daughter). 'There, now we've dried them up—no we haven't! there's one left—And now that's gone, let's have a little talk about this business, my dear, and see what's to be done. In the first place, what's all this I hear about a plaster cast being broken?'

Annie would have given the world to open her heart about the mask of Shakespeare, to Mr Colebatch; but she thought of her promise, and she thought, also, of the Town Council of Stratford, who might hear of the secret somehow, if it was once disclosed to anybody; and might pursue her grandfather with all the powers of the law, miserable and shattered though he now was, even to his hiding-place, at Tidbury-on-the-Marsh.

'I've promised, sir, not to say anything about the plaster cast to anybody,' she began, looking very embarrassed and unhappy.

'And you'll keep your promise,' interposed the Squire; 'that's right—good, honest little girl! I like you all the better for it; we won't say a word more about the cast; but what have they taken? what have the infernal scoundrels taken?'

'Grandfather's old silver watch, sir, and his purse with seventeen and sixpence in it, and my brooch—but that's nothing.'

'Nothing— Annie's brooch nothing!' cried the Squire, recovering his constitutional testiness. 'But, never mind, I'm determined to have the rascals caught and hung, if it's only for stealing that brooch! And now, look here, my dear; if you don't want to put me into one of my passions, take that, and say nothing about it!'

'Take' what? gracious powers! 'take' Golconda! he had crumpled a ten pound note into her hand!

'I say, again, you obstinate little thing, don't put me in one of my passions!' exclaimed the old gentleman, as poor Annie made some faint show of difficulty in taking the gift. 'God forbid I should think of hurting your feelings, my dear, for such a paltry reason as having a few more pounds in *my* pocket, than you have in *yours*!' he continued, in such serious, kind tones, that Annie's eyes began to fill again. 'We'll call that bank note, if you like, payment beforehand, for a large order for lace, from me. I saw you making lace, you know, yesterday; and I mean to consider you my lace manufacturer in ordinary, for the rest of your life. By George!'—he went on, resuming his odd abrupt manner,—'it's unknown the quantity of lace I shall want to buy! There's my old housekeeper, Mrs Buddle—hang me, Annie, if I don't dress her in nothing but lace, from top to toe, inside and out, all over! Only mind this, you don't set to work at the order till I tell you! We must wait till Mrs Buddle has worn out her old stock of petticoats, before we begin— eh? There! there! there! don't go crying again! Can I see Mr Wray? No?— Quite right! better not disturb him so soon. Give him my compliments, and say I'll call tomorrow. Put up the note! put up the note! and don't be low-spirited—and don't do another thing, little Annie; don't forget you've got a queer old friend, who lives at Cropley Court!'

Running on in this way, the good Squire fairly talked himself out of the room, without letting Annie get in a word edgewise. Once on the stairs, he fell foul of the housebreakers again, with undiminished fury.

The last thing the landlady heard him say, as she closed the street-door after him, was, that he was off now, to 'trounce' the two Tidbury watchmen, for not stopping the robbery—to 'trounce them handsomely', as sure as his name was Matthew Colebatch!

Carefully putting away the kind old gentleman's gift, (they were penniless before she received it), Annie returned to her grandfather's room. He had altered a little, as the morning advanced, and was now occupied over an employment which it wrung her heart to see—he was trying to restore the mask of Shakespeare.

The first words he had spoken since the burglary, were addressed to Annie. He seemed not to know that the robbers had effected their retreat, before she got down stairs; and asked whether they had hurt her. Calmed on this point, he next beckoned the carpenter to him, and entreated, in an eager whisper, to have some glue made directly. They could not imagine, at first, what he wanted it for; but they humoured him gladly.

When the glue was brought, he opened his cash box, with a look of faint pining hope in his face, that it was very mournful to see, and began to arrange the fragments of the mask, on the bed before him. They were shattered past all mending; but still he moved them about here and there, with his trembling hands, murmuring sadly, all the while, that he knew it was very difficult, but felt sure he should succeed at last. Sometimes he selected the pieces wrongly; stuck, perhaps, two or three together with the glue; and then had to pull them apart again. Even when he chose the fragments properly, he could not find enough that would join sufficiently well to reproduce only one poor quarter of the mask in its former shape. Still he went on, turning over piece after piece of the broken plaster, down to the very smallest, patiently and laboriously, with the same false hope of success, and the same vain perseverance under the most disheartening failure, animating him for hours together. He had begun early in the morning—he had not given up, when Annie returned from her interview with Mr Colebatch. To know how utterly fruitless all his efforts must be, and still to see him so anxiously continuing them in spite of failure, was a sight to despair over, and to tremble at, indeed.

At last, Annie entreated him to put the fragments away in the box, and take a little rest. He would listen to nobody else; but he listened to her, and did what she asked; saying that his head was not clear enough for the work of repairing, today; but that he felt certain he should succeed tomorrow. When he had locked the box, and put it under his pillow, he laid back, and fell into a sleep directly.

Such was his condition! Every idea was now out of his mind, but the idea of restoring the mask of Shakespeare. Divert him from that; and he either fell asleep, or sat up vacant and speechless. It was suspension, not loss of the faculties, with *him*. The fibre of his mind relaxed with the breaking of the beloved possession to which it had been attached. Those still, cold, plaster features had been his thought by day, his dream by night; in them, his deep and beautiful devotion to Shakespeare— beautiful as an innate poetic faith that had lived through every poetic privation of life—had found its dearest outward manifestation. All about that mask, he had unconsciously hung fresh votive offerings of pride and pleasure, and humble happiness, almost with every fresh hour. It had been the one great achievement of his life, to get it; and the one great determination of his life, to keep it. And now it was broken! The dearest household god, next to his grandchild, that the poor actor had ever had to worship, his own eyes had seen lying shattered on the floor!

It was this—far more than the fright produced by the burglary,—that had altered him, as he was altered now.

There was no rousing him. Everybody tried, and everybody failed. He went on patiently, day after day, at his miserably hopeless task of joining the fragments of the plaster; and always had some excuse for failure, always some reason for beginning the attempt anew. Annie could influence him in everything else,—for his heart, which was all hers, had escaped the blow that had stunned his mind,—but, on any subject connected with the mask, her interference was powerless.

The good Squire came to try what he could do—came every day; and joked, entreated, lectured, and advised, in his own hearty, eccentric manner; but the old man only smiled faintly; and forgot what had been said to him, as soon as the words were out of the sayer's mouth. Mr Colebatch, reduced to his last resources, hit on what he considered a first-rate stratagem. He privately informed Annie, that he would insist on his whole establishment of servants, with Mrs Buddle, the house-keeper, at their head, learning elocution; so as to employ Mr Wray again, in a duty he was used to perform. 'None of those infernal Tidbury people will learn,' said the kind old Squire; 'so my servants shall make a class for him, with Mrs Buddle at the top, to keep them in order. Set him teaching in his own way; and he must come round—he *must* from force of habit!' But he did not. They told him a class of new pupils was waiting for him; he just answered he was very glad to hear it; and forgot all about the matter the moment afterwards.

The doctor endeavoured to help them. He tried stimulants, and tried sedatives; he tried keeping his patient in bed, and tried keeping him up; he tried blistering, and tried cupping; and then he gave over; saying that Mr Wray must certainly have something on his mind, and that physic and regimen were of no use. One word of comfort, however, the doctor still had to speak. The physical strength of the old man had failed him very little, as yet. He was always ready to be got out of bed, and dressed; and seemed glad when he was seated in his chair. This was a good sign; but there was no telling how long it might last.

It had lasted a whole week—a long, blank melancholy winter's week! And now, Christmas Day was fast coming; coming for the first time as a day of mourning, to the little family who, in spite of poverty and all poverty's hardening disasters, had hitherto enjoyed it happily and lovingly together, as the blessed holiday of the whole year! Ah! how doubly heavy-hearted poor Annie felt, as she entered her bedroom for the night, and remembered that that day fortnight would be Christmas Day!

She was beginning to look wan and thin already. It is not joy only, that shows soonest and plainest in the young: grief—alas that it should be so—shares, in this world, the same privilege: and Annie now looked, as she felt, sick at heart. That day had brought no change: she had left the old man for the night, and left him no better. He had passed hours again, in trying to restore the mask; still instinctively exhibiting from time to time some fondness and attention towards his grandchild—but just as hopelessly vacant to every other influence as ever.

Annie listlessly sat down on the one chair in her small bedroom, thinking (it was her only thought now,) of what new plan could be adopted to rouse her grandfather on the morrow; and still mourning over the broken mask, as the one fatal obstacle to every effort she could try. Thus she sat for some minutes, languid and dreamy—when, suddenly, a startling and a wonderful change came over her, worked from within. She bounded up from her chair, as dead-pale and as dead-still as if she had been struck to stone. Then, a moment after, her face flushed crimson, she clasped her hands violently together, and drew her breath quick. And then, the paleness came once more—she trembled all over—and knelt down by the bedside, hiding her face in her hands.

When she rose again, the tears were rolling fast over her cheeks. She poured out some water, and washed them away. A strange expression of firmness—a glow of enthusiasm, beautiful in its brightness and purity—overspread her face, as she took up her candle, and left the room.

She went to the very top of the house, where the carpenter slept; and knocked at his door.

'Are you not gone to bed yet, Martin?'—she whispered—(the old joke of calling him 'Julius Caesar' was all over now!)

He opened the door in astonishment, saying he had only that moment got upstairs.

'Come down to the drawing-room, Martin,' she said; looking brightly at him—almost wildly, as *he* thought. 'Come quick! I must speak to you at once.'

He followed her downstairs. When they got into the drawing-room, she carefully closed the door; and then said:—

'A thought has come to me, Martin, that I *must* tell you. It came to me just now, when I was alone in my room; and I believe God sent it!'

She beckoned to him to sit by her side; and then began to whisper in his ear—quickly, eagerly, without pause.

His face began to turn pale at first, as hers had done, while he listened. Then it flushed, then grew firm like hers, but in a far stronger degree. When she had finished speaking, he only said, it was a terrible risk every way—repeating '*every way*' with strong emphasis; but that she wished it; and therefore it should be done.

As they rose to separate, she said tenderly and gravely:—

'You have always been very good to me, Martin: be good, and be a brother to me more than ever now—for now I am trusting you with all I have to trust.'

Years afterwards when they were married, and when their children were growing up around them, he remembered Annie's last look, and Annie's last words, as they parted that night.

IX

The next morning, when the old man was ready to get out of bed and be dressed, it was not the honest carpenter who came to help him as usual, but a stranger—the landlady's brother. He never noticed this change. What thoughts he had left, were all preoccupied. The evening before, from an affectionate wish to humour him in the caprice which had become the one leading idea of his life, Annie had bought for him a bottle of cement. And now, he went on murmuring to himself, all the while he was being dressed, about the certainty of his succeeding at last in piecing together the broken fragments of the mask, with the aid of this cement.

It was only the glue, he said, that had made him fail hitherto; with cement to aid him, he was quite certain of success.

The landlady and her brother helped him down into the drawing-room. Nobody was there; but on the table, where the breakfast things were laid, was placed a small note. He looked round inquisitively when he first saw that the apartment was empty. Then, the only voice within him that was not silenced—the voice of his heart—spoke, and told him that Annie ought to have been in the room to meet him as usual.

'Where is she?' he asked eagerly.

'Don't leave me alone with him, James,' whispered the landlady to her brother, 'there's bad news to tell him.'

'Where is she?' he reiterated; and his eye got a wild look, as he asked the question for the second time.

'Pray, compose yourself, sir; and read that letter,' said the landlady, in soothing tones; 'Miss Annie's quite safe, and wants you to read this.' She handed him the letter.

He struck it away; so fiercely that she started back in terror. Then he cried out violently for the third time:

'Where is she?'

'Tell him,' whispered the landlady's brother, 'tell him at once, or you'll make him worse.'

'Gone, sir,' said the woman—'gone away; but only for three days. The last words she said were, tell my grandfather I shall be back in three days; and give him that letter with my dearest love. Oh, don't look so, sir— don't look so! She's sure to be back.'

He was muttering 'gone' several times to himself, with a fearful expression of vacancy in his eyes. Suddenly, he signed to have the letter picked up from the ground; tore it open the moment it was given to him; and began to try to read the contents.

The letter was short, and written in very blotted unsteady characters. It ran thus:—

'Dearest Grandfather,—I never left you before in my life; and I only go now to try and serve you, and do you good. In three days, or sooner, if God pleases, I will come back, bringing something with me that will gladden your heart, and make you love me even better than ever. I dare not tell you where I am going, or what I am going for—you would be so frightened, and would perhaps send after me to fetch me back; but believe there is no danger! And oh, dear dear grandfather, don't doubt your little Annie; and don't doubt I will be back as I say, bringing something to make you forgive me for going away without your leave.

We shall be so happy again, if you will only wait the three days! *He*—you know who—goes with me, to take care of me. Think, dear grandfather, of the blessed Christmas time that will bring us all together again, happier than ever! I can't write any more, but that I pray God to bless and keep you, till we meet again!—ANNIE WRAY.'

He had not read the letter more than half through, when he dropped it, uttering the one word, 'gone', in a shrill scream, that it made them shudder to hear. Then, it seemed as if a shadow, an awful, indescribable shadow, were stealing over his face. His fingers worked and fidgeted with an end of the tablecloth close by him; and he began to speak in faint whispering tones.

'I'm afraid I'm going mad; I'm afraid something's frightened me out of my wits,' he murmured, under his breath. 'Stop! let me try if I know anything. There now! there! That's the breakfast table: I know that. There's *her* cup and saucer; and there's mine. Yes! and that third place, on the other side, whose is that?—whose, whose, whose? Ah! my God! my God! I *am* mad! I've forgotten that third place!' He stopped, shivering all over. Then, the moment after, he shrieked out—'Gone! who says she's gone? It's a lie; no, no, it's a cruel joke put upon me. Annie! I won't be joked with. Come down, Annie! Call her, some of you! Annie! they've broken it all to pieces—the plaster won't stick together again! You can't leave me, now they've broken it all to pieces! Annie! Annie! come and mend it! Annie! little Annie!'

He called on her name for the last time, in tones of entreaty unutterably plaintive; then sank down on a chair, moaning; then became silent—doggedly silent—and fiercely suspicious of everything. In that mood he remained, till his strength began to fail him; and then he let them lead him to the sofa. When he lay down, he fell off quickly into a heavy, feverish slumber.

Ah, Annie! Annie! carefully as you watched him, you knew but little of his illness; you never foreboded such a result of your absence as this; or, brave and loving as your purpose was in leaving him, you would have shrunk from the fatal necessity of quitting his bedside for three days together!

Mr Colebatch came in shortly after the old man had fallen asleep, accompanied by a new doctor—a medical man of great renown, who had stolen a little time from his London practice, partly to visit some relations who lived at Tidbury, and partly to recruit his own health, which had suffered in repairing other people's. The good Squire, the moment he heard that such assistance as this was accidentally available in the town, secured it for poor old Reuben, without a moment's delay.

'Oh, sir!' said the landlady, meeting them down stairs; 'he's been going on in such a dreadful way! What we are to do, I really don't know.'

'It's lucky somebody else does,' interrupted the Squire, peevishly.

'But you don't know, sir, that Miss Annie's gone—gone without saying where!'

'Yes, I happen to know that too!' said Mr Colebatch; 'I've got a letter from her, asking me to take care of her grandfather, while she's away; and here I am to do what she tells me. First of all, ma'am, let us get into some room, where this gentleman and I can have five minutes' talk in private.'

'Now, sir'—said the Squire, when he and the doctor were closeted together in the back parlour—'the long and the short of the case is this:— A week ago, two infernal housebreakers broke into this house, and found old Mr Wray sitting up alone in the drawing-room. Of course, they frightened him out of his wits; and they stole some trifles too—but that's nothing. They managed somehow to break a plaster cast of his. There's a mystery about this cast, that the family won't explain, and that nobody can find out; but the fact appears to be, that the old man was as fond of his cast as if it was one of his children—a queer thing, you'll say; but true, sir; true as my name's Colebatch! Well: ever since, he's been weak in his mind; always striving to mend this wretched cast, and taking no notice of anything else. This sort of thing has lasted for six or seven days.—And now, another mystery! I get a letter from his grand-daughter—the kindest, dearest little thing!—begging me to look after him—you never saw such a lovely, tender-hearted letter!—to look after him, I say, while she's gone for three days, to come back with a surprise for him that she says will work miracles. She don't say what surprise— or, where she's going—but she promises to come back in three days; and she'll do it! I'd stake my existence on little Annie sticking to her word! Now the question is—till we see her again, and all this precious mystery's cleared up—what are we to do for the poor old man?—what?—eh?'

'Perhaps'—said the doctor, smiling at the conclusion of this character-istic harangue—'perhaps, I had better see the patient, before we say any more.'

'By George! what a fool I am!'—cried the Squire—'Of course!—see him directly—this way, doctor: this way!'

They went into the drawing-room. The sufferer was still on the sofa, moving and talking in his sleep. The doctor signed to Mr Colebatch to keep silence; and they sat down and listened.

The old man's dreams seemed to be connected with some of the later scenes in his life, which had been passed at country towns, in teaching country actors. He was laughing just at this moment.

'Ho! Ho! young gentlemen'—they heard him say—'do you call that acting? Ah, dear! dear! we professional people don't bump against each other on the stage, in that way—it's lucky you called me in, before your friends came to see you!—Stop, sir! that won't do! you mustn't die in that way—fall on your knee first; then sink down—then—Oh, dear! how hard it is to get people to have a proper delivery, and not go dropping their voices, at the end of every sentence. I shall never—never—'

Here the wild words stopped; then altered, and grew sad.

'Hush! Hush!'—he murmured, in husky, wandering tones—'Silence there, behind the scenes! Don't you hear Mr Kemble speaking now? listen, and get a lesson, as I do. Ah! laugh away, fools, who don't know good acting when you see it!—Let me alone! What are you pushing me for? I'm doing *you* no harm! I'm only looking at Mr Kemble—Don't touch that book!—it's *my* Shakespeare—yes! mine. I suppose I may read Shakespeare if I like, though I *am* only an actor at a shilling a night!—A shilling a night;—starving wages—Ha! Ha! Ha!—starving wages!'

Again the sad strain altered to a still wilder and more plaintive key.

'Ah!' he cried now, 'don't be hard with me! Don't for God's sake! My wife, my poor dear wife, died only a week ago! Oh, I'm cold! starved with cold here, in this draughty place. I can't help crying, sir; she was so good to me! But I'll take care and go on the stage when I'm called to go, if you'll please not take any notice of me now; and not let them laugh at me. Oh, Mary! Mary! Why has God taken you from me? Ah! why! why! why!'

Here, the murmurs died away; then began again, but more confusedly. Sometimes his wandering speech was all about Annie; sometimes it changed to lamentations over the broken mask; sometimes it went back again to the old days behind the scenes at Drury Lane.

'Oh, Annie! Annie!' cried the Squire, with his eyes full of tears; 'why did you ever go away?'

'I am not sure,' said the doctor, 'that her going may not do good in the end. It has evidently brought matters to a climax with him; I can see that. Her coming back will be a shock to his mind—it's a risk, sir; but that shock may act in the right way. When a man's faculties struggle to recover themselves, as his are doing, those faculties are not altogether gone. The young lady will come back, you say, the day after tomorrow?'

'Yes, yes!' answered the Squire, 'with a "surprise", she says. What surprise? Good Heavens! why couldn't she say what!'

'We need not mind that,' rejoined the other. 'Any surprise will do, if his physical strength will bear it. We'll keep him quiet—as much sleep as possible—till she comes back. I've seen some very curious cases of this kind, Mr Colebatch; cases that were cured by the merest accidents, in the most unaccountable manner. I shall watch this particular case with interest.'

'Cure it, doctor! cure it; and, by Jupiter! I'll—'

'Hush! you'll wake him. We had better go now. I shall come back in an hour, and will tell the landlady where she can let me know, if anything happens before that.'

They went out softly; and left him as they had found him, muttering and murmuring in his sleep.

On the third day, late in the afternoon, Mr Colebatch and the doctor were again in the drawing-room at No. 12; and again intently occupied in studying the condition of poor old Reuben Wray.

This time, he was wide awake; and was restlessly and feebly moving up and down the room, talking to himself, now mournfully about the broken mask, now fiercely and angrily about Annie's absence. Nothing attracted his notice in the smallest degree; he seemed to be perfectly unaware that anybody was in the room with him.

'Why can't you keep him quiet?' whispered the Squire; 'why don't you give him an opiate, or whatever you call it, as you did yesterday?'

'His grandchild comes back today,' answered the doctor. 'Today must be left to the great physician—Nature. At this crisis, it is not for me to meddle, but to watch and learn.'

They waited again in silence. Lights were brought in; for it grew dark while they kept their anxious watch. Still no arrival!

Five o'clock struck; and, about ten minutes after, a knock sounded on the street door.

'She has come back!' exclaimed the doctor.

'How do you know that already?' asked Mr Colebatch, eagerly.

'Look there, sir!' and the doctor pointed to Mr Wray.

He had been moving about with increased restlessness, and talking with increased vehemence, just before the knock. The moment it sounded he stopped; and there he stood now, perfectly speechless and perfectly still. There was no expression on his face. His very breathing seemed suspended. What secret influences were moving within him now? What dread command went forth over the dark waters in which his

[266]

spirit toiled, saying to them, 'Peace! be still!' That, no man—not even the man of science—could tell.

As the door opened, and the landlady's joyful exclamation of recognition, sounded cheerily from below, the doctor rose from his seat, and gently placed himself close behind the old man.

Footsteps hurried up the stairs. Then, Annie's voice was heard, breathless and eager, before she came in. 'Grandfather, I've got the mould! Grandfather, I've brought a new cast! The mask—thank God!—the mask of Shakespeare!'

She flew into his arms, without even a look at anybody else in the room. When her head was on his bosom, the spirit of the brave little girl deserted her for the first time since her absence, and she burst into an hysterical passion of weeping before she could utter another word.

He gave a great cry the moment she touched him—an inarticulate voice of recognition from the spirit within. Then his arms closed tight over her; so tight, that the doctor advanced a step or two towards them, showing in his face the first look of alarm it had yet betrayed.

But, at that instant, the old man's arms dropped again, powerless and heavy, by his side. What does he see now, in that open box in the carpenter's hand? The Mask!—*his* Mask, whole as ever! white, and smooth, and beautiful, as when he first drew it from the mould, in his own bedroom at Stratford!

The struggle of the vital principle at that sight—the straining and writhing of every nerve—was awful to look on. His eyes rolled, distended, in their orbits; a dark red flush of blood heaved up and overspread his face; he drew his breath in heavy, hoarse gasps of agony. This lasted for a moment—one dread moment; then he fell forward, to all appearance death-struck, in the doctor's arms.

He was borne to the sofa, amid the silence of that suspense which is too terrible for words. The doctor laid his finger on his wrist, waited an instant, then looked up, and slightly nodded his head. The pulse was feebly beating again, already!

Long and delicate was the process of restoring him to animation. It was like aiding the faint new life to develop itself in a child just born. But the doctor was as patient as he was skilful; and they heard the old man draw his breath again, gently and naturally, at last.

His weakness was so great, that his eyelids closed at his first effort to look round him. When they opened again, his eyes seemed strangely liquid and soft—almost like the eyes of a young girl. Perhaps this was partly because they turned on Annie the moment they could see.

Soon, his lips moved; but his voice was so faint, that the doctor was obliged to listen close at his mouth to hear him. He said, in fluttering accents, that he had had a *dreadful dream*, which had made him very ill, he was afraid; but that it was all over, and he was better now, though not quite strong enough to receive so many visitors yet. Here his strength for speaking failed, and he looked round on Annie again in silence. In a minute more he whispered to her. She went to the table and fetched the new mask; and, kneeling down, held it before him to look at.

The doctor beckoned Mr Colebatch, the landlady, and the carpenter, to follow him into the back-room.

'Now,' said he, 'I've one, and only one, important direction to give you all; and you must communicate it to Miss Wray when she is a little less agitated. On no account let the patient imagine he's wrong in thinking that all his troubles have been the troubles of a dream. That will be the weak point in his intellectual consciousness for the rest of his life. When he gets stronger, he is sure to question you curiously about his dream; keep him in his self-deceit, as you value his sanity! He's only got his reason back by getting it out of the very jaws of death, I can tell you—give it full time to strengthen! You know, I dare say, that a joint which is dislocated by a jerk, is also replaced by a jerk. Consider his mind, in the same way, to have been dislocated by one shock, and now replaced by another; and treat his intellect as you would treat a limb that had only just been slipped back into its proper place—treat it tenderly. By the bye,' added the doctor, after a moment's consideration, 'if you can't get the key of his box, without suspicion, pick the lock; and throw away the fragments of the old cast (which he was always talking about in his delirium)—destroy them altogether. If he ever sees them again, they may do him dreadful mischief. He must always imagine what he imagines at present, that the new cast is the same cast that he has had all along. It's a very remarkable case, Mr Colebatch, very remarkable: I really feel indebted to you for enabling me to study it. Compose yourself, sir, you're a little shaken and startled by this, I see; but there's no danger for him now. Look there: that man, except on one point, is as sane as ever he was in his life!'

They looked, as the doctor spoke. Mr Wray was still on the sofa, gazing at the mask of Shakespeare, which Annie supported before him, as she knelt by his side. His arm was round her neck; and, from time to time, he whispered to her, smiling faintly, but very happily, as she replied in whispers also. The sight was simple enough; but the landlady, thinking on all that had passed, began to weep as she beheld it. The honest carpenter looked very ready to follow her example; and Mr Colebatch probably shared the same weakness at that moment, though he was less candid in betraying it. 'Come,' said the Squire, very huskily and hastily, 'we are only in the way here; let us leave them together!'

'Quite right, sir,' observed the doctor; 'that pretty little girl is the only medical attendant fit to be with him now! I wait for *you*, Mr Colebatch!'

'I say, young fellow,' said the Squire to the carpenter, as they went down stairs, 'be in the way tomorrow morning: I've a good deal to ask you in private when I'm not all over in a twitter, as I am at present. Now our good old friend's getting round, my curiosity's getting round too. Be in the way tomorrow, at ten, when I come here. Quite ready, doctor! No! after *you*, if you please. Ah, thank God! we came into this house mourners, and we go out of it to rejoice. It will be a happy Christmas, doctor, and a merry New Year, after all!'

X

When ten o'clock came, the Squire came—punctual to a minute. Instead of going up stairs, he mysteriously sent for the carpenter into the back parlour.

'Now, in the first place, how is Mr Wray?'—said the old gentleman, as anxiously as if he had not already sent three times the night before, and twice earlier in the morning, to ask that very question.

'Lord bless you, sir!'—answered the carpenter with a grin, and a very expressive rubbing of the hands—'He's coming to again, after his nice sleep last night, as brave as ever. He's dreadful weak still, to be sure; but he's got like himself again, already. He's been down on me twice in the last half hour, sir, about my elocution; he's making Annie read Shakespeare to him; and he's asking whether any new pupils are coming—all just in the old way again. Oh, sir, it is so jolly to see him like that once more—if you'll only come up stairs—'

'Stop, till we've had our talk'—said the Squire—'sit down. By the bye! has he said anything yet about that infernal cash box?'

'I picked the lock of the box this morning, sir, as the gentleman told me; and buried every bit of plaster out of it, deep in the kitchen garden. He saw the box afterwards, and gave a tremble, like. "Take it away," says he, "never let me see it again: it reminds me of that dreadful dream." And then, sir, he told us about what had happened, just as if he really *had* dreamt it; saying he couldn't get the subject quite out of his head, the whole thing was so much as if it had truly taken place. Afterwards, sir, he thanked me for making the new box for the cast—he remembered my promising to do that, though it was only just before all our trouble!'

'And of course, you humour him in everything, and let him think he's right?'—said the Squire—'He must never know that he hasn't been dreaming, to his dying day.'

And he never did know it—never, in *this* world, had even a suspicion of what he owed to Annie! It was but little matter; they could not have loved each other better, if he had discovered everything.

'Now, master carpenter,' pursued the Squire, 'you've answered very nicely hitherto. Just answer as nicely the next question I ask. What's the whole history of this mysterious plaster cast? It's no use fidgeting! I've seen the cast; I know it's a portrait of Shakespeare! and I've made up my mind to find out all about it. Do you mean to say you think I'm not a friend fit to be trusted? Eh, you sir?'

'I never could think so, after all your goodness, sir. But, if you please, I really did promise to keep the thing a secret,' said the carpenter, looking very much as if he were watching his opportunity to open the door, and run out of the room; 'I promised, sir; I did, indeed!'

'Promised a fiddlestick!' exclaimed the Squire, in a passion. 'What's the use of keeping a secret that's half let out already? I'll tell you what, you Mr—, what's your name? There's some joke about calling you Julius Caesar. What's your real name, if you really have one?'

'Martin Blunt, sir. But don't, pray don't ask me to tell the secret! I don't say *you* would blab it, sir; but if it *did* leak out, like; and get to Stratford-upon-Avon,'—here he suddenly became silent, feeling he was beginning to commit himself already.

'Stop! I've got it!' cried Mr Colebatch. 'Hang me, if I haven't got it at last!'

'Don't tell *me*, sir! Pray don't tell me, if you have!'

'Stick to your chair, Mr Martin Blunt! No shirking with *me*! I was a fool not to suspect the thing, the moment I saw it was a portrait of Shakespeare. I've seen the Stratford bust, Master Blunt! You're afraid of Stratford, are you?—Why? I know! Some of you have been taking that cast from the Stratford bust, without leave—it's as like it, as two peas! Now, young fellow, I'll tell you what! if you don't make a clean breast to me at once, I'm off to the office of the 'Tidbury Mercury', to put in my version of the whole thing, as a good local anecdote! Will you tell me? or will you not?—I'm asking this in Mr Wray's interests, or I'd die before I asked you at all!'

Confused, threatened, bullied, bawled at, and out-manoeuvred, the unfortunate carpenter fairly gave way. 'If it's wrong in me to tell you, sir, it's your fault what I do,' said the simple fellow; and he forthwith retailed, in a very roundabout, stammering manner, the whole of the disclosure he had heard from old Reuben—the Squire occasionally throwing in an explosive interjection of astonishment, or admiration; but, otherwise, receiving the narrative with remarkable calmness and attention.

'What the deuce is all this nonsense about the Stratford Town Council, and the penalties of the law?'—cried Mr Colebatch, when the carpenter had done—'But never mind; we can come to that afterwards. Now tell me about going back to get the mould out of the cupboard, and making the new cast. I know who did it! It's that dear, darling, incomparable little girl!—but tell me all about it—come! quick, quick!— don't keep me waiting!'

'Julius Caesar' got on with his second narrative much more glibly than with the first. How Annie had suddenly remembered, one night, in her bedroom, about the mould having been left behind—how she was determined to try and restore her grandfather's health and faculties, by going to seek it; and how he (the carpenter), had gone also, to protect her—how they got to Stratford, by the coach (outside places, in the cold, to save money)—how Annie appealed to the mercy of their former landlord; and instead of inventing some falsehood to deceive him, fairly told her whole story in all its truth—how the landlord pitied them, and promised to keep their secret—how they went up into the bed-room, and found the mould in the old canvas bag, behind the volumes of the *Annual Register*, just where Mr Wray had left it—how Annie, remembering what her grandfather had told her, about the process of making a cast, bought plaster, and followed out her instructions; failing in the first attempt, but admirably succeeding in the second—how they were obliged, in frightful suspense, to wait till the third day for the return coach; and how they finally got back, safe and sound, not only with the new cast, but with the mould as well.—All these particulars flowed from the carpenter's lips, in a strain of homely eloquence, which no elocutionary aid could have furnished with one atom of additional effect, that would have done it any good whatever.

'We'd no notion, sir,' said 'Julius Caesar', in conclusion, 'that poor Mr Wray was so bad as he really was, when we went away. It was a dreadful trial to Annie, sir, to go. She went down on her knees to the landlady—I saw her do it, half wild, like; she was in such a state—she went down on her knees, sir, to ask the woman to be as a daughter to the old man, till she came back. Well, sir, even after that, it was a toss-up whether she went away, when the morning came. But she was obliged to do it. She durstn't trust me to go alone, for fear I should let the mould tumble down, when I got it (which I'm afraid, sir, was very likely!)—or get into some scrape, by telling *what* I oughtn't, *where* I oughtn't; and so be taken up, mould and all, before the Town Council, who were going to put Mr Wray in prison, only we ran off to Tidbury; and so—'

'Nonsense! stuff! they could no more put him in prison for taking the cast than I can,' cried the Squire. 'Stop! I've got a thought! I've got a thought at least, that's worth—Is the mould here?—Yes or No?'

'Yes, sir! Bless us and save us, what's the matter!'

'Run!' cried Mr Colebatch, pacing up and down the room like mad. 'No. 15 in the street! Dabbs and Clutton, the lawyers! Fetch one of them in a second! Damn it, run! or I shall burst a blood vessel!'

The carpenter ran *to* No. 15; and Mr Dabbs, who happened to be in, ran *from* No. 15. Mr Colebatch met him at the street door, dragged him into the back parlour, pushed him on to a chair, and instantly stated the case between Mr Wray and the authorities at Stratford, in the fewest possible words and the hastiest possible tones. 'Now,' said the old gentleman at the end, 'can they, or can they not, hurt him for what he's done?'

'It's a very nice point,' said Mr Dabbs, 'a very nice point indeed, sir.'

'Hang it, man!' cried the Squire, 'don't talk to *me* about "nice points", as if a point was something good to eat! Can they, or can they not, hurt him? Answer that in three words!'

'They can't,' said Dabbs, answering it triumphantly in two.

'Why?' asked the Squire, beating him by a rejoinder in one.

'For this reason,' said Dabbs. 'What does Mr Wray take with him into the church? Plaster of his own, in powder. What does he bring out with him? The same plaster, in another form. Does any right of copyright reside in a bust two hundred years old? Impossible. Has Mr Wray hurt the bust? No; or they would have found him out here, and prosecuted directly—for they know where he is. I heard of the thing from a Stratford man, yesterday, who said they knew he was at Tidbury. Under all these circumstances, where's there a shadow of a case against Mr Wray? Nowhere!'

'Capital, Dabbs! capital! you'll be Lord Chancellor some day: never heard a better opinion in my life! Now, Mr Julius Caesar Blunt, do you see what my thought is? No! Look here. Take casts from that mould till your arms ache again; clap them upon slabs of black marble to show off the white face; sell them, at a guinea each, to the loads of people who would give anything to have a portrait of Shakespeare; and then open your breeches' pockets fast enough to let the gold tumble in, if you can! Tell Mr Wray that; and you tell him he's a rich man, or—no don't, you're no more fit to do it properly than I am! Tell every syllable you've heard here to Annie, directly; she'll know how to break it to him; go! be off!'

'But what are we to say about how we got the mould here, sir? We can't tell Mr Wray the truth.'

'Tell him a flam, of course! Say it's been found in the cupboard, by the landlord, at Stratford, and sent on here. Dabbs will bear witness that the Stratford people know he's at Tidbury, and know they can't touch him: he's sure to think *that* a pretty good proof that we are right. Say I bullied you out of the secret, when I saw the mould come here—say anything—but only go, and settle matters at once! I'm off to take my walk, and see about the black slabs at the stone masons. I'll be back in an hour, and see Mr Wray.'

The next moment, the impetuous old Squire was out of the house; and before the hour was up, he was in it again, rather more impetuous than ever.

When he entered the drawing-room, the first sight that greeted him was the carpenter, hanging up a box containing the mask (with the lid taken off) boldly and publicly over the fireplace.

'I'm glad to see that, sir,' said Mr Colebatch, shaking hands with Mr Wray. 'Annie has told you my good news—eh?'

'Yes, sir,' answered the old man; 'the best news I've heard for some time: I can hang up my treasure there, now, where I can see it all day. It was rather too bad, sir, of those Stratford people to go frightening me, by threatening what they couldn't do. The best man among them is the man who was my landlord; he's an honest, careful fellow, to send me back my old canvas bag, and the mould (which must have seemed worthless to him), just because they were belonging to me, and left in my bedroom. I'm rather proud, sir, of making that mask. I can never repay you for your kindness in defending my character, and taking me up as you've done—but if you would accept a copy of the cast, now we have the mould to take it from, as Annie says—'

'That I will, and thankfully,' said the Squire, 'and I order five more copies, as presents to my friends, when you begin to sell to the public.'

'I really don't know, sir, about that,' said Mr Wray, rather uneasily.

'Selling the cast is like making my great treasure very common; it's like giving up my particular possession to everybody.'

Mr Colebatch parried this objection instantly. Could Mr Wray, he asked, seriously mean to be so selfish as to deny to other lovers of Shakespeare the privilege he prized so much himself, of possessing Shakespeare's portrait?—to say nothing of as good as plumply refusing a pretty round sum of money at the same time. Could he be selfish enough, and inconsiderate enough to do that? No: Mr Wray, on consideration, allowed he could not. He saw the subject in a new light now; and begging Mr Colebatch's pardon, if he had seemed selfish or unthankful, he would take the Squire's advice.

'That's right!' said the old gentleman. 'Now I'm happy. You'll soon be strong enough, my good friend, to take the cast yourself.'

'I hope so,' said Mr Wray. 'It's very odd that a mere dream should make me feel so weak as I do—I suppose they told you, sir, what a horrible dream it was. If I didn't see the mask hanging up there now, as whole as ever, I should really believe it had been broken to pieces, just as I dreamt it. It must have been a dream, you know, sir of course; for I dreamt that Annie had gone away and left me; and I found her at home as usual, when I woke up. It seems, too, that I'm a week or more behindhand, in my notion about the day of the month. In short, sir, I should almost think myself bewitched,' he added, pressing his trembling hand over his forehead, 'if I didn't know it was near Christmas time, and didn't believe what sweet Will Shakespeare says in *Hamlet*—a passage, by-the-by, sir, which Mr Kemble always regretted to see struck out of the acting copy.'

Here he began to declaim—faintly, but still with all the old Kemble cadences—the exquisite lines to which he referred; the Squire beating time to each modulation, with his forefinger:—

'Some say, that ever 'gainst that season comes,
Wherein our Saviour's birth is celebrated,
This bird of dawning singeth all night long:
And then they say no spirit dares stir abroad;
The nights are wholesome; then no planets strike,
No fairy takes, nor witch hath power to charm,
So hallow'd and so gracious is the time.'

'There's poetry!' exclaimed Mr Colebatch, looking up at the mask. 'That's a cut above my tragedy of the *Mysterious Murderess*, I'm afraid. Eh, sir? And how you recite,—splendid! Hang it! we havn't had half our talk,

[274]

yet, about Shakespeare and John Kemble. A chat with an old stager like you, is new life to me, in such a barbarous place as this! Ah, Mr Wray!' (and here the Squire's voice lowered, and grew strangely tender for such a rough old gentleman), 'you are a happy man, to have a grandchild to keep you company at all times, but especially at Christmas time. I'm a lonely old bachelor, and must eat my Christmas dinner without wife or child to sweeten the taste to me of a single morsel!'

As little Annie heard this, she rose, and stole up to the Squire's side. Her pale face was covered with blushes (all her pretty natural colour had not come back yet); she looked softly at Mr Colebatch, for a moment—then looked down—then said—

'Don't say you're lonely sir! If you would let *me* be like a grandchild to you, I should be so glad. I—I always make the plum pudding, sir, on Christmas Day, for grandfather—if he would allow,—and if—if you—'

'If that little love isn't trying to screw her courage up to ask me to taste her plum pudding, I'm a Dutchman'—cried the Squire, catching Annie in his arms, and fairly kissing her—'Without ceremony, Mr Wray, I invite myself here, to a Christmas dinner. We would have had it at Cropley Court; but you're not strong enough yet, to go out these cold nights. Never mind! all the dinner, except Annie's pudding, shall be done by my cook; Mrs Buddle, the housekeeper, shall come and help; and we'll have such a feast, please God, as no king ever sat down to! No apologies, my good friend, on either side: I'm determined to spend the happiest Christmas Day I ever did in my life; and so shall you!'

And the good Squire kept his word. It was, of course, noised abroad over the whole town, that Matthew Colebatch, Esquire, Lord of the Manor of Tidbury-on-the-Marsh, was going to dine on Christmas Day with an old player, in a lodging house. The genteel population were universally scandalized and indignant. The Squire had exhibited his levelling tendencies pretty often before, they said. He had, for instance, been seen cutting jokes in the High Street with a travelling tinker, to whom he had applied in broad daylight to put a new ferrule on his walking stick; he had been detected coolly eating bacon and greens in one of his tenant farmer's cottages; he had been heard singing, 'Begone, dull care,' in a cracked tenor, to amuse another tenant farmer's child. These actions were disreputable enough; but to go publicly, and dine with an obscure stage-player, put the climax on everything! The Reverend Daubeny Daker said the Squire's proper sphere of action, after that, was a lunatic

[275]

asylum; and the Reverend Daubeny Daker's friends echoed the sentiment.

Perfectly reckless of this expression of genteel popular opinion, Mr Colebatch arrived to dinner at No. 12, on Christmas Day; and, what is more, wore his black tights and silk stockings, as if he had been going to a grand party. His dinner had arrived before him; and fat Mrs Buddle, in her lavender silk gown, with a cambric handkerchief pinned in front to keep splashes off, appeared auspiciously with the banquet. Never did Annie feel the responsibility of having a plum-pudding to make, so acutely as she felt it, on seeing the savoury feast which Mr Colebatch had ordered, to accompany her one little item of saccharine cookery.

They sat down to dinner, with the Squire at the top of the table (Mr Wray insisted on that); and Mrs Buddle at the bottom (he insisted on that also); old Reuben and Annie, at one side; and 'Julius Caesar' all by himself (they knew his habits, and gave him elbow room), at the other. Things were comparatively genteel and quiet, till Annie's pudding came in. At sight of that, Mr Colebatch set up a cheer, as if he had been behind a pack of fox-hounds. The carpenter, thrown quite off his balance by noise and excitement, knocked down a spoon, a wine glass, and a pepper-box, one after the other, in such quick succession, that Mrs Buddle thought him mad; and Annie—for the first time, poor little thing, since all her troubles—actually began to laugh again, as prettily as ever. Mr Colebatch did ample justice, it must be added, to her pudding. Twice did his plate travel up to the dish—a third time it would have gone; but the faithful housekeeper raised her warning voice, and reminded the old gentleman that he had a stomach.

When the tables were cleared, and the glasses filled with the Squire's rare old port, that excellent man rose slowly and solemnly from his chair, announcing that he had three toasts to propose, and one speech to make; the latter, he said, being contingent on the chance of his getting properly at his voice, through two helpings of plum-pudding; a chance which he thought rather remote, principally in consequence of Annie's having rather overdone the proportion of suet in mixing her ingredients.

'The first toast,' said the old gentleman, 'is the health of Mr Reuben Wray; and God bless him!' When this had been drunk with immense fervour, Mr Colebatch went on at once to his second toast, without pausing to sit down—a custom which other after-dinner orators would do well to imitate.

'The second toast,' said he, taking Mr Wray's hand, and looking at the mask, which hung opposite, prettily decorated with holly,—'the second toast, is a wide circulation and a hearty welcome all through England, for the Mask of Shakespeare!' This was duly honoured; and immediately Mr Colebatch went on like lightning to the third toast.

'The third,' said he, 'is the speech toast.' Here he endeavoured, unsuccessfully, to cough up his voice out of the plum pudding. 'I say, ladies and gentlemen, this is the speech toast.' He stopped again, and desired the carpenter to pour him out a small glass of brandy; having swallowed which, he went on fluently.

'Mr Wray, sir,' pursued the old gentleman, 'I address you in particular, because you are particularly concerned in what I am going to say. Three days ago, I had a little talk in private with those two young people. Young people, sir, are never wholly free from some imprudent tendencies; and falling in love's one of them.' (At this point, Annie slunk behind her grandfather; the carpenter, having nobody to slink behind, put himself quite at his ease, by knocking down an orange.) 'Now, sir,' continued the Squire, 'the private talk that I was speaking of, leads me to suppose that those two particular young people mean to marry each other. You, I understand, objected at first to their engagement; and like good and obedient children, they respected your objection. I think it's time to reward them for that, now. Let them marry, if they will, sir, while you can live happily to see it! I say nothing about our little darling there, but this:—the vital question for her, and for all girls, is not how *high*, but how *good*, she, and they, marry. And I must confess, I don't think she's altogether chosen so badly.' (The Squire hesitated a moment. He had in his mind, what he could not venture to speak—that the carpenter had saved old Reuben's life when the burglars were in the house; and that he had shown himself well worthy of Annie's confidence, when she asked him to accompany her, in going to recover the mould from Stratford.) 'In short, sir,' Mr Colebatch resumed, 'to cut short this speechifying, I don't think you can object to let them marry, provided they can find means of support. This, I think, they can do. First there are the profits sure to come from the mask, which you are sure to share with them, I know.' (This prophecy about the profits was fulfilled: fifty copies of the cast were ordered by the new year; and they sold better still, after that.) 'This will do to begin on, I think, Mr Wray. Next, I intend to get our friend there a good berth as master-carpenter for the new crescent they're going to build on my land, at the top of the hill—and that won't be a bad thing, I can tell you! Lastly, I mean you all to leave Tidbury, and live in a cottage of mine that's empty now, and going to rack and ruin for want of a tenant. I'll charge rent, mind, Mr Wray, and come for it every quarter myself, as regular as a tax-gatherer. I don't insult an independent man by the offer of an asylum. Heaven forbid! but till you can do better, I want you to keep my cottage warm for me. I can't give up seeing my new grandchild sometimes! and I want my chat with an old stager, about the British Drama and glorious John Kemble! To cut the thing short, sir: with such a prospect before them as this, do you object to my giving the healths of Mr and Mrs Martin Blunt that are to be!'

Conquered by the Squire's kind looks and words, as much as by his reasons, Old Reuben murmured approval of the toast, adding tenderly, as he looked round on Annie, 'If she'll only promise always to let me live with her!'

'There, there!' cried Mr Colebatch, 'don't go kissing your grandfather before company like that you little jade; making other people envious of him on Christmas Day! Listen to this! Mr and Mrs Martin Blunt that are to be—married in a week!' added the old gentleman peremptorily.

'Lord, sir!' said Mrs Buddle, 'she can't get her dresses ready in that time!'

'She *shall*, ma'am, if every mantua-making wench in Tidbury stitches her fingers off for it! and there's an end of my speech-making!' Having said this, the Squire dropped back into his chair with a gasp of satisfaction.

'Now we are all happy!' he exclaimed, filling his glass; 'and now we'll set in to enjoy our port in earnest—eh, my good friend?'

'Yes; all happy!' echoed old Reuben, patting Annie's hand, which lay in his; 'but I think I should be still happier, though, if I could only manage not to remember that horrible dream!'

'Not remember it!' cried Mr Colebatch, 'we'll all remember it—all remember it together, from this time forth, in the same pleasant way!'

'How? How?' exclaimed Mr Wray, eagerly.

'Why, my good friend!' answered the Squire, tapping him briskly on the shoulder, 'we'll all remember it gaily, as nothing but a STORY FOR A CHRISTMAS FIRESIDE!'

Solution of the Endgame in 'A Happy Solution'
(See page 26)

1. . . . P to K6; 2. Q to R 6 [a], Q to R 5, check; 3. Q (or B) takes Q, B to B 5; 4. Kt to Kt 3, B takes Kt and mates, very shortly, with R to R 8.

[a] 2. Kt to Kt 4, Q takes Kt; 3. Q (or P) takes Q [b], B to B 5 as before.

[b] If 3. Q to R 6, Q to R 5, check, as before. If 2. P to K Kt 4, B to Kt 6; 3. Kt takes B, Q takes Kt and wins.

The following is the proof, from the position of the pieces that a white queen must have been taken by the pawn at Q Kt 3: All the black men except two are on the board; therefore White made only two captures. These two captures must have been made with the two pawns now at K 5 and B 3, because they have left their original files. White, therefore, never made a capture with his Q R P, and therefore it never got on to the knight's file. Therefore the black pawn at Q Kt 3 captured a *piece* (not a pawn). The game having been played at the odds of queen's rook, the white Q R was off the board before the game began, and the white K R was captured on its own square, or one of two adjacent squares, there being no way out for it.

Now, since Black captured a *piece* with the pawn at Q Kt 3, and there are no white *pieces* off the board (except the two white rooks that have been accounted for), it follows that whatever piece was captured by the pawn at Q Kt 3 must have been replaced on the board in exchange for the white Q R P when it reached its eighth square. It was not a rook that was captured at Q Kt 3, because the two white rooks have been otherwise accounted for. The pawn, on reaching its eighth square, cannot have been exchanged for a bishop, or the bishop would still be on that square, there being no way out for it, nor can the pawn have been exchanged for a knight for the same reason (remembering that the capture at Q Kt 3 must necessarily have happened *before* the pawn could reach its eighth square).

Therefore the pawn was exchanged for a queen, and therefore it was a queen that was captured at Q Kt 3, and when she went there she did not make a capture, because only two captures were made by White, both with pawns. QED.

ACKNOWLEDGMENTS

The editor would like to thank Andrew Gasson (Wilkie Collins Society), John Hogan (Edgar Wallace Society), and David Rowlands, for their helpful advice and assistance.

Grateful acknowledgment is made for permission to reprint the following:

'The Trinity Cat' by Ellis Peters, copyright © Ellis Peters 1976 (first published in *Winter's Crimes* 8, Macmillan).
'An Upright Woman' by H.R.F. Keating. Reprinted by permission of the Peters Fraser and Dunlop Group Ltd.
'A Pair of Muddy Shoes' from *Eight Short Stories* by Lennox Robinson, published by T. Fisher Unwin, part of HarperCollins Publishers.
'The Unknown Murderer' from *Mr Fortune's Practice* by H.C. Bailey, reproduced by permission of Tessa Sayle Agency.
'A Christmas Tragedy' by Agatha Christie, taken from *The Thirteen Problems*. Copyright © 1932 by Agatha Christie Mallowan.

The following stories are reproduced by permission of the authors:
'A Book for Christmas' © 1991 by Christopher Hallam
'The Grotto' © 1991 by Pamela Sewell
'The Show Must Not Go On' © 1991 by David G. Rowlands